13

An Anthology Of Horror and
Dark Fiction

13: An Anthology Of Horror and Dark Fiction

Limitless Publishing, LLC
Kailua, HI 96734
www.limitlesspublishing.com

Formatting: Limitless Publishing

ISBN-13: 978-1-68058-825-5
ISBN-10: 1-68058-825-7

Table Of Contents

Méchante Reine

By Savannah Blevins

Chapter One

Sanctuary 1802

"Lake." Abram held his hand above his eyes, squinting through the darkness. Even though the sky was clear and the moon bright, reflecting off the snow-covered mountain, it would be hard to see Lake sitting in the shadows, draped in her ragged

1

black cape. Abram stepped around the sparks of the fire he'd just spent two hours smoldering into a gallant flame. "C'mon, Lake. Come sit by me and warm up."

She didn't move. Not even a single inch.

Abram and Lake were like Romeo and Juliet. If Juliet wanted to fling a harpoon through Romeo's rich, privileged heart every day.

"I'm fine, Abram."

Abram tugged the bottom of his perfectly tailored winter coat around him and stuffed his hands in his pockets before leaving the warmth of the fire to step closer to her. "Don't be stubborn on me, Lake. You'll get hypothermia up here. Do you want to lose your toes?"

Lake looked the other way. She couldn't be cruel and look at his stupid, perfect face. "I've always looked good in blue. And who really needs toes anyway?"

"Lake." Abram's voice dropped two octaves.

Lake's teeth clenched together. She hated when he said her name like that, like she was supposed to listen to him, no questions asked. Mostly she just hated when he said her name at all. It was a constant reminder of who she was, or rather who she wasn't. Lake didn't belong to one of the four founding families of Sanctuary. She'd been found abandoned on the fountainhead shoreline by none other than Abram's father. They'd given her the name Lake and that was it. No surname.

In Sanctuary, your last name was a big deal. Like Abram, for example. His last name was Daniels. That meant his family owned Frog Hollow, one of the largest pieces of land in town. He had everything a nineteen-year-old boy could want. Power, money…girls. Abram Daniels could get any girl he wanted.

Lake had nothing but the clothes on her back.

The wind whistled in her ears, rattling the barren trees around her. Her toes were numb and probably blue. The snow had seeped through her shoes hours ago, the holes and worn leather no match for the frigid temperatures of an Appalachian winter, especially one at the top of Red Crane Mountain.

"Come sit by the fire or I swear I'll drag you off this mountain kicking and screaming. I promised you I wouldn't stop you from this suicide mission, but I won't sit here all night and watch you freeze to death."

Lake's gaze rose to Abram. He was absolutely serious. She knew that look all too well. The take-no-prisoners glare. For a spoiled rich kid, Abram had a big heart. For some ridiculous reason, he'd always chosen her as his charity case. She hated it. Most days, when she could convincingly lie to herself, she hated him too.

Today wasn't one of those days.

Lake grudgingly stood up and stomped toward the fire.

"Thank you," Abram said, throwing his hands out in victory. He turned back toward the fire too, rubbing his hands together above the rising flame.

Lake watched him closely. The way his breath blew out in a white puff between his lips. The way his nose wrinkled when the flames would dart up too high and sting his fingertips. She wanted to remember those things. Even though they were small and insignificant, it's what she would recall at the end.

When the shadow took her, she would think of Abram.

She would hear his laugh as they sat next to the stream and fished until the sun hung low in the sky. She would hear his footsteps sneaking up the back alley of the Inn to bring her fresh strawberries during lunch. It would be his face, his voice, and his life that would live on because of her.

"Are you crying?"

Lake tucked her long, frozen hair behind her ear as she tried to wipe away the tear on her cheek. "Don't be ridiculous, Abram Daniels. You know I don't cry."

Abram stepped toward her around the fire. "You don't have to do this. In fact, you shouldn't do it. We should go home, right now."

Lake bit her lip and turned away. "You don't understand."

"The Méchante Reine is out there. We all know that. She comes and she wreaks her havoc on us, but that doesn't mean we should go looking for her, Lake. This notion that you can save us from her is stupid."

"It's not stupid!" Lake screamed. She didn't mean to, but it came out that way.

Hearing the witch's name like that, said so casually in conversation, caused a fire to rise in her gut.

Méchante Reine.

That's what the Cote family called the witch. It

meant wicked queen. And she *was* wicked. She was evil, pure incarnate.

The Méchante Reine didn't just wreak havoc on Sanctuary. She wreaked havoc on Lake. Every day. It used to be only in her dreams, but recently, the shadow followed her every step. Sometimes she would whisper in her ear. Horrible things. Every type of sin imaginable.

Kill.

Kill them all.

They deserve it.

Lake tried to ignore it. She sat back and watched as the Méchante Reine took possession of the patrons of Sanctuary. One by one, every time a new moon appeared in the sky, magnifying the darkness, hiding the shadows that swallowed you whole. Innocent people lost their minds. Their screams could be heard through the silent night, echoing down the abandoned streets. They turned on their families. They slaughtered their best friends. Blood would mark the door of every house the wicked queen visited. It was all for one reason.

Lake.

The Méchante Reine wanted to get Lake's attention. Now she had it.

Yesterday, Lake heard only one word whispered in her ear. She stood in the kitchen at the small Inn in town. She busied herself washing dishes, hoping Mrs. King, the owner, would give her an extra helping of potatoes for staying late. Abram's family came in last minute, and Mr. Daniels brought in ten new bags of meal he had delivered from Charleston to help supplement the waning winter rations. Mrs.

King demanded they stay for dinner. Lake stayed in the back, knowing better than to ask to sit out front with the others. She peeked through the window, admiring the smiling boy sitting at the end of the table.

Abram.

The witch whispered it so low, Lake thought she imagined it. It wasn't her mind playing tricks on her though. A dark shadow appeared behind Abram's shoulder as a high-pitched laugh rang in her ears.

Abram Daniels is mine.

A hand touched her shoulder, and Lake jumped back. Abram stood in front of her, blocking the radiating heat from the fire, his head cocked to the side. "Let's go home, Lake. Please."

Lake took a step back. "Home? I don't have a home, Abram."

His eyes narrowed. "Is that what this is about? I told you, in another year I'll be old enough to have my own house. My dad will give me my own piece of land. We can get—"

Lake held up her hand. She couldn't let him say it. "Your father would never let you marry me. We both know he wants you to marry Estelle Cote."

Abram grabbed Lake's shoulders, forcing her around to look at him. "I don't love Estelle Cote."

The tears come back. Abram's face transformed into a blur. "I have to do this, Abram. Trust me."

"What can you do? Look me in the eye and tell me what *you* can do to stop the witch."

Lake jerked away from Abram, slinging her black cloak around, stalking away from the fire. "She wants me. She taunts *me*."

"Why would you think that?"

Lake couldn't bear to look at him. What would he think of her if he knew the truth? The witch talked to her. Lake would be tainted even more, as if a homeless orphan with no name wasn't enough shame to bear.

The wind shook the limbs in the trees, and the flame of the fire danced low to the ground. The Méchante Reine was there. Listening.

Lake pulled her cloak tight around her. "I think you should go back to town, Abram."

"No." He pressed his lips tight together. "I won't leave you on this mountain alone. Not with her."

"You said you would turn back once we got close to her cavern. You promised."

"I lied."

The darkness shifted behind him. Lake looked up at the sky. The waxing crescent moon was the only thing that saved them from the witch's immediate wrath. The Méchante Reine could only take possession of humans during the New Moon when the light was hidden from Earth. Tonight she'd merely have to suffice with Lake's tortured soul. Lake's heart didn't break at the thought of leaving Abram.

It died.

Every part of her died at the thought of the moments she'd lose with him. No more secret talks. No more smiles that hinted at more than mere friendship. No kiss...not even her first. Lake squeezed his hand, willing him to listen to her. She had to make him listen.

"Go back to Sanctuary, Abram. Go back to your

big, warm house. Go back to your friends."

"Seriously? That's your argument right now? I don't want to go back to George and Luther any more than I want to go back to my house. What good is anything there without you?"

"No, Abram." Lake started to back away, to pull away from his desperate grasp. "You have to go back."

Abram tightened his grip. He wrapped his arms all the way around her, squeezing her close to his chest. "I'm not going anywhere without you."

"I have to stop her." Lake cried openly, the sobs echoing deep in her chest. She'd cried a lot in her lonely existence, but it was the first time Abram ever witnessed it. "I don't have a choice."

"Then we go together. We stop the Méchante Reine together."

Lake shook her head. "Abram, no."

He only held her tighter. "I'm not leaving you, Lake. Ever."

She held onto to him too. Again she had no choice. She couldn't make herself let go. This moment…this small space in time would be all she had with him.

Tomorrow night the new moon would rule the sky, and Sanctuary would belong to the Méchante Reine.

Chapter Two

The fire was a soft glow of embers by morning. The sun beamed high over Lake's head, but it did little to knock off the chill that felt like it froze down to her very core. She wouldn't have survived the night if not for Abram and his fire. She nuzzled her face closer to his chest, listening at the steady rhythm of his heart. She hated how much she lived for that sound. He was awake too. His fingers played with the end of her hair that lay at the small of her back. Lake turned her face into his chest, her fingers intertwining in the wool sweater beneath his jacket.

His lips brushed the top of her temple. "It's still a long way to the top of the mountain."

"I know."

They needed to leave now if they wanted to make it to the witch's cavern before nightfall. Lake needed a few more moments with him, though. A

9

few more seconds to listen to the soft beat of his heart. She pressed the tips of her fingers against the thrum and closed her eyes. In a dream, one that would never exist, she would wake up next to Abram like this every day. They'd live in a small house next to the fountain head, right off the shoreline. It would be summer, and the morning dew would cling to the railing of the porch. She wouldn't be working at the Inn anymore, and there would be no long, cold nights huddled in a corner in hope of merely surviving the night.

Abram pulled away and stood up, helping her to her feet. Lake's legs were stiff, causing her to stumble. He grabbed the bag he'd brought with him and pulled out a canteen of water. He shook it and smiled when a sloshing sound could be heard inside. "Good," he said, relieved. "It didn't freeze."

He unscrewed the cap and took a drink, passing it to Lake. Her lips were so cold she could barely manage to make them work to press against the container's opening. The water felt good, though. It was even a little warm after sitting next to the fire all night. Lake screwed the lid back on the container, not wanting to drink too much. Abram would need it for his journey back down the mountain tomorrow.

She looked around them at the thick tree line that surrounded the clearing at the cliff base. A cold morning breeze snaked through the maze of pines, brushing across the exposed skin at her collar. The witch would be hidden deep in the shadows of the cave right now, but that didn't mean she couldn't reach Lake if she wanted.

"Look," Abram said, stuffing all his gear back into his bag. He stood up and pointed at the skyline above them. A stream of gray smoke was floating just above the treetops.

Lake's chest contracted. "You don't think it's a burial, do you?"

"I don't know." Abram walked through the trees toward the overhang that stood above the town. He slid down the hillside toward it, and Lake followed.

Once on the large piece of rock that protruded out of the cliff face, they could see Sanctuary in the valley beneath the mountain. Smoke rose up from the town's center. Lake was right. It was a burial. Abram reached out to her, and she immediately accepted his offer.

"The new moon wasn't in the sky. It couldn't have been the witch," Lake said, trying to convince herself.

"People die of natural causes all the time," Abram agreed, shaking his head. "It was probably old man Johnson. That nagging cough finally took him."

They stood there quietly. It wasn't old man Johnson. They both knew that. The witch stretched her reach. The Méchante Reine wanted to prove a point. Sanctuary was her town. The people there were her playthings. They existed merely for her to toy with and torture.

Abram.

Lake jerked at her ears, threatening to rip them off her head. That voice. It was so confident and cold. It echoed inside her head.

"No." Lake pulled at her hair, whirling around as

11

her fingernails clawed at the side of her head. "You can't have him."

"Lake, what's wrong?" Abram rushed to her, his hand held out for her.

She looked like a madwoman, her eyes wide and dark. Similar to all those helpless souls the witch took possession of through the years. She wanted to dig the voice out of her head.

"Get out of my head."

Abram grabbed her, holding her tight while she thrashed and kicked. No matter how hard she tried, she couldn't get that voice to go away. It was there, rooted deep inside of her. It poked at her every day, taunting her with her worst nightmares.

Lake finally started to calm down as she realized the witch wasn't going to push the issue. At least not right now.

Abram studied her face. "Tell me what's going on."

"I hear her." Lake sounded devastated because she was. She didn't want Abram to know. "The Méchante Reine talks to me."

His brows knit together. "What do you mean she talks to you? How?"

Lake looked down at her hands. She didn't want to see his face. She couldn't bear to witness the disgust and fear that would be there. "I hear her inside my head. I've always heard her." She gritted her teeth at the memories. "She used to talk to me when I was a young girl. She tried to convince me to do such mean things. Some nothing more than cruel practical jokes, but others…were not."

Abram cupped Lake's face in the palm of his

hands and tilted it up. "Why didn't you tell me?"

She couldn't meet his gaze. "You already pity me so much."

"Geez, Lake." Abram pulled away, turning his back on her. "I thought we were a team. I thought that we told each other everything. What was the point of all those nights out on the dock, sharing secrets until the sun rose, if it didn't mean you couldn't trust me enough to tell me when you're in danger?"

Lake stood her ground, her shoulders straight. The thought gutted her. "I am not the one in danger."

Abram slowly turned around, his beautiful boyish face full of fear. "What did she say to you?"

"It doesn't matter. I am going to end it tonight. Once and for all."

Abram stepped closer. "What did that witch say to you?"

Lake bit her lip. The bitter taste of blood filled her mouth. "You, Abram. The Méchante Reine wants *you* because she knows what it would do to me. Those people down there…they can strip me bare. They can starve me. They can neglect me and forget I even exist. It doesn't matter what they've done. I've survived it all. They can't break me, and neither can she. Trust me, she's tried over the years."

Abram looked at her, his eyes round. It was too late now. Lake might as well tell him the whole dirty truth of it.

"That night at the Inn last summer…when Estelle kissed you. She told me to kill her."

"But you didn't."

"Of course I didn't. My defiance is the only upper hand I have on her. She's raised the stakes now. I can no longer turn a blind eye to her madness."

Abram is mine.

Lake clawed at her ears again, screaming, cursing, ready to tear her own thoughts out one by one. "Shut up! You're not taking him from me. I'll kill you first!"

Abram grabbed Lake, holding her steady until the mania passed. She fisted her hair, tugging at it as if it might help keep her mind quiet. Abram pressed his hand to her cheek. "Who does she want?"

Lake looked up at him. The answer was in her stare. "The only person who can break me."

"You're going to face the Méchante Reine because of me?"

"Yes."

Lake loved him. Abram Daniels was the one single good thing in her life. He was the reason she fought to live another day. The reward of seeing his smile one more time was enough to suffer through the pain of the loneliness, to survive when all she wanted to do was give in.

Abram's fingers brushed away the long strands of hair that blew across her face. His forehead fell down against hers, his thumb raking across her bottom lip. "I love you, Lake. And one day I promise you, I will give you a last name."

Abram's lips were soft.

She'd always imagined they would be. However,

14

she didn't expect it to take her breath away.

Lake gasped into his mouth, and it was quickly followed by a sigh. Abram only pulled her closer, held her tighter. She clung to him too. She'd waited so long for this. She'd dreamed about it. She'd hoped for it.

When Abram lifted her chin with his thumb, she melted into him. She forgot the cold. Her once-numb limbs lit on fire with the lust and yearning she'd held in for too long. She enjoyed the taste of him. She savored each brush of his lips. Even if nothing else in the entire world could be, this moment was perfect.

Abram pulled back enough to whisper against her shivering lips. "Will you marry me?"

"Abram." A lump formed in Lake's throat. "You know we can't. Your father—"

"I'm a grown man. I don't need my father's permission to get married." Abram pulled her face back so he could look her directly in the eyes. "Will you marry me?"

Tears leaked down Lake's face. "It's not that simple."

"But it is, Lake. It is simple. I love you. I want to marry you. I want to give you my name." Abram held her steady by her shoulders. "I'm going to ask you again, and I want an honest answer. Will you marry me?"

Lake touched his face, his soft brown hair that fell in his eyes. "Yes. Of course."

He kissed her again. She could really get used to that. His lips were warm despite the frigid air he gasped in between breaths. They stood there like that under the morning sun, the snow a bright light all around them. Abram pulled back, his hands suddenly searching his coat pockets. He pulled out a piece of white paper and folded it in half.

"Here." He ran his hands down her cloak, searching for a pocket. He found it on the inside and shoved the note in it. "Keep this just in case."

"What is it?"

"Just keep it." Abram looked up at the sun that slowly moved toward its noon position. "Come on, we have a long way to go before dusk."

Abram pulled her hand, but Lake remained rooted to her spot. Abram looked back at her. "What's wrong? Have you changed your mind?"

Lake fought back the smile, but it was useless. "Are we engaged?"

Abram smiled too. It was contagious. "Yes." He walked back to her and took her hands and held them tight between their stiff, shivering bodies. "We're engaged."

She kissed him a third time. And a fourth. Abram Daniels was everything she would die to keep.

Chapter Three

The hike up the mountain was long. Lake's feet bled as the bottom of the worn soles of her shoes gave out against the unforgiving rocks of the mountain. Her fingers were dirty and her nails broken from digging in the dirt to pull herself up the steep incline that led up to the cavern's entrance.

Darkness approached. Not a single star dared to shine in the blank sky. Blackness consumed Sanctuary. Evil would reign the helm tonight. She imagined all the patrons were locked up in their houses, eyeing their closest loved ones with steady suspicion. Would they turn on them? Would tonight be the night they fell to the darkness?

Abram pulled her up the last few feet, and she crashed onto the open ledge of the jagged rock. Blood soaked through the sparse cotton of her pants leg. She grabbed her knee as the pain turned into a burning sting, jerking her hand away from it when

Abram turned around. She didn't want him to see that she was hurt.

"I need a second to catch my breath," he said, throwing his bag off his shoulder to bend down on one knee, gasping for air.

The light of the day slipped away minute by minute. Lake could hear the witch laugh in her head. A slow, deadly lullaby.

"Stay here," Lake said, shoving herself up to her feet.

She was out of breath too, but it didn't matter. Nothing mattered except saving Abram.

Abram stood up too. He looked so much taller in the fading light. Older too. He wasn't the bright-eyed boy playing hide and seek in the clearing, or the one who tossed stones at the fountainhead shore. Abram was a man. He was her fiancé.

"I refuse to argue with you about this. We either go together, or I go alone."

Lake glared at him.

He walked toward her, smiling at her hateful face. "I was always a sucker for that grimace of yours, but don't think it's going to change my mind."

Lake rolled her eyes.

Abram reached down and twisted a strand of her hair between his fingers. "It's true. It was the first look you ever gave me. Do you remember?"

"We've known each other our entire lives. How could I possibly remember the first look I gave you?"

He eased closer to her, whispering against her ear. "I remember."

She gave him a skeptical look, and he laughed. "I do," he said, grinning down at her. "It was your first day of school. Mrs. King had thrown a fit until they let you join our class. You had on a faded blue dress that was at least two sizes too big and these little brown-soled shoes that had a hole on the back left heel."

Lake's lips parted. "You remember that?"

"Of course. You sat by yourself under the big oak tree during lunch, and I came over to introduce myself. I told you that I liked your shoes, and you gave me that face. That grimace you reserved from then on just for me."

Lake sighed. "I hated those shoes. I knew you only felt sorry for me."

Abram laughed quietly. "You're wrong. I really did like those shoes. They were mine. I put that hole in the left heel the previous summer, climbing a tree up on the ridge."

"What?"

"My mother had a fit when she saw the hole and replaced my beloved shoes with a brand new pair that wasn't broken in and they left blisters on my feet for a week. She donated the old ones to the church. I really liked those shoes, but mostly, I really liked you, and those shoes were a good excuse for me to talk to you."

Lake scoffed. "How could you have liked me then?"

"You lit up the room, Lake. No matter where you were, you brought the light with you. Your face shined above the others. Your smile, though rare, was the only one I could see."

Lake bit her lip to keep from crying. Abram had always been so good to her. He'd been her only friend in the world. Even when she pushed him away and told him to leave her alone, Abram was there. His words always kind, his touch always gentle.

Abram was the kind of perfect she wished she could be.

He grabbed his head with both hands. The last spark of light disappeared behind the mountain's peak. The new moon was up. Lake tried to jerk his hands down so she could see his face. "What's wrong?"

"A ringing," he said, jabbing his fingers into his ears. Pain. There was so much pain on his face. "It's so loud. Like a high-pitched wail."

The wicked queen was ready to play.

"Block it out. Don't listen to it."

Abram began to scream, louder and louder. The Méchante Reine took him down to his knees.

"You're a coward!" Lake said, yelling it into the night. "I'm the one who came for you. Face me!"

Abram was on the ground, pinned to the hard rock beneath him as if a knife had been pierced through his chest. Lake let go of him and stood up. She spun around, searching the night for the shadow she knew would be there. "Come out," she demanded. "Show your face."

A face did appear in the black hole of the cavern's entrance. Pale white skin and black eyes. It faded into the cave.

Lake bent down and kissed Abram's temple, patting him as he lay writhing in torture. "Stay here.

I'll come back for you if I can. If I don't…go home." It hurt so much to admit the truth. To finally succumb to the reality of what would happen. "Never come back here."

He tried to reach for her, but she made herself step away. "I love you, Abram. I always have. Remember that. Forget everything else, the pain and the torture the witch has caused us all, but remember that I loved you."

Lake hurried into the cave, the darkness enveloping her. The blackness in front of her shimmered. She was there. Right in front her. "Show yourself," she said, heaving in a breath as her heart threatened to beat out of her chest. "Stop hiding in the back our minds like a snake in the grass."

The white face flashed in the darkness. A shadow in human form. Her black hair stood at the ends, her body moving in a fluid motion as if the wind could blow her away. A black fog lingered around her, forming the black garments that draped over her skeletal frame.

Lake stood her ground. "It's time you leave this town."

Sanctuary is mine.

The witch's lips didn't move for her to speak. They couldn't. Her mouth was sewn together. She could still her words in her head, though. Clear and perfectly cruel. Lake gritted her teeth and took a brave step forward. "I won't let you have it."

The witch cocked her head to the side, studying Lake.

Why do you care for it? Those people have done

nothing but shun you. They turn their nose up at you, give you nothing but scraps to eat and bare threads to wear.

"It doesn't matter."

With me you could ruin them all. Bring them to their knees and make them serve you.

Lake stood there, her mind steady. She knew better than to even consider the Méchante Reine's offer. She would get no pleasure out of watching the downfall of others.

"There are good people down there."

Are there?

"Yes." Lake looked back at the beautiful boy behind her. Abram lay motionless at the cavern's entrance. That boy was the one who stood up for her when Estelle Cote tried to soil her reputation. The one who brought her food when he knew she had none. "Abram is good. He doesn't deserve your threats."

The Méchante Reine tried to smile, stretching the corners of her threaded mouth.

Abram.

Abram stood up on command and walked into the cave. He moved past Lake, shoving into her shoulder as he went by like she hadn't been standing there at all.

"Abram, no!"

Lake grabbed him, but he continued to move forward. The Méchante Reine guided him, possessing him now just like she said she would. It would only be hours before the manic state would set in. Abram would see visions, twisted versions of the truth that would turn him against the ones he loved the most. He'd probably come after Lake first, his favorite blade with the ivory handle held in the air, prepared to take her apart limb by limb.

"Let him go. He doesn't deserve this. Abram is good."

Abram stopped halfway between them, turning around to face her. His eyes faded to a coal black. The emotion, the love that she saw there only minutes ago, was gone. Abram was simply an empty void waiting to be filled with the Méchante Reine's hate.

Lake ran to him and pulled him back away from her. "What are you doing to him?"

Nothing. He invited the darkness in. They all did. It dwells inside of them now. It will take them one by one.

"No. You're wrong. Abram is good."

"Ahhh!" Abram grabbed his chest and collapsed to his knees. He started clawing at it, ripping his jacket and shirt apart.

Lake tried to hold him still, to steady him, but it was no use. She lifted up his shirt and there was a visible black spot on his chest, beneath the skin, deep down into the fibers of his heart. It started to spread like a poison through his veins. Lake cupped her hand over it.

The seed of evil has been planted in him. He belongs to me.

"No." Lake pressed against his skin, pushing down, trying to stop the blackness from snaking through his veins. The spot in his heart grew too. It consumed him second by second. Lake held his face in her hands. This wasn't what was supposed to

23

happen. Abram was supposed to be the one who lived. She held his shoulders as he started to cough and jerk, his limbs flailing out beside his body.

She pressed her face against his, squeezing him tight. "Take me."

What?

Lake looked up, her tears ice water in her veins. "I said take me instead. I'm really who you want. Let Abram go home to his family. Let him live a life free of you. Take me."

The darkness grew around the Méchante Reine, excitement and victory in her cold stare. The blackness started to fade from Abram's eyes. He struggled to gain a breath, but when he did, he grabbed onto Lake's cloak, pulling her down to him. "No." He gasped in another breath. "I won't accept your sacrifice."

The witch's eyes blazed red, but she remained in her spot. Lake took Abram's hand, holding it to her cheek. "Yes, you will. You will take it and go home."

Abram shook his head, the blackness inside of him gripping him, threatening to consume his very next breath. "The witch talked to me too." Abram's eyes squeezed together as he fought through the searing fire inside of him. "Except I wasn't as strong as you, Lake. I was weak. Too blinded by everything that doing things her way would afford me."

Abram held her hand tight. "Don't you see? The witch talked to us all. You were the only one in this entire cursed town she couldn't break."

He reached up and touched her face, his fingers

24

running down her cheek, across her lips. "The world needs more of you…more of your light. It needs your goodness, Lake. Sanctuary needs you and your defiance against the evil that wants to take us all."

Abram reached over and jerked a granite-colored ring off his finger. It was his family ring. It had the Daniels family crest on it. He took it and cupped the ring into the palm of her hand. "Take my name. Use it for better good than I would have done."

"I need you," Lake sobbed, tears blurring her vision. "I need you with me."

Abram reached up and touched her chest, his fingers pressing against the soft thrum of her heart. "You have me, Lake Daniels. Always."

She kissed him. It would be the last time. She knew that now. "I love you, Abram. I want to save you."

"You did. Without you, she would have taken me years ago. Saving you is the only good thing I'll ever do."

The darkness bore down on them, and the Méchante Reine screeched in her ears. The wicked queen wanted her prize. Abram pulled on Lake, and she helped him up to his feet. She held onto him tight. His fingers brushed her hands that dug into his arm. "Let me save you."

She shook her head, and Abram kissed her temple. "I love you too. You remember that. I always loved you."

He pried her fingers off his arm, patting them gently. He stumbled toward the witch, his hand covering the black spot in his heart. "Take me," he said to her. "Take me and leave Lake alone."

There shouldn't have been any goodness left in Abram. The venom of the Méchante Reine had spread through every inch of his soul, yet it didn't stop him from loving Lake. It didn't stop him from allowing that love to let him see through the darkness, through the evil that consumed him.

The Méchante Reine dove forward, her long, bony fingers seared through his chest. He clutched his heart, and the blackness bulged out of his chest like it might rip itself out of his ribcage. And it did. At least a dark, shadowy form of Abram's heart. The witch held it up in her hand like a trophy, squeezing it in her grasp. The black venom in Abram's veins surged through his body. His feet lifted off the ground until he stood on the tips of his toes. Abram fought at something at his neck, an invisible noose that ripped away each breath.

The witch crushed the shadowy heart in the palm of her hand, the black venom leaking down her wrist, and Abram's neck cracked.

"Abram!" Lake dove for him.

It was too late. Abram fell to his knees, his eyes fading black to match the evil inside of him. Lake caught him as his lifeless body surrendered to his fate. She touched his face. His stupid perfect face.

The evil inside of Abram started to retract. It had its prize. There was no reason to linger. The shadow, the Méchante Reine, loomed over her, leaving nothing but her shattered dreams in her wake. The wicked queen stared at her. She wasn't satisfied with her bounty. She never would be unless she had Lake.

She couldn't touch her, though. The voice inside

Lake's head was gone. Abram's sacrifice for her had whittled away the Méchante Reine's power over her. Lake could feel it inside of her. A warmth that stirred deep down in her very soul. It tingled her fingertips and unthawed her toes. There was no darkness inside of her…not even a shadow that could taunt her and tempt her with whispers of false promises.

Lake stared at the queen. Was that fear behind the anger buried inside her coal black eyes?

They stood there like that. Faced off against each other. The dark and the light, each unwilling to yield. Even in her drastic sorrow, when the hate could have filled her to the brim, Lake remained firm in her cause. The Méchante Reine wouldn't break her. Not now, not ever.

"Sanctuary is *mine*."

The witch's scream was silent, but it ripped the threads that held her bloodstained lips together. Her shadowy body broke into pieces, multiplying until black flames engulfed her cracking bones. An unholy trinity of shadows rose from the ground. Three sets of footsteps could be heard walking out of the cave as the darkness moved past Lake. She threw herself over Abram's body, but this new form of malevolence didn't touch her. It went down the mountain into the town she'd promised to save.

Lake knew that kind of evil wouldn't just pack up and leave, but she was ready. She'd face anything the Méchante Reine wanted to throw at her and she'd win. She'd do it for Abram. She'd conquer the darkness in Sanctuary so his light would live on.

Chapter Four

In the morning, when the sun paused the war, Lake picked up the body of her fiancé. She carried Abram down the mountain. She carried him down the middle of the road that carved out the main street of the town. It was there, in the town's center, where every Sanctuary patron could see, Lake wept. She laid her tear-stained face against Abram's still heart and grieved for the boy she loved.

What would she do without the boy who talked to the girl everyone ignored? The boy who fed the girl everyone watched starve? The boy who loved the girl no one wanted?

People peeked out their doors and stared out of their windows.

It was a scene that would be remembered for ages. Lake lay over Abram's body, her screams taunting the Méchante Reine. No one dared to interrupt them, not even Mr. Daniels when he saw his heir's lifeless body on display.

Lake stayed like that, protecting Abram until the darkness came again. Sanctuary stayed quiet in the wake of the chaos. The wicked queen did not appear a second night. She did not take possession of any more patrons who allowed the evil to take root inside of them. She dared not fan the flame of Lake's light that shined to the heavens and back in that spot on the street.

Even evil knew its limits.

It was only in the light of the next dawn that Lake let Mrs. King pry her away from Abram's body. Mrs. King took her to the Inn, frozen and numb with pain. She put her in a bed with clean sheets, a glass of fresh water on the night stand. Accommodations fit for a queen.

Lake woke up with tears still in her eyes. Her tears would never subside as long as Abram was gone. She heard voices arguing outside the door. They whispered and hissed. She heard her name countless times. The gossip and the rumors wouldn't matter to her. Lake sat up in the bed. She recognized the room. She'd cleaned it a thousand times. Her clothes and cloak lay freshly washed on the arm of the chair next to the bed. Lake tugged at the white cotton gown she wore. Her bruises and cuts were still fresh but no longer ached.

She quickly threw on her clothes and opened the door. Mrs. King and Abram's father stood outside the door. Others stood behind them down the hall, all watching. Mrs. King held a single sheet of white paper in her hand. It was folded in half.

Lake jerked it away from her. "That's mine."

Mr. Daniels glared at her. "Did you write that?"

She clasped the note tight to her chest. "No. Abram wrote it. He gave it to me and told me to keep it just in case."

Mrs. King eyes softened. "Lake, do you know what that note says?"

Lake shook her head. It didn't matter what it said. It belonged to her. "He wouldn't let me read it."

Mrs. King reached out and gently touched Lake's arm. "We found Abram's ring in your possession as well. Did he give it to you?"

Lake nodded. They wouldn't believe her if she told them the truth. A man of Mr. Daniel's prestigious honor would never believe his son proposed to a girl like Lake.

Mrs. King looked back at Mr. Daniels. "I told you how your son felt about her. I've told you for years."

Mr. Daniel's face contorted into grimace. "The marriage isn't legal."

Mrs. King scoffed. "Chief Justice," she said, calling back to Mr. Holloway, the judge. "Caleb here is trying to contend that his son's last will and testament shouldn't be upheld by the law. What do you say?"

Mr. Holloway stepped through the crowd, his face solemn and serious. "I'm sorry," he said to Abram's father, "but your wife confirmed that the note was indeed Abram's handwriting. I will uphold the will as law."

"Will?" Lake looked down at the note in her hands. Why would Abram have written a will that

30

first night at the fire? She opened it up, clasping her hand over her heart as she read the scrawling writing on the note.

I, John Abram Daniels, as my last will and testament on this day, November 14, 1802, hereby grant, upon my death, all my possessions, including my inheritance of land, to my wife, Lake Daniels.

She covered her mouth to keep the sobs that ripped her apart inside. Abram had planned to marry her all along. He planned to give himself up to the witch to save her.

"Where is he?" Her voice was barely a squeak. Her knees started to go weak. "Where did you take his body?"

Mrs. King came over and wrapped her arms around her. "They took him to the chapel. They'll prepare his body for the funeral this afternoon."

Mr. Holloway cleared his throat. "Technically, as Abram's wife, you would choose where he should be buried."

She hadn't even thought about it. Usually, when a person died, their body was burned in a ceremonial event. Only members of the four founding families were granted the honor of a true burial.

Lake looked at Mr. Daniels. "Do you have a suggestion?"

Mr. Daniels, who was torn between his own grief for the loss of his only heir and anger, nodded. "His mother and I wish to bury him in Frog Hollow. We have a section of land there plotted off to be our family cemetery."

Lake looked back at Mr. Holloway. "I agree. Abram belongs in Frog Hollow with his family."

Mr. Holloway nodded and backed out of the room.

Mr. Daniels looked up, his lips pressed tight. "Thank you."

Lake merely nodded. Mr. Daniels left, and the crowd disappeared with him. Lake returned to her room to wash up. She placed Abram's family ring on her finger. It was big, but she didn't care. She'd wear it every day. People watched her as she left the Inn, their eyes following her down the street on her way to the chapel. She took the long way around, crossing through the field. She wanted time to think, to collect herself. People already started to gather at the entrance. Mr. Daniels stood at the door in his three-piece suit. He looked like he'd just finished another one of his famous business deals. Abram's mother sat on the bottom step, surrounded by her sister and niece. Her eyes were red and swollen. She looked up and spotted Lake as she approached.

Mrs. Daniels whispered something to her sister before standing up. She came to meet Lake outside of the crowd. She grabbed her hand and turned it over, looking at Abram's ring on her finger. She touched her fingers to her mouth and then her heart. "I'd hoped it was true."

Lake's eyes rounded at her words. Mrs. Daniels smiled through her tears. "You are family now. You will keep the room at the Inn I rented until my husband can finish Abram's house. Then you will move to Frog Hollow into to your home."

"Abram started building a house?"

"It's only a foundation. He started it with his father this past spring. I think my son had this—" she held up Lake's hand, showcasing the ring, "—on his mind for quite some time now."

Lake twisted the ring around her finger. Even in death Abram managed to take care of her.

Mrs. Daniels touched Lake's wrist, squeezing it tight. "One more thing. There is something else I want to give you." She searched in her pockets and pulled out a small silver chain. She placed it in Lake's palm. "When I found you by the fountainhead, this was wrapped in the blanket with you."

Lake held it up, admiring the round charm that dangled from the end. **"Alphine,"** she said, reading the inscription.

Mrs. Daniels smiled. "That's your name. One of the workers at the Inn wanted to take that necklace, and I wouldn't let them. I thought it best to save it for you."

Lake looked up, her breath halted in her throat. "I have a name."

"My husband tried to say it probably meant something else, but I know it's your name. It suits you. Alphine Daniels."

Lake held the necklace and charm to her chest. "Thank you for saving it."

Mrs. Daniels nodded. "I apologize for keeping it so long, but it was hard to find the right time." Her voice broke. "Not that today is the right time, but…"

Lake hugged her. She didn't know what else to do. "It's okay. You saved it; that's all that matters."

Mrs. Daniels tried to get herself under control and wiped her eyes on the sleeve of her dress. She nudged Lake forward. "Go on. As his wife, you get to see him first. We will follow in after you."

Lake stepped toward the chapel, staring at the open door. She wasn't ready to say goodbye to Abram Daniels. She wasn't ready to admit to herself that he wouldn't be waiting for her back at the Inn with a fishing pole and a grin.

She walked up the steps slowly. The soft light of the evening spilled through the stained glass windows. Beautiful shades of red and blue filtered through and decorated the wooden coffin. The walk up the aisle to him felt like miles.

Although he looked peaceful, it did little calm the madness that tore her heart apart.

Lake laid down a single flower, a simple yellow dandelion she'd picked from the fields were they used to play. It was a symbol of her. The flower merely a weed to some, left alone to be stomped over or pulled up by its roots. Abram saw more in her. He loved her. Because of that love, she would live each day of this life for him. She would take that goodness that he shared with her, and like the dandelion's seed, she'd let it blow in the breeze and spread throughout this dark town. She would bring the light back to Sanctuary.

Lake touched Abram's hand one last time.

She turned around and stood above the others, looking down at each face that through the years of her life had looked down upon her. Abram's mother took a seat at the front with her sister and niece as her brother played a slow tune on his guitar in the corner. Mrs. King found a seat in the back corner, and the other patrons slowly filled in the space in between. George, Luther, and Estelle stood in the back of the room. They were supposed to be Abram's best friends, each an heir to one of the founding families' land. Not a single tear stained their eyes. A black rim shimmered around the iris, though.

The Méchante Reine was here. She lived in each of them. This war between them wasn't over.

For the first time in Lake's life, she walked out of a room with her head held high.

She had Abram's last name and she had his love. She had everything she needed to survive them all. The wicked queen was in for a rude awakening.

Sanctuary belonged to Alphine Daniels.

About the Author

Savannah Blevins is an author of Fantasy and Contemporary Romance from Corbin, Kentucky. *The Méchante Reine* is a legend told in her *Witches of Sanctuary* Series. She was born and raised in the Appalachian Mountains that inspired her series and still lives there with her husband John and her two wonderful daughters, Delilah and Gracie.

Facebook:
https://www.facebook.com/savannahblevinsauthor

Twitter:
https://twitter.com/vannajodee

Website:
http://www.savannahblevins.com/

ROOM 313

By: Thomas S. Flowers

The roars from the airport could be heard well past Court Avenue as jet engines landed on the squeal of tires at Des Moines International. It would be easy to imagine the airport as something much larger than what it was, something like O'Hare, Dallas, or Hartsfield-Jackson Atlanta International even. Flights coming and going from airports like Atlanta catered to such destinations as Frankfurt, Paris-Charles de Gaulle, London, Istanbul, and even certain restricted locations, like Kuwait.

Will Fenning had flown through Atlanta only once before, on his way back home from his last deployment in Iraq. Before, it was always Bangor, Maine.

Things change, he supposed. *Things always change*.

Will Fenning hadn't been doing much flying of late. In fact, he drove most everywhere nowadays. As far as his last sale would take him, which typically wasn't very far. Careline Safety Supply was a con, nothing more than phone number to some desk nobody sat at. CSS hadn't always been a con, of course. The business had been just that, a business, struggling to compete in a market as volatile as a match struck near a gas leak.

To say Will was a failure would be unfair. He'd done as much as anyone could expect. He loved his customers, always sent out gift baskets during the holidays, birthday cards to owners, and he paid nearly twenty percent higher than most employers in Houston. Everyone loved him. Life was good. But when you catch your wife in bed with the guy who was supposedly *just* her gym trainer, and she off and takes the kids back to Birmingham without so such as an explanation, other than an *"it's not you it's me"* speech, which we all know is utter bullshit, well...without the ones you love, life just doesn't seem worth living anymore, does it?

Gradually, CSS suffered along with Will. Customers began to drop accounts, new customers dried up like dew on the desert sand, bills began piling up, overdrafts, last notices. Eventually he had to let his staff go, what little he had left. In the end, there was nothing left but one empty desk with a somehow still-connected landline and one framed photo of the Fenning family, frozen in time: wife, husband, ten-year-old son, and seven-year-old daughter smiling as if nothing in the world could touch their little happy moment.

Things change, he surmised. *Things always change*.

His last "sale" was two days ago. The check he cashed (faster than a sneeze through a screen door) was meager at best, but it was something. Enough to get him and his bald tires, yellow check engine and red oil lamp warning, 1993 dented gray Buick Sedan north from Dallas to Des Moines, Iowa. North from Route 75 to 69 and Route 69 into Interstate 44, which wound through Kansas City, hoping and praying like a born again Christian his last twenty dollar bill would get him up Interstate 35 and into Polk County, Iowa.

His low fuel light came on a few miles before the Des Moines International airport started rolling out of the horizon. Knowing how his Buick was, Will knew he couldn't risk more than another couple of miles before the engine would begin to heave and sputter until finally collapsing somewhere on the side of the road. Court Avenue stretched past the airport terminal and out towards a group of huddled hotels, typically catering to weary business travelers. Without much hope of actually being able to get a room in one of them, Will drove his dusty gray Buick down Pinewood Boulevard anyhow. Night was coming on fast. The angry red sun was snuffed by purple clouds and wisps of blue. He wondered for a brief moment how his kids were doing, if they were in bed yet, or if their Babylonian mother was letting them do whatever they wanted, before his car started giving him trouble.

"Shit," Will hissed, listening to the Buick start to rattle. "Come on, baby. Just a little bit farther." He patted the dash gently.

Sitting forward, Will surveyed all the hotels. He passed the DoubleTree with its marble finished entryway. Beside the Hilton was a Jordan Creek. Farther along, a Holiday Inn Express & Suites looked promising, but with a full parking lot, there wasn't much hope in finding a room there.

Listening to the engine putter, Will spotted a hotel at the end of Pinewood Boulevard. A quaint-looking place among the glitter and marble and glass door entryways, the Twin Pines Hotel was anything but fancy. Mostly made of thick log wood, dark maple and pine, about four floors high. Best of all, only four cars were in the parking lot. The Buick made it into one of the open spots near the entrance before giving one final breath of gray smoke and dying.

Will turned the key, just to see.

Nothing.

The car was done.

"Well, I guess this is it." Will patted the dash one last time. "Thanks for the ride." He jumped out and walked to the trunk, pausing briefly. Looking around, Twin Pines seemed somewhat of an oddity. Hidden almost among the glitz and glamor of more modern places to lay your head. The hotel's existence was more likely thanks to the overflow of travelers coming in on late flights. Those with secretaries with forgetful memories failing to book ahead. Judging by the outdated models of cars in the parking lot, there was a good chance he was probably right.

Popping the trunk, Will slung his green duffle over his shoulder.

At the entrance, he stopped and smiled up at the looming stuffed black bear.

The kids would have loved this place, he thought.

Inside, there was a woman sitting behind the front check-in counter just past the comfy recliner and the roaring stone-mantled fireplace. With short, wavy, ginger-colored hair and bright blue lipstick and matching eyeliner, if not for her somewhat masculine black blazer and button-up, she was oddly placed in a business that was designed to look like a flannel-loving log cabin. She was too modern, too deco, even for the more expensive-looking places on Pinewoods. On the wall above the counter hung a large taxidermied moose head with thick, wide reaching antlers.

"Hello. Welcome to Twin Pines. How can I help you?" The odd ginger spoke cheerfully enough to be considered polite, but there was something in the way she was looking at Will that gave him the impression she was struggling to suppress what his wife used to call "resting bitch face." She folded her hands together and smiled painfully.

Will let his duffle fall to the floor. The metal box inside clinked on the tile. He rested his arms on the high vaulted countertop. "Any rooms available?" he asked.

The woman didn't even look at her computer. "Of course."

"I'll take one. One night. Somewhere…quiet, please."

"Absolutely."

"Take Visa?"

"Yes."

Will pulled his wallet from his back pocket. Opening it, he paused on a photo inside, one of his kids smiling at him. His wife's face was no longer recognizable, not since he'd scratched it out with a knife. He tugged on his fading credit card wondering just how much was left before it would bounce. Enough for tonight? Doubtful.

The deco woman began clicking away on her keyboard. She took Will's outstretched card slowly, carefully, as if some deadly pathogen grew like black-purple moss on the damn thing. Typing some more, she finally looked back at Will.

"The room is eighty-five a night," she reported, pausing her long red fingernails over the keys, her *resting bitch face* spasming.

Will whistled lowly.

"Do you want the room, mister…?"

"Fenning."

"Fenning?"

"Yes."

The woman resumed entering Will's credit card information, her thumbs massaging the brail-esque digits.

"Okay. All set." She handed back Will's card.

Will exhaled in relief. He would have slept in the Buick, if push came to shove. He would have done what he came here to do, what the final stretch of road had brought him to do, if he had to. But it wouldn't have seemed right. Not tonight. No, tonight called for the luxuries of push button lamps, single cup Mr. Coffee brews, to long over some reprint art piece, some painting depicting maybe a girl who looked eerily like his own daughter, laughing on a swing roped to a thick oak branch in front of a white picket fenced two-story farmhouse. He even deserved the luxury of thumbing through the Gideons' Bible in the bedside table drawer and the twisted sense of humor of leaving one of the his last Careline Safety Supply business cards stuck between Exodus and when God told Moses of a breed of darkness that could be felt.

Would someone dial the number? Would the line still be connected? Nothing was impossible. Improbable, though. Maybe whatever detective mulling about the room would discover its hiding place. Or perhaps they wouldn't find it at all. It would be a piece of himself, surviving still in the world long after he was gone.

"Mr. Fenning, I've got you in room 313, on the third floor. Plenty of privacy. You'll be all alone up there. We don't expect our next rush to be until the weekend." The deco ginger slid Will his room keycard with the number 313 inked in bold handwritten black ink.

Will picked it up.

"Check out is at noon, please."

He nodded.

"Have a nice night, Mr. Fenning." The ginger smiled, politely fake.

"Thanks." Will picked up his duffle and headed toward the elevators, pushed the up arrow button, the bell chimed, and the door slid open. He walked inside, jabbing the number three button. The bell chimed again and the doors closed with the sound of iron bars clanking together. Or perhaps that was simply his imagination after such a long day on the road and the dark and lonely plans he had for himself later in the night.

The elevator lifted off with a hum.

No music.

Only silence.

Dead and cold.

The elevator came to a stop. The bell chimed again, and the doors opened. The third floor held no surprises. The carpet, with its zigzag pattern, seemed infinite. Diamond after triangle and more diamonds, as blue as the deco woman's lipstick downstairs at the receptionist desk, accented with a shade of plum rose, blending fantastically with the mock-oak walls and faux wood-paneling. More taxidermied critters were molded in the hall, placed on top of rich-looking corner tables. Some beavers, a few badgers, and one stuffed peacock.

Besides the frozen corpses of animals, Will was alone.

No surprises.

Privacy to enjoy himself, one last time.

Sliding his keycard through, the lock blinked green. The hinged popped, releasing the door, which opened slowly, as if fixed by disuse and time. A cold breeze whipped at his neck, prickling his flesh with goosebumps, carrying with it the smell of stale air and the faint hint of dead flowers. This was a tomb. His tomb. Filled with the same amenities he had imagined before. He walked inside and the door thudded shut, but he paid no mind.

Will gazed at the last of the Earthly possessions he would enjoy. A large LG TV sat on a swivel on top of the mahogany drawers; a loveseat matching the carpet in the halls; an ottoman; lamps; Mr. Coffee; cheap arthouse reprints hanging on the walls. And sure enough, one was of a little girl swinging back and forth, smiling with little care of worldly concern, and behind her, a farmhouse surrounded by a white picket fence. Best of all, a Gideon Bible sat waiting inside the bedside nightstand. Laughing quietly, he pulled out his last ruffled card belong to his failed business and thumbed to that part in Exodus, the part about darkness, and gently placed the card between the pages.

The bed was a queen, plenty large for one. Will tossed his green duffle, another relic from a bygone life, onto the bed. A life of BDUs, ACUs, yellow dust, sand, IEDs, and the odor of burning trash, rubber, and the screams of hundreds of mothers lamenting the loss of some son or daughter foolishly caught by the cross hairs of the world. Laments, as he was now, pondering the meaning of it all. If you pulled back the walls, you'd find swine. Did it really matter what happened in it? Was there any meaning in watching the world burn?

Will sat on the bed. Patting his duffle bag, his fingers traced the bulge of the square metal lockbox inside. He'd never been to Des Moines before. The drive had been a quiet twelve hours or so, listening to his own troubled thoughts of "what now?" Endless hours reminding himself there was no turning back. His wife didn't love him. His kids, who once ran to the door every time he came in from work, dashing into his open arms, hugging and smiling and laughing, probably hated him now, no doubt coached by their *jezebel* mother. He'd changed since the war. He'd lost control of himself and his business when the one person he depended on most betrayed him so insidiously.

Now there was nothing left. Nothing to cling on to. No reason for hope.

He drove with those thoughts, like molten stew, singeing his soul. He drove and drove. Will had never been to Des Moines, but still, here he was, chasing the last morsels of sanity and willingness to go on. And there was the dream, of course. He dreamt of a hotel made of log and wood, eerily similar to this place called Twin Pines. An oddity among modernity. Puzzling as it was, though the hotel itself held no foreboding qualities, he felt drawn to this place, or maybe it was the place that was drawn to him.

The dream had come following the night of a rather scrupulous bender of Jack Daniels, the same night he'd put all his worldly documentation inside the shredder, the sharp-toothed guzzler that ate all his tax information, his 401K paperwork, his sales receipts, bills, and last notices. And finally, his marriage certificate. When he awoke, soaked in sweat and purpose, he collected what was left, leaving behind his last family photo, and drove.

He drove to Des Moines.

Good a place as any.

Still on the bed, Will unhooked the latch on his green duffle bag. Carefully. Slowly. As reverently as if performing some religious rite, he took out the metal lockbox. Placing the box on his lap, he punched in the four-digit code, the same number matching his wife's birthday. Looking up at him from the inside was a dull black 9mm Beretta. The serial number had been rubbed clean. Ceremonially, he closed the lid and placed the box on the bedside table. Standing, he unpacked a change of clothes from his duffle. Blue jeans, black button- shirt, dark gray blazer. Tenderly, he folded the clothes, spreading them out on the bed. A part of him wondered why he was going through such motions. In the end, did it even matter what you wore?

"There has to be dignity in dying," he said aloud.

Or maybe this is all habit.

Satisfied with the arrangement, Will walked to the bathroom, shedding his clothes on the way. Unwrapping the hotel complimentary soap and shampoo, he set the shower to hot and bathed himself. Scrubbing hard until his skin glowed red and raw. Again he wondered, *Why?* Did cleaning himself really matter?

"Why not?" he said. "Why not enjoy it, one last time?"

Will started scrubbing his hair.

"Perhaps this will be like a baptismal. Washing away my sins before…"

He rinsed.

Shutting off the water, Will dried with a posh

white hotel towel. He then shaved his month-long stubble, splashed on aftershave, brushed his teeth, gargled mouthwash, and applied lotion to his relaxed and still red muscles.

Finished, he rejoined his Beretta beside the bed.

He opened the box.

—Wait!

Why?

—Don't!

Will picked up the gun. He pressed the barrel against his temple, finger resting on the trigger. He closed his eyes and imagined in his mind's eye all he had lost. His business, his dignity, his friends, his kids. Even his wife. Despite how she had ruined him, he loved her still.

Deeper, he saw all the things he never cared to see. The things that were a part of him, regardless of how far he buried them. How cruel he'd been in the war; how terrible he was. He saw them, eyes, countless eyes pleading with indifference. And the people at home who chanted and howled "*Hero! Hero!*" though he was not. He deserved what had happened to him. Recompense for his sins. It was his wife's fault. It was his own.

Pressing the barrel harder against his skull, Will screamed. Clenching shut his eyes, he held his breath, making a fist with his free hand.

Moaning, he threw the gun on the bed.

"*Coward*," he hissed, punching himself.

Will sat, weeping into his palms.

Scratching at an itch on his shoulder. His shoulder was hot.

Hot.

Itching like a fever, the flesh burned.

What is this?

Will scratched and rubbed, to no relief of the growing pain. His skin broke, inking his fingernails with dabs of red.

Something was opening along his shoulder, just within peripheral. His flesh was coming apart like a seam, revealing...

A large wet eye was blinking up at him between the folds of his crimson skin. One bloodshot eyeball with a sky blue iris, as blue as his own eyes, looking up at him with a gesture of hunger unlike anything Will had ever seen before.

"Jesus fucking Christ!" Will howled and ran for the bathroom. Tripping on his own feet, he fell, thumping against the zig-zag patterned carpet. He could feel The Thing bulging, struggling to...what? To get out?

Of...me?

Picking himself up, Will dashed for the mirror. He watched with a strange expression of horror and curiosity as the wound opened, ripping skin and creaking bone like old wood. More of a face was coming out, as bloodied as some fetus coming into the world. Hair sprouted.

More ripping.

Tearing.

Pulled by the pain, Will smashed the bathroom mirror with his fist. He ran out, losing control of his right side to some kind of bizarre mutilation. The impossible making itself possible. A red painted face, fully emerged, was glaring and smiling and hooting and howling. In its voice, he could taste a sense of lustful freedom. It whispered in his ear in rolls of hot hissing sounds.

"Let me free," it said.

"Let me out," it begged angrily.

And more of it came, pulling itself out and opening his flesh. Will believed his body would split wide open, revealing to the morning maid a mess, his dark red heart and bluish-purple guts, and veins and whatever remained of his roadside dinner, pooled together in a slush of what was once a husband and father of two, a soldier and failed salesman. All the things he hated of himself, his failures puddled on the floor of his ruin.

Rolling now on the bed, Will begged and pleaded with whatever gods were there to end the pain, to break his spine, to *something*, whatever it took. But he couldn't ignore the hideous laughter of his conjoined *other*. His twin, for the monstrous creature shared his eyes, his nose, his mouth, his teeth, his everything. It was like looking into a mirror slick with afterbirth.

More came.

The wound split further, opening wider and wider like the mouth of a fish. It was…impossible and too horrifying to describe.

The *other* came into the world in one final spasm, as bloodied as a newborn baby. Birthed on white sheets and a cheap flannel bedspread covered in a thick mucus with milky red membranes, a girth of something otherworldly and insane. Will exhaled, relieved. The pain was gone. He was free. He opened his eyes to look at the horror of his wounds.

My skin?

He glanced at his shoulder. Lingering. In awe. Nothing there, the wound was sealed. Closed somehow. All that remained of proof of his agony was the gore and the now-standing *other* version of himself, naked and wet with muck. And smiling.

"How?" Will asked without any real hope of an explanation.

The *other* kept a blissful glee. Wicked somehow in its perverse nativity.

"Who are you?" Will pressed.

The *other* reached for the Beretta.

"Are you me?" Will asked, feeling tired from the event. Drunk on endorphins.

The *other* aimed the gun at Will's head, thumbing the safety.

As if just waking, Will glared wide eyed at his *other* and then at the barrel of the gun.

"Wait!" he shouted.

The *other* shrugged and pulled the trigger. The shot thundered, vibrating off the simple painted walls, filling the room with the smell of shower soap and sulfur. The reprint painting frame shifted. The tableside lamp jiggled. But nothing else. No shouts down the hall. No banging on the doors, *"Are you alright in there?"* None of that. He— *they*—were alone.

Will's corpse lay spiraled on the bed, his genitals shriveled like a useless balloon. His pupils filled his eyes in a spreading black pool. The sheets beneath him soaked in red.

The *other* showered, washing the gore and afterbirth fluids down the drain. He dressed in the clothes Will had laid out. Replacing the Beretta into the lockbox and repacking the duffle bag, he stood at the door, giving one last look at the body that he freed himself from, the place of sorrow and parturition. Sighing with a sense of calm satisfaction, the new Will Fenning closed the door and walked out into the great and wonderful unknown.

About the Author

Thomas S. Flowers is the author of several character driven stories of terror, including *The Subdue Series*, and *Reinheit*, among others. He grew up in the small town of Vinton, Virginia, but in 2001 left home to enlist in the U.S. Army. Following his third tour in Iraq, Thomas moved to Houston, Texas, where he now lives with his beautiful bride and amazing daughter. Thomas attended night school, with a focus on creative writing and history. In 2014, he graduated with a Bachelor of Arts in History from UHCL. Thomas blogs at machinemean.org, where he reviews movies, books, and other horror-related topics.

Facebook:
https://www.facebook.com/ThomasSFlowers?fref=ts

Twitter:
https://twitter.com/machinemeannow

Goodreads:
http://machinemean.org/

The Devil's Daughter

By Marissa Farrar

Chapter One

The tiny propeller plane bumped down onto the makeshift runway, red dust bursting up around the aircraft as it bounced and jolted its way to a halt.

Erika Porter cautiously unfurled her stiff fingers from the armrests of her seat, trying to ignore the faint white line circumnavigating her ring finger, and waited for her heart rate to slow. She was a seasoned traveller, although most of her flights involved having more than three people on the aircraft and an engine that didn't cut out every ten minutes.

Still, she was on solid ground now.

Exhaling a sigh of relief, she undid her seatbelt and got to her feet. Her stomach felt loose, her legs still weak from the frightening flight. She knew she'd feel better as soon as she got out of the metal can.

"We are landed safe, Miss Erika," the pilot called back to her in his broken English.

"Yes, thank you." She resisted adding, *Thank God*.

Her rucksack was wedged between the seats behind her, so she leaned over and hauled it up and onto her shoulders. A number of years had passed since her backpacking days, yet she still experienced that same sense of exhilarating freedom of having all her belongings on her back. Except these weren't *all* of her belongings. She had a whole flat full of things back in London, or at least half a flat full of things. She still hadn't managed to fill the empty spaces that had appeared six months earlier.

Erika thrust away the memory of home. These next few days would be good for her. She'd go home refreshed and energised, ready to start again.

The co-pilot wrenched open the door of the plane. The heat hit her like a smack in the face, and she reared back, her lungs tightening. The blinding bright light made her squint, and she lifted a hand to shade her eyes.

The co-pilot nodded at her encouragingly. "You okay? You go now?"

She smiled. "Yes, I'm going now."

Clutching the straps of her backpack, she exited the plane, pausing at the top of the steps which led down to solid ground. Other than the patch of red soil where they'd landed, the only other things around were tall trees, the canopy of which seemed to stretch on as far as the eye could see.

Carefully, Erika descended the narrow set of metal steps and her feet touched the dusty Peruvian ground. Still squinting against the fierce sunlight, she slid her sunglasses from the top of her head down over her eyes and immediately relaxed.

Breaking through the line of trees, a tall man, flanked by two Indians, lifted his hand in a wave as he strode towards her. He appeared at ease in a loose white shirt and khaki shorts. His glasses were the kind where the lenses changed tint depending on the strength of the sunlight, and she knew he needed them for reading.

Erika smiled as he approached. "Shaun! It's great to finally meet you in person."

He put out his hand and shook hers. His palm was warm and strong. "And I finally get to meet the legendary Erika Porter."

She laughed. "Hardly legendary. Perhaps 'occasionally recognised in Brick Lane' would be more accurate."

He grinned. "Bullshit. Most of London reads your blog and your column."

"Not right now, they're not. I finally ran out of things to write about."

He nodded. "Sure, the divorce, and…everything. I'm sorry to hear about that."

"Yeah, so was half of London. I think that was one of the things my husband hated about me—the fact I insisted on writing about our lives for everyone else to read about." She brushed it off. "Anyway, I decided I wanted to write about a real news story, so here I am."

Shaun was a freelance photographer who sold his pictures to numerous London publications, including the newspaper she worked for. They'd chatted online on several occasions over the past couple of years, and when he mentioned chasing down a story in a remote Peruvian village, madness had gripped her and she'd asked if he needed a writer.

Before her head had a chance to question what she was doing, she'd found herself at Heathrow Airport with her backpack on her back and her passport clutched in her hand.

"So how far away is the village?" she asked.

He glanced at her feet. "Let's just say I hope you've got sturdier shoes than that." She looked down at her flip-flops. "It's a good three-hour hike," he continued, "so we need to get moving if we're going to reach the village before dark."

"It's going to get dark in three hours?" she said, doubtfully, taking in the heat and bright sunshine.

"When it gets dark here, it does so suddenly and completely. Believe me, we don't want to be caught out in the middle of the forest when the sun goes down. The bugs alone are enough to send you screaming back to England."

"Hey, I backpacked through most of South East Asia when I was in my twenties. I'm not a complete urbanite."

"Even the most remote places in Cambodia are still more used to seeing tourists than here. Trust me, this is nothing like you've ever experienced before."

Erika didn't know whether to be excited or turn around and go back to the plane. No, the thought of getting back on that plane anytime soon was too much to stand. She'd prefer to face the bugs.

"Don't worry," she told him. "I'm tougher than I look."

She pulled the bag off her shoulders and dropped it to the ground, pulling open the top and delving inside. She had a pair of strong walking boots, something she'd debated due to their weight and was now glad she'd brought, and tugged them out along with a pair of socks. Feeling self-conscious, she changed her footwear and then lifted her bag onto her back.

"You sure you don't want me to get that for you?" Shaun offered.

She shook her head. "Not for the moment. Ask me in an hour or so, and I might have changed my mind."

He grinned. "Sure, will do." He reached into his own rucksack, took out a couple of bottles of water, and handed one to her. "Here, you're going to need this. The heat and humidity can be pretty overwhelming."

"Thanks."

"This is Raphael and Teodoro," he said,

introducing the two men who had stayed back. "They're from the village we're heading to. Their English is only minimal, mainly from what I've taught them since I've been here."

She smiled over at them. Both men were dressed in the same way—belts of feathers around their waists and further bands of feathers secured around the tops of their thighs, calves, and ankles. Both men wore their black hair long, down to their shoulders, with a fringe across their foreheads. Neither man would meet her eye, instead staring over the top of her head.

"I'm not sure they've seen a white woman with blonde hair before," Shaun explained. "You must look kind of strange to them."

"Oh, right," she said, unsure how to ease the awkwardness.

Shaun jerked his head back toward the line of trees and started walking. As soon as he did, the two tribesmen strode ahead, leading the way.

"The people we're staying with aren't a completely uncontacted tribe," he explained as they stepped into the forest and were immediately engulfed by shadows. "Some tribes have no contact with the outside world at all, and just coming into contact with Westerners can have devastating effects on their community. A simple cold can wipe out half of them. This one isn't as secluded as that. They've had contact with the loggers and oil miners for some time now. As far as hair colour goes though, you don't get many blondes around here."

She laughed. "No, I guess not."

They trekked at a steady pace. The ground

through the forest was worn in a groove, the foliage hacked away to allow a relatively direct walk. On occasion, she found herself tripping over exposed roots or being whipped in the face by low-lying branches she hadn't noticed. Shaun hadn't been kidding about the bugs. They buzzed and flitted around her face, so she felt she was constantly swiping them away, and the spider webs which stretched from one side of the trail to the other were the size of compact cars. While she wasn't someone who would burn down her flat at the sight of a spider, she didn't want one crawling under her shirt either.

The longer they walked, the less intense the heat of the sun felt. The change was partially down to the thick canopy of foliage above their heads, though it was also due to the waning of the day. The shadows grew thicker and darker, until she felt like she could step into one and sink right through it and into another world.

"How much longer?" she called out to Shaun. The straps of her backpack were cutting into her shoulders, and sweat poured down her back and into her cleavage, creating dark circles on her clothing.

"Almost there," he called back, almost too cheerfully.

He was right. Within fifteen minutes, the forest opened out into a clearing, and Erika was able to take in the sight of the tribal village that would be her home for the next few days.

She didn't know what she'd been expecting. The village's appearance was what she'd imagined— numerous wooden homes with straw roofs, all placed around a central meeting house. However, it was the atmosphere of the place that Erika found strange. People caught sight of them approaching and hurried into their homes, snatching up the children who had been playing in the dirt as they went. Chickens squawked and flapped at the sudden commotion.

"Are they frightened of my weird hair?" she asked, only partially joking.

Shaun drew to a halt and turned to her. "No, it's not you, or us even. It was just bad timing that we arrived now."

"At sunset?"

"No, it's nothing to do with the time." He raised his eyebrows and nodded toward the open doorway of the meeting house.

Erika glanced over. A little girl stood in the doorway, watching their arrival with huge, dark eyes. Erika guessed her to be about six years old. Rags hung off her skinny frame, and her feet were bare.

"What's she doing?" Erika asked. "Where are her parents?"

"She doesn't have any."

"Oh, the poor thing." Her heart broke for the little girl. She looked so alone and frightened, standing there while everyone else disappeared into their homes.

No, Erika realised. *That's wrong.* The girl looked alone, yes. Frightened? Had Erika just projected how she might feel herself onto the child? She didn't look scared at all, in fact, the opposite. Her dark eyes fixed on Erika, locking her in her stare, and she stood stock still, while most of the other villagers hurried away.

Despite the heat, a flash of cold raced through Erika's body, and she shivered.

"So who looks after her?" she asked Shaun, tearing her gaze away from the child.

He shrugged. "No one and everyone. She's the village's child now, though from what I've seen, she's pretty self-reliant." He jerked his head toward one of the huts. "This is where we're staying. The family has been kind enough to move in with a cousin for the time that we're here."

Erika glanced back towards the girl, discovering the space where she'd been standing was now empty. "Shouldn't we ask the child to stay with us, if she's got nowhere to go?"

"I wouldn't do that. It'll be seen as extremely bad luck."

"Why?"

"It's to do with the reason you're here."

"The villagers who are going missing?"

"That's right. The girl's parents were the first to disappear. It's part of the reason no one will take her in. They think she's responsible."

She shook her head in amazement. "That's crazy! She's a little girl. She must barely weigh twenty pounds. What possible harm could she cause anyone?"

"Superstitions and spiritual beliefs are powerful things out here. Just because she might not be physically capable of hurting someone doesn't mean she's not responsible."

"So the poor girl has lost both her parents and

then is turned into an outcast by the village? She must be so traumatised."

He reached out and touched her shoulder. "Erika, you can't walk into this situation and judge these people. Remember, you're here to report on what has happened—is still happening—and allowing your views to blinker you will only mean you'll get a narrow-minded view of the story. Yes, in England, allowing a six-year-old girl to fend for herself would be seen as child cruelty. Here, they're far more self-sufficient, even from a young age. There aren't the same dangers as there are back home. There're no cars, and no one is a stranger. She has a roof over her head, and she knows how to forage."

"But...but she's alone, and she's just lost her parents. Don't you think she'd be scared?"

"Did she look scared?"

"No, but..."

"Look, it's been a long day. Normally, the village would have a welcome gathering for you; however, they've lost five of their members over the last couple of weeks, and they're more frightened than in the partying mood. Raphael has gone to get us something to eat. His wife knew we were coming and has cooked for us."

Erika's stomach rumbled. "That's wonderful. I'm starving."

Outside the hut, Shaun got a fire started to keep off the worst of the mosquitoes, though they continued to buzz and whine around Erika's head. Within ten minutes, Raphael was back, carrying two banana leaf wraps in each hand.

He smiled, exposing startlingly white teeth, and bobbed his head at them, handing them a parcel each. The smell drifting up was amazing, and she quickly opened it. Rice and some kind of fish, together with a type of savoury banana.

They both ate with their fingers, and Erika found herself licking off the banana leaf to catch the last grains of rice on her tongue.

Her eyes grew heavy. "That was amazing, and I want to learn more about this place later. Right now I can barely think."

"Don't worry." He motioned toward the doorway with his hand. "Your bed is the one on the right. You brought a sleeping bag and a mosquito net?"

She nodded.

"You won't want to get into the bag as it's too warm, but it'll help make the bed softer."

"Okay, thanks." She hesitated, suddenly embarrassed. "This is going to sound like a stupid question…where's the bathroom?"

He laughed. "The jungle is your bathroom. If it's a number two, just bury it."

Her mortification deepened. "Ugh. Wonderful."

"I thought you'd done a whole heap of trekking in your twenties."

"Turns out I didn't care in my twenties. I guess the thirties bring with them a whole new sense of self-awareness."

Chapter Two

Erika walked away from the firelight, and immediately the absolute blackness of the night swallowed her. It pressed from every side like a living creature, threatening to lure her in and never let her out again. She'd brought a roll of toilet paper from her backpack and a torch. The light of her torch felt like a pinprick of illumination against the total dark, a pathetic attempt at conquering something that could not be conquered.

Hurrying her pace, she stepped into the bushes. Other than the beam of her light, she knew no one would be able to see her, and they probably wouldn't care if they did. Still, she felt self-conscious. A quick scout with the light reassured her that no giant spiders were waiting to creep up her backside while she squatted.

Holding the toilet paper in one hand and the torch in the other, she had no free hands. "Shit."

She wedged the roll under one arm and put the end of the light between her lips, trying to hold it firmly. The light wobbled as she undid the button of her shorts and quickly wriggled them down, together with her underwear, and squatted awkwardly.

The hot gush of urine hit the heated dirt beneath, and her relief was palpable as she let out a sigh.

Finished, Erika moved to pull her shorts back up.

Crack!

She froze. The buzz of insects masked her hearing, and her ears strained. The crack had been that of a large twig snapping, exactly as if broken beneath foot. Her mind flipped over what kind of large creatures lived out in the jungle. A big cat about to pounce, perhaps?

Erika waited to see if anything else happened, half expecting something to leap out of the darkness and attack her. Nothing did. Her heart racing, she fumbled with her clothes so she wouldn't be found half-eaten with her pants down. She exhaled a shaky breath, trying to pull herself together. She could see the firelight of the village not far away. They'd hear her if she shouted out for help. Wouldn't they?

Shaking off her paranoia, Erika took a step forward, intending on heading back to the hut.

She didn't get any further.

A strange noise echoed through the jungle, like a giant's teeth chattering together. It caused all the hairs on the back of her neck and down her arms to stand on end. She stared into the darkness in horror.

What the hell type of animal would make a sound like that?

The strange noise ended without her able to tell which direction it had been coming from. An animal, it must have been, some jungle animal calling to its mate. Only the sound had reminded her more of the character from *Silence of the Lambs* than any kind of animal. Panic clutched at her, and she hurried, stepping away from where she'd urinated, only wanting to be back in the hut, with the fire and Shaun close by.

Something stepped into the torchlight's beam.

Erika let out a scream, and then she realised who the figure was. "Oh my God. You just scared the life out of me."

The little girl with the big dark eyes stood staring up at her. Her face was utterly expressionless, blank even, her head tilted slightly to one side.

"Are you okay?" Erika asked, trying to shake off the chill that had run through her and calm her crazily beating heart. She was still shining the light directly in the girl's face, though she hadn't squinted or lifted her hand to protect her eyes, and Erika jerked the beam lower. The shadows the light created only served to make the girl's eyes even darker, as though they were mere hollow black holes in her skull.

Erika pushed the thought away. "Let's go back into the village," she said, though she knew the girl wouldn't understand her. She lifted the hand not holding the torch and pointed. "Village? Home?"

"Erika?" a male voice broke out of the darkness, calling to her. "I heard a scream. Is everything okay?"

She lifted her gaze from the child and held out

the flashlight to try to get a glimpse of Shaun approaching. "I'm fine. I'm here with—" As she said the words, movement slipped from beneath her. When she looked back down, the girl had vanished, only a slight rustling of the bushes to the right giving any indication she'd gone that way.

God, that was weird. No wonder the villagers think she's responsible for the disappearances.

No, Erika couldn't allow herself to think like that. She was a young child, probably traumatised and frightened by everything that had happened. For all Erika knew, the girl might know who was responsible for the tribe's missing people and that was what was causing the strange behaviour. Someone could be threatening her or abusing her to keep her quiet.

"Are you decent?" Shaun called again.

"Yeah," she said, continuing toward the village. "I'm coming."

She stepped out of the line of bushes and found Shaun waiting for her, a concerned expression on his face. "What's going on?"

For some reason, she didn't want to mention the girl, worrying that she was only adding to the child's bad reputation. "Oh, nothing. I thought a spider was crawling up my leg, and I freaked out."

He laughed. "You're going to have to get used to that. There are a lot of spiders around here."

"Yeah, I know. I'm fine, honestly. Just tired."

Moving past him, she headed to the hut. Her sleeping bag was laid out on the bamboo bed, the mosquito net hung in a canopy from the low ceiling.

Without saying anything else, she climbed

beneath the net and lay down. Exhaustion crept up over her, claiming her limbs to its weight. As sleep took over, she tried not to let those black holes of eyes follow her into her dreams.

Erika woke to a scream shattering the otherwise still night.

She bolted upright in bed and fumbled down the right hand side where she'd left her torch. Before she found it, a light illuminated from the other side of the hut, and she glanced over to see Shaun standing beside his bed.

Her fingers finally touched the cool metal of her torch, and she flicked the switch, the light joining the beam from Shaun's.

"What's going on?" she hissed over to him.

He glanced her way, his expression serious. "I don't know."

Another wail sounded through the night, and Erika fought with the mosquito net to get to her feet, tangling herself up in it before breaking free.

She and Shaun stood, staring at one another in the dim light.

Movement and shouts from more people came from outside, and both she and Shaun ran for the door. They stepped out to find half of the village standing in a group outside the central meeting house. An older woman cried in great, whooping wails, her hands covering her face. The men all stood with various weapons, mainly spears, held in their hands. The tension was high, and even though she couldn't understand a word that was being said, Erika knew enough about body language to ascertain something bad had happened.

"What do you think is going on?" Erika asked Shaun, keeping her voice low so as to not attract any attention. Although no one was paying any attention to them at the moment, they were still strangers in this situation. And everyone knew strangers weren't to be trusted.

Shaun spotted Teodoro, one of their guides from the previous day. "Give me a minute."

He went over and spoke to the man in a mixture of languages and hand gestures and then walked back to Erika. "The woman's son is missing. He's only fourteen years old. They went to bed with all of them in the hut, and when she woke during the night she discovered him gone."

"Could he have just gone to use the bathroom or something?"

"They found blood in his bed, quite a substantial amount it seems. It's not looking good."

Erika looked back over to the wailing woman and brought her hand to her mouth. "Jesus."

Shaun's lips thinned. "This is the reason we're here. To see if we can figure out what's going on and help these people."

Erika surveyed the group of men holding spears, their voices growing raised and more agitated the longer they stood together. "Are they going to try to find the boy?"

"Yes…and no."

"What do you mean?"

"They're going to find the person they think took

him."

Something suddenly occurred to Erika, and she quickly glanced around, trying to see if someone else was missing. Her heart lurched. "You don't mean the little girl, do you? They surely don't think she's responsible for pulling a teenage boy out of his bed in the middle of the night without any of his family noticing?"

"It's the explanation they believe. I can understand a few of the words they're muttering around here. They're calling her the Devil's daughter."

Her stomach churned, her muscles tensing with anger. "You've got to be fucking kidding me. We can't let a group of grown men with spears hunt a little girl down. This is goddamned barbaric. Can't they see this must have been done by an animal of some kind? A big cat or something!"

Shaun pushed his glasses higher up his nose. "We're just here to observe. We can't interfere."

Erika clenched her fists. "If you say that one more time, I'm going to grab one of those spears and stab you myself."

The men began to head off, moving in a jog as a huddled group. When Erika moved to follow, strong fingers wrapped around her wrist and pulled her back.

"What good do you think you're going to do running off into the jungle in the dark?" Shaun hissed. "All you'll do is get lost or killed. Do you think you can help the girl then? Use your brain, Erika. I thought you were smart? If you want to help her, think before you act. Besides, the girl is a lot more capable than you are out there. She's small, and if she wants to hide, I'm sure she'll find somewhere. The jungle is a big place."

Though she didn't want to admit it, Shaun had a point. She *would* get lost out there. Still, the thought of the girl being hunted down like some kind of animal broke her heart while making her want to rage at the tribespeople.

"They should be hunting for whatever animal is big enough and strong enough to pull people from their beds in the middle of the night," she muttered, "or even try to find the poor boy who's gone missing."

"I agree," said Shaun, "but there's nothing we can do right now. Let's go and try to get some more sleep. We'll think on things again in the morning."

Erika didn't have much choice. She allowed him to guide her back to the hut, promising herself she'd do something at first light.

Assuming the girl wasn't already dead by then.

Chapter Three

As soon as the first shafts of light crept through the open doorway, Erika climbed from the hard bed and left the hut, leaving Shaun snoring quietly on the other side of the room. The village was quiet, people sleeping later after all the activity in the middle of the night. While part of her had been aware of the tribesmen returning during the night, she hadn't heard any more commotion, and exhaustion from all the travelling had dragged her back into sleep.

Erika had intended on heading into the bushes to relieve the pressure on her bladder, then something caught her eye and her heart lurched. From where she was standing, she could see the front of the meeting house, and curled up on a woven mat in the doorway was a tiny figure.

Instantly, her thoughts jumped to the worst conclusion—the girl had been hurt and dumped there by the tribesmen. Erika hurried over, realising the girl was sleeping peacefully, her thin shoulders barely lifting with each breath, her expression serene.

Did the tribesmen even know she was back? Asleep out here in the open, the child obviously had no idea she was in danger.

Or else she knows they can't harm her.

Erika shook her head at herself. Where had that thought come from?

Though she wanted to grab the girl and run far away with her, she held herself back. She had nowhere to go, and perhaps she simply wasn't seeing the bigger picture. Shaun might have misunderstood what the tribesmen had been saying last night. Perhaps they had no desire to hurt her at all and instead had been concerned for her whereabouts?

Then why do they call her the Devil's daughter?

Erika pushed the thought from her head. She couldn't allow herself to be drawn into this madness. A couple of strange incidents in an already strange situation meant nothing. The girl was just a child.

The tribespeople began to stir in their huts, waking to ready themselves for the day. She didn't want to imagine how the mother of the boy must feel right now, waking to an empty, bloodied bed. Still, Erika wondered how an animal had made it into the hut and taken off with the boy without him making a sound or anyone noticing until after he was gone. And it wasn't only the boy who'd been taken. Grown men and a woman had gone missing before him. Even though the tribespeople were small in stature, far smaller than their British visitors, it would still take an animal of considerable strength to drag them away with no commotion.

A hand on her shoulder made Erika jump, and she barely managed to hold back the scream threatening to burst from her throat.

"You okay?" Shaun asked.

She spun around, her hand clutched to her chest. "Jesus. You just scared the shit out of me."

"Sorry. You've been standing here staring at the meeting house for ages. I was getting worried."

She blinked. "Have I?"

It hadn't felt like that long. When she looked around, she discovered the village was up and about. She turned back to where the girl had been asleep on the mat in the doorway, and the space was empty.

She pointed at the spot. "Did you see her?"

"Who?"

"The little girl. She was curled up asleep on the mat, right there. That's who I was watching."

Shaun slowly shook his head. "Sorry, Erika. I didn't see anyone."

She ran to the meeting house. One of the elder tribeswoman was inside, busying herself with sweeping the dirt floor. There was no sign of the girl.

She went back outside to Shaun, her fingers at her mouth, gnawing away at the nail, a habit she'd give up a long time ago. "She must have run off."

"I can't say I blame her," he replied. "Now let's go and get some breakfast. We need to keep our energy up."

"What's the plan for the day?"

"We're going to accompany one of the tracking groups. They'll be able to see more in the light, and hopefully we'll get some idea of what's going on. I'll take my camera, if you want to take your notebook?"

Erika nodded. She needed to remember she was here to do a job.

They ate a simple breakfast of rice and plantains and then gathered their things to join the trek. They each carried a backpack containing water, insect repellent, and a first aid kit. Shaun's camera hung from around his neck, and he held a machete in one hand.

She gestured to the knife. "Protection?"

He grimaced. "Let's hope not. It's more for hacking away at any foliage blocking the way."

She nodded, only partially relieved. "Right."

The group who had gathered was all men, the women staying behind to watch the children and tend to the livestock. Erika felt like even more of an outsider, tall and blonde and obviously female. She could sense the men's disapproval of her accompanying them, which only served to heighten her anxiety.

As they left the village and hiked into the jungle, she did her best to remain calm and professional, though both the events of the night and seeing the little girl asleep that morning haunted her. Being in the depths of the jungle didn't help her frame of mind either. It was hard to believe the concrete buildings, cars, and people of London existed when all that stretched for miles were trees. She felt like she'd been transported back to a prehistoric time, where the insects were the size of small mammals, and the foliage surrounding her was thousands of years old. Once more she was plagued by the idea that the depths of the shadows held something more sinister than simple darkness. Something was taking these people. And even though it had only happened at night so far, the thought that something could snatch her from behind wouldn't leave her mind.

Commotion sounded up ahead, the tribesmen shouting to one another.

Erika looked to Shaun, her stomach tightening in a knot. "What's going on?"

"I guess they found something."

They ran to the spot where the tribesmen had gathered. A big track ran through the mud, vanishing into the undergrowth. Clearly, something heavy had been dragged. In the distance, Erika heard the sound of running water. They must be somewhere near a river.

"A crocodile," she guessed. "Surely this points to a croc being responsible."

"I've never heard of one going into huts before."

"They're very open. Walls of sticks and bamboo, some not even that. How would a hungry crocodile even know it was a house it was going into?"

"That's true." He lifted his camera, snapped some images, and then used the recording facility to film himself, holding the camera at arm's length. "We're searching for the remains of the sixth member of the tribe to go missing…"

Erika froze, her ears straining. From somewhere

nearby came the same strange chattering she'd heard before, a mixture of teeth clacking together and lips smacking. She didn't know how else to think of it. It was a sound that sent fingers crawling up her back and across her neck.

"Can you hear that?" she hissed at Shaun.

He frowned and tilted his head as though to listen, although the moment she'd spoken, the sound had stopped.

A high-pitched scream suddenly issued through the jungle.

Erika stared at Shaun. "Oh my God. What now?"

Shaun grabbed her arm, and they hurried through the undergrowth to where the tribesmen stood together in a group, shouting and gesturing at one another.

Erika noticed they were one man down. "It's happened again, hasn't it?"

Someone else had been taken.

Chapter Four

They got back to the village just before nightfall.

They still didn't have any answers, and there was no sign of the sixth tribesman who'd gone missing. It was as though someone was plucking the people from the face of the Earth. While Erika still believed that a crocodile was the most likely explanation, it was strange no one had seen the reptile, who must have been huge in order to snatch a grown man like that.

Right now, Erika only wanted to be able to get a full night's sleep. Between the broken sleep the previous night and the full day's trek, she was exhausted.

While Shaun sat on the edge of his bed inspecting the images he'd taken during the day, Erika prepared herself for sleep and prayed no one else went missing during the night. If this continued, within a couple of weeks the tribe wouldn't have anyone left.

"Erika," Shaun called from the other side of the hut, a chill to his tone. "Come look at this."

The growingly familiar feeling of dread settled over her, her heart rate tripping. She got to her feet and crossed the hut to sit beside him on the bamboo bed.

"Watch," he said and played back the footage he'd recorded of him speaking while they'd been in the jungle. He pointed at the screen. "Look, there. In the background."

Icy fingers ran up her back, her hairs standing on end. "Oh my God."

Standing not far behind him was the girl from the village. She stared directly into the camera with her large, almost black eyes, her expression solemn.

"She must have followed the search party," said Erika.

He lifted his eyebrows. "You think? Why didn't we see her?"

"I don't know. Like you said, she's self sufficient and she must be good at finding her way around the jungle. A child as slight as she is must be able to move pretty silently."

"She must have been completely silent. How did we not even hear her?"

Erika remembered the sound, the same strange chattering she'd heard when she'd gone to the bathroom the previous night, right before she'd seen the girl. Although her bladder tightened, suddenly feeling full, there was no way she'd be heading into the bushes alone that night.

"I don't know," she whispered. "Maybe we did."

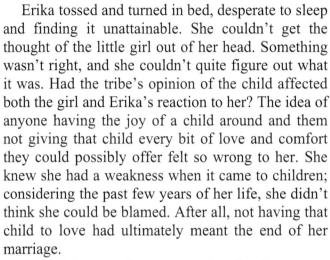

Erika tossed and turned in bed, desperate to sleep and finding it unattainable. She couldn't get the thought of the little girl out of her head. Something wasn't right, and she couldn't quite figure out what it was. Had the tribe's opinion of the child affected both the girl and Erika's reaction to her? The idea of anyone having the joy of a child around and them not giving that child every bit of love and comfort they could possibly offer felt so wrong to her. She knew she had a weakness when it came to children; considering the past few years of her life, she didn't think she could be blamed. After all, not having that child to love had ultimately meant the end of her marriage.

They'd been trying to conceive for five years. They'd started when she'd been twenty-seven, young and naive, with no idea that this exciting journey would turn into one of disappointment and heartbreak and eventually divorce. She'd imagined that by now they'd have had at least two children and would have sold their city flat to move out into the countryside, thinking about green spaces and potential schools. Instead, she was in the same flat, now on her own, with no possibility of a family anywhere in the future.

People could be happy without children, at least that's what she tried to tell herself. She could live a life doing what she was doing now—writing interesting stories from far-flung parts of the world with no ties or baggage. She could have the time of her life travelling the world and having wild, whirlwind romances with inappropriate men. Some women would love to have such a life. Except it had never been Erika's dream. The hollow ache in her heart told her that.

She hated that there was a child out here who not only didn't have anyone who loved her, who was being persecuted. For her to be responsible for the missing people was simply ludicrous.

Erika had only ever wanted a child to love, and here was a child who had no one.

Chapter Five

They woke the next morning without further event.

Erika was relieved no one else had gone missing in the night, and she'd finally managed to get a full night's sleep. Her stomach growled audibly and Shaun, who was changing his t-shirt on the other side of the hut, laughed at her.

"I assume it's time we go and find some breakfast," he teased.

She nodded. "Definitely." She was also desperate to pee, not having wanted to venture into the forest at night. Before she did anything else, she needed to relieve her poor bladder.

Picking up a roll of toilet paper, she said, "I'll meet you in a minute."

Erika headed into the bushes, taking care to watch out for spiders or anything larger that might bite. She emptied her bladder with relief and then made her way back into the village.

She frowned. The villagers stood at a distance, in a semi-circle in front of the meeting house, looking at something and speaking in quiet tones to one another. Shaun stood at the back of the group, his height, clothes, and color of his skin making him stand out. He also held his camera in one hand, pointed over the heads of the tribespeople.

Erika hurried over. "What's going on?" she whispered to him.

He nodded to the front of the meeting house. "The girl is back."

Her line of sight followed his. The little girl was asleep on the mat in the doorway of the meeting house, exactly as she had been the previous day. The child appeared completely unaware of the crowd gathered around her. The voices of the tribespeople grew louder, the men appearing to discuss something of importance. Erika's heart picked up its pace, and a sickening dread settled in her stomach.

"What are they doing?" she asked Shaun.

He shook his head. "I don't know."

Several of the men suddenly broke from the semi-circle, hurrying toward the girl. One of the men stooped and yanked the girl upright, dragging her from sleep.

"Hey!" Erika shouted. No one paid her any attention.

More men stepped forward, until the tiny figure of the girl was barely visible between the bodies. They grabbed her and began to haul her away from the meeting house.

Shaun spotted one of their guides and hurried over, Erika close behind.

"What is happening, Raphael?" Shaun asked the other man. "What are they doing with the girl?"

Raphael looked between them and the group of tribesmen with worry in his dark eyes. "They take her out. Leave her. Girl is bad luck to village."

Erika's mouth dropped open. "What? Take her out where? Into the jungle?"

"Girl is not good. Devil's daughter."

"Bullshit, she's just a little girl!"

The group of tribesmen carried the child, who didn't struggle. They passed the huts, broke through the line of trees, and vanished into the jungle.

Erika stared after them, unable to believe what was happening. They weren't really about to leave a six-year-old girl in the middle of the jungle alone, were they?

"No," she said, shaking her head in disbelief. "I can't let this happen."

Focused only on the spot where the tribesmen had vanished with the child, she broke into a run and took after them, vaguely aware of Shaun calling to her.

"Erika, wait!"

She wasn't going to wait. She needed to find the tribesmen before they lost the girl somewhere out in the depths of the jungle for good. While she knew Shaun would tell her that the girl was able to take care of herself, the tribesmen wanted to get rid of her. They would take her far enough away that she wouldn't be able to find her way back again.

Moving as quickly as she could, within minutes

she found herself tangled up in creepers that strung from the trees like Halloween decorations. By the time she managed to fight free, she could no longer discern the sound of the men moving through the jungle from all the other noises. The trees were alive with the crashing of birds and other wildlife, animals and insects hooting and tweeting and buzzing. She had no idea what direction she should go in next.

A hand on her shoulder dragged a scream from her throat.

"It's okay, it's only me."

She allowed Shaun to pull her against him, emotion flooding out of her. She didn't want to cry against his chest. Although she hated being weak, her reaction came from frustration, and this outpouring was the result of the last five years of disappointment and heartbreak. She had wanted a child so badly, and now here was a girl being thrown away as though she was no more than a disobedient dog no one had time for anymore.

"Come on," he said gently. "Let's go back to the hut. We can't do anything more."

Erika nodded and wiped away her tears, hating herself for giving up so easily. She had no survival skills and didn't know the jungle. She'd only end up getting herself lost if she tried to search any further.

With his hand on her lower back, Shaun guided her back to the hut. She drank some water and splashed her face, trying to figure out what to do.

"We have to tell people," she said eventually. "I know we shouldn't want to make trouble for the tribespeople, but we can't do nothing. What if, now that particular girl is gone, people still go missing, so they single out another girl, and another?"

"You're right. I've got it all on camera, them hauling her away," Shaun said. "Although I know I'm a photographer, not a filmmaker, I felt like we should have proof to take back with us about what's happened here."

"Can I see it?"

He nodded. "Of course."

Shaun retrieved his camera and scrolled through until he reached the clip he'd taken outside of the meeting house. They watched the elder tribesmen grab the girl, her appearing confused and frightened, and then the screen greyed out into static, then cleared again.

Erika stared at the screen, unable to believe what she was seeing, her heart in her throat. The doe-eyed young girl was gone, replaced by a pale-faced creature with burning red eyes and razor sharp teeth. The face was blurred, as though she was looking at a still image that had been captured while the subject had been moving, except Erika was watching a video.

The static returned, and the spectre was gone.

She turned to Shaun, tears of fear and disbelief blurring her vision. "Did you see that?" she said, her voice barely a whisper. "Please tell me you saw that too?"

He scrolled back through the footage. Where the... *thing*... had been was now filled with static.

"I saw it," he admitted. "I saw it."

"The footage is wrong," she said. "That... that *thing* wasn't her. Something happened. The footage must have got muddled up with footage of an animal or something."

"You've got to be kidding me. An animal? That wasn't an animal on the screen, Erika. That was her. That was the girl."

She shook her head, frantic. "No, that's what they want us to believe. The tribespeople must have done something to us—spiked our food and drink with some kind of a hallucinogenic maybe."

Shaun paled and slowly shook his head. "I don't know. Maybe that's what's happened. Perhaps there's something in our food that the tribespeople are used to, so it doesn't affect them, but makes us see things."

"Play it again."

He scrolled back. This time all they saw was static.

"I saw something," she whispered. "I know I did."

"We're both tired. Let's just try to get through the rest of the day. One more day and we can get out of here."

"Okay," she agreed, knowing she didn't have much choice. "One more day."

Chapter Six

The next morning, a shriek from outside the hut had them both clambering out of bed and racing for the door. A woman was jabbering in fear, her panicked screams quickly joined by more voices, all filled with dread.

Erika and Shaun exchanged a glance. *What now?*

If someone else had gone missing, at least they'd know the girl hadn't been responsible. Would the tribe then choose another child to blame? Thoughts rushed through Erika's head as they ran out into the village to find a group of the tribespeople once more gathered around the meeting house.

Erika stopped short, her eyes wide. She didn't know whether to be terrified or relieved.

The girl was back.

Just as she'd been each morning, the little girl was curled up on the mat in the doorway of the meeting house.

How had she found her way back here? Had she simply followed the tribesmen back?

One woman pointed and called out a name in her language. A second woman joined the cry, and then another, and another. Even though Erika didn't understand their language, she knew exactly what they were crying over and over.

Devil's daughter.
Devil's daughter.
Devil's daughter.

A couple of the elder tribesmen pushed through the crowds. They grabbed the girl as they'd done the previous day, yanking her from sleep. She barely struggled, her dark eyes wide.

"Hey, leave her alone!" Erika shouted, terrified of what they would do next. Would they take her out into the jungle again, knowing she was clearly capable of making her own way back?

None of the tribespeople even glanced her way, focused on the child they thought to be to blame for their missing relatives.

One of the women approached, holding out something to one of the men who had hold of the girl. In the sunlight, Erika saw the flash of a large knife, the same one she'd seen being used to kill a chicken for dinner during her stay.

Adrenaline burst through her. "No!"

When she lunged toward the group, numerous hands caught her, holding her back.

She struggled against them. "Get off me!"

Erika twisted toward Shaun, reading the concern on his features.

"Hey, that's enough now!" he shouted to the

tribesmen. "Put her down." He strode towards the girl, then found himself with several spears pointed at his chest. He put up his hands in surrender. "Please, let her go. This has gone too far."

Erika and Shaun locked eyes in desperation, completely helpless to do anything.

Tears filled Erika's eyes as she watched the knife brought to the girl's throat. A chant started up among the tribespeople, a haunting song.

No, no, no.

A flash of silver, and then blood, too much blood.

A scream echoed in Erika's ears, and she realised it was her own.

The girl's body slumped to the ground. The men scooped her up. They wouldn't want to keep her body in the village, wouldn't bury her. They probably worried her vengeful spirit would continue to torment them.

The hands released Erika, and she fell to her knees, sobbing. How could they do that to a child? She couldn't be here any longer. She needed to get away.

Erika staggered to her feet and ran blindly to her hut. She grabbed her belongings, stuffing her clothes and toiletries into her bag, rolling up her sleeping back, and attaching it to her rucksack.

A shadow fell over her. "What are you doing, Erika?" Shaun was standing in the doorway of the hut.

"What does it look like? I'm getting the hell out of here!"

"Where do you think you're going to go? The

plane doesn't arrive to pick you up until tomorrow. You can't just run out into the jungle."

"I think I'd rather take my chances with the trees than with a bunch of child killers."

He lowered his voice. "How do you think it's going to look if they see you run away? Do you think that's going to make it look like you're on their side?"

"I'm *not* on their side!"

"Our reaction out there was bad enough. I'm saying that I don't think we should do anything else to make them fear us."

Realisation dawned, and she paused in her packing. "You think they might hurt us?"

"I don't know. I do think we need to be careful though."

She laced her fingers in her hair, knotting the strands to pull at her scalp until it hurt. "Fuck. Fuck, fuck, fuck!"

"Just one more night," he said, taking hold of her wrist and pulling her hand from her hair. He took her other hand too, holding both in front of her, grounding her. "We keep our heads down and leave at first light, as planned."

"What are we supposed to do when we get home?"

His expression remained serious. "We report the story, just as we were always supposed to."

She took a shaky breath and nodded. "Okay. I guess we'd just better hope none of the villagers go missing in the night, or we might find *we're* the ones who end up with our throats cut."

She slept fitfully. At some point, she thought she heard the sound of teeth chattering, but it might have been a dream...

Chapter Seven

Erika woke with faint morning light filtering through the open doorway of the hut. She sat up, instantly alert, the events of the previous day immediately at the front of her mind. She glanced over to Shaun's side of the sleeping space and frowned.

Empty.

Alarm spiked through her. Where the hell was he? Had he already gone to see if Raphael would still be able to guide them back to the airstrip? Although their guide hadn't been directly involved with the girl's murder, he had been standing by, just like them. Yes, that must have been where Shaun had gone.

She'd gone to bed in her clothes, so she sat on the edge of the bed and pulled on her walking boots, which she'd purposefully left on the ground at her bedside. Her bags were already packed, so all she

94

needed to do was grab her rucksack.

Something across the room caught her eye, and she paused. Shaun's bag was still on the ground at the end of his bed. And that wasn't all. A streak of red stained the bed, and drag marks scarred the dirt floor.

Her hand flew to her mouth as she staggered back, holding in a shriek of fear.

Oh, God. Not Shaun, too?

The thing that frightened her the most was that if Shaun was dead, it meant she was here alone.

Not wanting to give up on him so easily, she ran from the hut.

Erika drew to a halt outside of the meeting house, staring in shock, her heart pounding, her head swimming. She blinked, hard, wondering if she was seeing things right or perhaps if she was still in bed, dreaming. However, she'd never felt more awake. She was hyper-alert, the world painfully bright and defined around her.

There, lying curled up on the mat in the doorway of the meeting house, was the girl they called the Devil's daughter.

"Oh my God."

Her paralysis broke and she ran to the little girl's side. Was she dead? While Erika couldn't see any sign of blood, there had been so much before, with the knife... She couldn't even bring herself to think about it.

The girl was definitely breathing.

Panic gripped Erika. What would the tribespeople do if they saw her here? She couldn't face going through them trying to hurt her again.

She couldn't explain how the girl was still alive or why she didn't appear to have a mark on her. She did know she had to get her away. A fierce protectiveness swept over her, a determination and need like nothing she'd ever felt before.

"Hey," she hissed, placing her hand on the girl's shoulder and shaking her awake. The girl's big, dark eyes blinked open, looking up at Erika with pure innocence. "You can't be here. If they see you, they'll kill you."

The girl unfurled, still dressed in no more than rags, her feet bare. She put her little hand out to Erika, and Erika's heart just about broke. She knew what the girl was saying even though they didn't speak the same language…

Help me.

Erika nodded. "I will. I swear. We need to get to the airstrip. I have a plane coming today. Do you know it—the airfield?" She put out her arm like a wing and made airplane noises.

The little girl nodded and stood, tugging on her hand.

What about Shaun?

Despite the guilt gnawing at her, she couldn't wait and try to find him. If what had happened to him had been the same as the other villagers, he was most likely dead, and if she stopped long enough to try and find him, they would kill the girl, and most likely kill her too for trying to help.

Noises were already coming from the surrounding huts as the tribespeople woke.

The little girl tugged on her hand, pulling her towards the line of trees that led to the forest.

"Yes," said Erika, understanding. "I know. We have to go."

She broke into a run to keep up with the child, her bag bouncing on her back. She didn't even notice its weight, the adrenaline coursing through her veins making her oblivious to everything except her need to get the girl to safety. Her life was literally in Erika's hands.

A shout came from behind them.

Forcing herself to run as she never had before, she picked up her pace, crashing through the undergrowth. Within minutes, she was soaked with sweat as it rolled down her back, gluing her backpack to her spine. Salt ran into her eyes, stinging, and she didn't even have any water with her. Even though the possibility she would die out here occurred to her, she couldn't allow herself to stop. The little girl ran slightly ahead, still holding Erika's hand, leading the way. The run barely affected the girl, her breathing no deeper, never seeming to tire.

"I can't do it!" Erika cried, feeling herself flagging, her legs so heavy she could barely lift them. She wanted to cry but didn't think she had enough fluid left in her body to allow the tears to form. Every part of her hurt.

The huge dark eyes stared up at her, the lower lip poking out. She tugged again on Erika's hand and pointed ahead.

It's not much further.

Erika nodded. "Okay. Okay." She forced her legs to keep going. She felt like they'd been running forever. Her lungs burned, like she was trying to breathe through warm treacle, and she couldn't catch a breath. She thought it would never end, then finally the trees opened out into a clearing and she held back a sob when she saw the plane waiting for her on the red patch of dirt.

The pilot stood beside the open doorway, and his eyes widened when he saw her with the child.

"I am sorry, Ma'am," he said in his broken English as they approached. "I cannot take girl."

"Please," she begged, gasping for breath. "I'll pay you. Whatever it takes. Her life is in danger and I need to get her somewhere safe."

He paused. "You pay? How much?"

She snatched a random figure out of the air. "One thousand pounds."

His lips tightened and he nodded. "Okay. You go now. You go quick."

She didn't need to be told twice. She helped the little girl up the stairs and onto the plane, marvelling the child showed no fear about being put onto an aircraft when it was clearly her first time flying.

They took a seat and the door slammed shut. The propellers started to spin, and before she knew it, the plane was bumping down the red dirt runway.

Erika sat back in her seat and finally took a deep breath. The airplane lifted and climbed into the sky, leaving the jungle as a sea of green far below.

Tiny fingers touched her hand. Instead of the warm touch she'd held during her run through the jungle, the child's skin was ice cold.

Goosebumps crawled up over her neck, tears of fear pricking the backs of her eyes.

With her heart in her throat, Erika forced her

head to turn and look down at the girl. Only this time she didn't see the child. She saw the creature who lived behind the innocent guise. The eyes were no longer dark, but blood red.

Erika squealed in terror.

The girl's fingers around her hand tightened, making her freeze. She was the girl's guardian now—*girl,* if that's even what she was. This was her new role in life. She would take the child away to a place where she would be safe, where whatever was inside her would be protected, and she would continue to kill.

Erika stared down at her in numb horror, and as she did, the girl's mouth stretched open wide. Beyond her lips, numerous sets of sharp teeth chattered…

THE END

About the Author

Marissa Farrar is a British author who has penned more than twenty novels. She predominantly writes paranormal romance and horror but has branched into contemporary fiction as well. When she's not writing, she's fighting off the sticky fingers of her three young daughters and looking forward to a glass of wine.

If you want to know more about Marissa, please visit her blog at www.marissa-farrar.blogspot.com. You can also find her at her Facebook page, www.facebook.com/marissa.farrar.author. To stay updated on all new releases and sales, sign up for her newsletter! http://forms.aweber.com/form/61/19822861.htm

Haverly Insane Asylum

By Taylor Henderson

Part 1

"Turn the flashlight back on," Lacey screeched, slapping her boyfriend Jace's arm roughly. "Come on, Jace. This isn't funny."

Despite Lacey's words, Jace and his friend Corey both began to laugh hysterically.

"Come on, Jace. This isn't funny," Corey mocked her, his imitation of her voice a high trill. "You're such a wimp, Lacey."

Just then, both of the boys flicked their flashlights back on and shone them around the room. Lacey let out a sigh of relief at the sudden light. Without it, the room was so dark that it seemed like the darkness was swallowing her up whole, suffocating her and touching even the darkest corners of her mind.

"Fine, I'll admit it, I'm a wimp. Does that mean we can leave now?" she questioned, hugging her torso. Her pleading voice sounded desperate even to her own ears. Lacey knew this was a bad idea from the start. She had been scared when Debra Wilkins first mentioned it in the cafeteria a few days ago. Debra was the type of girl who owned only dark clothing and ringed her eyes in black eyeliner every day. Maybe *her* idea of fun was breaking and entering in an insane asylum, but it wasn't Lacey's.

"No, this is awesome," Corey said, walking around slowly. The light from his flashlight bounced around the room to show broken gurneys and spray-painted walls. The words, "Death awaits you," were tagged on the inside of the door they'd just passed through.

Jace tossed his arm over his girlfriend's shoulder and put his mouth near her ear. "Don't worry, babe. I won't let anything happen to you."

Lacey shivered at his touch and nodded, ignoring the nagging feeling in her gut that told her they should leave.

Placing a wet kiss on her cheek, Jace added, "We can leave after we find the others."

"No the hell we can't," Corey chimed in, overhearing Jace's statement. "I think we should spend the night in here. Wouldn't that be awesome? We'd be legends. The first group of high schoolers to spend the night in Haverly Insane Asylum." He spoke as if he were broadcasting a headlining title to millions.

"I am *not* spending the night in here," Lacey insisted. "This place gives me the creeps," she said, shivering at the thought of being here for even another hour. In the dim lighting, Corey didn't see the glare she gave him.

He laughed. "No shocker there, princess," he spat. "You don't have to stay. If we find the others, I'm sure one of the girls in that group would volunteer in a heartbeat to cuddle up with Jace for the night."

"Come on, man. That's enough," Jace spoke up. "Let's just keep looking for them." He flashed his beam on the next door and pulled an unwilling Lacey along with him.

The floor creaked ominously as they exited the room and proceeded down a hallway. Lacey tried to ignore the daunting sounds she kept hearing. Coming from behind them she heard the sound of a door closing softly, and if she listened intently, she could swear she heard a shrill scream coming from up ahead.

My mind is playing tricks on me, that's all. She willed herself to believe that was true, but it was hard. Giving up, she held onto Jace's arm tightly.

As they made their way through the abandoned corridors, Corey flashed his light on the walls. They were tagged with sayings like, "Turn back," and, "Forbidden ground." The group walked together in a close pack until they reached an intersection of hallways.

The signs labeling where the halls led were peeling and faded. The only one that could be made out was the one leading to the examination room. Corey screeched like a child when he saw the sign. "Sweeeeet!" he said, stretching out the word.

Lacey bit her lip and held fast to Jace's arm.

Corey leaned into Lacey's side as they walked. "I hear they used to cut out the tongues of their more severe patients."

Lacey rolled her eyes. "That's not true."

"Oh, but it is, sweet cheeks. It was their way of preventing them from sharing their hallucinations with the other patients." He placed a hand on Lacey's slender shoulder, and she moved away quickly, her grasp on Jace never faltering. Everyone in town knew that Haverly had specialized in the treatment and care of those who were suspected of having schizophrenia, as well as those who were actually diagnosed with it. "It's rumored that if you listen hard enough, you can still hear the screams of the patients just before their tongues were cut from their throats."

"Just shut up, Corey. You aren't going to scare me."

Corey shone his flashlight beam on his face and grinned sinisterly. The light created dark shadows that stretched across his usually boyish face, making him look gaunt and hollow-eyed. He came to a stop in the center of the hallway, next to a rickety old gurney.

The couple came to a stop as well. Lacey groaned, while Jace just looked amused with his friend's antics.

"Just listen for a moment. Maybe we can hear the final screams of the patients who had their tongues removed from their mouths." Corey closed his eyes, listening to the eerie silence mixed with the sound of Lacey's heart pounding in her chest.

After merely a second that seemed to stretch on for an hour, Lacey stuttered, "T-this isn't funny, Corey."

Corey opened his eyes and glared at Lacey. "Stop whining for a moment and just listen to the screams of the once mentally unstable."

Lacey chewed her bottom lip and squeezed Jace's arm for the umpteenth time since they entered the asylum. Her heart pounded loudly in her ears, yet she still was able to hear the sound of a high-pitched scream as it tore through the air, causing her to scream in response and propel her body into Jace's. The force of Lacey's body made Jace lose his footing, and the pair ended up on the old linoleum floor that was covered in a layer of mouse droppings, shattered glass, and paint chips. Lacey was too horrified to care. Her body began to shake as the screaming continued. A few tears leaked from her eyes as goose bumps rose along her arms and legs. The scream was deafening in comparison to the once stark silence that filled the empty halls.

"I want to leave. I want to leave. I want to leave," she chanted under her breath, clinging to Jace for safety.

The screaming grew louder, and the owner of the voice began to plead for help. Lacey's voice was barely audible to even herself now. All she could hear were the tortured screams of pain that filled the air. The scream had torn through her ears and muddled her brain to the point that she didn't know if it was her screaming or not. Unsurprisingly, it was.

Jace held his girlfriend's shaking body to his chest, ignoring the glass that was cutting into his calf. He needed her to stop screaming. His flashlight had fallen from his hand, hit the ground and shattered, leaving them in more darkness than before. Although he didn't want to admit it, he was a little scared now too.

"Lacey, stop. You're okay," he said in an attempt to comfort her. When that didn't work, he got Corey to pull her off of the ground so he could stand up, then placed both hands on her shoulders and shook her. Her short hair was frazzled and raised at the ends. "Lacey! Snap out of it!"

Finally, her scream died and she collapsed a little, only to be caught by both guys. She looked weaker, like what had just happened had made her physically tired.

Jace hugged her body to his chest, kissing her face lightly until she nuzzled her head into the crook of his neck. He was only worried about her, and he knew how to get a reaction out of her.

"We need to find the others," Corey finally spoke up. "Think she's going to be alright?" While Corey liked to pick on Lacey, he truly didn't want anything bad to happen to her.

"I'm okay," Lacey answered, leaning away from Jace slightly. "You're right, we should find them. Then we can get the hell out of here."

Jace and Corey nodded, and the group walked down the hall toward where the scream came from. As they walked further, Lacey tried to hide her fear, but it was etched all over her face. The corridor seemed to stretch on longer than before, and with the absence of Jace's light everything was enveloped in shadows. Walking down the hall was more daunting now than it was before. The scream still echoed in the hall and in Lacey's mind. She was by far the most scared out of them all, evident by the viselike grip she had on Jace's arm.

"Maybe they went up to the third floor," Jace suggested.

Finding the others and getting out of the building was the best option in his mind. They already had been courageous enough by venturing inside the building at all, not to mention at night. That alone would be good enough to use to brag about and hold over the heads of everyone at school, including the wimps in his group of friends who had chickened out.

"Maybe. We've been everywhere on this floor already, and we know they wouldn't have gone back down to the main level," Corey rationalized.

When they all had first entered the building, they stayed as one group and explored together. Then Debra, Quinn, Kyle, and Chelsea decided that they wanted to find the morgue. Corey and Jace wanted to see everything, so they had decided to split up, and Lacey wanted to stay with Jace. When they finished seeing the entire main level, they went up a floor and found the morgue empty.

"We can go up and check the higher levels. They

probably wanted to see something else."

Jace glanced at Lacey, even though he could hardly make out her expression in the dark. Noticing that he looked her way, she nodded, knowing that he was waiting for her take on Corey's suggestion.

"All right, let's go back to the stairs," Jace said.

The walk back to the stairwells was harder than they had expected it to be. The hallways and rooms had turned them around, messing with their sense of direction. When they finally made it to the stairs, they all let out a sigh of relief and began to ascend the stairs with Corey in the lead and Jace bringing up the rear. They tread softly, watching their steps. The building was old and decrepit, and the last thing they wanted was for one of them to fall through a rotted away piece of the stairs.

Once they all reached the third level, Lacey latched onto her boyfriend and pressed her side against his. "Where to next, Corey?" she asked, staring off down a dark hall and feigning bravery.

Corey turned from side to side, flashing his light down each corridor. His light beam landed on the ground not far from a large rat whose eyes glowed red in the darkness. Corey grimaced in disgust and turned the opposite direction, away from the rat, and pointed the light back down the first hall.

"We'll go this way."

"We could just scream, you know. See if they hear us?" Lacey suggested.

Jace shook his head. "I've had enough screaming for one night."

"I second that," Corey said. "They have to be in

here somewhere. We'll find them. If they aren't on this level, then there's only one more level for them to be on." He flashed his beam at the ceiling.

"That's not true," Jace countered. "This place has a basement. Before they got shut down, they had to open a second morgue down there because of the excess bodies. They even installed a chute on each floor that would take the dead bodies to the basement."

Lacey gagged, feeling sick to her stomach at the thought of rotted, dead bodies piled up in the basement. "That's disgusting."

"They wouldn't go down there," Corey said.

"I don't know." Jace shrugged. "I think Debra would. She's into all of that morbid type of stuff."

"All right, well, let's just check this floor before we have to worry about anything else," Corey said. Then he proceeded to walk down the hallway, leading the way.

The hallways on this level were filled with far less junk than the other two floors had been. The first two floors were covered in debris, broken glass, cigarette butts, dead animals, paint chips, beer bottles, and more. This floor had some glass here and there, as well as the big chips of paint from the walls, though for the most part it wasn't so bad. These were probably the levels that fewer people ventured to, and that thought alone made pride swell inside of Corey.

The group pushed past old metal gurneys and rickety-looking wheelchairs. When they made it halfway down the hall, peeking into rooms to check for their friends, Lacey heard the sound of a girl's voice coming from farther down the hall. She couldn't make out who it belonged to, but they all set off toward the room she heard the sound from.

Corey entered first, walking slowly and cautiously despite his macho man attitude. Lacey and Jace followed closely behind, leaning around Corey to see who or what was in the room. The beam of Corey's flashlight flicked around the room, until a dull amber glow caught his eye. He aimed his flashlight at it, and the beam landed on a raven-haired girl huddled in the corner of the room. Her long, dark hair was parted down the center and hung on either side of her thin, pale face. She looked up at them, smiling for a second before taking a final long pull from her cigarette and putting it out on the wall.

"Debra?" Lacey chimed.

"In the flesh," Debra replied, pushing herself to her feet. She brushed her butt off and raised both hands to tuck her hair behind her ears. "Can you *not* shine that light right in my eyes?" she snapped at Corey.

Corey obliged and lowered the light to the ground. "Where is everyone? Why are you in here alone?"

The shadow from Corey's flashlight was still raised enough to create a haunting shadow on Debra's face. Debra smirked and shrugged her bony shoulders before she walked toward them.

"I wanted to be alone to fully embrace this experience. Besides, I needed a cigarette and Quinn has bad asthma, so we split up and she went to find you guys."

Jace pulled his arm free of Lacey's grip and slipped his arm around her shoulders. "Where are the others?" he asked.

Debra chuckled and shook her head. In the dim lighting, her wide, black eyes looked desolate, and the smile on her thin lips looked almost sinister. "They left less than half an hour after we split up. They were so scared." The way she said it was as if she were holding back laughter. "I don't know why." She kicked a rotten mattress that was lying on the ground. Dust particles billowed through the air, only visible in the beam from the flashlight. "Everything in here is either old and broken or dead."

"Do you know where Quinn is now?" Corey asked.

Debra shrugged. "No. I've been sitting in here since she left. She said she wanted to explore some more. Her flashlight's battery died, so I let her take mine."

Corey nodded, as if that was the logical thing to do. Split up and find a dark corner in a supposedly haunted asylum to smoke a cigarette. Debra was just that kind of person. Always looming in the shadows, laughing at crude humor, keeping everything in her life a mystery even to her supposedly closest friends. She was probably unfazed by the decrepit building surrounding her, unlike Lacey.

"Well, can we find her and get out of here? This place is seriously giving me the creeps." Lacey shivered. Although she felt weak for asking, and for being afraid, she had a gnawing feeling in the pit of

111

her stomach. She was always the type to trust her gut feeling, and this time her gut was telling her to get the hell out of dodge. She didn't want to be here any longer, but they couldn't just leave without Quinn.

Debra walked forward and placed a hand on Lacey's narrow shoulder. "Chill out, Lace. Nothing's going to happen to you in here." Her breath smelled acrid, and the overpowering smell of stale cigarettes weaved around Lacey, the scent almost choking her. "Let's just call out to her."

Jace chuckled. "This place is huge. No way she'll hear us."

"She will if she's close," Corey countered.

"It's worth a try," Debra said, sliding past them and heading out the door and into the hallway.

The group followed her lead, Corey keeping his flashlight trained on the hallway in front of Debra as she went.

"Quinn!" Debra called, her voice high and playful sounding. "Come out, come out, wherever you are!" she chanted. She cupped her hands around her mouth as she shouted, spinning in a slow circle. "Quinn!"

"Maybe she took the stairs up?" Corey asked aloud. He pointed his beam at the cracked ceiling.

"She could've. We'll find her eventually." Debra shrugged, as if finding her friend wasn't a priority. "You know, it's rumored that entering this building can make you go crazy," she said, stopping at the stairs. "Not only have we entered it, but now we're going to have been on every level."

Lacey's heart hammered in her chest. "We-we

never went in the basement," she pointed out, trying to keep her voice from shaking.

"There is no basement anymore. They filled it with cement years ago. The first floor is the lowest level," Debra answered, turning to take the stairs up. She didn't take her time or check the steps before she ascended. She clomped up them, not worried even the slightest that they could cave in at any second.

"Are you guys coming or what?" she called from the top. As the rest of the group slowly made their way upwards, she said, "I did a lot of research on this building before tonight. I've been planning this for a long time. If you guys didn't come, I would've come alone."

Lacey scowled when she reached the landing of the fourth floor. "That would've been so dumb. What if something happened to you and no one knew where you were, and you had no one here to help you?" Lacey questioned, her hands on her hips, now far angrier than she was scared. While she didn't consider Debra as one of her best friends, she did care about her, and she didn't want anything bad to happen to her either.

"Well, I guess that's kind of inconsequential now, isn't it?" Debra mused. She turned away from Lacey and walked down the hallway, trailed by Corey.

"Jace," Lacey whispered when the others were far enough away to not overhear her, "if they don't want to leave, I think we should get out of here."

Jace smoothed his girlfriend's hair down, leaning slightly to be on the same level as her face. "We're all leaving as soon as we find Quinn. I promise. She has to be on this level. As soon as we find her, we're out of here." He pulled Lacey close to him and hugged her tightly. She nearly melted in his embrace, relaxing in the safety of his arms.

"I love you," she murmured against his chest.

"I love you too," he replied, kissing her forehead. "Let's go." Jace took Lacey's hand in his, and they proceeded down the hallway in the direction that their friends had gone. It didn't take them long to find the others. When they entered the room, Lacey sighed loudly in relief when she saw Quinn standing next to Debra in the center of the room.

Corey stood near the door, holding his flashlight to the floor. It appeared as if his light was reflecting all over the room. Shards of glass of all sizes were scattered on the ground. Two long windows near the far wall were empty of glass and gave a wide view of the trees and overgrown grass that surrounded the building outside.

"Isn't it beautiful?" Quinn asked. She was staring out the window. The moon above was full and opaque. It was mesmerizing.

"It is," Debra responded. "Is this where you've been the whole time?"

"No," Quinn answered. "I was exploring, then I found this. I was going to come and get you guys to show you, then you came in here." She turned and smiled at her friends. The moonlight reflected off her glasses and the shards on the ground alike.

Quinn was a petite girl, often mistaken as much younger because of her cutesy style, short stature, and narrow frame. With her blonde hair and positive outlook on things, she was almost the exact opposite of Debra. It was a wonder that they were even friends.

"It really is beautiful," Lacey agreed, "and I'm glad I got to see it. Now I think we should all get out of here." She pulled her outdated flip phone from her pocket. Although the service bar still showed that she had no service inside the building, that wasn't her goal. She looked at the time. "It's half past midnight, and I have to be home before one or I'm so dead."

Quinn flipped the switch on her flashlight, filling the room with a bright glow and lighting everything up. "I kind of want to stay longer. I don't think I've seen everything yet," she said timidly, as if she didn't want to make Lacey mad.

"I'll stay with her," Debra volunteered quickly, still staring out of the window. "I have some unfinished business to take care of in here."

"I kind of want to stay too," Corey said. He set his flashlight on the floor and slid his backpack off of his shoulder. He crouched down, digging in the bag for a moment before pulling out a can of spray paint and holding it up for everyone to see. "I can't leave until I mark that I've been here." He smirked. "I got red so that it'll look kind of like blood."

Debra grinned. "Cool. You have to let me borrow that."

Corey nodded. "Sure."

Lacey could feel the anger building up inside her. "Seriously? Fine. Jace and I will leave, but don't come crying to us when something bad happens!" she yelled, stomping her foot down and crushing small shards of glass beneath her feet. Breathing heavily from her outburst, she said, "Come on, Jace, let's get out of here."

"Sure, let me just take a picture of the view from the window before we go."

Lacey scowled and crossed her arms in annoyance. Ignoring her, Jace crossed the room. Once at the windows, he slipped his phone from his pocket and snapped a few photos of the view. "This will be good proof that we actually came inside and went all the way up," he said under his breath. He stared at his phone screen, flicking through the pictures he'd just taken as he crossed the room again.

Everything happened in slow motion then. It was as if Lacey's gut feeling was coming alive into something even more horrible than she'd anticipated. She watched with her mouth agape as Jace lost his footing on a piece of glass and fell forward, dropping his phone and landing in the shards of broken glass on his hands and knees. His face came inches from hitting the ground before his hands caught him. Instantly, she ran to him, dropping down to help.

Shards of glass impaled his hands and legs, but worst of all was a long, jagged piece of glass that stuck out of his throat. Jace tried to scream, causing the glass that was lodged into his neck to bob. The only sound that came out was a garbled gurgling.

"Help him!" Lacey screamed at her friends, who were all in shock, just staring at Jace as he struggled to breathe. Lacey knew it was up to her to act quickly. She reached out slowly, afraid to hurt the guy she loved so much, and touched the end of the cool glass that pierced his neck. Jace's eyes widened fearfully. "I'm going to make it stop," she told him, gripping the glass. She yanked it free in one swift tug, cringing at the sucking sound that came as she pulled it from Jace's throat.

His blood came fast, spurting a crimson red. Lacey hastily tried to block the flow of blood, her tears blurring her eyes. "Help me!" she screamed to her friends, but her words fell on dead ears. "Please God, someone help me!" Jace's body fell forward, his weight knocking Lacey backwards into the broken glass. Pieces of glass pierced her legs in multiple places, but she didn't care. All she was worried about was Jace. She applied pressure to his neck, staring deep into his eyes and sobbing hysterically as he gagged on his own blood, straining for a breath. It wasn't long before his lifeless eyes stared back up at her.

Lacey cried harder, leaning over Jace's body, hugging him to her chest tightly. She wasn't sure how long she sat like that, hunched around him, with tears flowing down her cheeks. When she finally stopped shaking and looked up, her friends stared back down at her with horrified looks on their faces. She started to stand, still gripping the glass in her hand that she'd yanked from Jace's throat.

"We need to get out of here, guys, but we can't leave Jace here," she said, realizing that she had to take control of the situation.

Quinn looked like she was going to be sick, Corey looked broken, and Debra was frozen in shock. Lacey got to her feet, pulling a piece of glass from her calf, and stepped toward Corey. She needed his help to carry Jace. They couldn't just leave him like this. "Corey," she pleaded, "you have to help me."

Corey shook his head hurriedly. "I'm getting the hell out of here," he said, turning and running from the room.

Lacey's mouth dropped open in shock. "Corey!" she screamed after him. He didn't respond. She stooped to grab Jace's shoulders, trying to pull his body toward the door. It was useless. She wasn't strong enough to carry his weight alone. She looked at Quinn and Debra, who had edged closer to the door. Quinn was pulling Debra along.

"Help me!" she screamed, trying to snap them out of it. At her outburst, they both ran from the room, their footsteps echoing on the hallway floor. The room was now empty of her friends and their flashlights. The moon left a haunting glow on Jace's face. Lacey broke down, sobbing again and hunching over his body.

How could they just leave him like that?

For the first time since she entered the building, she was alone. She held onto Jace like her life depended on it. Her grip was tighter than it had been all night as she continued crying over his still warm body and wishing that they'd never entered the building. She'd known something bad would happen, and she was right all along.

Part 2

Lacey's footsteps were loud as she walked down the hallway slowly. The darkness was thick, and her mind played tricks on her at every corner. Her priority was to find her friends and then get as far away from Haverly Insane Asylum as possible. Her heart thudded loudly in her chest and felt like it was seconds from breaking through her ribcage. She was terrified. She couldn't remember a time when she'd been alone like this before. Especially not in an old, decrepit building like the asylum.

Leaving Jace had been one of the hardest things she had ever had to do, but she wasn't strong enough to carry him on her own. She couldn't believe that Corey had left him like that. He and Jace had been best friends since elementary school, and he didn't even try to help him. Lacey shook her head in disbelief. People reacted differently in certain situations. Corey must just be the type who

119

couldn't handle tough situations and had the impulse to flee. She needed to find him and the others and make sure they were all okay. Then they needed to leave and go to the police so that they could come back for Jace.

She felt resolve, knowing that she would be out of there soon and would be sending someone back for Jace. Her thoughts were still muddled about exactly what had happened. It was like a horrible nightmare. One second he was fine, and the next he was collapsed on the ground with a shard of glass lodged into his throat.

We should have never come here, Lacey thought for the hundredth time that night.

Why hadn't anyone listened to her? Why did no one take her seriously?

She huffed, feeling a surge of anger building up inside of her.

It's all their fault, she thought as she gripped a doorknob and opened a door rougher than she had intended to. The door creaked loudly, and she jumped back, screeching in fright when a large shadow on the floor scurried over her shoe and down the hall. When the silence had settled again, Lacey heard a voice at the end of the hallway. Her head snapped to her right, and she focused her attention on the sound. It sounded like Quinn.

Her heart lifting at the sound of her friend, Lacey hurried toward the direction where she heard the voice. When she rounded the corner to the room, she walked in to see a large, open room with old-fashioned bathtubs lined up in rows. With the help of the flashlight her attention was directed toward

Quinn, who was kneeling beside one of the bathtubs, trying to force Debra out of the tub. Debra's head was leaned back on the rim of the tub with her dark hair spilling over the edge. She had a glowing cigarette in her hand that she lowered to her mouth and took a long drag from.

Hearing her enter, Quinn looked up with wide eyes. She stood to her feet quickly and backed away from the bathtub Debra was laying in. Lacey frowned. They'd left her alone, not caring about Jace even the slightest, and were now hanging out in the washrooms. Did they care about Jace that little? Was smoking a cigarette more important to Debra than her own friend?

Lacey crossed her arms over her chest and scowled. "I can't believe you two left Jace like that," she said loudly.

Quinn tugged at the scarf that was draped around her neck uncomfortably. "Debra, get out of the tub," she said, ignoring Lacey.

Debra ignored Quinn and puffed on her cigarette. "This is the reason we came here, Quinn," she droned ominously.

Lacey eyed them both in confusion. Quinn slowly backed up until she was near a tub that was against the wall. She placed her hands on the rim of the tub and stood up on it. She removed her long infinity scarf and tossed it over a beam that hung low from the ceiling, pulled the scarf toward her, and hooked it around her neck.

Lacey's mouth dropped open when Quinn stepped away from the edge of the tub. Hanging from the ceiling, her small body bounced and swayed. Lacey charged toward her, ignoring the pain in her legs from where the glass had stabbed into her. When she reached Quinn, she wrapped her arms around her legs and tried to lift her out of the self-made noose, but she was much heavier than she looked.

"Debra, help me!"

Debra merely climbed out of the tub and sat on the edge, watching them while she continued to puff on her cigarette. She made no attempt to help, and Lacey realized that she was on her own. She stooped lower, gripping Quinn's legs below her knees, then stood up. Quinn gasped, taking in a breath of air before she kicked Lacey roughly, her foot connecting with Lacey's face and sending her stumbling backwards. Lacey winced, cradling her head in her hands, the taste of blood flooding her mouth. Woozy, she tried to maintain her balance, but she never took her eyes off of Quinn's dangling body for even a second.

Once she recovered from the blow, she tried to pull Quinn down again. She gripped her legs and lifted, to no avail. After a few minutes of trying to pull her down, she finally gave up. Her breathing heavy she slumped to the floor, crying harder than she ever had.

The sound of Debra's footsteps stomping toward her caused her to look up. Debra stood over her, pointing the flashlight up at Quinn's face. Her usual complexion was now replaced by a bluish tint, and her eyes were wide open as if they were frozen in fear.

"There was nothing we could have done to stop

her," Debra said, turning the light downwards to shine it on Lacey.

Lacey shielded her eyes until Debra crouched down and placed the light on the floor. She took one final pull of her cigarette, blowing the smoke into Lacey's face, then she stood up and dropped the butt, stubbing it out with the toe of her combat boot.

"What do you mean?" Lacey questioned as Debra walked toward one of the glassless windows.

Debra didn't even turn around. "When someone wants to die, it's hard to stop them." Her words sent chills through Lacey. "I'm sorry I brought you all here. I didn't want any of this to happen. The only person who was supposed to die tonight was me."

"What do you mean?"

Debra turned around, and the moonlight that poured through the window highlighted her expression. She looked...*broken*. "I've been planning this night for a long time. I invited you all here because I wanted my friends to be the last people I saw before I did it. I didn't plan for things to go this way."

Her words were finally beginning to make sense. Lacey held onto the edge of a tub nearest to her and pulled herself to her feet. Her legs were wobbly like overcooked noodles. "Why would you want to do that?" she asked, stepping toward Debra with an expression of genuine concern on her face.

Debra stepped backward, nearing the window. "Don't come near me," she demanded. A crystalline tear dripped down her cheek, and she hurriedly wiped it away. "You wouldn't understand."

Lacey crossed her arms over her chest. "Try

me."

Heaving a sigh, Debra shook her head. "Everything is just so *hard.* Not everyone can live a perfect, happy life like you do, Lacey."

My life isn't perfect, Lacey almost corrected her, then thought better of it, not seeing how that would make any difference.

"My foster parents hate me," Debra continued, her voice sounding choked up now. "I overheard them talking about getting me transferred to a new house. They think I'm a bad influence on their son." She wiped another tear away. "They don't know that *he's* the one they should be sending away. The guy is a creep." She shuddered, and Lacey wondered what was going through her mind.

Lacey took another step forward, thankfully unnoticed by Debra, who was wiping her tears with the sleeve of her black sweater dress. "Did he try something with you?"

Debra let out a shaky, forced laugh. "What *hasn't* he tried? I sleep with my freaking desk chair wedged under the doorknob just to keep him out at night."

Lacey shook her head, feeling bad for Debra. She couldn't believe she hadn't seen it before. Debra's foster brother, Archie Powell, was pretty popular at school. He was friends with everyone, although whenever he came around Debra, her mood always changed instantly. She never wanted him around. Lacey had always just thought that it was sibling rivalry. Now she knew that that wasn't the case.

"Did he ever…?" Lacey didn't want to ask the

question on her mind.

Debra looked physically sick at the thought of it. "If you're asking if he *raped* me, then no, but he did touch me." She looked away, wrapping her arms around herself as if she was trying to hold herself together. "He's a creep," she repeated.

"Well, maybe the best thing is to get moved to a new house then. One where he can't get to you," Lacey suggested.

Debra shook her head. In the moonlight, Lacey could see that tears were now streaming down her cheeks. For the first time, Debra looked lost. She always seemed to have an air of maturity about her that no one else their age had. She had an effortlessly cool style about her, and she always seemed so sure of everything. Now she looked like she needed someone to take care of her. Lacey didn't know why Debra was in a foster home, as she didn't disclose much information about herself; however, she wondered if the toll of having to grow up so quickly had finally hit her. Standing by the broken window, in her black sweater dress, torn stockings, and beat-up combat boots, she looked like a child in need of guidance.

"I actually like my foster parents," Debra said with a sniffle. She hugged herself tighter. "This is the first time since my mom died that I feel like I'm a part of a family, and now they don't even want me." She wiped her face again. "What's wrong with me?" she asked, her voice breaking.

"Nothing's wrong with you, Debra."

"Yes there is. You hardly know me. You just know the fake me that I want everyone to see. You don't know anything real about me."

Lacey stood frozen, realizing that her words were true. "Well, tell me something then."

Debra stepped backwards, sitting on the window's ledge. "My dad was a heroin addict who left my mom and me when I was pretty young. I never even got to know him, and he just left us. I wasn't good enough for him to stay, I guess." Debra hung her head low. "It was just my mom and me for a long time, and then she met Zeke when I was thirteen. She loved him, and he said he loved her too, but that was just bullshit," she spat angrily. "He used to hit her, and she just let him. It was like that for years until one day he wouldn't stop. He just kept hitting her. So I stepped in, and then he turned his anger on me."

"That's awful."

Debra shrugged. "I probably deserved it."

"Don't say that."

"Anyway, after he hit me my mom was done. She didn't want to be with him anymore if he couldn't control his temper. The next day I came home from school and all of our bags were packed and sitting in the living room. I was *so* happy." Her breath escaped in a strangled sob. "I called out for her, but there was no response, so I went looking. When I found her, she was already dead. Apparently Zeke came home early from work and saw her packing to leave and he killed her."

Lacey couldn't even imagine the pain Debra had gone through. "I'm so sorry," she whispered just loud enough for Debra to hear her.

"Why are you sorry? You didn't kill her. You

didn't leave me when I was little. You didn't hit me or sneak into my room and touch me. You didn't kill my mom and then put me into the foster system at fourteen. You didn't put the thought in my foster parents' minds to get rid of me. You didn't slap me around or treat me like shit like all of my other foster parents did."

Lacey held her hand out and stepped toward Debra. She wasn't far. If she ran to her, she could grab her. "Let me help you."

Debra shook her head and swung her leg over the ledge so that she was straddling it now. "I don't deserve to live." She focused her eyes behind Lacey on Quinn's hanging body. "I killed Jace and Quinn."

Lacey frowned. "No, you didn't."

"I did. I'm the one who brought you here, and being in here makes you go insane. You start to see things that aren't real. It can make you behave in ways that wouldn't normally behave." Debra pushed her dark hair back off of her face and tilted her head up to the sky. The moonlight made her skin appear to glow. Her chest rose slowly as she took in a deep breath, and then she swung her other leg over.

Lacey ran forward just as Debra began to slip away. She screamed, watching in horror as Debra fell like a rag doll, plummeting toward the ground in slow motion. Lacey's knees buckled when Debra's body hit the ground, her limbs and neck bent at unnatural angles. A broken cry escaped her throat, and she slumped to the floor, sitting in glass for the third time that night. Her body ached as if she was the one who'd just plummeted four stories to her untimely demise.

She pressed her back against the wall beneath the window, breathing heavily. This night had quickly turned into a nightmare. Jace, Quinn, and Debra were all dead. The only people left were her and Corey, and she was sure that he had left the building already. Now her worst fear had come true; she was alone in Haverly Insane Asylum. She should have trusted her gut instinct and never come inside this Godforsaken place.

Her heart raced, and she had to press her hand to her chest and focus on her breathing to calm herself down. She tried to keep her eyes focused on her shoes, afraid to look up and see Quinn's lifeless eyes staring back at her. Once she had collected herself, she stood up on shaky legs and crossed the room, heading toward where Quinn's body dangled from the ceiling beam. She kept her eyes low, going around the body to grab the flashlight from the ground near the tub that Debra had been sitting in not long ago. Her heart ached at the thought.

She grabbed the cold handle of the flashlight and made a beeline for the door. She needed to get out of here and fast. There was no point in staying anymore. Debra and Quinn were gone, and Corey was more than likely halfway back into town now. She hoped that he would be headed for the police station. She didn't want her friends' bodies to be left on the hospital's premises for any longer than they had to be.

Lacey gripped the handle of the flashlight tightly, shining the beam down the hallways on her way toward the staircases. They creaked, groaning under the weight of her descent. The blood rushing through her ears created eerie sounds that made the hair on the nape of her neck stand on end. Lacey moved faster, and when she reached the second level, she heard the sound of a gurney rolling and footsteps. While her mind told her to run, her body froze. She stood completely still, flicking the switch on her flashlight off and allowing the darkness to consume her.

She listened, trying to calm her breathing. The gurney stopped rolling. The footsteps continued, and to the left of her, at the bottom of the next set of stairs, she saw the beam of a flashlight. At the sight of the light, Lacey instantly perked up. Corey had the other flashlight. He had waited for her. They could go to the police together.

"Corey!" she called out as she hurried down the next flight of stairs, following the direction that the light had been going in.

Why is he going away from the exit? Lacey wondered, heading further down the hallway. At the end of the hall, there was a door with a plaque on it that labeled it as the examination room. It was the room that Corey had wanted to visit earlier. Lacey saw the light beam go past the bottom of the door for a second. Even after what happened upstairs, he was still interested in seeing the building.

Shaking her head, she opened the door. As she entered the room, the flashlight beam hit her face, momentarily blinding her, before it was clicked off.

"Corey, turn the light back on," Lacey demanded. She didn't want to be there for a second longer. She was going to have nightmares about this night for the rest of her life.

Lacey neared the corner of the room where the light had come from. When Corey didn't flick the light back on, she fumbled with hers for a moment, turning the light on and shining it in front of her. A strangled scream left her instantly at the sight before her.

Standing in the corner of the room wasn't Corey. Instead, there was the figure of a pale, skinny man standing not even a few inches in front of her. The look of pain was evident in his eyes, and he held a tan straitjacket in his red-stained hands. The part that made her skin crawl and her stomach churn was his mouth. His jaw was hanging open, and crimson blood was dripping down his chin, onto the front of his shirt. She noticed in horror that there was no tongue in his mouth.

Corey's words from earlier that night hit her like a ton of bricks. *"I hear they used to cut out the tongues of their more severe patients."*

Knowing that she was probably just seeing things, Lacey stepped back slowly, keeping her flashlight trained on the figure in front of her. She backed up, terrified. She hoped that she could get to the door without anything happening, but that thought was quickly erased from her mind when suddenly the man ran at her, dropping the straitjacket and shoving her backwards. Lacey hit the ground hard, screaming. He was on top of her. She kicked and flailed her limbs, swinging her flashlight around wildly as the man on top of her gripped her throat roughly. The blood dripping from his chin landed on her face, mixing with the blood that was already smeared across her skin.

Lacey swung her flashlight hard into the man's temple. She slammed it into the side of his head until he fell off of her. When he hit the ground, she climbed on top of him, slamming the flashlight down repeatedly. She continued to cry out, letting her anger out with each hit she took. The sound of the flashlight slamming into the man's skull was horrific. Still, she wanted to make sure that there was no way he was coming after her when she was done. She continued to sit on the man's chest, hitting him with the flashlight until his face no longer resembled a face. When she was finished, she rolled off of him, breathing heavily and sobbing. Her hands shook, and the flashlight was covered in warm blood.

She stood and ran from the room. The blood on her flashlight created a red glow as she ran through the halls on the main floor in search of the doors that she and her friends had entered through earlier that night. Her legs were shaky and weak, and she ran out of breath fast, hunching over and vomiting in the center of one of the hallways. She felt sick to her stomach, and she knew she had to get outside.

Standing back to full height, Lacey pointed her flashlight in front of her, instantly recognizing a grouping of old gurneys in front of her. One of them was lying on its side, and she remembered that when they first came inside the asylum, Debra had hopped onto a gurney and had Corey push her around. When they got to the group of gurneys, she had gotten off and had shoved it over, laughing.

131

"Sometimes it's fun to leave a disaster zone behind. Especially if you know no one will care in the end," she had said, running toward one of the rooms excitedly.

Lacey felt relieved that she knew she was close to getting out. She pushed past the gurneys, rolling them out of her way and walking briskly down the hall. Her attention was caught by rows of pictures that lined the hallway. When she and her friends entered that night, there had been nothing there but chipped paint and graffiti.

Lacey shone her flashlight up at the first picture, stopping to look at it. What she saw sent a chill down her spine. Her hand shook as she stared at the picture that showed Jace standing near the two long windows on the fourth floor. The picture came to life, moving and showing Jace snapping a photo of the view before turning around and flicking through the pictures. He had a cute smile etched onto his face as he looked at them, and then he tripped, landing on his hands and knees in the glass.

Lacey saw herself in the picture screaming and running forward, grabbing Jace's shoulder. The Jace in the picture looked up, smiling and assuring everyone that he was okay.

"I'm fine, I'm fine," his voice said in her ear.

The image of herself reached for a long shard of glass lying by Jace's leg and stabbed it into his throat. His eyes went wide in terror as she pushed the glass farther and then proceeded to pull it out. Jace slumped over onto her, blood spurting all over her face and hands. She screamed for her friends to help her. Then everyone fled.

Lacey's mouth dropped open, and she shook her head vehemently as the picture froze again. "That's not how it happened," she said aloud, looking all around her. The walls seemed to be closing in on her. Gasping for breath, she squatted down and hung her head between her legs.

That's not what happened. He fell onto the glass. I was trying to help *him.*

"That's not what happened!" Lacey screamed, standing upright. She turned her light on the next picture that had begun to move. "No, that's not right either," she mumbled, shaking her head slowly. The image depicted a different story than she had witnessed of Quinn's death.

In the image, Lacey was standing on the bathtub, yanking Quinn backwards by her scarf. Quinn was so small she barely had a chance as Lacey hooked the scarf over the beam and hoisted her upwards. Quinn flailed her limbs, trying to grab onto any and everything to save herself. All the while, Debra was sitting on the edge of the tub, frozen in fear.

"Debra, help me!" The cry for help hadn't come from Lacey's mouth but rather from Quinn's.

Tears welled up in Lacey's eyes as she saw herself kill Quinn. She knew it hadn't happened that way. Quinn had killed herself, hadn't she? Yet Lacey couldn't shake the feeling of how heavy Quinn had seemed earlier. Quinn was tiny. Rationally, there was no way that Lacey couldn't have saved her, unless she hadn't really been trying to in the first place.

The moving image turned to show Lacey and Debra talking after she'd hung Quinn. Debra was backing away toward the window, and Lacey was taking tentative steps toward her. Bits of their conversation floated through Lacey's mind. Debra was telling her why she wanted to die and about her childhood, except in this version Lacey was egging her on, daring her to take her life. Lacey heard herself telling Debra to jump, saying that was the best decision and that Debra could never fix things. It was as if Lacey was verbally pushing her friend over the window's ledge.

One part finally registered in her mind.

"I killed Jace and Quinn," Debra said, straddling the window's ledge.

"No you didn't," came Lacey's response. Her voice sounded sinister even to her own ears.

"I did," Debra said fervently. *"I'm the one who brought you here, and being in here makes you go insane. You start to see things that aren't real. It can make you behave in ways that wouldn't normally behave."*

Lacey finally understood what Debra's words meant. She was saying that she killed Jace and Quinn by bringing them to Haverly, not that she had *actually* killed them. In fact, Lacey had. Debra felt responsible for Lacey's actions because she had known that coming inside of Haverly could make you go insane. Lacey had been seeing things all night long, and now she couldn't determine what was real and what was just figments of her imagination. She thought about the scream she heard when she was with Corey and Jace. They had looked terrified too, but now she wondered if they were just scared because she had begun screaming

134

for seemingly no reason.

Lacey began to breathe heavily, her heart breaking. She looked at the next picture, watching an image of Corey tug on the doors, unable to get out. Then he took out his can of spray paint and began to spray the doors. Afterwards, he turned around and walked down the hallway, looking for another way out. As he neared the staircase, Corey looked up, hearing Lacey call his name from the top of the steps. Looking scared, he hurried down the hall into the examination room. He was frantically looking for something when Lacey entered and he turned his flashlight off. She watched herself turn her light on, scream, and then back away from Corey, who ran forward and shoved her backwards. Then she watched in horror as she rolled over him and began to smash his face in with her flashlight until he was no longer recognizable.

Lacey began to shake uncontrollably. Her emotions hit her all at once when she realized that *she* had killed Jace, Quinn, and Corey. She may have even been able to stop Debra from jumping if she had been in the right state of mind. She dropped her flashlight, and it hit the ground, shattering.

Wracked by uncontrollable sobs, she ran toward the exit. Maybe if she got outside, she would be in control of her thoughts. Lacey ran, the dark making it hard for her to see where she was going and causing her to stumble over different objects that littered the floor. Finally, after running for seemingly forever, she saw a weird red glow flicker in front of her. She slowed, staring at the flickering sign hanging from the ceiling. Making out the word,

"Exit," relief swept through her.

She walked forward, keeping her eyes trained on the sign. With every step she took, the sign lit up more. When she was standing just beneath it, the sign was glowing a bright red, lighting up Corey's spray paint that was tagged across the two large main entrance doors.

In red spray paint, the words, **"No escape,"** were written in big, blocky letters.

The exit sign above her winked off, plunging her into a thick, inescapable darkness.

About the Author

Taylor Henderson is a psychology major at the University of Mary Washington who was born and raised in Northern Virginia. She has been an avid reader and writer since she was young and has always found solace in the worlds and characters other authors have brought to life in their works. Taylor plans to continue writing and hopes to expand to different genres in the future.

Facebook:
https://www.facebook.com/profile.php?id=10000
8525042075

Twitter:
https://twitter.com/TayMHenderson

Goodreads:
https://www.goodreads.com/author/show/988521
4.Taylor_Henderson

Anesthesia

By D.A. Roach

"Justin, I'm putting in my two-week notice."

"You're joking, right?"

I wasn't, and after a moment he realized that too.

"Mary Norfolk, half my crew heads home for summer break. You were one of the few I was counting on being around to pick up the slack."

I enjoyed my job at Ferment, the hottest club near campus. And the tips were amazing. At night, the club came alive with successful 20-30 somethings who'd found themselves with more money than they knew what to do with. They came to Ferment to work business deals, drink heavily, interact with gorgeous girls, and have their egos inflated. It was a part-time job I worked to make ends meet until I finished school. Graduation day was nearing, and I had a great job in my field lined up to start in July.

"I'm sorry. I received a letter yesterday informing me I got the apprentice architect job at Archetype. I start in mid-July."

"Archetype? Where is that located?"

"Austin, Texas."

Justin's jaw dropped. "That's, like, a two-day drive from here. I thought you applied at Allied? They're only a ten-minute drive from here."

"I know. But the job at Archetype is a chance of a lifetime." I set my hand on his arm. "I promise I'll come back to visit. I gotta give this a try."

"Why are you quitting a month and half before the new job?"

I knew Justin would have to scramble to find another bartender that could handle the busy crowds of the Ferment weekends, and with only two weeks' notice, the pressure was on to find a suitable replacement.

"I'm scheduled for surgery the week after graduation and will need time to recuperate."

"Oh my God, is everything okay?" The defensive Justin stepped aside, and the caring one that I'd come to love took his place.

"I'm okay. I decided to have a breast reduction."

His eyes trailed down to my breasts then back up to my face. "You're crazy. Sorry, what I meant was, you're beautiful. Why pay someone to change you?"

Justin wasn't the one caring these tits around all

day long. The mornings after a shift were the worst. My back would spasm as I lay in bed breathing through the pain, and only after a half hour of stretching could I manage getting out of bed. The pain wasn't even the half of it. For the past ten years of my life, guys would talk to my tits. Their eyes were instantly drawn to that part of my body, and once they locked on, the conversation was as good as dead. I hated it; I hated my tits. I had saved for the day to be free of them.

"You're a guy. You wouldn't understand. If you had big boobs, you'd never leave the bathroom mirror. You'd be like," I started running my hands up and down my breasts in a sensual way, "oh yeah, look at my titties. I'm so hot." We both chuckled.

"True," Justin said. "That'd be so awesome. By the way, that was pretty hot. Can you show me again what I'd be like?"

I threw my bar towel at him. He caught it mid-air and smiled at me, then set it back on the counter in front of me. "I still don't think you should do it. Aren't you worried about the risk of surgery? This is a totally elective procedure. What if they mess up and you kick the bucket? Or what if you end up losing a nipple?" His face contorted in disgust.

"Justin, it's not open heart surgery, so the risk of dying is fairly low. But thank you for the concern. The surgeon has a good reputation."

Justin was a decent guy. Even though he was surrounded by scantily clad women all day long, he wasn't slimy like the guys you see working clubs on TV shows or movies. In fact, he opened Ferment as a way to get more potential clients and connections for his own startup company. *"You have to give to get,"* he once told me. And it was true; nothing in life was free.

Ferment was a place where the geeky, smart, socially awkward crowd joined the handsome, charismatic, salesmen type and many successful ventures were launched. Justin once shared that many of the new companies formed under his roof gave him substantial stock shares as a gift in return for making the connection happen. Although he could probably retire tomorrow with the money that Ferment brought in along with that stock, Justin was a social bug and enjoyed mingling.

"Anyway, if you find a new bartender soon, I'd be happy to go over some of the tips and tricks I learned along the way." I grabbed the bar towel and mopped up the water droplets from the last washed glass.

Fray walked over in a tight white tee. She had the best boobs in the house. If mine turned out half as good as hers, I'd be happy.

"Hey, Mary." Fray nodded at me. "Justin, Tonya is gonna help close tonight. The sitter called and said my little guy woke up with a fever."

"Okay, thanks for makin' the switch. I'll put it in the books. Are you taking one of her closings in exchange, or is she only covering tonight?"

"She's covering tonight." She leaned in and gave Justin a hug. "'Night."

"'Night. Hope Leo feels better soon," Justin said.

"Thanks!" Fray pulled a sweatshirt over her top, pulled her hair into a messy bun, then headed out.

Looking at my work station, there was nothing

more that needed to be done. The bar had slowed down an hour ago, allowing me time to get it fully stocked and ready to go for the next night's crew. "I gotta get home for some sleep before my afternoon classes. I'll see you tomorrow, Justin."

He looked up from his scheduling book. "See ya, Mary."

I drove to my studio apartment on campus and took a quick shower, drew the blinds, and attempted to sleep, hoping to get at least four hours of rest before class.

Although two o'clock Econ was my least favorite class, it was a requirement for graduation. With only two weeks left of school, I could count the number of Econ classes remaining on one hand.

"We have a group project to take us to the end of the semester. You and three others will run a pharmacy. You will get a packet of info that includes sales, customer satisfaction, inventory, and overall rank against your neighboring pharmacies, or in our case, competing groups." Mr. Chassey flicked on the overhead projector. "Here are the groups. The first name in the group must come retrieve packets for each group member. Oh, and this is worth thirty percent of your final grade."

Ugh. I hated working in groups, and of course I was not a fan of two of my group members. John Stame and Jackson Demear had both had their fair share of wisecracks about my boobs this semester. I ignored them. Still, their wisecracks hurt, and I was not excited to spend extra time with them during these last weeks of school.

Lily Patrick, the fourth member of our group,

was a mousy, petite girl. She hadn't said a word all semester. She walked up to us with packets in her hand.

"Thank you, Lily," I said, and she nodded in reply. This wasn't looking hopeful. John and Jackson laughed and shoved at each other as they slid into two nearby seats. Lily passed them each a packet.

"It says we need to have a name and pick a manager. Suggestions?" I asked the group.

"How about Titty Drugs?" John suggested, and Jackson started laughing.

I pinned them with a stare. They were so childish, always having to play their little teasing game.

"Or Dope Knockers," Jackson chimed in, sending him and John into another fit of laughter.

"Are you done?" I asked them both, because I was. "Seriously, we have three weeks to get this done."

"She sounds mad," Jackson said to John, pleased he'd irritated me.

"I'm not mad. Let's forget the name for now. Any volunteers for managers?"

"You're the one talking. I think it should be you," Jackson suggested.

Although I did not want to lead this group of mismatched people, I couldn't see any of them stepping up to make it work.

"Any objections?" No one objected. "Okay. Can you all meet at the library reference center in the afternoons on Monday, Wednesday, or Friday?"

We made a standing date to meet up Monday and

Wednesday afternoons to discuss our ideas. "Lily, I want you to work on the name. John, look at the inventory for the past two weeks and make the inventory order for the next week. Jackson, you'll need to look through the customer satisfaction and comments to see what we are doing good and where we can improve. I'll look at sales. Questions?"

"Lily, seriously, give Dope Knockers some consideration."

Jackson was such a tool.

"Lily, come up with your own ideas," I said. "Okay, we'll meet Wednesday afternoon." Lily headed for the door and John ran after her, whispering in her ear as they left the classroom. John was also a tool. Hopefully Lily would not bend to their influence.

Psych was my last class of the day, and I enjoyed it the most of all my classes. There was a little bit of crazy in all of us, and I enjoyed thinking of real life examples of the different neuroses.

My appointment at ten in the morning had me nervous. The day of the surgery was approaching quickly, and Dr. Spangler wanted to take some measurements and discuss options.

The one-way streets of the downtown area pushed my anxiety level to an all new high and made me ten minutes late for my appointment. The Plastiques office was in a tall building at the corner of 3rd and LaBroix. Thankfully there was parking along the street. The lobby of the building was grand and expensive looking, with marble floors, modern glass doors, and beautiful wood accents. I stared at the unique and beautiful décor of the office building while I waited for the elevator to descend. A month's rent for one of these offices was probably more than I could dream to make in a year working full time with tips at Ferment. The elevator arrived, and I stepped in and pressed 3. It ascended and opened not to a hallway, but an entire office. The Plastiques office took up the entire 3rd floor and was decked out with lush deep purple velvet furnishings dotted with gold nailheads. A solitary woman sat at the enormous white, backlit desk. Her soft brown waves framed a gorgeous face and flawless skin, not a blemish or wrinkle in sight.

"Hello, I'm Mary Norfolk. Sorry I am late for my appointment with Dr. Spangler. I got a bit turned around."

"That's okay, we understand. Let me see…" She scanned something on her computer then looked up at me. "Okay, I have you checked in. Have a seat and they'll call you when they are ready."

I took a seat on one of the comfy couches. My phone beeped in my pocket. It was a text from Justin:

Justin: Still think you should leave those girls alone. What did they ever do to you?

Me: You already know how I feel about it.

Justin: I do. I didn't want to miss the chance to talk you out of it. Change is hard.

Me: I know.

"Mary?" A pretty blonde nurse came out to summon me. She looked like a fashion model. I couldn't help but wonder if all the office staff got discounts on plastic surgery and treatments or if Dr. Spangler only picked pretty girls to work for her. "Dr. Spangler is ready to see you." She led me down the hall to a cozy exam room, also with plush seating, carpeted floor, and large framed pictures on the walls. In fact, it felt less like a doctor's office than like a cozy reading room with an exam table in the center of it. "Take off your shirt and bra and put this gown on, tie goes in the back. Dr. Spangler will be with you in a moment."

After she left the room, I undressed. The large mirror on the wall was all the motivation I needed to know I was making the right choice. I had grown to hate my 36F breasts that did not fit my 130-pound frame. Shoot, my breasts probably weighed ten pounds on their own. My breasts were not perky like a typical twenty-three-year-old's breasts should be. Mine drooped and laid flat across my stomach, making me look older and heavier than I actually was.

I put on the gown and walked about the room. On a corner table sat a small flat screen playing a video about breast reductions, and next to the screen were three clear ovals filled with different liquids. Breast implants. I picked each one up and fondled them while chuckling to myself. I could probably ask Fray to feel hers, but she might think I was crushing on her. Nope, this was the only time I'd feel what a breast implant felt like.

"They feel kinda funny, don't they?" Dr. Spangler entered the room, and I was taken aback by her beauty. While the receptionist and nurse were pretty, Dr. Spangler stole the show. Never had I seen anyone as stunning as her, beauty that enraptured you, beauty that inspired poetic prose. "I prefer the silicone ones myself. What about you?"

I squeezed each of them once more gently and agreed. "The silicone feels more natural."

"Hop on up so I can take some measurements." She pointed at the exam table and took out a tape measure. "What size bra do you wear now?"

"36F."

"And you want to go to what size?"

"36C."

"Okay, I recommend a lift while we are in there so you get a more balanced and youthful look." After taking measurements, she wrote down a bunch of notes and numbers on a clipboard, then helped me put the gown back on.

There was a knock at the door. "Come in," she called.

The girl at the door had several freckles assembled in a pattern under her right eye that vaguely resembled the constellation Cassiopeia.

"Sorry to interrupt, Dr. Spangler. I need a signature on this chart."

Dr. Spangler glanced at the young nurse briefly before taking the chart to sign. She handed the clipboard back to the nurse and returned her attention to me while the nurse slipped out. "Sorry about that interruption. Where were we?" She scanned the chart in her hands. "Oh yes, have you noticed that one breast is larger than the other?"

"What? No."

"Come over to the mirror and have a look." I undid the gown and saw for the first time that my right breast was indeed larger. I looked horrified.

"It's quite common," Dr. Spangler explained. "They are sisters, after all, not twins. I wanted to show you because I'll need to take more tissue from the right breast. It will help even out the size, though there still may be a slight difference between the two after surgery. The incision site is prone to opening, so no pushing or pulling for six weeks, not even lifting a gallon of milk."

"What about driving? I live alone so I'd like to drive as soon as possible."

"As soon as you are no longer taking the prescription pain meds that I'll prescribe you, you can drive. Speaking of driving, you'll need a ride home after the surgery from someone you know. Some patients Uber or taxi here and then have us call a friend when they are ready to go home. Just let us know the day of the surgery." She stood to leave. "Go ahead and get dressed and Patricia will take you to the scheduling desk. See you soon."

Alone in the room, I took off the thin medical gown, stood in front of the full-length mirror, and really looked at myself. I wasn't one to spend a lot of time in front of the mirror, especially naked. My breasts were so disproportionate compared to the rest of my body and shape. They unevenly hung low and laid flat against my belly. I put on my bra and fastened it, then worked to shove my breasts into each cup, pulling and tugging until they looked the same and pointed in the same direction. Then I pulled my stretchy tee over my head.

There was a knock at the door. Another beautiful girl peeked in and introduced herself as Patricia. "Congratulations on making this decision. Breast reduction surgery has a high patient satisfaction rating, and I'm sure you won't regret it." She held the door open for me and then briskly walked down the hall to another office.

"Have a seat," Patricia said and sat on the other side of the desk, looking through a stack of papers. "Okay, looks like you are scheduled for a few weeks from now. We require two-thirds of the payment by next Wednesday. The rest you will pay the day of the surgery."

"What if I get sick right before the operation? Will they still do it?"

"Depends what you have. Give us a call and we'll figure it out."

Everything seemed to be moving so quickly; maybe they did that so you didn't have time to second guess yourself.

"Here's some information to take home and read. Call me with any questions. My info is at the top of the first page. Now, I'll need your signature on a few pages."

She passed a packet over to me. I skimmed it, seeing the words "Plastiques" and "breast reduction" on the paper, reassuring me that I was not signing my life savings away, only my permission for the procedure.

"Excellent," Patricia said when I handed her the

signed packet. "Any questions?"

"No. I'll call you if I think of any."

Patricia stood and walked me toward the reception room. The receptionist was busy taking a phone call but smiled and waved a farewell as I entered the glass elevators to descend to the lobby.

I needed to head home for some sleep. This weekend was historically the busiest of the year. Seniors were getting ready to graduate, and the regulars at Ferment wanted to poach the top grads before recruiters could sway them. The club would be packed. Justin had his A list lined up to work, the best-looking girls with the tightest bods and best personalities, and he had me on three nights in a row. Although it would be an exhausting weekend, I'd probably clear $1,500 by the end of it. Thankfully, Justin agreed to bring Cooper, Ferment's other bartender, on board to help with Saturday's crowd. Cooper worked the club during the weeknights when I was home studying. He was a good worker, but he was slow. This Saturday, I needed someone reliable who could make a strong drink, and Cooper did that well.

I laid down and set an alarm for three hours. Ferment opened at 6PM, and I wanted to get there early to set up and talk to Justin about driving me home from the surgery.

When my alarm woke me, I got ready for my shift. A black stretch mini skirt and a drape-necked batwing shirt would be my uniform for the night, along with ankle boots and a wrist covered in bangles. I set some loose curls in my long, dark blonde hair and went heavy on the eyeliner and mascara.

The club was already buzzing with preparations for the night when I arrived.

"Holy crap, someone wants good tips this weekend." Justin came over to the bar and pulled up a stool.

"You like?"

He answered with a smile and nod. "Stunning. How'd your appointment go?"

"Good, I like the surgeon. She seems real knowledgeable and thorough. And she and her staff are beautiful. That's a good sign, right?"

"Yeah, I guess." He didn't sound too enthused.

"You guess?"

"I mean, if the doctor was hideous and said she could make you look better, I'm not sure I'd believe her."

"Exactly. Oh, hey, Justin, they said I need a ride home from the operation. Do you think you can take me home? As long as I can get an early surgery spot for the day, that is. I don't wanna mess up your opening that evening."

"Huh? Yeah, yeah. Do you need a lift there too?"

"No, I have that figured out already. I'll take an Uber."

"Okay, text me the date and I'll put it on my calendar."

Fray hopped over to the bar. "Mary, did you see the doc?"

"I did. I like her."

"Sorry I couldn't recommend someone to you. I love my doc, but he's a good two-day drive from here. Not very convenient."

"No, that's okay."

"Ladies, please excuse me. I need to go over the reservations for the private seats." Justin stood and walked to his office.

"What day is the surgery?" Fray asked.

"The 13th. So that's what…two and a half weeks away? They said they'd call with the time of the surgery a few days before."

"I'm so happy for you. I know you've been wanting to do this for some time. When are you moving to Texas?"

"I can't lift, push, or pull anything for six weeks after the reduction, so the soonest would be end of June or early July. I start the new job on the fifteenth of July."

"I'm happy to help you pack. I have to bring Leo, but we could put on *Sesame Street* for him while we work."

"Thanks, Fray, that sounds great."

Fray was my favorite of all the girls that worked at Ferment. She always stopped by the bar to chat with me and see how I was doing. The girls of Ferment were supposed to mingle with the guests, keep the drinks full at the private tables, and make sure the patrons were entertained. It was a classy establishment where the girls were fully clothed and earned their tips based on their charisma and waitressing abilities. Once in a while, those tips would be very generous if a good business deal was made.

Fray was the only girl that had a group of regulars who came to the club to hang out and chat with her. They weren't after a new business deal; they simply came to enjoy the company and drinks with their friends and Fray.

"How's Leo feeling? He was sick last time I saw him."

"All better. The little stinker was back to full energy today and made a huge mess of my kitchen." She laughed. "Thanks for askin'. Doors open in ten, and I need to find Valerie. Have a good night, doll."

"You too."

"Hey, get me a drink. Hey dumbass, I'm talkin' to you." A cocky thirty-something with a suit and tie was barking orders at Cooper. He was drunk and belligerent.

Cooper's fist hit the bar top, his face showing every bit of anger he wanted to unleash on the guy. Poor Coop was used to the mellow weekday crowds. I needed to step in since this was Justin's big night. I wouldn't let this drunk ruin it.

"Coop, I got this one." I gently touched Cooper's shoulder. His body was rigid under my palm. "The guy with the plaid button down at the other end wants a screwdriver." I gently nudged Coop away from the irritating guy in front of me who now wore a wolfish grin. "What can I get you tonight, sir? A Coke, Sprite, water?"

The guy looked me up and down and laughed. "I'll take a gin and tonic...and your number."

Smiling at him while cringing inside, I grabbed a glass and fixed a watered-down version of his drink.

"Here you are. Shall I put it on your tab?"

"Yes, last name is Kent."

"Very good, Mr. Kent. Can I get you anything else?"

He looked at me with an intensity that made me uneasy and then, like almost every guy walking on the planet, he found *the girls*. Staring at my boobs, he replied, "Yeah, you never gave me your number."

"Mary, I need one of the chilled bottles of Dom." Justin to the rescue. I went to retrieve the champagne and saw Justin turn to the drunk patron. "James, haven't seen you in a while. Everything okay?"

"Today was rough. Nothing a few drinks won't wash away."

Justin chuckled and clapped his hand on James' back. "Be sure you don't get behind the wheel intoxicated." Justin turned toward me. "Mary, how's it goin' up here?"

From the corner of my eye, I could see Cooper had the situation under control and we did not need to alert Justin of James' rudeness from a few moments ago. I gave Cooper a quick, meaningful glance and then said to Justin, "It's been a great night."

"Good to hear." Justin took a tray with champagne flutes and the bottle of Dom and walked over to the private tables.

"Mary, huh?" James said, eying me.

"That's the name, don't wear it out. Excuse me

for a moment." I walked over to Cooper and excused myself for a trip to the bathroom. I needed a moment to breathe before dealing with James again. Letting pushy guys down nicely was a challenge. The quiet of the bathroom helped me decide that I would play the boyfriend card. Surely once he heard I was taken he would back off. I left the stall and checked myself in the mirror to make sure my hair and makeup were holding up to the hustle and bustle of the night.

Fray came in the bathroom, laughing hysterically.

"Everything alright?" I asked.

"Everything is awesome. Howie's here. Have you seen him?"

Howie was one of Fray's regulars. He was a nice guy, though a little bit old for Fray. He treated her well and tipped her even better.

"I didn't. Is he responsible for putting you in this state of hysterics?"

"Yes, of course! How's the bar going?"

"Busy. Cooper's a big help, though. Which reminds me, I need to head back. Have fun."

"Thanks, doll!" Fray said as she applied more lip gloss to her lips.

I walked out of the bathroom hallway. The club was packed. Hoping that James would get distracted by some of the other pretty girls in attendance tonight, I looked over to where he had sat at the bar, but the seat was empty. I scanned the rest of the patrons surrounding the bar to see if he was hitting on some girl. He was nowhere in sight. Cooper was busy tending to orders and seemed relaxed. Maybe he left? Scanning the crowd for either James or Justin, I did not expect to feel hands come from behind me and fondle my breasts. I whizzed around to find James wearing a satisfied grin.

"You're so beautiful."

I slapped his face so hard that my palm stung.

Fray popped out of the bathroom behind him, shocked at the scene before her. "Mary, are you okay?"

I nodded. James was rubbing his face while Fray ran past me and out into the crowd.

"Don't you dare put your hands on me again!"

Justin was suddenly in front of me, with Fray behind him looking concerned. "Mary, are you all right?" he asked.

"I am." Dammit. I hated that this went down on his busiest night. "Justin, I'm sorry. I don't want to ruin your night, but I won't let a strange guy touch me."

"It's okay. I'm not upset. Not with you. Fray, can you take Mary in the back for a moment? I'll be there shortly."

Fray led me off to the back of the club. I started shaking from the adrenaline surge.

"Here, Mary, drink this." Fray handed me a bottled water and urged me to sit down.

"Fray, I'm good. I need a minute to settle down. You don't have to stay with me."

"Nah, I'm gonna stay till Justin comes back here."

I nodded. "Thanks for getting Justin."

"Fray," Justin said, stepping into the room, "I'm back. I'll hang with Mary."

Fray came over and kissed the top of my head.

"Love you, Fray."

"Love you back, Mary." She grabbed a sequined headband and headed toward the club's main room.

Justin pulled up a chair in front of me. "Did he hurt you?"

"No. He felt me up without my permission, so I slapped him." Would Justin fire me for hitting a customer? I hoped not, but it was his establishment.

Justin nodded. "Good. I kicked him out and told him he's not welcome back. I'm sorry he did that to you, Mary." He pulled me in for a hug, and it felt nice to have Justin care for me and stick up for me. "Think you can finish out the night, or do I need to ask Coop to man the bar solo?"

This made me chuckle. We both knew that Cooper couldn't handle the bar nights on a normal weekend, let alone the biggest weekend of the year. "I don't know. I feel kinda nauseous. Maybe I should head home and get some sleep."

He pulled back. "Uh, okay." He rubbed his chin, looking knocked off balance. "Think you can drive yourself or should I get an Uber?"

I shoved his arm. "I'm kidding. I'll be fine. Just make sure that jerk doesn't come back in."

"Agreed." Justin looked relieved. "You had me there, scared the crap out of me."

"I know." I smiled at Justin. "I've been groped before, but there's something slimy about that guy. I don't know what it is; he just rubs me the wrong way. Having his hands on me…"

Justin put his arm around me protectively, and we walked toward the club floor. "He's gone now.

157

If you need to stop for the night at any point, you let me know."

"Thanks, Justin."

The rest of the night was busy and blessedly free of creeps. While Cooper and I washed the glasses and restocked the bar, Justin and Fray came over for a drink.

"Isn't James Kent that rich kid that lives up on Mason Hill?" Fray asked Justin.

"Yeah, he comes from money. Both his parents are doctors, so he's had money his whole life."

"I'm surprised he didn't become a doctor like his folks," Fray remarked.

Justin took a sip of his scotch. "He was. He once told me he liked the money but hated the gore, although I'm not sure if that's why he switched occupations. I wouldn't doubt if he had his license taken away from one of his run-ins with the law."

"Oh yeah?" I prompted.

"Yep. Mom and Dad were able to bury some of the charges with bribes, though not all of them."

"Did he do jail time?" Fray sat at the edge of her seat, anxious to hear the dirt on the rich guy.

"No, they only fined him because they know he has lots of money."

"How do you know all of this?" I asked.

"It's my business to know about the people coming through the door. Besides, when you sit long enough with a drunk, you'll soon find you become their personal sounding board."

"What kinda charges does this guy have?" Cooper came around and leaned against the bar.

"Mostly DUIs. There were a few times, when he

was younger, that he got in trouble for being a peeping tom."

"Perv," Fray said, a disgusted look crossing her face.

"Well, good riddance to him now." Justin raised his glass in cheers.

"Thank you for standing up for me, Justin." I was so grateful that he took my side. My previous employer would not have had my back as Justin did, as he firmly believed the motto, "The customer is always right."

"Anytime."

The four of us helped close up the club then we headed our separate ways.

The rest of the weekend was a blur. We had so many customers coming through the doors of Ferment that we had to worry about occupancy codes and began filtering guests in as others left to ensure we were not in violation of those codes.

I skipped classes Monday to reward myself for surviving the weekend. My grades were good, and missing one day of lectures wouldn't hurt me. I laid in bed watching trashy talk shows all morning until I got a text from Justin.

Justin: Are you avail between 1-2pm today?

Me: Yeah, why?

Justin: Fray says I owe you lunch–you game?

Me: Yeah, sure.

Justin: I'll pick you up at 1pm.

That gave me one hour to pick up and make myself look like a living person and not like the zombie I currently resembled.

Justin promptly knocked at my apartment door on the hour. I was used to seeing him dressed in slacks and button-down shirts for work each day, and the guy standing in my doorframe was the casual version of my boss. Justin wore gray cargo pants and a black Motley Crue t-shirt. His hair was styled as always, slicked back with the sides and back shaved close, but he'd skipped his morning shave and had a little scruff on his face. He looked good, really good.

"You look so different." My cheeks heated as I checked him out. "I'm not used to casual Justin."

"Sorry, I didn't put much effort into my appearance. Guess I'm still dragging from the busy weekend." He looked me up and down and smiled. "You look amazing. You ready to go?"

"Yeah, let me get my purse." I returned a moment later and locked the door behind us. "Where are we going?"

"Do you like sushi?" he asked as we headed down the front walk toward his car.

"Yeah."

"Great, there's this place that has the best sushi in town." Justin opened the car door for me and closed it once I was in, then ran to his side and got in. Justin's BMW X3 was a nice set of wheels as well, far nicer than my used Dodge Charger.

For all of one moment, I worried the

conversation between us would be awkward, but it ended up being so easy and fun to chat with Justin. I teased Justin for his Motley Crue shirt. He told me his older brother was a huge fan in the 80s and had turned him onto their music. He played a few songs on the drive to the restaurant, and I admitted to previously hearing several of the songs and liking them.

At the restaurant we talked about our families. He spoke very highly of his older brother and said his parents' marriage was dysfunctional. Both his folks had remarried several times and were obsessed with looking perfect. He took out his phone and showed me a picture of them. I was stunned. Justin's parents were flawless, like runway models. As he spoke of them, his face and voice hinted that he harbored some ill feelings toward them.

"Hey, I'm a member of the crappiest parents' club too!" He almost choked on his sushi when I told him my mom OD'd on heroin when I was in high school and I had never met my dad.

"How are you able to go to college? It's so expensive."

"I sold our house and all our belongings. I have loans for the rest."

"I'm impressed with you, Mary. You could have given up or turned to drugs. You didn't. Instead you're honest, bright, gorgeous..." He stopped and looked at the table. "I'm sorry. That was inappropriate." He looked at me; his cheeks had pinked up with embarrassment.

"It's okay. I heard nothing after 'honest'," I lied.

A wide smile spread across his face, then he shook his head, "No, it's okay. It's the truth. Doesn't matter anyway, you'll be leaving in a month." The moment was awkward between us. "Don't worry, I'm not into groping."

"Oh, that's too bad." I wanted to see how red I could make him.

He blushed. "No, I mean, I grope, though only with girls I'm involved with."

"Uh huh, sure," I teased. "Okay, okay. I'm only teasing you. Thank you for the compliments. I guess seeing my mom wither away in front of me motivated me to have a different life."

"I'm glad you have a different life, Mary."

"Me too."

I'd miss Justin when I moved; it's too bad my job offer was so far away.

Justin paid the bill, and he dropped me off at home.

"Thanks for the lunch. It was nice spending time with you outside of work," I said before exiting the car.

"I had a good time too. And you're welcome."

"I guess I'll see you Thursday. My last weekend of working."

"God, that came up so fast." He looked down at his steering wheel. "Guess I'll see you Thursday then. Bye, Mary, have a good week."

I waved to him before climbing the steps to my apartment.

Tuesday morning, I drove downtown to a repurposed goods store called Trash. The ad in the local entertainment paper boasted that they had unique gift items from local artists. I hoped to find farewell presents for Fray and Justin. Unfortunately, I didn't drive downtown often and was frazzled by the one-way streets. I eventually found the store and realized I would have to parallel park if I wanted to shop there. Although I had not parallel parked since my driver's license test, I managed to maneuver my Charger between two sedans in only two tries.

Trash was located in an older building. The store had a grass green wood door with big window panes on the top half. Inside, the wood floors had knots and cracks, giving the dark wood character. The walls were a bright golden yellow and barn red, which was merely the background to the awesome art that filled the room. Artists had combined old, used items, like bicycle wheels, barn wood, glass doorknobs, ornate spindles, and old tools to craft new items. Trash to treasure. I meandered through the aisles and nooks taking in all the beauty.

I ended up finding a hand-painted sign made out of reclaimed barn wood that read *"I blossomed in your sunlight."* It was perfect for Fray, as it applied to how she treated me and her son. For Justin, I found a cool bottle opener made out of a railroad spike and a wind chime made out of bottle caps. While they weren't very sentimental, I hoped that every time he heard the wind chime tinkling in the wind, he would remember me. After purchasing my items, I headed toward my car that was now sandwiched between two different cars with almost no space between them. Crap. I walked around the cars and decided I wouldn't be able to maneuver without someone visually assisting me, so I'd have to sit tight until one of the car owners returned. At least this was a two-hour parking zone so I was sure they'd return in the next two hours or be ticketed.

I got in the car and turned on the air and radio while I waited. Justin texted that Cooper was sick and couldn't do tonight's shift, asking if I could come in. As I was about to text back, I noticed someone in my periphery approaching the car in front of me.

The guy wearing the black suit looked back toward my car and locked eyes with me. Why did he look familiar? He approached my window and knocked on it. Crap. I rolled down the window, and the realization hit me…it was James Kent, the drunk who copped a feel last weekend.

"Mary? I thought that was you. What are you doing on this side of town?" He seemed a little less slimy when sober.

"A bit of shopping. I'm actually in a bit of a hurry and am blocked in. Think you could move your car so I can be on my way?"

He looked at his car then back at me and smiled. "Sure. First, I wanted to apologize for last weekend. I was in a shitty mood and had too much to drink. I'm not a nice guy when I drink." He pushed his hair back. "Anyway, hope you'll consider forgiving me. Good seeing you, Mary."

He walked back to his black Jag and drove off, his arm extended in a wave out his window.

Before pulling out into traffic, I texted Justin about the interaction I had with James, as well as telling him I'd be in to work tonight.

I walked into Ferment at 7:30PM. Justin came over and wrapped me in a hug.

"Life. Saver."

"What are you gonna do when I'm gone?"

"That's a good question. My brother might come help me out until I find a replacement. He's gotta wrap up some business first before heading out this way."

"That's really nice of him. Will he be taking a break from his job?"

"No. He's a software engineer and can work remotely. He'll work this day job and help me out when needed at night." Justin tried to look confident in the replacement setup, yet it was evident he was worried.

"Is he any good?"

"He was a bartender at the local bar at his college. But you know, college kids mostly drink shots and beer."

"Ferment's clientele mostly drinks mixed drinks and hard liquor."

"I know, we'll figure it out." He let out a worried chuckle. "Anyway, so James…that must have been awkward."

"That's an understatement."

"He apologized?"

"Yeah, he did. He even sounded sincere. He said he turns into a jerk when he drinks and that night he had too much liquor."

Justin made a face like the explanation seemed reasonable to him. "You okay?"

"Yeah. I'm good."

"Good, I need to head in the back and check in the rest of the liquor delivery. Thanks for fillin' in tonight, Mary."

"Glad I could help."

Justin told me James came by the club and apologized to him Monday afternoon. Justin had agreed to permit him in the club again. I wasn't surprised when James showed up at Ferment that night. While he spent some time at the bar making small talk with me, he kept his drinking to a minimum.

"Did you grow up around here or are you a transplant?" I asked James. My goal was to keep him talking about himself so that he wouldn't ask me a ton of questions or get flirty with me.

"I'm sure you already know the answer to that. Hasn't Justin filled you in on me?" He gave me a knowing glance. "What'd he tell you?"

"He said both your parents were doctors and you weren't a fan of the gore."

"That's true. Now I make my living in the international and domestic trading realm."

"Well, there's no gore in that." I chuckled.

"Only a little," he said seriously before taking a drink.

Just as I was about to ask him what would make that job gory, Justin came up and asked James to join him at a private table. He probably wanted to review club rules so that he wouldn't have to kick

James out again.

Tuesday nights at Ferment were slow, and this wasn't even Fray's night to work. The time was dragging past so slowly, it was torturous to watch the second hand slowly tick each dash on the clock again and again. Justin approached the bar, and I noticed James left.

"Everything alright? With James?" James didn't look drunk or mad when he left. Still, I was surprised he didn't stop by the bar to say goodbye.

"What? Oh, yeah. I think everything is going to work out fine. Hey, Mary, what if I manage to set you up with a good company in town? Would you consider staying?"

"I don't know, Justin. This is my dream job and a chance to explore a new town. It's like a fresh start, and I got nothin' here tying me down."

He looked hurt by my words. I didn't mean to hurt him, but I had a plan for my future, and I was excited to start on that path.

"I see. Well, would you at least reconsider having your body altered? You know there are risks to every surgery and—"

"Are you worried I'll become obsessed with it like your parents?" He looked up at me but said nothing. "You don't have to worry about that. I'm happy with who I am, but these breasts are too big."

"That's how it starts," he mumbled.

He was wrong. I had no interest in reshaping anything else on my body; I just did not want to deal with my large mismatched breasts any longer. I chose not to continue the argument and went about wiping down the bar. Justin walked away looking deflated, and I felt bad. Maybe having lunch the other day was a bad move this close to my departure. Maybe it gave him the wrong idea about us.

Justin was a nice guy. If we would have started something months ago, this all might have had a different outcome. If we were in a committed relationship, I might have tried one of the local companies he offered to set me up with. However, what we had was a friendship and one flirtatious lunch, not enough to sway me away from the potential that awaited me in Austin.

"Justin, my surgery is scheduled for 9AM. They said it should be about five hours before you can pick me up. Can you make it tomorrow at 2PM?"

"I can. I'd like to drive you in the morning as well."

"No. I don't want you sitting around here all day. Honestly, I am going to Uber in to the appointment." I heard a sigh on the other end of the phone.

"Okay. Only if you meet me for dinner tonight." He sounded less defeated and more hopeful of my answer. How could I let him down?

"Sure. Name the time and place."

"Gulliver's on the west side. How about 6PM?" From the sound of his voice, I could tell he was smiling.

"See you then." I spent the day cleaning and restocking everything since I knew I would not be driving or up to any chores for the first week after surgery. Then I cleaned up and headed to Gulliver's. I saw Justin's black BMW and parked next to it.

He was already seated and looking at the drink menu when I walked in.

"This is nice. Have you been here before?" It was a cozy restaurant with white tablecloths and dim lighting.

"A few times, yes. Would you like to see the drink menu?"

"I can't, surgery tomorrow."

"Right. Sorry. Do you mind if I get a cocktail?"

"No, not at all." I picked up the food menu and looked at the options. "Why are there no prices on the menu?"

"They are on mine. You have a 'blind' menu so you don't have to worry about the cost of the food during our meal."

"Well, that's silly. How will I know what to get if I don't know how much I'll have to pay?" I asked, surprised that I never knew about this concept before.

"If I had intended on having you pay for your meal, I would've asked for you to have a priced menu. Tonight is my treat." He set down the drink menu and picked up the dinner menu.

"Why is it your treat?"

"Employers often take an employee out for a meal when they are resigning on good terms. Since I don't know if you'll be up for a dinner out after your surgery, I didn't want to miss the chance to enjoy this time with you."

169

"Well, thank you. In that case, I'll order the lobster and steak platter for two."

He chuckled. "The most expensive menu item?" He peeked over his menu and saw me quietly giggling.

"I'm kidding."

"I'm not. If you really want it, order it." I decided on a simple chicken, orzo, and asparagus dish.

The conversation felt a bit strained at times. Justin seemed bothered by something, yet when I asked if something was wrong, he was quick to change the subject. My guess was that he wanted to try and talk me out of my surgery or leaving and was battling his desire to voice his opinions versus keep quiet and enjoy the evening. I was impressed and thankful he kept quiet because it was a most enjoyable evening.

The waitress came and took our plates away and left the bill for Justin. "Excuse me, I need to use the ladies room." I went to the restroom and heard a text message ping on my phone.

Fray: Good luck tomorrow. I'll be thinking about you.

Me: Thanks!

Back at the table, Justin was typing on his phone and quickly slipped it into his coat pocket when I approached.

"Are you ready to go?" I asked.

"Almost. I'm waiting for the waitress to bring

back my card. Have a seat."

I sat down and drank some of my water. "When does your brother arrive?"

"He's gonna try to come down this weekend. It all depends on where he's at with his work. He's trying to get his client visits out of the way so he can come help me." Justin raised his wine glass. "Shall we toast? To tomorrow." I clinked my water glass with his wine glass and took a sip. "In Russia the custom for toasting is you have to drink it all and place your glass on the floor." He chuckled. "Are you up for the challenge?"

"You're on." I downed my water and set the glass on the floor.

The waitress came by a moment later. "Here you go. Top copy is yours."

"Be careful of our glasses." Justin pointed to the floor where both our glasses sat. "Russian tradition."

She nodded and hurried away.

"Okay, let's go." Justin put his wallet away.

When I stood, the room spun, and I felt a bit motion sick.

"Are you okay?" Justin asked with concern. "You look a little pale."

"Give me a second. Maybe I got up too fast." Justin came over and supported me around my waist. I was glad I was in his company. He'd help get me home safely.

"Maybe you need some air. Let's get outside." He helped me out the door into the cool night air. I felt less nauseous, but the dizziness was still there. "You don't look so hot. Where's your car?"

I pointed at my car, and Justin led me to it and helped me in. He sat next to me in the driver's seat. "Give me your keys and I'll drive you home."

"What about," yawn, "your car?" I felt so tired, like I was about to pass out.

"Don't worry about my car. I can Uber to it and get it later."

Leaning my head against the car window, I said, "Thank you. I hope I'm not getting sick. I don't want them to cancel the surgery."

My heartbeat drummed loudly in my head as the crushing headache made me wonder if my head was about to explode. I didn't dare open my eyes, for the nausea was barely being held at bay.

I had the most fitful sleep with haunting nightmares. I dreamt of a terrified girl, naked and caged in a dark basement. She cried out my name over and over, and I couldn't move or speak. Then the room would grow darker, consuming me in the darkness. The voices faded to a whisper, and I would think it was over, that my nightmare had gone and I could rest peacefully.

Then the screaming would start. Her panic, her sobs, the sounds of a girl losing her innocence against her will...and then it was silent.

I'd give anything to forget that awful dream, but I knew that was the kind of nightmare that stuck with you for a while. I went to stretch my limbs, discovering my range of movement was limited on the squeaky bed beneath me. I opened my eyes for a moment and saw the room from my nightmare. Everything was spinning. The nausea peaked, and I vomited to the side of the bed. For a moment I felt better. My temperature cooled, and the sweat that covered my body now provided relief from the heat wave I had just endured. I was in a dark and dingy basement. The only light source came from a small window above my head. It was enough for me to see an empty cage a few yards away. My wrists and feet were bound with rope. What the hell was going on? My heart started beating faster, making my crushing headache worse.

"Help!" I screamed, though my voice sounded strained. "Help! Anyone. I'm down here!"

I heard footsteps walk across the floor above. Then there was the sound of a door opening and footsteps walking down wooden steps. It was too dim to make out the details; I could only see that the person approaching was tall and trim—masculine. My fear grew as the fog in my brain parted. I realized that I was awake in my nightmare, tied up in a basement, God only knew where. Kidnapped by someone, possibly this guy approaching. Who was he? What did he want with me?

As he approached, the light from the window illuminated the face of a smirking James Kent. "You look so pretty tied up like this."

"You sick pervert. Let me go!"

James chuckled and pulled up a seat beside me. He removed a ball gag from his pocket. "You know what this is?" I remained silent. "It's the 'shut the hell up or I shove this in your mouth' toy. I'd love to use it on you, though somethin' tells me *he* wouldn't like it. So I advise you to keep your pretty little mouth shut."

"Why are you doing this?"

"I told you I do international and domestic trading. Guess I forgot to mention I trade pretty girls for money." He shrugged. "I gotta make a living somehow, and the money is good." He put his hand in mine to hold, and it triggered a cloudy memory of rough hands on my body, *his* hands. Disgusted, I shook my hand loose and balled it into a fist.

He tsked. "Relax. You're so angry."

"Don't touch me!"

"Why? What are you gonna do about it? You're a little helpless laying there all tied up. I think," his fingers trailed down my leg, making my skin crawl, "you might be the prettiest thing we've caught so far. I'm not sure Mr. Baumann should get you. He'd pay well for you, and you are his type, sure." His fingers trailed up my other leg, inching slowly up my inner thigh. "I might rather keep you for myself."

He put his rough hands on the sides of my face. "Such a beauty you are. No wonder he is so protective over you. He probably could have had you for himself. The second he included me in the plan, he lost that option, only he doesn't know it." James was talking in riddles, and I couldn't keep up. He referred to a Mr. Baumann and someone he called "he", and I had no idea who he was talking about. His hand trailed down my neck and continued to my breast. His fingers circled the nipple until it became erect.

"Stop, please."

He chuckled and then palmed my full breast in his hand. "You are so beautiful."

Tears quietly fell down my face as he fondled me. I tried to escape in my mind since there was no physical escape from this Hell. Finally, I could not bear to have the creep's hands on me another moment. "Stop touching me, you sicko!" The yell that came out of me sounded feral.

Footsteps bounded down the stairs and quickly came over. "Hey, what's going on? I told you not to touch her." The voice was familiar.

Justin!

Justin was here to save me. Relief came over me as he charged James and shoved him hard in his chest. James backed off with hands in the air.

"Justin, Justin, please help me. Help me get me out of here," I pleaded.

Justin walked over to the bedside and stared down at me with concern on his face. "Shh, shh, shh. Don't cry." Justin wiped my tears away. "It's gonna be okay, Mary."

"Justin, please untie me."

He continued looking at me, his face turning sympathetic. "You poor thing, you think *James* brought you here?" He shook his head. "No, Mary, I am the one who loves you. I brought you here to save you."

I looked over at James, who was lurking in the darkness of the room, and Justin followed my eyes. "I wouldn't worry about James. I paid him to…retain you." James chuckled in the darkness.

"Retain me? What do you mean? What's going on? Why do you want to keep me here?"

Justin paced back and forth at the foot of the bed. "See, I tried to make this work. I tried. I didn't want to do it this way. You left me no other choice. When you told me you were leaving for Austin, something switched inside of me." He came over to me and placed both hands on the pillow on each side of my head and bent close to my face. "I love you, Mary. Can't you see that?"

"Justin, stop. Please help me."

"I couldn't let you leave." He stood and began walking away from me. "And I couldn't let you massacre your body and sink into the self-mutilating trap that my parents fell into. Don't you see? I had to save you from yourself, from your bad decisions." Justin pulled a sheet off the wall, revealing a large corkboard of pictures of me. There were large photos of memories I had posted on Facebook, photos taken from a distance of me around town, and Polaroids of me in my bra and panties tied to this bed.

"You are too perfect the way you are, Mary. Can't you see that?"

"Why?" It was the only thing I could think to say at that moment.

"Because I love you. You needed to be saved," he said matter-of-factly.

"You *saved* me, by kidnapping me?" I shook my head, and it felt like a bunch of broken glass rolling around in my head. "God, my head is gonna break open! You drugged me, didn't you?"

"Well, technically that was James. He made a cameo at the restaurant last night when you stopped in the ladies' room."

My mouth fell open with his confession. "Stop before this goes too far. Let me go. I won't tell anyone. We can forget all of this happened and go back to life as we know it." This had his attention, but I needed to sell him on the idea and get him to release me. "You want me to cancel the surgery, I'll cancel it. You want me to stay in town, I'll stay. I'm sorry I made those selfish choices in the first place. I'm sorry. I love you, and I want to stay with you."

His face lit up. "You mean that, don't you?" He glanced at James and then turned back to me. "This is good. I knew you had feelings for me too, but hearing you say them means so much more. We're good together, Mary. I wish you could have realized this before and accepted my help finding a job in town. Sometimes it takes an extreme situation to see the light. Just as I knew what I needed to do when you told me you were leaving. I knew we belonged together. Now you see it too."

I nodded quickly. "Please untie me."

"Don't do it, man. You have her right where you want her." James paced in the background and shook his head. "She's lying and manipulating you. And like some lovesick puppy, you are buyin' her crap."

"LIAR!" Justin screamed at James. "You shut up, you stupid liar!"

"Seriously, she is playing you. I could catch a pretty dollar for her, and we could split the money. You'll never need to work again."

"I'm not a sick fuck like you. I don't want to hurt her, and I don't need your damn money. I love her, and all I want is to be with her!" Justin yelled at James.

This was a bad situation to be in. Both of these guys were mentally sick in their own way, and I was tied down and helpless.

"Your loss." James smiled at me with his sick grin and winked.

"Don't listen to him. Justin, we can be together. We can have a future together." I was convincing Justin and just needed a few more moments, preferably without James and his comments, to convince him to untie me.

The doorbell upstairs rang.

"Shh!" James came over and put a knife to my neck. "Not a word, gorgeous. Go get rid of whoever that is." Justin bounded up the steps, and I heard him speaking with another man. It was hard to make out the conversation, but I could clearly hear a male voice asking for James.

"Be back soon, little lady." He kissed my forehead then took the stairs two at a time. Laughter and greetings could be heard between James and the man. The men remained upstairs talking for a while. The withdrawal from whatever drug they had given me was kicking my butt. If I wasn't nauseous and feeling like my head was going to explode, I was dead tired. Right now, I felt like Mr. Sandman had delivered a two-ton truck of sleep sand just for me.

"She's pretty. Mr. Baumann will be interested in her for his personal collection. Is she a virgin?"

The men's voices stirred me awake. How long had I been out?

"She's wakin' up. Better check now before she is all the way conscious. She might start screamin'."

I felt coolness on my legs and a calloused hand scratching up my inner thigh. My eyes jolted open. "No! Stop." James and a new man stood on each side of me. "Justin!"

"Justin's gone to get his car from last night. He can't help you," James said.

"Stop! Please stop."

The hands of the strange man continued up my legs, and James pulled out the ball gag and fastened it around my mouth. "Check her now. Don't worry about being gentle. We are running out of time," James commanded.

The other guy stuck his fingers in me forcefully. I did not want to give them the pleasure of screaming, of letting me know they affected me so much. The tears fell from my eyes; I could not stop them no matter how hard I tried. A moment later, he pulled out his fingers and held them up to me. "I think she liked that. Look who was nice and wet for me." The creep licked his fingers. I had to turn away and shut my eyes, horrified at his violation of my body. "You have yourself a huge catch here, James. She's a virgin, and Mr. B. pays 20% more for them. I'll call Jimmy and have him bring the van around."

"Better hurry, Tucker. I'm not sure how much longer before Justin comes back." James undid the ball gag and removed it. "The nut job is a little psycho for this one."

Justin, the nut job they spoke of, was now my best chance of surviving this and I could only hope he arrived home in time to stop them from shoving me in a van and selling me off.

Tucker spoke briefly on the phone, then said to James, "He's close, said he'll be here in five minutes. I'm gonna wait outside for him."

Tucker climbed the stairs, and a door closed a moment later. James came over to stand by me. "You liked him touching you, didn't you? Guess you got a bit of pervert in you too."

"Screw you." I spat the words like out like they were venomous.

"You know what? I think I'll tell Mr. B. to keep his 20% in exchange for—"

A mechanical sound interrupted him, followed by the sound of a door being shut. Footsteps came down the stairs, and I hoped and prayed it was not James's friend.

"I'm back. Is everything alright here?"

It was Justin. He had saved me again.

"Uh, yep. We're good."

"I'm gonna make some soup. Hope you like split pea, Mary."

I lay there with my eyes shut, wishing all of this could be over and I could be safe in my apartment, sleeping in my own bed.

Justin went upstairs.

"Crap. Lover boy got here too fast." James began texting furiously. "I can't have Jimmy and Tucker come back with that van. Justin will know what's up and go ballistic."

The doorbell rang.

"Dammit. Did he not get the text?"

I expected to hear footsteps across the floorboards overhead. There was nothing, not a sound. It rang again, followed by someone pounding at the door. James came over to me and held a knife close to me in warning. A door opened.

"Hello?" a female voice called out. "Justin, are you home?" Footsteps across the floor above could be heard. "Oh, hey! Your garage was open. I tried the doorbell, but no one answered." It was Fray.

"Sorry, I didn't hear it. What are you doing here?"

"I got a call from the surgery center, and they said Mary never showed. They called me since I was her emergency contact. She's not at home, so I came here hoping you might know where she is." She paused. "That's her car out front, isn't it? Is she here?"

"What? Um, n-no. Uh..." Justin nervously stammered.

"Don't screw it up, jerk-face," James muttered. He walked closer to me, holding the blade tight against my neck. I had to do something. Fray being in this house put her in danger. I had to warn her to get out. I turned to the left where the fleshy part of James's hand was positioned and bit down on his hand with as much force as I could gather. His blade nicked my skin before falling away.

James howled in pain. "Dammit. You bit me!"

"What's going on down there?" Fray asked, coming down the steps to the basement. She froze when she saw me. "Mary?"

James slapped my face hard. Justin, who followed quickly behind Fray, pushed past her and jumped at James with his fist raised, ready to strike. The two exchanged punches and fell to the floor.

"Fray! Help!" Fray grabbed the knife James had been holding to my neck and began cutting the ropes. "Hurry!"

James and Justin continued fighting. Fray undid the last ropes, and we ran for the stairs. The sound of our feet hitting the steps caught their attention, and they stopped their brawl to pursue us.

"We've got to get out of here!" I yelled. Fray ran through the garage and started her car. I jumped into the passenger side. "Go, go, go!"

She put the car in reverse and gunned it out of the neighborhood. Justin and James stood on the driveway looking pissed as we put distance between us and them.

"Go to the police station," I said.

"Are you hurt? Did they rape you? Maybe a hospital would be better."

"I'm fine. Please, police station." I kept checking the rearview mirror to make sure I didn't see any sign of them or Jimmy and Tucker's van.

My adrenaline eventually subsided, and another wave of nausea hit. I shut my eyes and leaned my head against the cool window, hoping the sick feeling would pass. I was so tired, and I finally gave in to sleep and didn't wake up until we reached the station.

Officer Riggs took my statement. He asked me to get a rape test done as soon as I left the station.

Fray sat with me and held my hand while I gave my statement and endured the rape test. The cops put me up in a safe house until they had both Justin and James in custody. Officer Riggs assured me that James would go away for a long time and that Justin would be treated in a mental hospital.

Once the cops caught James, Tucker, and Justin, Officer Riggs had me identify James and Justin in a lineup. Officer Riggs told me that they found my classmate Lily's body in a lagoon east of campus. Her clothes had blood that matched Tucker's DNA. James and Tucker were denied bail and placed in a high security prison. Justin faced jail time, though Officer Riggs had arranged for him to begin meeting with a mental health counselor while awaiting trial. Riggs seemed to believe Justin could be helped and would benefit from therapy instead of rotting away in a cell.

After graduation, Fray and Leo came over to help me pack for Austin. I gave Fray the gift I picked up from Trash and extended an open invitation for them to come to Austin and stay with me whenever they wanted. She was a good friend to me, and I promised myself I would make sure she was always in my life in some way.

Austin ended up being a welcome change that helped heal some of the scars that James and Tucker inflicted on my soul. Justin's feelings for me were bittersweet. On one hand, he cared very deeply for me and kept me safe from the perverted hands of

James. On the other hand, his affections were so intense that they consumed him, making him obsessed and wanting to keep me for himself.

The new job was as exciting as I had hoped. I loved the team I was a part of and the work they assigned me. Doing what I loved and settling into my new home were welcome distractions from the memories of that nightmarish day.

Six months later, I had the surgery for my breast reduction. Fray and Leo came out and took care of me while I healed. Ferment had closed, and Fray had had a hard time finding a job that allowed her to be home with Leo in the day.

After living with me in Austin for three weeks, she and Leo decided to move out to Austin permanently. I told Fray she was welcome to stay with me as long as she needed, but she quickly found work at one of the local bars and was able to afford an apartment a few doors down from mine.

It was the perfect setup. I helped watch Leo while she worked, and Fray was there for me as I healed emotionally. She had become a sister to me.

"I should be home by two. The baby monitor is already turned on, so just lock up when you want to go to bed and keep listening for him."

"Okay, have a great shift."

"Bye, Mommy!" Leo ran up to his mom and hugged her leg.

"Bye, my little bug-a-boo. Be good for Auntie Mary. I'll see you in the morning."

Fray kissed him goodbye, then walked toward the apartment door. She looked up at the sign that hung above her door, the one I'd bought her from

Trash.

"You know, Mary, I've blossomed in your sunlight too."

"Love you, Fray."

"Love you too, Mary."

I locked up after her and went into Leo's room to lay out his pjs.

Knock, knock.

"What did you forget this time, Fray?" I unlocked the door and stopped breathing the moment I saw him.

"Hello, Mary," Justin said with a smile.

The End

About the Author

D.A. Roach has been telling stories since she was a young girl in the suburbs of Chicago. In college she met the man of her dreams, her happily ever after, and married him two weeks after graduating. They have three children together and two pet cockatiels named Gimli & Poppy.

D.A. discovered her love of reading and writing after college. Her preferred genres are YA/NA drama, romance, or paranormal. D.A. has a treasured collection of fiction that includes works by Rebecca Donovan, Larissa Ione, Jojo Moyes, Sylvia Day, Nicole Williams, Stephanie Meyer, Richelle Mead, and E.L. James.

Facebook:
http://www.facebook.com/DARoachDA

Twitter:
http://www.twitter.com/daroach12books

Website:
http://daroachbooks.blogspot.com/

Goodreads:
https://www.goodreads.com/juozupaitis

This One's Broken

By Bradon Nave

Chapter One

Billy

Her gaze, dancing about the scorching and crumbled sidewalk, appeared to be longing for attention, yet yearning to remain hidden from all around her. Unpolished and in need of shade, her brow showcased a steady production of sweat beads. Her forearm wiped the perspiration and stringy blonde bangs to one side of her pretty head.

Perhaps some might assume her the tragic

outcome of an existence teetering on the edge of poverty, a sad story with a pretty smile attached. Those people, those assumers, were not listening contently night after night as pretty little Savannah played such enchantments as Pachelebel's Canon on her family's secondhand upright piano. Billy was always listening.

Cash-poor and never one to roam far from the sanctuary of her paint-peeled family home, little Savannah had been left to her own devices. The late months of summer had been spent managing a pathetically constructed lemonade stand out front of the house. The tiny street, lined with modest homes on one side and clad with thick brush and tall cottonwood trees on the other, was less than the optimal site for conducting such business. Luckily, the county fair was changing that.

The fairgrounds were located two miles south of Savannah's home. The street was a straight shot to candied apples, prized hogs, and a small-town-Kansas conservative crowd of large smiles and larger voices.

To reach this delight afoot, however, one would have to first walk past Savannah and her stand, past her humble home, and past Billy.

Crouched low in the thicket on the opposite side of the street, Billy intently watched the eleven-year-old girl waiting in the baking heat for her next customer.

She was scrawny and lacked much pigmentation, other than her sun-kissed cheeks. Billy's gaze rarely left Savannah's face. Hours had become days. Billy was always in Savannah's company, although the girl never saw him.

His dry tongue dragged across his cracked and jagged lips. She wasn't too young. It was time. He'd taught her before; he'd teach her again. She cried last time, but she enjoyed it. The fractured bits of excitement in her eyes assured Billy that she enjoyed it.

"Well, hello there…" The thin, middle-aged woman reminded Billy of a teacher of some sort. She seemed kind as she stood in front of Savannah's stand. The awkward little girl didn't verbally respond, and the woman was obstructing Billy's view.

It was nearly noon; the heat was oppressively unbearable. The woman accepted the paper cup of lemonade from Savannah, and Billy was quick to observe the woman's reaction to tasting the mixture. As with all the customers, the woman appeared somewhat taken aback by the first gulp.

"Oh…my. Well, this is…my. Well, thank you kindly!" Handing the cup and a few cents to Savannah, the woman walked briskly away.

Billy was left once more with his thoughts, as twisted as the vines entwined about the trees and rotting branches at his feet. Sweat stinging his eyes, he attempted to remain as quiet as possible.

A much-welcomed breeze brought with it the scent of stale popcorn and scattered leaves. Enjoying the brief reprieve, Billy took notice of the flyer that drifted in with the leaves:

1972 Chili Contest

Reading a few more lines, he briefly reflected a few fair days past from his childhood. He rarely partook in such occasions now. Billy's days of social gatherings were typically left only to recall from a long line of memories half-tucked.

Turning his attention once more to Savannah, Billy looked upon only a shabby lemonade stand. "Goddammit!"

Carefully maneuvering the tall grasses from his view of the front door, Billy's anxious gaze searched the parched property waiting for Savannah's return. Minutes dragged by at a Sunday sermon's pace.

Perhaps it was the previous night's misadventures, or perhaps the hours of discomfort spent in the vegetation and summer heat, but something had Billy's eyelids heavy and aching for a moment's rest. Resting his head aside a tall cottonwood, he closed his eyes and drifted off.

"Because, sir. It's busted. It's broken."

Billy's attention was immediately snared by the raspy voice of Savannah. Judging by the position of the sun through the trees, he estimated it to be at least one in the afternoon. Sweat pouring from each armpit, he shifted himself slightly.

"Busted, huh? Is that so? Well, what's so busted about it, little lady?" Reaching in his trouser pocket, the man produced a handful of coins for the young girl.

"I'm not too sure." Savannah graciously

accepted the coins.

The man appeared to be in his thirties, balding and moderately overweight. After a generous sip, the man eyed the cup with a disgruntled look. "This needs something."

"Sorry. I just want my bike fixed."

"If ya don't know what's wrong with it, how'd ya know it's busted?"

"It's in that cellar if you wanna take a look at it, mister."

Sitting forward silently, Billy saw the man's sour look turn to one of curiosity.

"In the cellar? Well, you could bring it up here. I'd take a look-see at it for ya."

"It's okay. It's pretty heavy. Maybe some other day or something."

"Yeah. Some other day. I've got to get down to the fair before the rabbit judging takes place or my young'n will have my hide."

"Hide?"

"My daughter. She's eleven. She's certain that fat rabbit of hers is gonna bring home the blue ribbon. I won't be surprised none if that thing kicks over plum dead of a heart attack."

"You better get then."

Scratching his head, the man turned from Savannah, pouring the remainder of the lemonade to the dried grass beneath him. Billy felt the man's gaze piercing through the thicket as if he were mere seconds from total exposure. Tossing the cup near the stand, the man walked in the direction of the fair.

Savannah raised her mason jar of pennies to her

disappointed-looking face. Turning from her stand, she retreated once more from the heat to the comforts of her home.

Drenched in sweat and harboring a mounting frustration in his gut, Billy opted for a heat retreat at this point as well. Standing from his cramped quarters, he sunk deeper into the brush.

Chapter Two

Savannah

Ragdolls, dominos, and a chalkboard were more than enough to keep her boredom at bay during the blistering winter months. However, the sweet smell of honeysuckle, the call of robins, and the rushing creek near her home frequently coaxed Savannah from her tiny bedroom. But that was before.

Sitting on the corner of her worn mattress, her gaze anchored to the hardwood flooring, she found herself once more contemplating an outdoor adventure. Each time she mounted the ambition to rise, something secured her tight to the bed, a reluctance of a cruel and macabre origin.

With each passing day, the screams in her head were muffling. She prayed each night they would continue to do so, that they would continue to fade to nothing more than a soiled memory, tattered and tainted with regret and blood splatter.

After a deep and forceful exhalation she stood, walking toward the bedroom door. Reaching for her butterfly net, she envisioned tadpoles, minnows, and possibly a racerunner lizard if she was fast enough.

Leaping from the front porch with a smile, she was quick to glance about the area to ensure there were no predatory eyes resting upon her.

The boisterous sounds of the fair were alluring. Savannah, however, sought entertainment of a more organic nature.

A child of nature, a lover of sod—finds peace and contentment in the meadows broad.

It was something her mother would often whisper to her when she'd return home in the evening with soiled clothing and a mason jar of toads, lizards, and other small wildlife.

Darting across the yard and narrow city street, she leapt into the brush. With each step into her outside sanctuary, her heavy heart shed sorrow and her broken smile widened. The thick grass blanketed the floor of the wooded area, and the trees provided a canopy of heavy shade. Within moments she was at her destination, babbling and teeming with life.

Removing her shoes, scuffed from jumping rope, she slid her tiny toes into the moving water. It was then she saw it. Inhaling deeply and holding it, she eyed the baby snapping turtle basking a mere three feet from her. Not much larger than a quarter, the creature offered no resistance when Savannah cautiously picked it up. She'd come across large specimens of this sort, but each became wildly belligerent when the curious girl approached. She'd heard that Jed Johannsson's absent index finger was the result of a noodling adventure gone awry. The man had blindly violated the lair of large snapper, resulting in the loss of his finger. This baby turtle, however, didn't even offer a hiss.

Holding the tiny turtle on her flattened palm, she brought it closer to her face to examine it. Quickly, she tucked the turtle in the net and secured it by twisting it tightly. The perfect pet, something different with a tinge of danger.

Her mind was all but free of any hint of the tribulation that had previously held her captive to her room. She thought only of her new pet—what she would name it, how she would house it. It was then she heard a disruption among the twigs and fallen leaves behind her.

Quickly, Savannah sprang to her feet, her fists clenched as though she were prepared to battle a foe. She was then looking upon him.

"Hey, young'n."

"B…Billy. Why are you here? You scared me."

"Why aren't you at your stand, Savannah?"

Unsure of Billy's intentions, Savannah stepped backward into the cool water. He was eighteen and every bit a man. Broad and boasting a chiseled physique, in Savannah's eyes Billy was as much an adult as any other of the townsmen.

"What do you want, Billy?"

Stepping closer to her, Billy smirked. "You know what I want, Savannah. You want it too. I know you do."

"I don't…I don't know if I can, Billy. I don't know if—"

"You have to, Savannah. You know I love you, right?"

"Billy, I—"

"Don't be scared, Savannah. You know it's right, sweet girl. You know this is how it's supposed to be."

Breathing heavily, Savannah turned her attention to the waters beneath her. She found herself wishing she could magically turn in to one of the many minnows swimming about her feet. She could then swim away from Billy and his words.

"What if it's not? What if Jesus don't think it is, Billy? What if God don't think it's right?"

Stepping even closer, Billy placed his hands on the girl's shoulders and brought her closer to him. Kissing her atop the head, he squatted to make eye contact. "Jesus loves this…this I know."

Chapter Three

Billy

The sinister plot churned in his mind. Beautifully crafted with a gritty aftertaste that left him longing for more. More heart-pounding euphoria and wild-eyed excitement. This pastime was now his addiction, one that kept his hands dirty; he loved the dirt.

The heat index was even greater on this day. Billy sought to observe from a covered point rather than the brush and tick-infested woods across the road from Savannah's stand. The cool cellar offered the perfect hideaway. He peered out onto the lawn from beneath the metal door, watching Savannah complete a few exchanges with passersby. Two high school boys, one with a puppy, stopped to try her lemonade. They seemed nice enough. An elderly couple offered a few cents as a donation rather than in exchange for the product, blaming the husband's uncontrollable blood sugar.

Waiting patiently on the cement steps of the cellar next to Savannah's home, Billy saw an odd-looking fellow approach. Lanky and alone, the man stood with his hands tucked in his pockets, a sinister-looking mustache, and a crooked smile.

"Hello, mister."

"Hello, my little lovely. What are you selling here today?"

"The sign says lemonade…my guess would be lemonade."

"Indeed. I'll take a cup to sip."

Pouring the man's drink, Savannah wasted no time in pleading her case. "My bike is broken. I need to fill this penny jar to fix it. I appreciate you helping me out."

"Broken, you say? Your parents aren't here to fix it?"

Eyeing the man cautiously, Savannah stepped tentatively in his direction. "No one's here but me, sir."

"Oh. Well isn't that a predicament? A broken bicycle and no one here to help you. Where is this bike, young lovely?"

Reaching her hand to take his, Savannah nodded toward the cellar door. "In the cellar. You could have a look at if for me if you wanted. I'd sure appreciate it."

"Oh…I'm sure you would. Lead the way, darling."

Hand in hand, Savannah escorted the man in the

direction of the cellar. Leaping from the stairs and into the darkness of the large cellar, Billy hid behind fishing equipment and a weathered canoe.

"Right down them stairs, sir."

Footsteps made their way to the cement under the lair. Savannah turned to the tall, thin man. He looked scrawny and weak.

"It's…it's right there, mister." Pointing to the corner of the cellar, Savannah and the man looked upon a worn-looking ten-speed bike.

"Oh my. That bike looks awful big for you."

"I manage."

"I'm certain you do. What is your name?"

"Savannah."

"Have you gotten any boo boos, Savannah?"

"A few."

"Where?" The man appeared red and wild with some sickening anticipation. He was perfect, the perfect customer.

"My tummy." Savannah pointed to her belly, covered by her light yellow sundress.

"May I see the boo boos, Savannah?"

"Yes."

Crouching down, Billy saw the man's trembling hands inch their way to the bottom of Savannah's dress. He appeared to be salivating at the sight of the young girl. Billy was overcome with a nauseating disgust for the wretched specimen before him. Savannah turned her head toward the cellar stairs.

"Oh Billlllly! This one's broken!" Her shrieking voice sent the would-be violator stepping back in confusion.

"What? What is broken? Savannah, who is Billy?"

"I'm Billy, you sick sonofabitch. And you're the one that's broken!" Leaping from the shadows with mallet in hand, Billy struck the dumbfounded man aside the head, knocking him to the ground, out cold.

"You did it, Savannah! I told you we'd do it again!"

Peering down at the hideous monster at her feet, Savannah looked to Billy, swallowing hard. "I know, Billy…I …I don't know if I can do what comes next. I don't think I'm ready to do what comes next."

"Look at me, baby sis. Have I ever led you astray? Have I ever done wrong by you? This man is a bad egg. He ain't right in the head. He has to be punished, like before. He has to die screaming."

"But Billy, it's all I can think about. What we done…I can't think about nothing else!"

"Baby girl, we're taking care of varmints. These ain't people; this is pest control. This scum has probably hurt other little ones like you. Just like…just like the last one."

"You sure?"

"Yes, honey. When this bastard goes to hollerin' in pain, you remember what Henry did to you. You take that and you use it."

"Don't say his name, Billy!"

"Okay…okay. Are you with me?"

"I am. I love you, Billy."

"Love you too, sis. Help me get him strapped to the table."

A rusty bucket of old newspapers and a metal side table of malicious hardware sat next to a rickety operating table in the cellar of the basement. Billy and Savannah's father had been a coroner in the army prior to his death several years before. The cellar housed an array of old surgical tools and a worn and weathered bed, complete with leather straps.

Billy waited patiently for the man to awaken. The evening was fast upon them, and Billy was uncertain if the man would ever regain consciousness.

Strapped to the bed with only a sheet to cover him, the side of the man's head bled profusely. Not from being struck, but from where Billy had removed a portion of his ear.

Contemplating which tools would be used when and where, Billy was startled to hear Savannah call his name from outside the cellar door. Ascending the stairs, Billy met his sister when he opened the heavy door. The sounds of the fair and woodland life were heavy in the air.

"Hey there, Savannah. Your turtle like that earlobe?"

"Oh, Billy! She loved it! She's eating! She's really eating!"

"That's great news! That means it's time you pick her out a name. Am I right?"

"I did! Her name is Petunia! And I love her."

Billy was overjoyed by his sister's excitement, and then a soft moan echoed up the stairs. "He's awake. You about ready for some fun?"

"I am, Billy!"

"Well, hot dog, little-bit! Let's go get Petunia some more of that good grub!"

Descending into the cellar, Billy looked upon the poorly pedophile, stunned and coming to.

"Hey there, Mister! How you doin'?" Billy's excitement overflowed in his mannerisms and boisterous voice.

Gagged and squirming, the man looked wildly about the room with a fearful look in his eye. Reaching for the top of the sheet, Billy pulled it down to the man's hips, exposing inked lines all about the man's abdomen and thorax. Developing a look of intense fear, the man began screeching as he looked at trunk.

"Hey! You hush that!" Billy blatantly struck the man across the face, silencing him. "Them are just for guidance so I know where I'm cuttin' at."

Breathing heavily, the man bucked his hips in an effort to escape. As if on cue, Savannah handed Billy a pair of pliers.

Placing the pliers near the man's nipple, Billy clamped down on a hefty portion of the man's skin, twisting it as he pulled. The action removed the screaming man's flesh and sent him into a chaotic frenzy, much to Billy's delight.

"You see how this works? You act up, we hurt you real good. Now if, and *only* if you behave, I'll slit your throat after we take your fun parts off. But by God, you're gonna be fully awake for that."

Sheer horror shot through the man's eyes as he stared at Billy in horror, shaking his head in disbelief.

"If you don't behave, then you'll get a front row seat to the whole show. First things first." Billy patted the man's crotch under the thin sheet, giving him an evil smirk. Pulling the sheet back to the man's knees, Billy shook his head in disappointment. "Ain't much here to work with, mister. Savannah, looks like Petunia's gonna get more ear than she will pecker."

"Here ya go, Billy." Savannah happily handed her brother a surgical scalpel.

The gagged man's eyes bugged.

"Oh no, sweetie. That there hacksaw will work just fine. He's gonna feel the slow cut and think about each little girl he done put his hands on."

Billy took the saw from his sister and the man's nether parts in his other hand. Bringing the hacksaw to his crotch—much to the horror of the captured sufferer, all three of them seemed surprised to hear a loud knocking on the cellar door. The interruption sent the man screaming through his gag.

"Shut up!" Billy squeezed the man in his hand until he stopped screaming. His eyes rolled back in his head in sheer misery. Billy turned his attention to the intrusion.

"Hello? Children, are you down here?"

The door flung open; a portly sheriff, Officer Golay, reached the bottom of the stairs.

"What the hell do you kids have here?" The officer's stunned shout sent a slight relaxation through the shoulders of the confined and condemned man. He wailed into the gag as though he were on the verge of rescue.

"Wha…what?" Billy stepped backward, holding his hands up after setting the saw aside.

"This ain't enough! He ain't enough!" Stepping closer, the smiling sheriff poked and prodded the bound man. "You done good, kids. I'm right proud of you."

"You mean that, Golay?" Smiling, Billy boasted a look of pure pride.

"I surely do, son. You'll be behind a badge in no time at all."

"Sheriff! We was just about to cut the fun parts off before you showed up!" Savannah's excited shrieks sent a smile across the sheriff's face. He reached his hands under her arms, lifting her up to hold her.

"Is that right? I got here just in time!"

Stepping closer to his sister and the sheriff with the hacksaw, Billy shot the man an appreciative look. "Would you like to do the honors? It'd mean the world to me and little-bit."

"Billy, I don't know what to say. I know how hard you two have been working to trap this prize. And now you're gonna offer me first cut? If that ain't tellin' of the kind soul you got housed in there, then I don't know what is."

"Well, sir, we appreciate all you've done for us. Payin' for piano lessons and helpin' me put food on the table and whatnot."

"That's the way of the Lord, Billy. All God's children…all of them. Now either you hand me that there hacksaw or grab me a glass of sweet tea, young man! Let's get this bastard to squealin'!"

"Yes sir!" Billy happily handed over the

hacksaw, grinning widely. "I told him we'd cut his throat if he behaved before we really went to work."

"What? Oh no, Billy. Do you know who this is? This is Trent McFaver from the southwest. He's been known to touch young'ns for a while now. Oh no. He's be fully conscious while we harvest this good tripe."

"Whatever you say, sir! Nothin' gets my blood pumpin' better than doin' right by the law and riddin' this land of vermin like this."

With a heavy hand, the Sheriff took the man's personals in his grasp and began sawing away while the man screamed and bucked in pain. Billy and his sister looked on with pure pleasure.

The night was a colorful one and a long one for Trent. Billy and Golay took the time to show young Savannah the proper way to harvest a good capture, piece by piece. Parts were individually wrapped in newspaper and set aside until finally the man was no longer breathing.

Billy noticed Savannah had a certain excitement during this escapade, something that was absent during the last live butchering. The girl had a twinkle in her eye and a grin that Billy couldn't get enough of. Seeing his sister enjoy herself while spending quality time delighted Billy. She was his pride and joy, and he would do anything for her.

This new excitement for their joint venture couldn't have come at a more opportune time. Billy understood he and Savannah had a lot of work to do in the days ahead since the fair would bring greater crowd numbers and hopefully more "broken ones."

With a large smile and blood-covered clothing,

Billy looked to his precious sister. "You did good, little-bit. You did real good, and I'm real proud of you."

"I love you, Billy. And I tell you right now I had a whole heap of fun!"

Chapter Four

Savannah

Savannah couldn't wipe the smile from her face. At last the shower water was clear, no longer pink with blood. It was nearly morning. There was no feeling of guilt or disgust brewing in her belly. Savannah had thoroughly enjoyed each detail of the previous evening. The bonding effect of each cut and every scream was something magical. She truly felt the night had been a fantastic family affair. Sheriff Golay was an honorable man, and Savannah found herself charmed by his fatherly presentation.

Drying off quickly, Savannah thought of the many potential broken ones she might possibly miss if she were to take anything more than a morning catnap.

With a towel snugged securely around her waist,

she tiptoed to her room. The large punch bowl housing Petunia sat near the window. The tiny turtle sat contently by its small mound of fresh flesh.

Crawling into bed with a mind of wild ideas, Savannah soon drifted off to sleep.

The knocking at the front door was disruptively loud. Savannah sprang from her bed, momentarily unsure of where she was. Throwing her nightgown on, she quickly made her way to front door. Opening it, she looked upon Sheriff Golay and an obese woman with shoulder-length brown hair. She was smiling, holding a folder, and her clothing was covered in what appeared to be white dog hair.

"Hi, Sheriff."

"Hello, Savannah. How are you?"

"Sleepy."

"I understand. Savannah, this is—"

"My name is Bria Clancey. How are you today?"

Savannah was instantly taken aback by how fake and disingenuous this large woman seemed. Even at eleven, Savannah was more than capable of spotting a bullshitter. When the woman extended a hefty hand, a disgruntled Savannah shook it briefly and then stepped out onto the porch, closing the door behind her. "What is it you need?"

"Well, young lady, I need to see the inside of this house. I need to make certain you're being properly cared for."

"Ma'am? My brother cares for me just fine."

"I'm certain. But I'll need to see just the same."

"I don't understand." Savannah reached backward for the door handle.

"Young lady, I have recently been assigned the task of assuring all children in this county are properly cared for."

Disgusted with the woman, Savannah opened the door and allowed the two inside. The house was found to be in pristine condition.

"Very clean, young lady. Where is the ice box?"

"What, you didn't get enough for breakfast?" Savannah's crass question had Golay choking on his coffee.

"Well, I never! Young lady, I need to be assured you are properly nourished."

"It's in the kitchen! Where else would an ice box be?" Savannah led the way to the kitchen.

"Where is your brother right now, young lady?"

"He's at work, old lady."

With this, Bria Clancey became clearly outraged. "You are a disrespectful little heathen child!"

"My brother does right by me. He works hard to take care of me."

"Who is with you during the day?" The obese woman stepped closer to Savannah.

"No one. No one is with Rebecca when her papa is at work either."

"I have to know!"

"You can just come back. We'll treat you to a home-cooked meal and you can meet my brother this Friday."

Bria looked at the girl in state of shock, as if she'd been outwitted by the sarcastic eleven year old. "You are just too big for your britches."

"You're one to talk." Savannah's smile had the woman fuming with anger. "Seven o'clock. Friday night. Now get."

Chapter Five

Billy

"You gotta let it simmer in them good juices. Can't let it burn none. Keep tendin' to it."

Stirring the greasy mixture within the blue and white speckled metal pot, Golay invited an eager Billy to smell the slow simmering meat.

"That smells heavenly, Golay. Damn near brings tears to a man's eyes."

"These is hard times, Billy. Waste not, my boy…waste not."

"You're gonna have the best damn chili them folks has tasted in years."

"Dern tootin'! Billy-boy, we gotta get that freezer stocked. This here won't last but till December. You're a workin' man. You gotta keep that tank full of that good fuel. This here sweet meat

211

will keep your belly full this winter."

"My mouth is just a watering away, Golay."

"Makes a mean sandwich when you slap it 'tween two pieces of thick white bread." Golay licked his lips as the oils in the pot accumulated atop the heated water.

"Savannah is almost ready. That silly girl. I still can't believe she asked that woman to the meal table with us."

"Oh, Billy. That girl is too smart for her own good. She had that ole gal fit to be tied. She was just about as steamed as a pot of beans!"

"Well, sir, we'll make sure she gets treated right to a home-cooked meal that she won't soon forget."

"We gotta get that hefty heifer off our case, Billy. She's gonna have her snout so deep up your backside she can sniff what you done ate for breakfast."

"So what we gotta do, Golay? I can't let that big bitch take my baby sister away. I'm all she's got. She's better off here. You know she's better off here growin' up in the light of the Lord."

"I know it and you know it. After that two ton sits herself down to family feast in this here kitchen, she'll know it too."

"I sure do hope so, Golay."

"Trust me, boy. Now hand me that there can of spice. This here smells like it needs a kick of somethin'."

Manning her stand, Savannah flashed an

ambitious smile as she greeted people walking past her and her concealed brother. So many potentials, yet Billy looked upon normal and functional members of society as they migrated toward the organ music of the fair.

Witnessing the excitement in her eyes, Billy beamed with pride as his little sister did her part for the family.

"Hello, sir. Some lemonade on this here hot morning?"

"I got me a raspberry soda pop callin' my name."

Biting his bottom lip, Billy cautiously eyed the young man. Watchful and seemingly spooked, the man, who appeared in his early twenties and remarkably dirty and thin, stood close to Savannah.

"I fell down. I could show you my boo boos if you want."

"What? Are you hurt or something?"

Noting his sister's overzealous approach, Billy grasped the moist earth in his fists, praying Savannah wouldn't come on too strong.

"I'll take you down to the cellar."

The man's sunken eyes didn't settle on Savannah for longer than a mere second at a time. Billy's jaw went agape as he witnessed the man sporadically reach for the jar of pennies and began running from the stand.

Quick to his feet, Billy sprang from the thick brush in pursuit of the man, who was more than likely only a few years older than he was.

Soon upon him, Billy tackled the frail thief to the dried front yard.

"No!" The man's stunned yelp was met with

Billy's fist.

"Get him good, Billy! Get him good!" Savannah's happy cheers were heard behind the scuffle. The man offered little resistance, only attempting to block his face from Billy's blows.

"Get him to the cellar, Billy! Let's put that good hurt on him!"

"I'm sorry! I'm hungry!" The man's shrieking proclamation halted Billy's assault immediately.

Looking upon the near-anorexic man beneath him, Billy developed an overwhelming sense of guilt. This man wasn't broken—he was desperate. He was a desperate child of God.

"You can't just go around stealing from folk!" Billy's forceful tone was met by a wailing of tears.

"I'm so hungry!"

"Get him to the cellar, Billy!"

"No, Savannah." Standing from the pummeled man, Billy offered a hand to assist him from the ground. "You get dusted off. Come inside and I'll fix you a damn fine sandwich with the best-tasting sweet meat you ever tasted."

"I got no money for it." The man's tears cut through the dirt and muck on his face.

"Your money ain't no good here. That's how good Christian folk do. Now get dusted off; I'll show you inside."

"He weren't broken, Savannah. That wasn't vermin. He was hungry. Hungry folk do crazy things sometimes."

"You gave him all my pennies, Billy. Them was mine, and now I got none."

Sitting at the table, Billy attempted to calm his confused sister. After treating the stranger to two massive smoked meat sandwiches and a tall glass of sweet tea, Billy sent the man on his way with several pounds of smoked meat wrapped in newspaper and all of Savannah's pennies. The man had been completely taken aback by their generosity, shedding additional tears as he continued to apologize. The two men prayed for the man's wellbeing, and Billy sent him on his way with a full belly and at least four dollars in change.

"Savannah, we're catching demons. We gotta make sure, and I mean *damn* sure, that whatever we catch in our snare is indeed a demon. That man had nothing and has been living out of garbage pails from town to town. Do you think he was a monster? Do you really think he deserved to be strapped to our table?"

"No, sir."

"That's right. He just needed a helping hand, someone to get his belly full and get him pointed in the direction of the light."

"My pennies—"

"I think it might do you some good to get that Bible down. We got some readin' to do, little-bit."

"Okay, you're right, Billy. We got plenty of food. That poor man had nothing. He needed them pennies more than me."

"That's right, sis. I guarantee you, you will be rewarded for your generosity."

"I'll read the Good Book tonight, I promise. I

need to get back out there. I wanna do right by this family. Let's get that freezer full of that good meat."

"Now that's my girl!" Billy's large hand sat atop his sister's head as he grinned.

At nearly eight in the evening, the setting sun reminded the duo that their efforts would more often than not be unsuccessful. Preparing to rise, Billy looked through the brush to see a lowly face walking toward his sister's stand.

The man looked familiar, yet Billy couldn't quite place him. He appeared younger, in his mid to late twenties, and heavy.

"One cup, princess."

His breathless pants sent Savannah scrambling to pour him a watered-down beverage. "One cup, coming up." When she handed the cup to the man, Savannah appeared completely dumfounded. A stunned Billy witnessed the large man expose himself to the young girl in the twilight.

Rising to his feet in outrage, Billy saw his sister's hand go up, as if she were telling him to stay put momentarily.

"I know who you are, mister. You're Henry's nephew."

"And I know you know what happened to my uncle, you nasty little piece of trash."

"Don't got a clue. I like your uncle."

"Is that so?"

"Sure is."

"And why would that be? After what your greasy brother done said and did to my family name, now you say you like my uncle?"

"We were friends, your uncle and me. You come on down to my cellar and I'll show you the games we played."

"And then you'll go squealin' how I done you dirty. Tarnish my name how you done did his."

"It's you who'll be squealin'. I ain't the one that said nothing about any of that. I'm going to my cellar now."

Turning from the heavy man, Savannah bounced off in the direction of the cellar. The man followed her. As soon as he descended, Billy sprang from the woods, racing across the yard. Creeping down the stairs as quietly as possible, Billy stopped at the last step and looked upon two dimpled and pimpled ass cheeks. The fat man had already dropped his trousers around his ankles.

"My niece sure liked to play like this too. She grew up…junior high. If you can keep a secret, we can make this a regular outing, you and me."

"Oh Billlly! This one's broken!"

"Sure as hell is, little-bit!" Billy appeared in the cellar, and the stunned man nearly fell to the ground, tripping over his pants.

"What are you doin' here!" The man's scream brought a smile to Billy's face.

"Oh, Savannah. Look at them fun parts. You get to do the cuttin' this time, little-bit. I think you're ready."

"Really! Oh, Billy that's amazing! Will he be awake the entire time? Please?"

"What the hell are you crazy fuckers talking about?" The man backed into the wall as Billy reached for the mallet.

"Oh, he's gonna be good and awake." Billy playfully patted the horrified man's large belly. "Look at that good jiggle! Freezer's gonna be stocked tight for sure!"

"I don't understand! I gotta go!" When he bent over to reach for his trousers, Billy raised the mallet high, bringing it down on the back of the man's head.

Chapter Six

Savannah

"This here is the best jerky I've ever had, Golay. It really is!" Savannah savagely tore at the tough jerky, standing next to Billy and Golay in the cellar.

"I'm glad you like it. Momma's recipe."

"Golay, I sure am glad you happened here when you did. I was like to have never got that fat bastard up on the cuttin' table."

"Oh, Billy. You got us a good one…both you kids did. You done real good with this one."

"I sure can't wait for him to wake up. We're gonna have so much fun!" Savannah's excitement had her heart racing. Looking to her brother, she spotted a tear in the man's eye.

"Billy, are you okay? You ain't about to cry, are you?"

"No, little-bit. It's just…getting to spend this family time with the people I love. This is what it's all about."

"You kids, I love you both, and we're doin' right by this world. What else could we ask for? You're both as much blood family as my own kin." Golay offered Billy a full embrace.

Savannah's heart soared—and then they heard the magical moans, beckoning them to their captive's bedside.

"He's waking up, Billy." Golay peered down at the man, his smile showcasing his anticipation.

"Hey there. You with us?" Billy stepped closer, patting the man's stomach. The action elicited another moan, and the man opened his eyes.

"Peter, can you hear me?" Golay said into the gagged man's ear.

Peter finally responded. "Mmmmhhmmm."

"Good. We're just about to get started, ain't we, kids?" Golay patted Peter atop his sweating forehead.

Mumbling from behind the gag prompted Golay to pull the cloth from the man's mouth momentarily. "What you got to say, fat boy?"

"Sheriff! My head hurts somethin' awful. Help me!"

"Oh, Peter boy. Your head is the least of your worries." Slapping Peter's bare stomach loudly, Golay leaned down to Savannah. "How 'bout we break this puppy down and see what's inside?"

"What the hell are you talkin' about, Sheriff? Why you got me tied to this here bed?" Peter's gaze danced about the room, as if he were unable to absorb what was taking place.

"You, sir, are a threat to all that is holy and good. You have hurt God's children…little girls. Now it's time to pay." Golay's sinister smile widened as he pulled the stained sheet completely away from Peter's trembling body.

"Pay? Whatchu mean I got to pay? I didn't hurt no girls."

"Peter, your hands is dirty. You are a vile and nasty creature. You will be processed, harvested, and you will be breathing for as long as we can keep you that way."

"What? You mean to say you gonna kill me, Sheriff?"

"Oh, Peter, we're gonna do a lot more than that. Now you relax while we get everything rounded up."

"Help!" Like a belligerent swine, Peter squealed for assistance. *"Help me! Help! Help! Hellllp meeee!"*

When he attempted to force the gag back into Peter's mouth, Golay's finger was chomped down on.

"Let go! Billy! He gota hold of me!"

Rushing to the aid of his elder friend, Billy secured Peter's head within his arms. "Let him go, you fat piece of dung!" Attempting to maneuver the man's head, a sickening cracking sound was heard—and then Golay was released.

"You done snapped his neck, Billy."

"I'm sorry, Golay. I didn't…I didn't mean to."

"It's okay, boy. You didn't have no choice."

"What does that mean?" A disappointed

Savannah stepped closer, holding a rusty pair of tinsnips.

"Well, sis, he's dead. He was biting Golay, and I had to stop him."

"It was my turn to cut off the fun parts! That's not fair! You said I could—"

"Little-bit, them fun parts are still there waitin' on you to get to hackin'. You have at it."

"It ain't the same, Billy, and you know it!" Throwing the snips to the floor, Savannah bolted from the scene and up the stairs.

"I got her," Billy said to Golay as she fled the cellar.

When he entered the house, Billy heard Savannah's cries from her bedroom. Walking down the hall, he looked upon his said little sister, crying face-down into her bed.

"Little-bit, don't do this."

"This was my chance to prove myself! I wanted to do you proud. We don't know when we're gonna catch another one, and now it's all ruined!"

"You silly-head. Dry them eyes." Walking to the bed, Billy sat next to his wailing sister. "You make me proud every single day. You're the best part of my life. And you're plum crazy if you think that ole boy is the last catch we're gonna bring in."

"I wanted to put that good hurt on him, Billy."

"Little-bit, he's burnin' in the pits of Hell right now. He's screamin' away. He'll be suffering every single time you take a bite of ice cream or pick a

222

dandelion. He'll be ablaze in the hotspot of Satan's living room. He's hurting real good right now."

"You sure?"

"I am. And right now we got a whole mess of meat to get processed. It's still gonna be fun even though he ain't screamin' and thrashin' around."

"Okay."

"Little-bit, you done good. That freezer is gonna be plum full because of you. You caught us the grand prize."

"You mean it, Billy?"

"I do! I don't wanna do none of that without you there, though. This is about being a family. We caught this prize. Now let's go bag it up."

"Oh, Billy. You're the best big brother ever!"

Chapter Seven

Billy

The air hung thick and stagnant, heavy with the smell of butter, bacon, cotton candy, and the voices of countless patrons. At nearly five in the evening, the baking heat beat down relentlessly on Billy, Golay, and Savannah.

Long lines gathered near one of four large round top barns; it was chili-feed time. Anxiety was apparent in Golay's expression, and he fidgeted nervously among the various meaty morsel tasters.

"Billy…I want that top prize. I need me that top prize."

"Aww, Golay, don't you go to stressin'. That there sweet meat is the best damn tastin' business this side of Wichita!"

"What if they think it tastes off? What if they

know?"

"Know what, Sheriff? When you gonna share this secret recipe?"

A thin, middle-aged man boasting an extraordinary mustache and a tin bowl of steaming hot chili approached. "Sheriff, this here is *deeeelicious*!" The man's teeth were flecked with spices and streaked in red oil.

"Is that there mine? Is that my recipe? They's distributing already?" Golay's nervous questions were followed by his trembling hands resting behind his head, his elbows in the air as he breathed heavily.

"Oh yes, Sheriff. I do declare this is a true treat! What's in this, rabbit? Can't be venison...is it rabbit?" Taking another bite, the man waited patiently for an answer as the accumulation of sauce in either corner of his mouth coaxed his grease-ridden tongue to lick his lips clean.

"It's that lean beef. Seasoned just right and simmered long in them good juices."

"This here is the best damn beef I ever ate, Golay! You didn't buy this at no supermarket. This here is from the Johnson's herd, ain't it?"

"If I say any more, I'll have to kill you." Slapping the man on the back, Golay gently pushed the curious fellow in the opposite direction, away from him and Billy.

Billy grew increasingly nervous as more patrons presented with tin bowls, jaws working as they munched their meals in what appeared to be sheer bliss.

Spoons clanking, slurps, and sounds of

fulfillment were all about them as more and more fair-goers eagerly wolfed down the tastily prepared recipe.

"Look at them go to town on that like nobody's business. Ain't that something, Golay?"

"Billy, I want that ribbon. I need me that blue."

"It's yours, Golay. I can smell it in the air."

"I sure do hope you're right, Billy…I sure do."

"Where the hell did Savannah go running off to?" Looking through the sea of people, Billy was unable to spot his towheaded sibling.

"Ladies and gentlemen! I do believe Mayor Myers has an announcement to make!"

Diverting their attention to a large wooden table with chairs seating four plump county-men and the mayor as chili judges, Billy and Golay moved closer to hear the announcement.

"I do, I do, I do! As mayor of this here town, I would like to say that this year has produced a whole mess of delicious goodies. Everything from Suzan Harrolson's prized cinnamon rolls to Harvey Hinkles' preserves, my wife is gonna have to let out my trousers. Now, I know this is a happy time, a good time of year, but due to recent events, I am gonna have to ask the lot of you to keep an eagle eye out. We're missin' two boys of our own, and now a visitor from Morton County has done gone missin'. I want you all to eat, congregate, and be happy under the watchful eye of our sheriff, Officer Golay, but, dagnabbit, folks, be mindful."

The crowd looked about with curious eyes, and Billy was certain they were falling on him and Golay.

"And now for the good stuff, folks. I have been involved in the chili cook off in some fashion or another for years. Let me tell you, I have never in my life tasted anything like the bowl of beauty I done ate today. Sheriff Golay! Get on up here, boy! You're taking home the blue ribbon!"

The crowd erupted. Billy stepped backward, the pride for his friend's accomplishment overshadowed with worry over his sister's unknown whereabouts.

As Golay approached the smiling mayor, Billy melted into the crowd, his gaze wild with anxiety as it danced about the smiling faces. It was unlike Savannah to leave his side, especially after the incident with Henry.

Making his way to the hog stalls, Billy found himself initially relieved to find his sister poised near a sow at the end of the covered stalls, until he noticed him. Savannah was talking to an older fellow, more than likely in his sixties.

Approaching cautiously, Billy paid little mind to the conversation at hand. "Savannah, why did you leave?"

"Billy, this here is Albert Jacobson from Salina, Kansas."

"Hello, Mr. Jacobson." Billy extended his hand, attempting to gauge his sister's motives.

"Howdy, Bill."

"Savannah, I was worried about you. You just took off without no warning. You missed Golay's blue ribbon."

"I'm sorry, Billy. I got to looking at these fine sows and paid no mind to what was going on."

"Are you about ready to go back now?"

"Billy, did you know Mr. Jacobson here gets paid to bring bad guys to the law? Bad guys that can't no one catch? He catches them and brings them to the law."

"Is that right?"

"It is, Bill. That's why I'm here."

Crossing his arms, Billy waited for an explanation.

"I'm looking for a Trent McFaver. He was last seen around these here parts about a week ago. He's an ole boy I can't wait to personally get my hands on."

"Can you describe him for me?"

"Tall, thin, has an awkward haircut and a taste for little boys and girls. His momma ran a trashy daycare from her home outside of town. He had all the access in the world to little children."

"I hope you catch him, sir."

"Have you seen this fella?" He held a picture up for Billy to see.

Billy attempted to appear collected. "No sir." Looking at the smiling man in the picture, Billy's thoughts envisioned the bloodbath of muffled screams and countless newspapers.

"Well if you do, please let me know. I'm stayin' at the Inn."

"Will do, Mr. Jacobson. Savannah, let's get."

"Bless this blue! Oh, bless this grand prize, children!" Golay stared at his large and extravagant ribbon while Billy and Savannah grinned from the kitchen table of their home.

"You earn't that blue, Golay. That sweet meat had them people in hog heaven!" Billy patted Golay on the arm.

"I'm tickled pink we were able to reunite ole Jacobson with Mr. McFaver! Askin' for his whereabouts and whatnot. He's in your damn belly, fool!" Golay's boisterous comment sent Billy into a fit of laughter. Savannah grinned from the opposite side of the table.

"You don't think he'll come sifting through our business, do ya?" Billy asked.

"No, Billy-boy. I sent that man on his way. Right now we're looking cleaner than a virgin's honey."

"That's good. That's real good."

"I'll be right back." Excusing herself from the table, Savannah made her way down the hall.

"It's plum beautiful, Billy," Golay crowed. "We took the world's worst and we turned it into the grand prize."

"And we got a whole damn freezer full of that sweet meat. Imagine the possibilities!"

"Billy!"

Savannah's shriek sent both Billy and Golay rushing down the hall to the little girl's room.

"Billy…she's dead! I think she's dead!" Looking devastated, Savannah held up a lifeless Petunia, tears streaking down her face.

"Oh no, sis. I'm so sorry, little-bit."

"Savannah, honey, sometimes these things just happen." Golay attempted to comfort the little girl, resting his hand atop her shoulder.

"Let's have a service, Savannah. Let's put this pet to rest."

"Oh, Billy! This ain't fair! She was just a baby!"

"We are gathered here today to lay to rest little Miss Petunia. She wasn't but a baby turtle, but she was Savannah's friend and Savannah loved her. She was taken from this here Earth too soon, and she will be missed." Golay's words were soft yet gruff as the trio stood near the cellar door over a foot-deep hole and a small wooden cross.

"Oh, Billy!" Savannah buried her face into her brother's waist while he patted her on the back.

"There, there, little-bit. Petunia is up there with Jesus right now. Momma and Papa will take right good care of her."

"It ain't fair! Why does God take everything?" She released her brother and raced from the impromptu funeral site to the wooded area near the house.

"Should I chase her, Golay?"

"No, Billy. Let her work through her head on her own terms. Them young'uns ain't quite right upstairs till they hit about your age."

Chapter Eight

Billy

Long and dragging, the day had left a sense of angst in Billy's psyche. It was calm and windless, the air silent in the streets while the young man made his way home. He found himself worried what the evening's dinner with Bria Clancey would produce.

If he and Golay were unable to convince the woman that Billy was a good caregiver for his sibling, he might lose her.

Approaching his home, he was relieved to see Golay's vehicle was still parked in front. Rounding the side, his heart fluttered when he looked upon the open cellar door. He knew with absolute certainty that he'd shut the door after the last harvest clean up.

Racing down the stairs, Billy gasped at the horrific sight. His sister, sweet and loveable Savannah, was covered in blood, standing next to the cutting table.

"What the hell have you done?" Billy's hands involuntarily covered his mouth as he looked upon the mangled and lifeless body of a small brown animal, the companion dog of their elderly neighbor, Grace Thorton. The dead dog's digestive organs were hanging out; some had been set aside. Blood covered the table and a pile of newspapers at the girl's feet.

"Hi, Billy."

"Savannah! How could you do this?"

"This mutt done dug up Petunia. He dug up my pet...my little baby! I did it, Billy. I put a good long hurt on him. I put a hard hurt on him!" Savannah stared her brother down, her rage released in her tears.

"Oh my God, Savannah, you killed it! You killed this poor little dog. You killed Mrs. Thorton's dog!"

"Damn right I did! He *dug* up my turtle's grave and *ate* my Petunia. I got every last piece of her back." Savannah smiled, pointing to the bits of bloody turtle shell next to the intestines and other various innards.

"I can't...I just can't..." Turning from the carnage, Billy went up the cement stairs and to the house.

"Billy!"

Paying no mind to his screeching sister, Billy reached the porch and glanced back at the blood-covered girl emerging from the cellar.

"Savannah! They'll see you!" Racing to his sister, Billy grabbed her with one arm while slamming the door shut with the other. "Are you insane, Savannah? Damn you, girl!"

"Billy, please don't be mad with me. I was so angry. I still am! I had to put that good hurt on that dog for what he done."

"Savannah, you can't kill a dog for bein' a dog! That ain't Christian; it's demented. You tortured an innocent animal for digging up what it thought was a little bag a'bones. That's sick!"

"I'm sorry. You hate me now? You're gonna send me away with that fat ugly woman?"

His gaze resting on his trembling sibling, he quickly embraced her. "No, little-bit. Never. We got a whole lot of talking to do, though. And don't you ever go down to the cellar again without me, do you understand?" His fierce tone had the girl in tears.

"Yes, Billy."

The scents of home-cooked goodness wafting throughout the home were pleasant and thick. Peach cobbler, roasting-ears of corn, a fine green salad, and the focus of the meal—a mean slab of ribs.

The afternoon's events had Billy's mind abuzz as he and Golay worked hastily to prepare the bounty for their guest. Savannah had been banished to her room to read the Good Book and contemplate her actions after bathing the dog blood from her malicious hands.

Setting the large glass pitcher of tea on the table,

Billy froze when a heavy knock sounded on the front door.

"She's here, Golay. That big ole bitch is here."

"Settle yourself, boy. This is going to go only one way. The best way."

"Savannah! Please get the door!"

Savannah quickly opened her bedroom door and skipped down the hall. She was dressed appropriately in a summer dress with her hair brushed nicely. When she opened the door, Billy saw his sister flash a large smile. It almost passed for genuine.

"Hello, young lady."

"How are you, Miss Clancey?"

"I'm well, and yourself?"

When the woman stepped inside, Billy was surprised to find Golay and Savannah's description was not only accurate, but almost kind in comparison. This woman was much fatter than they'd described.

"I'm great. My brother and Sheriff Golay are in the kitchen."

"Splendid. You must be, Billy. I'm Bria Clancey."

"It's nice to meet you, ma'am."

"You as well. I need you to know that I'm here on your behalf and in your best interest. I only want what's best for you and your family. I'm on your team, Billy. Together we're dangerous."

"I'm pretty dangerous by myself, ma'am." Billy flashed a cocky smile and offered the woman a wink. He'd intentionally worn tight-fitting trousers that showcased his assets in detail and was pleased to find Bria's gaze continuously falling below his waistline.

"I see you have a gorgeous spread here. It looks and smells delicious."

"Nothing better than a home-cooked meal, ma'am. I know you must be busy as all get out and don't got much time to set at the dinner table. I hope this strikes your fancy. Me and my sister put a heap of effort into it."

"Well, it certainly looks delicious. I am beyond pleased that Savannah extended the invitation."

Pulling the chair from the table, Billy motioned Bria to sit. "Please, let's eat."

The group gathered at the table, and Billy found his anxiety easing slightly. Savannah seemed somewhat out of sorts, although her mood was nothing notable.

"This meat is so tender and juicy. I must say it is absolutely delicious." Her face covered in sauce, Bria devoured the ribs ravenously.

"I'm glad you let these kids treat you, Bria. I tell you, I love these two kids like family."

"I can see that, Golay. I think you're right. I think this here is anything but a typical family. Even though you kids have lost your parents, Billy, you have proven you are capable of caring for this young lady, and I see no reason for me to intervene in your care."

"That's great news, Mrs. Clancey!" Billy's excitement filled the room as his sister smiled proudly.

"It certainly is, Bria," Golay agreed. "I assure you I have these children's best interests at heart.

I'll be looking in on them daily. There ain't no need to worry about them none."

"I believe you, Officer Golay."

"That makes me so happy!" Savannah ran to her brother, hugging him at the table.

"Well, I'm happy you're happy," Bria said. "I do appreciate this hearty and delicious meal, but I have a long day ahead of me tomorrow. I'll be using your facilities and then excusing myself for the evening."

"Down that there hall, Mrs. Clancey."

"Please, call me Bria."

After Bria left the table, Billy looked to her sister. "We're gonna be okay, little-bit. It's gonna be okay."

"You kids is gonna be just fine. Both of you. We got a freezer full of meat and nothing but support from me."

"Thank you, Golay. Today is really a great day!" Billy's smile was interrupted by hefty footsteps coming from the bathroom down the hall.

"Sheriff Golay! Sheriff, I need you right now!"

As the group looked to the hallway, a disheveled Bria appeared. "*Now*, Sheriff!"

"Why, Bria Clancey. Woman, what the hell has got you troubled?"

"I couldn't find a cloth to clean the seat. I can't empty without cleaning the seat first. I looked in the dirty hamper!"

Billy's inside knotted.

"There's a bloody dress in the hamper! It's fresh blood! And it has animal hair on it!"

"Now calm down, Bria, we—"

"Don't tell me to calm down, Golay! What is

going on here?"

Searching his mind for an answer, Billy said the first thing that came to him. "She helped a dog what got hit by a car. It was dying and she took it from the street!"

Bria stared at the group. The explanation slowly erased the horror from her gaze, and her breathing settled. "Okay. That...that makes sense. I'm sorry, that had me in a tizzy."

"That's okay. I had to help that little ole dog. I couldn't save him, but I took him to the cellar to—"

"Show me." Bria's demand was solid.

"We buried it, ma'am." Billy swallowed. His saliva felt like rocks in his throat.

"Show me."

"We can't." Savannah's smile crept deviously across her face like a serpent in the garden.

"Why can't you? If you buried it, there should be a freshly dug—"

"Because I put that good hurt on that damn dog, and I made damn sure it was awake and breathing as long as I could!"

"Savannah!" Billy charged toward his sister, knowing it was already too late. It was over.

"Officer Golay, did this child harm an animal? Tell me this young girl is not that depraved."

"Bria, I...I don't know."

"If you don't know, then don't attempt to assure me this home is the optimal place for her. She is coming with me."

"No!" Billy stood defiantly between Bria and his sister.

"It's okay, Billy. Calm down. I'll take her to the

dog…trust me." Maneuvering around Billy, Savannah grabbed Bria Clancey's hand and pulled her in the direction of the front door. Billy and Golay reluctantly followed.

Hand in hand, Savannah opened the cellar door and escorted Bria Clancey to the macabre scene. The disemboweled dog immediately had the heavyset woman affected and at a loss for words.

"You see, Mrs. Clancey? I put that good hurt on that damn dog, just like I told you."

Appearing at the bottom of the stairs, Golay and Billy stood helplessly.

"She's unwell, Golay. She'll have to be institutionalized. This girl is insane!"

"So you'd take me from my brother and my family?"

"I have no choice, young lady."

"Well, that ain't no better than hurtin' kids. Wouldn't you say, Golay?"

"I guess I would, Savannah." Golay's response was absent enthusiasm. He looked to Bria with a sympathetic gaze as Savannah produced a rusty scalpel from the dog carnage, cutting the woman on the thigh.

Bria's screams sent a smile across Savannah's face. She found herself craving the screams of the condemned. Her gaze captured her brother's shaking hand reaching for the mallet near the bottom of the stairs. She looked to the men and grinned widely.

"Oh, Billlly! This one's broken!"

About the Author

Bradon Nave was born and raised in rural Oklahoma. He attended a small country school during junior high and high school and graduated with only three people in his class. After graduate school, he decided to devote his spare time to his passion of writing. Bradon currently lives in Piedmont, Oklahoma, with his wife and two young children.

Facebook:
http://www.facebook.com/bradonnavebooks

Twitter:
http://www.twitter.com/BradonNave

Google Plus:
https://plus.google.com/u/0/108823460188949641
774/posts?partnerid=gplp0

Website:
http://www.bradonnave.com/

Ricochet

By Carissa Ann Lynch

Chapter One

I don't remember my mother. Although she was around when I was little, I have no memories of her. She vanished in the night. Well, that's only part of the story…

"Dad would fucking flip if he found you in here." I jumped at the sound of my brother's voice, though I didn't turn around. I had to find the uniform.

My father's closet was full of them, although not the particular uniform I needed. His hung in rows, dull denim jump suits that stunk of fat and oil.

French-fry mechanic. Have you ever heard of such a ridiculous job?

For the past thirty years, my dad left for work at six in the morning and worked until long after dark. His job was to manage the conveyor belts and quality control of the fries. He always came home smelling like starchy water, fat, and oil. One benefit of the job was that there was no shortage of food in our house. Bags and bags of brown paper sacks filled our freezer. French fries. Bags and bags of fries.

Toby was breathing down my neck now. "Dad will fucking flip…" he repeated.

"Dad's drunk, Toby." I sighed deeply, pushing uniforms aside. What I needed was in the back of the closet.

Dad was always drunk by this time. He came home every night with a thirty-pack of beer and he drank until he passed out, like clockwork. Most nights we didn't speak.

He had a girlfriend, our "stepmom" as she liked to call herself, for five years or so. However, like Mom, she cut her losses and ran. Can't say I blamed her.

"What if he wakes up? I don't want to see that belt again."

"Found it!" I whipped around, holding out my prize for him to see. Toby gulped so loudly I could hear the lump in his throat.

"So the rumors are true." He stepped forward, running his fingertips across the buttons of my mother's uniform shirt.

I smiled. How could he even miss her? He was a baby when she disappeared. I barely remembered her myself, and I was seven at the time she left. Vague flashes, sounds, smells were my only memories of her, if you could even call them that.

"The rumor is true. Adventure Town is reopening. They offered me a job. Told me they'd pay me extra if I wore her old uniform."

Toby shuddered, jerking back from the garment in my hand. "Why? Why would they do that? Why would *you* do that? That's disgusting, Regan!"

"I need the money. One of us has to get out of this town. I can't live in Crimson County forever. I can't live with *him* forever," I grumbled. We both knew I was talking about our deadbeat dad.

I turned away from Toby, clutching my mom's Adventure Town shirt to my chest, trying to fight back tears. Try as I might, my eyes were burning and my cheeks were wet.

Toby placed his hands on my shoulders. "Okay. I'm with you."

"You can't work there, Toby."

"I didn't mean work there. Someone is going to have to cover for you."

I stared at the grimy knit shirt with its checkerboard pattern and loose, khaki-colored buttons. It smelled dusty. Forgotten. Fading.

Like my memories of my mother.

I walked toward my dad's bed, laying the shirt out flat across his crumpled sheets. The words **"Adventure Town"** were embroidered across the right breast pocket. The collar was stretched, loose strings of fabric hanging from the neck and arm holes.

It was an ugly shirt.

I flipped it over, trying to smooth the wrinkles out.

"What the hell is that?" Toby hissed in my ear, pointing at something on the back of the shirt. I leaned over, squinting at a small brown stain.

"Looks like blood," I whispered.

"Do you think she did it? Do you think she killed those kids?"

I gathered up the shirt, rolled it in a ball, and stuffed it beneath my own shirt. I couldn't take the chance of Dad seeing me carry it upstairs.

I took off for my bedroom, leaving my brother's question behind, pretending he never asked it in the first place.

Chapter Two

"What's this about you working at Adventure Town?"

I nearly choked on my beef stroganoff. At least, that's what I thought it was. The lunch ladies at Crimson High liked to come up with their own bizarre recipes. Today's was a mixture of flabby brown meat and slimy, too-soft noodles.

"So he told you. That little shit bag told you." I shoveled in a spoonful of the putrid meat as Jenny sat down beside me. My best friend. Also my tattletale brother's girlfriend.

"Why?" Jenny asked, prying open a carton of milk.

"Need the money, I guess." I shrugged, pushing my lunch tray aside.

"How did this come about?"

I shrugged again, glancing out the dusty cafeteria windows. The sun was beaming. Another lovely day in Crimson County.

I could hear sounds of saws and drills in the distance. Adventure Town being resurrected.

"I went up there the other day. To investigate. There was an old man there, caught me peering through the fence at all the construction. I thought he was going to yell at me, then he asked me if I was Ann's daughter."

Jenny's mouth fell open in shock. "He knew who you were?"

I nodded, glancing around to make sure no one else was listening.

"He said he knew my mom. They worked together."

"Did he defend her? Did he say he knew she didn't do it?" Jenny asked hopefully.

"No. Nothing besides what I already told you."

"Why do they want you to wear her old uniform?" Jenny pushed.

"I think he liked her or something. Said he wanted it to feel like old times, me working there."

Jenny shivered. "That's fucking creepy."

When she saw the look on my face, the anger and pain, she looked down apologetically. "I'm sorry, Regan. I know she didn't really do it. Even my parents said it wasn't her. That old place was haunted. We've all heard the stories…"

I rolled my eyes. "Carousel horses coming to life, ripping kids to bits and pieces. Rollercoasters that run their own courses, riders' heads sailing through the night sky, I've heard it all too, Jenny. It's stupid. All of it. My mom ran off because my dad's a drunk and she couldn't take it anymore. She went to work at Adventure Town, and she never came back that day. She's probably hanging out in California somewhere, drinking mojitos and eating steak."

I smiled. I liked the idea of her out there somewhere, living a life better than Crimson County could offer.

"How do you explain what happened that night then?" Jenny asked, her voice barely above a whisper.

"Rides malfunction. Shit happens. People die. And sometimes mothers leave."

I jumped up from the table and stomped off toward my next class. I didn't need Jenny. Or my stupid traitor brother. I was going to work at Adventure Town when it reopened, earn enough money to leave like she did. And then they'd all be sorry.

Chapter Three

Our old farmhouse was silent, Dad still at the factory and Toby with Jenny working on a science fair project. I dropped my backpack in the kitchen then walked around the house, flipping on lights and pushing back curtains. Soft light filtered in, fading with the presence of a full moon and creating dusty little streams in the air.

I stared out the window. From here, I could see across Langley Park. Steel monsters in the distance punched the skyline, and twinkling lights shone from the construction crew laboring to re-erect the old coaster and Ferris wheel.

Adventure Town was scheduled to reopen this Saturday.

I drained a glass of milk. Deciding I didn't want fries tonight, I climbed the creaky old stairs to my bedroom.

My room was boring and small, fitting only a

twin-sized bed and stout dresser that held a tiny TV set. No pictures. No posters.

I turned the TV on and kicked off my shoes, stretching my toes and lying back on my bed. I had chemistry formulas to solve and a shower to take, but after my argument with Jenny today, I didn't feel like doing anything.

Instead of watching the screen, I stared at the closed door to my closet.

I needed to try it on. Make sure it fit.

I got up and opened the closet, staring at Mom's Adventure Town shirt. It hung limply on a hanger in the dark closet space.

From this view, it didn't look scary. Ten years ago, she supposedly had it on when she...

I shook the images away. It wasn't true. None of it.

Slipping the shirt off the hanger, I carried it over to the bathroom across the hall. Toby's room sat dark and empty. I wondered when he would be home. I wondered if he and Jenny were talking about me.

What if she's crazy like her mother?

I'd heard kids at school asking that very same question, whispering to each other in the hallways and backs of classrooms. I didn't care.

However, I *would* care if Toby or Jenny started asking questions like that too.

Standing in front of the spotted bathroom mirror, I slipped my oversized t-shirt off and slowly unbuttoned Mom's shirt.

I expected it to be tight. In every picture I'd ever seen of her, my mom looked dainty and small.

Fragile and ghostlike. Surprisingly, my arms slid in easily. I buttoned it, mindful of the loose buttons and worn fabric.

I stared at myself in the mirror. With the shirt on and my dirty blonde hair swept back from my face, I almost looked like her.

I pressed my forehead against the mirror, squeezing my eyes shut. Ever since news of the reopening, my mom was all I could think about. She invaded my mind, memories tiptoeing through my head.

Fantasies, I corrected myself. *Not memories.*

"Regan?" My heart skipped a beat. I jumped back from the mirror, staring at the closed door in terror.

It wasn't my dad or Toby.

"Regan, it's Melvin. From Adventure Town Fun Park." I recognized the old man's voice. The man on the other side of the wired fence, who asked me to wear the shirt and come to work for the fun park.

Why the hell was he in my house?

"Your brother let me in. He said it was okay. I've been knocking and knocking. We need you to start work tomorrow. As soon as you get home from school. We have to get ready for the reopening."

I yanked the door open, grateful to see my brother in the hall, standing next to the man named Melvin.

"O-okay," I stammered. "I'll be there tomorrow."

The man nodded, his eyes staring at my shirt. Immediately, I covered myself, embarrassed for wearing it.

"Aren't you going to wash that thing?" my brother spat, a look of disgust on his face.

I stared at the man. "How did you know where I lived?"

"Well, this is where your mother lived so I figured…"

I put my hands up, not wanting to hear more about my mother. My dad would be home any minute now, and he would freak if he saw the shirt or this strange man in our house.

I followed the man out, nearly knocking him down the stairs as I rushed the process. He had to be nearly sixty, his skin cracked and leathery, his movements slow and painful.

I stared out the window until he disappeared, walking toward Adventure Town, the city of steel and lights.

When I turned around, Toby was looking at me, a worried look on his face.

"It's only a job," I said. "Stop looking so weirded out by it."

I hurried up to my room to strip out of the shirt. It went on so easily, and now it felt tight on my back. I jerked my arms forward and back, struggling to take it off.

By the time I did, I was sweating and panting. I glared at Mom's crumpled shirt on the floor. I scooped it back up, straightening out the wrinkles again and replacing it on the hanger.

Feeling strange, I pressed my face against it. Did it smell like her?

It smelled old and musty. There was something else too, a light flowery smell I didn't notice before.

Perfume? No, that wasn't it.

Roses.

It reminded me of a funeral.

Chapter Four

Adventure Town was a short fifteen-minute walk from school. Toby was supposed to cover for me with Dad, tell him I'd stayed after to work on the school yearbook committee. What a load of crap that was, but Dad didn't know me well enough to know I'd never join a club.

The front entrance to the park loomed ahead, a creepy clown mouth and painted murals of children and theme park rides.

Metal bars blocked my entry. Normally there would be a ticket taker or someone I figured, but there was no personnel in sight. I pressed against the bars. They didn't budge.

Sighing, I slipped between two bars, sucking in my gut and turning my head to the side in order to fit through.

I went inside the heart of Adventure Town. Booths were set up, food vendors and games. No

253

one was working yet. Some of the booths looked half-empty, like their owners were still in the process of setting them up.

Where was everyone?

Rides sat motionless like abandoned giants. A newly painted pirate swing, spinning teacups, a baby coaster, and the big main coaster lay ahead.

I reached the front of the old wooden coaster, staring at a freshly painted sign: **Ricochet.**

"You can change the name, but it's still the same. The Rollercoaster of Death," I muttered.

There were scuffling sounds behind me. I turned to see Melvin, hands on hips.

"You're right. It's still the same. Those are just stories, you know. Those boys were stupid. Not wearing their belts, standing when they were supposed to be sitting, drinking alcohol on the ride. Both boys got their heads cut clean off." He made a crude impression with his hand, like a knife slicing across someone's throat.

I pinched my eyes shut, trying not to picture flying heads in the sky.

I wonder where the heads landed.

"Where is everyone?"

"This way," Melvin said, pointing in the direction of a rectangular trailer. He moved speedily, zigzagging between the Scrambler, Tilt a Whirl, and a large set of spinning swings. For someone who moved so pitifully yesterday, he now appeared quite spry.

He led me through a door and inside the cold aluminum-sided building. Rows of tables were filled with employees, some young and some old, all dressed in regular clothes. I felt silly in the moth-eaten, old-fashioned uniform I'd quickly scurried into in the girls' bathroom after school.

Everyone was staring at me.

"She looks just like her," a plump lady gushed, walking toward us. I didn't have to guess who she meant. The woman stuck her hand out to greet me. I accepted it reluctantly, offering a tight smile. "I knew your mother," the lady added, searching my face for something.

"I didn't," I answered curtly.

The woman nodded knowingly. "I'm sorry, sweetie. I'm Maggie. Let me introduce you to some people. Some of us worked for the old theme park, and some of these guys are new. Either way, you'll fit right in."

"What will I be doing exactly?" I looked at her and then Melvin.

"I was thinking she could do her mother's old job." Melvin coughed nervously, staring at Maggie for an answer.

Maggie nodded, her eyes never leaving mine. I was watching the people, watching me, listening to whispers about Ann and how much I looked like her. I took a seat at the emptiest table I could find. I wasn't sure I wanted to meet my coworkers after all.

Jerks. Nobody wants to be told they look like a mass murderer, even if that murderer is their mother.

"What did my mother do here exactly?" I asked no one in particular. A girl sitting across from me, no older than twenty, stared at me, unblinking.

"I mean, what did she do for work? Did she do something in particular?"

"She took tickets for several rides, rotating shifts. And she managed the Mirror Maze," said Maggie. She stood behind me now, resting a casual hand on my shoulder. I wanted to brush it off.

"The Mirror Maze? You guys are bringing back the Mirror Maze? *Really*?" I looked around the room incredulously.

I couldn't believe it. Eight children found dead and murdered inside. You'd think they would have torn it down.

"We didn't change a thing. We want to bring Adventure Town back as it used to be."

"Minus all the death, I hope," I mumbled.

Chapter Five

Equipped with a cart of cleaning supplies, as well as a broom and a box of black trash bags, I set out to work, cleaning the seats of The Scrambler and the pirate ship ride. I kept my head down, humming as I scrubbed. When I was finished, I started sweeping the grounds and picking up any litter I could find.

Honestly, the park seemed pretty clean already, although it was apparent that most of the vendors still had some setting up to do, and there were nearly a dozen theme park employees painting signs or the rides themselves. It was amazing how much rust a coat of paint could hide.

The park had been closed for ten years now, ever since the tragedies, and I'd never ventured inside the theme park before. Sure, I'd been *dared* before, especially when I was younger. A few times I set out with intentions of sneaking inside but never got close enough.

I'd heard stories of kids coming to Adventure Town to smoke or drink, or to make out with boys twice their age. Mostly, however, the park sat empty all those years.

In the light of day, it didn't really seem all that scary, the way it looked in my dreams.

"Are you working hard?" a voice asked from behind me. Startled from my daze, I turned around to see a dark-haired girl I'd seen earlier in the meeting trailer. She was right around my age or younger. She had sleek, silky hair and a pretty complexion.

I smiled at her. "I guess so."

"Do you want to take a break? Go get a drink?"

I stared at my heavy cart of supplies, unsure what to do with it.

"Leave it for now." The girl, who told me her name was Nichole, led me across the midway.

In the distance I could see a creepy little makeshift house with crooked letters painted on its awning. The Mirror Maze.

"Want to check it out?" Nichole asked when she saw me looking.

"Hell no." Surely, she'd heard the stories about my mom. "Do you go to Crimson?" I asked, trying to determine if I'd seen her before.

"Nope. My mom homeschools me. I heard about the reopening though, and I couldn't resist the job." She directed me toward a woodsy spot with motionless train parked out front.

"I'm going to drive the train. Can you imagine how I'll feel after I've taken a hundred groups of snot-nosed brats in a circle? I'll be ready to kill them!" She grinned, then immediately froze, remembering her words and my mother. She cleared her throat uncomfortably.

"Want some water?" She tossed me a bottle from a small knapsack on the bench.

She stared at me while I drank it; all the while I was staring at workers as they bustled around, cleaning and arranging stations.

"At least you'll be in the shade," I remarked, staring at the old wooden coaster in the distance.

Suddenly, I saw the coaster whoosh by on the tracks.

What the hell?

"It's moving! The rollercoaster is running by itself!" I shouted, pointing.

Nichole gripped my arm steadily. "They're doing a test run. They'll be doing those throughout the day, with all the rides. To make sure they're safe."

Feeling silly, I finished off the water and tossed it in a nearby trash basket. "I'd better get back to work," I said, scurrying away from the girl. I could feel her watching me as I walked away.

I felt foolish. Listening to the roars of the coaster behind me, I cursed under my breath. I could feel workers' eyes on me and a couple whispers: "She's the one."

This place is as bad as high school, I thought, happily retrieving my cart and getting back to work so I could avoid their stares.

Three hours later, my wrists and fingers ached from scrubbing the fifty-something swings on the swing ride. I was relieved when Melvin came to me and told me I was all done for the night.

It was dark, past dinnertime, and Dad would be home now.

"Same time tomorrow?" I asked, remembering my reasons for wanting this job in the first place. I needed the money. Desperately.

Melvin smiled. "Yes, please." He handed me two twenty-dollar bills, my pay for four hours of work.

"Thank you." I headed toward the trailer to gather my backpack and change out of the shirt.

"Wait." I turned around, raising an eyebrow at Melvin. "Don't forget your extra money. For wearing the shirt." He whispered the last part.

I stared at the fifty-dollar bill in his hand. He was going to pay me fifty dollars for wearing a tattered old shirt? It seemed too good to be true.

I took the money, thrilled to realize that I had nearly a hundred dollars plus the two hundred I'd been saving up for the past couple of years. At this rate, I'd be able to buy a ticket out of Crimson County and have enough left over to get me on my feet. Perhaps by the end of summer.

Chapter Six

Walking home in the pitch-black darkness, I was flying high, the money I'd earned feeling good in my jeans pocket and my mind filled with fantasies of buying a plane ticket to go somewhere tropical, like Florida or South Carolina. Maybe even California, even though it was so far away.

The night air was cool and warm all at once, with sounds of approaching summer in the air. I was so happy I practically skipped, humming a song I'd heard once though couldn't recall from when or where.

I barely noticed the vehicle behind me.

A row of lights reflecting across the trees brought me back to Earth. I slowed down and made sure I was off the road so the approaching vehicle didn't swipe me as they drove by.

I peered over my shoulder. The car had its bright lights on, and I shielded my eyes, squinting in the dark. I stayed near the tree line, off the road, waiting for the car to pass.

It was moving slowly. I waited and then finally stopped.

Minutes passed and the car didn't move. Were they stopped in the road?

The headlights were so bright the driver was merely a silhouette behind the wheel. What the hell was he or she doing?

That's when it occurred to me: the driver was stalking me. They'd slowed down so they could follow me.

My heart pounding, I made a quick decision to take a shortcut through the woods. I darted through the gap between two trees. I was running now, blind in the dark, branches scratching my arms and catching my hair. I kept moving forward, trying to put some distance between myself and the car.

Out of breath and confused in the dark, I finally stopped and bent over, gasping for air.

What the hell is wrong with me? Why am I being so paranoid?

My eyes were adjusting to the darkness now. I was in the woods behind our farmhouse and other houses on our road. Even though it was dark, I only had to make my way through until I saw the back side of my house or a neighbor's house.

A twig snapped. I froze, straining to see or hear someone in the woods behind me. Had the driver of the car gotten out, possibly followed me? I couldn't hear the car in the distance or see its lights between the trees anymore.

My heart lurched in fear.

Although I wouldn't swear to it, I thought I heard brush moving, more branches shifting. Was I imagining things?

Then I heard a sound, like someone coughing or clearing their throat.

I whipped around, racing through the woods like my life depended on it. I don't know why I felt so scared, but something inside me knew I was in trouble.

Someone was chasing me. I could hear heavy footsteps pounding the ground.

Suddenly, I was jerked backwards. My arms flailed in my panic, then I realized my backpack was hung up on a tree branch. I jerked, trying to free myself.

Now that my feet were still, there was no doubt someone else was moving in the woods. I wiggled my arms out of the backpack, leaving it behind. Moments later, I saw Mrs. Estes' back porch lights and let out a sigh of relief. Our farmhouse was two houses down. I raced around the house toward our front porch, terrified to look back from where I came.

The front door was unlocked. I jerked it open, slamming it shut behind me.

After locking and securing the deadbolt, I let out a sigh of relief.

"What the hell are you doing, girl?"

I turned around to see my father, half dressed and inebriated, sitting on the living room couch. He stared at me expectantly, his hands resting over his underwear, looking like a sloppy drunk.

He had a can of beer on his lap and a scattering

of dozens more empties at his feet. I could barely stand to look at him when he got like this.

"Just running home, trying to get some exercise," I grumbled, walking past him as quickly as I could.

"Wait!" I froze, unsure what I was more afraid of—the stranger in the woods or him. "Where have you been?" my father demanded.

My thoughts were racing from what had happened, and for a moment I was stilted, unable to recall the lie I'd come up with in the first place. What was it I'd instructed Toby to tell him?

"She had yearbook, remember? I already told you," Toby barked from the kitchen.

Thank God.

When I looked back at my dad, his eyes were tiny slits. "Huh?" he asked, like he'd forgotten his own question.

"Good night, Dad." I mouthed *thank you* to Toby, heading straight for the stairs to my room.

Once inside, I sat on the bed, my hands and legs shaking uncontrollably.

What the hell happened tonight? Everything seemed so good, and then that freak in the car was following me. Maybe working at Adventure Town was messing with my head. Maybe I only imagined someone chasing me.

That's when I remembered my backpack, hung up on the tree in the woods. I felt for the money in my pocket, relieved to find the ninety dollars still there.

At least I had the money. That was the important thing.

Then I thought about Mom's Adventure Town shirt, folded up neatly in the bottom of my backpack and my expensive Calculus book and scientific calculator inside. Dad would kill me if I lost those things.

Sucking in deep breaths, in through my nose and out through my mouth, I tried to assure myself I could get the backpack in the morning. No one would be out in those woods. At least I hoped not.

I crept over to my window, peeking through the tiny gap in the curtains. Moonlight sparkled across our back lawn. My eyes drifted toward the tree line, imagining shadows everywhere.

Chapter Seven

Horses moving up and down. For a moment, I was watching from afar. The carousel moved in circles, playing that familiar song. I was riding the back of a beautiful porcelain horse with pale pink roses carved into its saddle and harness. I stroked its painted hair as though it were real, waving to someone on the sidelines.

Standing there was a girl who looked like me. But she wasn't me. It was my mother, smiling. Waving back at me. I nearly broke my neck trying to look back and see her as the carousel circled, leaving her out of sight.

When I came back around, she was still standing there. Now her face was contorted with a terrified expression. She wasn't looking at me. Rather, she was pointing at someone behind me. When I came around again, she was gone.

The ride was slowing, but my horse was up so

266

high. My legs were short, the legs of a child.

I heard a strange sound behind me, almost like a growl. A stationary tiger with blood dripping from its fangs. Suddenly no longer stationary, it growled at me and lunged. Its eyes turned from red to orange, tiny little angry flames. A mouth full of tiny pointed razors. I could feel its teeth ripping me limb from limb.

Chapter Eight

I jolted up from bed, traces of the dream lingering. My alarm clock buzzed.

I got on my feet, realizing I was late. I slipped into the same pair of jeans from last night and grabbed a long-sleeved tee from the closet. By the time I made it downstairs, Dad's pickup was long gone for work, and Toby was gone too, traces of his breakfast still on the table.

I nearly forgot about the backpack until I was headed out the door. Without giving myself a chance to reconsider, I raced back to the woods, looking around wildly.

I felt instant relief when I spotted something black and red beneath a broken tree limb. I practically dove to the ground, brushing the dirt off of it and swinging it around on my back. I ran the whole way to school, trying not to think about the car following me last night.

I was nearly ten minutes late for first period English. Luckily Mr. Oats cut me some slack, for which I was grateful.

After last night's incident, the day was going considerably well. Until I reached sixth period Calculus, that is.

As soon as I pulled out my heavy math book, a scattering of papers fell to the floor. Faded and dusty. Newspapers, dating back ten years.

I hurriedly scooped them up, already suspicious of their content. I stuffed them back in my backpack, staring straight ahead at the board.

I didn't know what Miss Singleton talked about or what my answers were for our weekly Calculus quiz. My mind was spinning.

What did the newspaper clippings say? And most importantly—who put them in my backpack?

As soon as the bell chimed, I made a beeline for the girls' bathroom. I waited in the stall for it to clear out, and then I took the clippings out. I was going to be late for work at Adventure Town, but I needed to read them, needed to understand what my "stalker" wanted me to see.

The first article contained the heading ***"Grisly Murders Shock the Citizens of Crimson County"*** and a collage of grainy photos beneath. Children, boys and girls, ages ranging from eight to thirteen. The kids from the Mirror Maze, found *"slaughtered like pigs"* according to the newspaper article. I shivered despite the stuffy, warm bathroom stall.

My eyes darting back and forth, I read as quickly as possible. The last thing I wanted was to get caught reading about my own mother in a bathroom stall. Wouldn't *that* give the kids something to laugh about?

Although there were no traces of a murder weapon, they did find a bloody pair of women's sneakers, as well as a pair of jeans, stuffed in a garbage can inside the operator's station of the Mirror Maze. Inside the back jeans pocket was my mother's name badge.

The next several paragraphs were about my mother, Ann Matthews. Age twenty-seven, she was the wife of local French fry mechanic, Frank Matthews, and the mother of two small children, ages three and seven.

My fingers rested on the word *children.* My brother and me. We'd been so small and my mother so young.

I stared at the black and white photos, innocent children murdered on a night when they should have been having fun. It was horrific to read about anywhere, especially so in a small town like ours.

"Things like this don't happen here," wrote the reporter who'd published the article.

I kept reading, more about my mother and her education. She grew up in Oklahoma and met my father when she moved to Indiana to attend college. She never finished. She never returned home to her parents, Mary and Nathaniel Schultz.

She was supposed to be manning the Mirror Maze when the bodies were discovered by several of the kids' parents, who came looking for their missing children. Police searched for my mother everywhere, thinking she may be dead, or worse—involved in the killings.

They wanted to question my mother.

Days later, after the murders, she still hadn't turned up anywhere according to the next article. At first there were rumors, that maybe the killer had kidnapped her and was holding her for ransom. Then a warrant to search the Matthews property—our family farm—revealed a startling piece of evidence. My mother's Adventure Town shirt. The one she'd been wearing that very same night.

Police found the shirt hanging in her closet. They immediately concluded that after murdering the children, she must have come home and changed clothes. After interrogating my father, he broke down and admitted that she was severely depressed and that money and jewelry were missing from their bottom drawer.

An APB was issued. Alas, my mother, the supposed murderer, was never found. I'd heard snippets of all this before but never the details.

I stared at the words on the page, letters blurring together as my eyes brimmed over with tears. The evidence was circumstantial. No one could prove she really did it.

Hastily, I flipped through the other articles, realizing some were older. Two were dated *before* the children's murders. A tragic accident, two boys' heads severed on the rollercoaster. A young girl named Ally Mae Fulkerson, whose parents claimed her arm was bitten off by one of the carousel horses. There was a gruesome photo, a bloody stub of an arm, and an obituary for the seven-year-old girl, who bled to death in her parents' arms.

The last article was the most current, dating exactly two weeks after the children's murders. *"Adventure Town closes in response to Crimson County's demands".* There was a picture of the old theme park and a man standing beside a **"Closed for Business"** sign. Although the man was younger, I recognized Melvin from the theme park.

He looked miserable to be shutting down, his eyes down and hand up, casting away the photographer. Beneath the theme park photo was the last photo ever taken of my mother. It looked like a creepy mugshot, her standing in front of the Mirror Maze, her arms flat against her sides, with a cold, blank expression.

She looked like me. Or rather, I looked like her.

I stared at her face and then specifically her lips, willing them to move.

Tell me what happened, Mom. Tell me, I begged the photo.

I wanted to rip the delicate paper to shreds.

No, no, no! It can't be true!

I struggled to remember my mother. Something, anything to help me understand. I came up empty. Blank.

The door to the bathroom slammed open and closed, jarring my thoughts. I folded the newspapers and dug around in the bottom of my backpack for the shirt. I could heard water running and then two girls laughing, so I took my time buttoning the shirt, waiting for them to leave.

I fumbled with the buttons, my hands shaky and

numb. When the girls were finally gone, I came out of the stall and quickly rinsed my face and hands in the sink.

I needed to hurry if I was going to make it to Adventure Town on time. I was already running late.

When I looked up in the mirror, I fought back the urge to scream. My mouth fell open. There was a small gold tag pinned to the front of my shirt.

The name on the tag was Ann Marie Matthews.

Chapter Nine

I jogged toward Adventure Town, my body buzzing. It wasn't fear or anxiety I felt; it was anger. Someone was trying to scare me off. The same someone who followed me and chased me through the woods last night.

I think I knew who that *someone* might be.

I slipped through the bars of the theme park, jogging across the midway to where Melvin was filling up a large aluminum tub with tiny rubber duckies.

"Why did you ask me to work here?"

He glanced up and then went back to setting up the game. "You're late, Regan. I told you to come right after school." When I didn't respond, he stood up, taking me by the elbow. "Let's talk somewhere else."

"I don't want to talk somewhere else!" I shouted, yanking away from his grasp. "I know you followed me last night. I know you knew my mother. Do you think hurting me will bring those children back? Do you think what happened to them is my fault?"

Melvin tried to shush me, but I got louder.

"She didn't do it! Why can't you people realize that! She wouldn't—"

"I *know* she wouldn't, Regan."

I stopped and stared, confused. "Then who followed me through the woods? And who put this tag on my mother's shirt?" I thrust the name tag at him.

He wasn't the only one looking. Workers in nearby booths stopped what they were doing, and everyone was gawking at me. In fact, a few of the older workers were walking toward us.

Melvin held up a hand, urging them to stay back. I was fuming, my cheeks flushed, and breathing so heavy I fought the urge to gasp for air. I clenched my fists, forming angry balls of hate.

"I know it was you in the woods," I repeated.

There was a small twitch, Melvin clenching his jaw. He was getting angry too.

"I don't know who was following you, though I can take an educated guess. Probably the same person who followed your mother to and from work ten years ago."

I stared at him, shell shocked.

"The same person who told the police she was deranged," Melvin added, getting louder.

"W-what you are t-talking about?" I stammered.

"I'm talking about Frank Matthews. Your *father*."

Chapter Ten

We were sitting in Melvin's office. It looked normal, with cheap plastic picture frames, a stack of invoices, and an even taller stack of unopened mail.

"It wasn't my father. He was home when I ran inside last night," I told Melvin matter-of-factly.

He sighed but didn't look surprised. "Honestly, Regan, the person who followed you could be anyone. There are a lot of people in this town who still remember, and even the kids your age know the stories. It was probably someone messing with you, although..." Melvin scratched his chin pensively, "I don't understand where the badge came from, 'cause that's not the one I made for your mother. If it *was* hers, I can think of only one person who could have it, and that brings me back to my original suspect—your father."

"What do you mean by *suspect*?"

"He was never considered a suspect in the

murder. Never, not even once. He cooperated with the police, played the role of mourning husband. He chose to keep you and your brother, although your mom's sister offered to take y'all in. In the townsfolks' eyes, he was a victim. The poor husband, left to fend for himself and his motherless children," Melvin spat.

"Aunt Marie. I know. I haven't seen her in years. I do remember that, I think," I said softly.

"Everyone likes to say that losing your mom is what sent him over the edge. That that's what led to all the drinking. Those of us who were close to your mom know the truth." Melvin pounded his fists on the desk in front of him.

Surprised by his reaction, I leaned forward. "You loved her, didn't you?" I couldn't help asking. I'd sensed it. Even that day, standing at the wire fence, I could feel the way he looked at me. Not in a creepy, perverted way, but with a look of nostalgia. Like I was a ghost from his past. A ghost he wanted to see.

"I loved your mother deeply. Yes, that's true. Your father knew it, and so did she. It wasn't the only reason…Your dad was always a mean man, Regan. Beat her with his fists once, did you know that? Well once that I know of, that is."

I don't know why I was so surprised. I tried to imagine him doing such a thing. I remembered him whipping Toby with a belt a few times, simply for forgetting his chores.

"I guess it's believable," I said, biting hard on my lower lip. I didn't like the way this conversation was going. Not one little bit.

"Do you really think your mother would hurt a child? Did she ever hurt *you*? Or your brother, for that matter?"

"I wouldn't know. I was too young to remember her."

"Is that your kneejerk response when the subject of your mother arises, Regan? Because it's a bold-faced lie, and you know it!"

His voice was so loud now, and no one had ever called me a liar when I told them I didn't remember my mother. I was stung by his words and confrontational demeanor.

"I was only—"

"Seven. Yes, I know how old you were. You weren't too young to remember. How could you *not* remember? You were so close, you and her. She took you everywhere with her. She even brought you to work!"

That part was *really* shocking. All those dreams about theme parks, riding on the carousel? Could they be…memories? I shook the thought away.

"No way! I don't believe it! I was too young to remember."

"Well, *I* remember it plain as day. She couldn't leave for work because you'd start kicking and screaming. You didn't want to stay with your dad. If I didn't know better, I'd think you hated him, even then. It got to the point where he couldn't handle it. Your brother was little, a baby, and he'd go to sleep in his crib at night. But you wouldn't let up. You'd pitch fits till your dad brought you to her. Once you even tried to sneak out and walk all the way here on your own. Ann was hysterical, her and your dad racing up and down the streets of Crimson trying to find you."

"And did they? Find me, I mean," I wondered incredulously.

"Yep. You were close. Less than half a mile from the park. We couldn't believe you made it that far. You were determined to be with your mother. You always were."

I stared at him, surprised by this. No one had ever told me stories of my childhood. It was all so secret, no one wanting to mention my mom and what happened. Hearing it now felt sort of good and relieving all at once.

"After that, she never left you with him again," Melvin continued. "You always came with her. You'd play in the Mirror Maze sometimes, but your favorite thing to do was ride the carousel."

I jerked, remembering my dream about the tiger, ripping me limb from limb.

"What about the night it all happened? Where was I that night?"

"You were here with me. She asked me to watch you for a bit until closing time."

When Melvin saw my horrified expression, he explained. "That was normal. She often brought you to me so she could finish up for the night. She always worried about you wandering around at dark. It made her nervous."

"My mother loved kids. She would never do what people are saying she did," I said, remembering her soft smile as she bent at the waist, handing out candy and small toys to the kids who came through the Mirror Maze, or any kid she saw at the park. She loved them as though they were her own.

"Yes, she did," Melvin said, smiling sadly. "She loved them very much. The feeling was mutual. Kids were drawn to her! She had this way of making them *all* feel like they were the most important kid in the world."

I could remember more: her laughter and the creases around her eyes; she would make up silly songs, changing the words of familiar ones to make them sound new and funny. I saw her face, smiling over at me in the passenger seat while I giggled and kicked my feet, singing along with her.

I can remember my mother.

"I can't believe it. I can't. I *do* remember some things about her," I said aloud, shocked by this revelation.

She loved silly games and questions. I remembered that about her.

If you had to do it again, what would you want your name to be? Would you still be Regan? Or would you change it to something else?

That's easy, Mommy! I'd pick my favorite flower and my favorite shape. And that's what my name would be! Rose and star. Rose Starr!

"She called me Rose sometimes. I remember that now," I whispered.

Melvin wasn't listening. His eyes were soft and misty, having memories of his own. His smile quickly faded. "Your father resented her. He made her feel guilty for her work. She was supposed to be a chef, you know. That's what she went to college for. She loved people, wanted to open her own restaurant. He put an end to that, he sure did! He didn't want her to be happy, you see, and that's why he followed her. Checked up on her. She was afraid of him. *Very* afraid of him, in fact."

I cleared my throat, trying to believe him because in a way, I wanted him to be right. I didn't want my mother to be a murderer.

I wanted to remember my mother for who she was—a lovely person. A good mother.

"He killed those kids in a violent rampage. While I can't prove it, I know he did. And then he killed her too. She's dead, Regan. I'm sorry, but she is."

Now that I actually remembered, I didn't want to let her go.

"I don't believe that. There would have been a body. She would have turned up!"

"She would have turned up if she was *alive*. She's gone, honey. I'm so sorry to tell you that. But *you're* here, and I'm so glad to see you, the spitting image of Ann."

I shook my head, tears flowing now. "My dad wouldn't kill her. She left! She's out there somewhere! *How* would he kill her? *How* would he make her disappear?"

Melvin coughed, fidgeting uncomfortably in his desk chair. "Have you seen those machines your father works with? The ones at the french-fry factory? He services them, knows all about them, and those machines could chop a body to bits."

I promptly vomited on my white sneakers, my chest filling with fear and disgust.

My whole life, all I wanted was for my mom *not* to be the killer. I had never considered it could be Dad.

Chapter Eleven

Melvin let me go home. In fact, he insisted upon it after I threw up on my shoes and his office floor. The reopening was tomorrow. He told me to come if I wanted to, but if not, he would understand.

He paid me a hundred dollars even though I didn't work. Unlike yesterday, the money didn't matter much. I walked home as slowly as possible, still reeling from my conversation with him.

I remembered my mother. No, that wasn't right, because in truth, I'd never forgotten her in the first place.

I had pushed her away. I didn't *want* to remember.

Well, now I do, I decided.

My heart was heavy, and my backpack felt like it weighed a thousand pounds. I had to fight the urge to plop down on the ground and cry. I felt like giving up.

283

All those years of not having my mother and few friends because of the stories…it felt like now all those years were catching up with me, all the pain slamming against me at once.

It was too much to handle. Too much to bear.

I heard sounds of a car behind me, though I didn't bother looking back.

Who cares if someone follows me? My mother is dead, and my dad might be the one who killed her.

A car roared past me, kicking up water from a nearby puddle. It splattered on my already-puked-on shoes.

About halfway home, the rain started to fall. Softly at first, then it came down in sheets, drenching my hair and clothes. I shivered, never once picking up the pace.

I felt defeated.

Just wash me away with the rain. All the way to the gutters and down below, below the dirt and earth.

I imagined my mother's voice. *"Rain rain go away, come again another day."* Although it sounded like she said, *"Pain pain go away…"*

I was crying now, my tears blending with the rainwater on my face. Finally, I stopped. Staring at my own house.

Never once did I think about the person who chased me yesterday. Why would I? The person to fear wasn't out here; it was the person *inside* my house I was afraid of.

Chapter Twelve

Nightmares. Not your run-of-the-mill falling off a cliff or being chased by a creep sort of nightmares. These were the feverish kind that feel so real you wonder if they really were when you wake up.

Me, as a young girl, running through hallways filled with mirrors. I could see a distorted version of myself, the way funny mirrors make things look. There was something else, someone standing behind me. This evil, black shadow chasing me. Was it my father? I turned a corner of the maze and saw him, standing over a pile of tiny legs and arms.

Then I was on the carousel, riding my favorite horse again. I heard the growl, and I knew what was coming. However, when I turned around, I didn't see a tiger. Rather, my father was crouched between two stationary horses, his teeth bared at me right before he lunged. He laughed manically as he gnawed on my arms and legs. My whole body looked like the stump in the picture.

I woke to the sounds of my alarm. This time, I let out a sigh of relief; it was Saturday. I could lay in bed all day if I wanted to. In fact, that's *exactly* what I wanted to do.

The sun was glaring through the curtains, and I remembered that today was opening day of Adventure Town. Melvin told me to come in at noon if I still wanted to work.

I groaned, sitting up to stretch, then headed for the bathroom across the hall. Toby's door was open, his room empty. He'd always been an early riser, like Dad. He'd probably already rode his bike to Jenny's. I wondered if they'd come to Adventure Town today.

I turned the water up as hot as it would go and stood under the scalding stream, willing it to strip away memories of last night. My conversation with Melvin; those terrible dreams; memories of things I'd tried so hard to forget.

Dad was downstairs making coffee. His face looked puffy and tired, the way it always did after a night of heavy drinking, which for him was every night these days. For some reason, he looked worse than usual.

He stirred the sugar in his cup, leaning against the counter. "Are you sticking around home today?" he asked gruffly, not even looking me in the eye. Sometimes I wondered if he hated me simply because I looked like her.

"I'm going to Melissa's." I tried to keep the lie brief. I wanted it to sound like the truth. Plus, I couldn't say I was going to Jenny's because she might turn up at our house to hang out with Toby.

"I don't want you near that place," my father said.

I swallowed the lump in my throat, my head ringing. How did he know I'd been at Adventure Town?

"*What* place?" I forced myself to ask, even though I already knew his answer.

My father turned around, his eyes focusing on mine. "Adventure Town, that's where. I'm not stupid. I live in this town too. I heard they were reopening today. It's hard to believe people have forgotten. Moved on from all that happened, but I haven't. I don't want you there. I'm not saying you would go, because I know you wouldn't, but I felt the need to say it. If your friends pressure you to go, come home to me." Although his voice was stern, it was edged with worry.

So he doesn't know about me working there.

I released an internal sigh of relief.

"I won't. I promise," I lied, pouring my own cup of coffee.

Chapter Thirteen

I waited until well past noon, after Dad had started drinking, and took off on foot for Adventure Town. I was late, but after yesterday, I didn't think Melvin would mind. He'd probably be shocked if I showed up at all.

The sun was shining—a perfect day for the reopening. The theme park looked like a brand new place. Even all the rain had dried up. People were lined up and the gates were open, welcoming in its new patrons. There were several workers stationed up front taking money, and I recognized the girl, Nichole, from the other day. She nodded for me to bypass the line.

I gave her a warm smile and entered the park. It was already filling with families pushing strollers and groups of teens arguing over which rides to ride first. The game booths were open, dings and bells and jolly music pouring out from them.

288

I felt happy. I don't know why considering all I'd learned; maybe because I knew my mother wasn't a killer. This wasn't a place of horror and dread for her. She had loved her job, and she loved bringing joy to children.

I was dressed in a tank top and jeans, so I quickly changed in the women's restroom, then headed to Melvin's office. He was indeed surprised to see me.

He smiled and nodded appreciatively at my mother's shirt. "It suits you," he said. Instead of the Mirror Maze, he sent me toward the old wooden coaster.

The line for Ricochet was a mile long, and every teen in town was eager to ride it first. The man checking armbands instructed me to make sure all safety bars were secured over riders' laps. For nearly three hours, I did just that. Pressing on safety bars and watching the old coaster roar to life as it whisked screaming kids and adults around its track. It looked like fun, and I felt the urge to ride it.

I saw plenty of people I knew, particularly kids from classes at school. I expected them to laugh or tease me, but they barely seemed to notice me as they were all so excited and nervous to ride.

At four o'clock, I was relieved for a lunch break. Glad for a break and starving, I grabbed my backpack from the operator's station and crossed the midway, looking for a place to eat. I spotted a red and green tent where a lady named Gladys was serving enormous, gooey slices of pizza, and I got in line.

I unzipped my backpack to take my wallet out

and saw the hatchet inside, gleaming in the bright sunlight. I immediately closed the pack, praying the people behind me didn't see it, or Gladys.

"Forgot my wallet," I mumbled, darting for a safe picnic area between two trees. When no one was looking, I opened up the backpack and peeked inside. Sure enough, it was still there.

I couldn't pull it out, so I carefully examined it inside the pack. It was a short-handled ax. I touched the edge of the blade then winced when I drew blood on the tip of my pointer finger.

It was sharp. Deadly sharp.

If anyone saw me with this, they'd send me to the nuthouse for sure. They'd probably think I was going to kill a bunch of kids like my mother supposedly did.

That's when I realized someone must have put it inside while I was working on the rollercoaster. I'd left it unattended for hours, and anyone who knew me from school would know it was mine. Someone was trying to fuck with me; that much was clear.

I considered tossing it in a nearby garbage can, but what if someone saw me doing it? Or worse, what if a little kid or someone got a hold of it?

I made a quick decision to keep it in my backpack. I pushed it deeper toward the bottom, beneath my tank top and wallet. That's when I saw something else. A white notebook card in the bottom. Had it fallen out of one of my school books?

I quickly received my answer. There were blood red letters written on the card, clearly not my own handwriting.

Regan Matthews had an ax. She gave herself forty whacks.
Just kill yourself and get it over with. We don't want you in this town.

So it *was* someone trying to run me off and scare me! For some reason, I felt a little relieved. It was a childish prank, like something one of my shithead classmates would do.

I threw the note card in the nearest trash can and went to Melvin's office.

It was nearly dark when Melvin sent me to work at the Mirror Maze. It was lit up, with strange, offbeat music pouring out from inside. For some reason, it gave me chills. The carousel sat less than a few yards away, playing happier music, though giving me chills all the same. I was starting to wonder if the money was worth it after all.

Kids poured into the maze, and some adults too, flashing their armbands at the door. I sat on a stool. It was a pretty boring job, really.

After an hour or so, I saw a group of classmates approaching. I kept my head down, trying to avoid their gaze.

"I didn't know this was the *freakshow* tent," a boy named Patrick said, laughing. He was standing mere inches from my face. I looked up finally, rolling my eyes.

"I need to see your armband," I told him, trying

to stay professional.

"Here's my armband, *freak*." He shoved me, and I toppled backwards off the stool, my tailbone connecting with the ground painfully. Patrick and three others, a girl and two boys, ran inside the maze howling with laughter.

I stood up, brushing off my skinned elbows and the butt of my pants.

Assholes.

"They're right, you know. You shouldn't be here." I was surprised to see Nichole standing a few feet away.

I sat back down on the stool. "Why not? Let me guess, you think my mother did it too?" I asked flatly.

After our encounter the other day, I was a little surprised to see her looking at me so angrily.

"My twin sister was one of the kids she killed," Nichole muttered, standing face to face with me now. "We don't want you in this town. None of us do," she snarled. Her words were the same words from the note card.

"So it was *you* in the car following me and putting that stupid hatchet in my backpack?" I stood up from my stool, ready to punch her lights out. Then I remembered her sister and felt a small pang of guilt. "I'm sorry about your sister. I am. My mother didn't—" My words were cut short by the sounds of screaming. A girl's scream, terrified and shrill.

"He's going to kill me! Don't, Patrick! Please, don't!" someone screamed from inside the maze. Without a second thought, I reached inside my backpack for the ax and took off inside to help the shouting girl.

Chapter Fourteen

I raced through the mirrored hallways, my own face reflecting back at me, confusing me. The girl's screams echoed through the maze. They were louder now, more panicked. Around another corner, I came face to face with Patrick. He was sneering at me, blocking my path while the two other boys assaulted the girl.

She was lying on her back, and I couldn't see her face. The boys were on top of her. Her screams were muffled, one of the boys using his hands to cover her face.

"Get off her!" I yelled, trying to push past Patrick. He was stocky and tall and smelled of booze.

"What are you going to do about it, *freakshow*?" As he said it, he saw the ax in my hand. I held it to my side, trying to hide what he already knew—I was going to kill him.

I swung the ax, the blade slicing him from cheek to cheek. He stared at me, horrified, raising his hands to his face as the wound split open, a river of bright red blood rushing down the lower half of face.

Before I could swing again, he grabbed my neck, squeezing hard. Tighter and tighter, his bloody face screamed obscenities in mine as he choked me.

My vision spotty, I kicked wildly with my right knee. Where was the blade? I'd dropped it when he grabbed me, but it couldn't be far.

I kicked and fought, screaming for air, my right knee finally connecting with his groin area. I brought my knee up again and again, collapsing to the floor when he released his grip.

The other boys were standing now, staring in horror at Patrick's sliced-up face. I gasped for air, holding my neck, feeling around for the blade as my vision struggled to return to normal.

"Let's kill this crazy bitch," one of the boys said, helping Patrick to his feet.

That's when I saw the ax. I dove for it, jumping back up and waving it around, letting them know I meant business. That's when a black bag came down over my face from behind me.

Nichole.

Chapter Fifteen

There was a garbage bag over my head. I struggled for air, sucking in plastic which each panicked breath. Then someone was punching me in my stomach and head, knocking me to the ground. Several people were kicking and punching me. They were going to kill me.

"What the hell is going on in here?" Melvin croaked, his voice the most beautiful sound in the world.

I fell to the ground, my assailants backing off.

"She tried to murder me!" Patrick screeched. "Nichole was trying to get her off me. See my face! See it? She's a murderer like her mother! Psychotic bitch!"

Melvin yanked the bag off my head. I took in gulps of air, too breathless to speak. Too weak to defend myself.

"The police are on the way. We'll let them sort

this out," Melvin said, his eyes never leaving mine.

There were sirens in the distance.

I should get up and run. Leave like my mother. They're going to put me away for life on attempted murder charges.

There was nothing I could do. Moments later, the police ran in, dragging me away in handcuffs.

Chapter Sixteen

"Your father is here to get you."

I was lying on a metal cot in a jail cell at Crimson County juvenile lock-up. It had been two days since I sliced Patrick with the ax. The longest two days of my life.

The sheriff repeated himself. "Your father's here, I said! Time to get up!"

"You're letting me go?"

"Yep. The girl you saved in the maze, the one who was raped, she collaborated your story. The boys involved have been arrested."

"What about Nichole?"

"She thought you were trying to kill those kids. She put the bag over your head to calm you down. She admitted she'd been bothering you some. Her sister was one of the victims in the Mirror Maze," the sheriff said, wincing.

I wasn't sure if I believed Nichole's excuse.

298

Nevertheless, she wasn't the one who hurt the girl or started the entire incident. That was Patrick.

I followed the officer out to the waiting room. My father and Toby sat silently in plastic chairs that were bolted to the floor. They stared at me incredulously. I must have been a sight, face bruised and hair a mess.

"Are you okay?" Toby jumped up, wrapping his arms around me. I remembered I was wearing Mom's shirt. My father stared at it momentarily, looking away in disgust.

He didn't talk the whole way home, but he made his feelings clear when we got there. He beat me so hard with his belt I could barely walk for days.

Chapter Seventeen

Two Months Later

I went back to work at Adventure Town, trying to forget the incident.

Today was my last day. Over the past eight weeks, I'd saved up nearly two thousand dollars. I finally had enough to leave town. Enough to get my own apartment.

I would miss seeing Melvin and Maggie, as well as some of my other coworkers. I'd miss my best friend Jenny. Most of all, I'd miss Toby.

I wanted to say goodbye but didn't have the heart to do it. Selfishness on my part, I guess.

I had to leave Crimson County; I no longer had a choice. I wouldn't be able to finish school, though I could eventually get a GED.

In the last hour of my last shift, I had to see the

one person I definitely wouldn't miss—Nichole. She was no longer working for the theme park, not after Melvin found out about her family and the grudge she held against me and Adventure Town for what happened to her sister.

And there she was, hanging out, laughing and having fun despite the fact she tried to kill me. She was standing with a guy. I could barely see them in the crowd. That's when I realized who it was. A fresh scar marked his face. He turned around, his eyes boring holes into mine.

Patrick.

I was working the swings, checking armbands, and securing belts. I tried to pay attention to my line of customers, but I could sense them getting close. They were headed straight for me.

They stood in line for the swings, both of them watching me with beady little evil eyes. I tried not to look.

The charges against Patrick were dropped after the young girl recanted her statement. I had no doubt he and his friends did something to scare her, convince her to change her story.

They were standing in line now, waiting for their turn on the swings. I wanted to puke, my stomach twisting in knots as the two got closer.

"Great to see you again, *freakshow.*" Patrick stared at me, his eyes menacing. Nichole was smirking, enjoying my discomfort.

"I checked your bands. Move on through and select your seats," I barked. I was through putting up with their harassment. After today, I'd never see them again.

People in the line behind them pushed forward, and finally they moved on, out of my sight for good. Once the swings were full of riders, I locked the gate and walked around doing belt checks. Nichole glared and Patrick snarled when I check theirs.

I flipped the switch, whirring the swings to life.

They rose higher and higher, suspended from a rotating top. At its fastest point, the swings would be nearly sideways, spinning so fast they looked like a blur from the ground.

"I'm out of here," I told the line of people, who were waiting for their turn to ride. "Someone will be here in a few minutes to take over."

I gathered up my backpack and made my way out of the park, ignoring the screams that followed.

"Someone just flew through the air!"

"What the hell was that?"

I heard people shouting, and several were running. I walked in the opposite direction.

"Oh my God! Don't look, honey! Don't look!"

I didn't need to look to know there were two bodies shattered to pieces.

I headed straight out of the park and away from Adventure Town Family Fun Park.

Good riddance, Crimson County.

Chapter Eighteen

Toby

The farmhouse was so empty, quiet. It'd been that way for weeks now, though even more so today. I'd seen the news at Jenny's house. Two teenagers, Patrick and Nichole, had been thrown from the swing ride at Adventure Town.

They were thrown nearly across the park, catapulted from fifty feet in the air, their bodies exploding against black asphalt.

"It's a gory scene," the reporter said, the expression on her face never changing. *"Officers on the ground report that the bolts securing their belts had been loosened. Possibly on purpose. Police have one suspect. A young girl who had a reason not to like the teens, and a gruesome family history to boot."*

303

Jenny and I stared at each other, our eyes widening in fright.

I raced home to see Regan. I needed to be sure she was alright. No way would she do something like that on purpose.

Would she?

It was nearly eight o'clock at night. Normally Dad would be home from work, but he'd left town weeks earlier to visit Aunt Marie. I couldn't help wondering if he was meeting with her to discuss Regan's future. After today's incident, Dad would really send her away.

I searched room to room, calling for Regan. If she wasn't at home or Adventure Town, where could she be?

Then I got to her room and found the answer. Her drawers were empty, and only a few lonely hangers were left in the closet.

Regan had left town. Just like our mother.

There was a loud knock on the front door. Startled, I was afraid at first, then eager to see if it was news about Regan.

Four police officers were standing on our porch.

"We need to talk to your father, Toby," one of the officers said sternly.

"He's not here. He's visiting my Aunt Marie in Manchester," I explained nervously.

The officers shook their heads. "We've talked to the factory and your aunt. In fact, she's on her way here. The factory said he never told them he was leaving. They reported him as missing. We're also searching for your sister."

I stepped aside, letting the officers inside. I sat at

the kitchen table while the officers searched the house, guns drawn. I tried to explain to them that she wasn't home; neither was my father. It was no use. They were determined to search the farmhouse themselves.

I sat at the table, my hands shaking. Why would my dad say he was going to my aunt's if he really wasn't? Now my whole family was missing.

Satisfied that neither of them were here, the police said their goodbyes, warning they'd be back soon and assuring me Aunt Marie was coming to stay with me.

I shouldn't have been hungry at a time like this, but I was ravenous. There was a package of cheese and carrots in the fridge, a couple of packages of meat in the freezer. And bags and bags of french fries, as usual.

I stared at the brown paper sacks. They looked...different. Like they'd been opened and taped back together.

I pulled the biggest bag out and set it on the table, staring at the extra tape on its top and sides. I lifted it again and set it back down. It felt heavy. Much heavier than the other bags.

I grabbed a steak knife from the kitchen drawer, slicing the bag open across the top.

I let out a bloodcurdling scream, leaping back from the bag.

It contained bits of flesh and human hair.

Epilogue

Laughing children, taunting me relentlessly. Pressing me against the walls of the maze, so tight I felt like I couldn't breathe. My mother was always nice to them, all the while ignoring me. I'll teach them next time. I'll bring a knife.

And then I was riding the carousel. No, not riding—watching. A little girl about my age. A girl my mother loved deeply. She always gave her candy and small toys. She had these little bitty braids I envied. Up and down, up and down, she was riding my favorite horse.

She always got to my horse first.

The little girl heard a growl and turned, and that's when I lunged, biting her, slicing her arm with the jagged saw I stole from my father's work shed.

I wiped her blood on the aluminum tiger's mouth and crouched in a bush behind the carousel, watching her bleed to death.

The scene changed. I was sitting on a scary ride. It jerked me around the track, up a steep hill and then swish, down through a tunnel. When I saw the boys fondling my mother, I thought they were hurting her. But actually, she appeared to be enjoying it. I followed them onto the ride, paying off Jimmy Carlito, the boy who operated it, and I sat behind the boys, whispering in their ears. Daring them to stand up at precisely the right time, when I knew the tunnel drop was coming.

It was amazing how fast it happened; their heads were attached and then on the other side of the tunnel—not. Those assholes deserved it.

My mother crying, saying she'd take the blame. She stripped off my bloody jeans, trying not to look at the dead kids in the Mirror Maze. Trying not to see what I'd done. She cleaned me up and took me to Melvin. She asked him to watch me while she finished up her shift. She told me goodbye, seeming so calm.

My father's face as he woke up, saw me holding the knife. His look of surprise was epic.

My "stepmother's" surprise when she found me in her closet, holding the jigsaw blade.

Bathtubs full of blood.

Knives lodging into bones, adrenaline pumping through my veins. And the perfect place for dad's raunchy pieces—in the bags he assembled himself.

I woke up shaking, panting from the scary dreams.

I got out of my bed, preparing my usual

breakfast of cereal and juice.

I looked around my apartment, smiling. It was tiny, barely big enough for a small bed, kitchen space, and raggedy armchair from the Salvation Army. But it was cozy. A little part of the world I could call my own. It was perfect, really.

By the time I finished eating, I could barely remember the dreams.

Tomorrow I'll write them down, and then maybe I'll remember, I decided.

I'd always had bad dreams. These were progressively worse.

They used to feel like tiny whispers, tiptoeing around in my head. Lately they'd become too loud to be ignored, tiptoes sounding more like stomps.

I dressed for the day, gathering my purse. Bright sunshine hit my face when I stepped outside into the beautiful California sunshine.

There was a diner down the road.

It was small like a trailer, a blinking neon sign attached to the top.

Rose Starr's Diner.

It had received rave reviews on Yelp.

I reached inside my purse for a tissue, unable to hold back tears. I'd finally found my mother.

Staring inside my purse, I was shocked to see a knife inside. I wondered who put it there, but I pushed ahead.

I was determined to be with my mother. I always was.

About the Author

Besides her family, Carissa's greatest love in life is books. She's always loved to read and never considered herself a "writer" until a few years ago when she couldn't find a book to read and decided to try writing her own story. With a background in psychology, she's always been a little obsessed with the darker areas of the human mind and social problems, so she tried to channel all of that into her writing. She is the author of *The Flocksdale Files*, *Grayson's Ridge*, *This Is Not About Love,* and the upcoming *Horror High* series. She resides in Floyds Knobs, Indiana.

Facebook:
https://www.facebook.com/CarissaAnnLynchaut hor

Twitter:
https://twitter.com/carissaannlynch

Website:
https://carissaannlynch.wordpress.com/

Goodreads:
https://www.goodreads.com/author/show/112045 82.Carissa_Lynch

Rest in Peace?

By Erin Lee

Lisa

In nine hours, my husband will be dead. He's oblivious, going about his day the best he can—house slippers on, paper open, shaking violently in his wheelchair with tremors he doesn't notice. His tremors make me, on the other hand, jump, especially at night. He can't even read. I think he simply likes the smell of the newsprint. It's familiar to him. He's read every article I've ever written, until he couldn't read any longer. I wish I could crawl inside his head and hear his thoughts.

Instead, I'm stuck with mine. *Does he care?*

Does he really *understand what's going on?* After more than half our lives together, you'd think he'd know that I like—no, *need*—to talk things out. Am I supposed to just give him this one? Let him do things *his* way on his final day?

Yes, I suppose I am.

I press my lips together and beg myself to be strong enough to handle what's to come.

Stop. The man can't talk anyway. What's he supposed to say, even if he could?

This isn't about me. It's about him. It's his story, for now.

This whole thing reminds me of the time we took our dog Samson to the vet to be put down. At only five years old, Samson had developed a rare and untreatable eye cancer. In six months' time, he went from a bouncy pup to a whimpering old boy, frail and delicate with the same big heart but much less of an appetite for Caesar's Kitchen treats. We didn't let him suffer, or we told ourselves that. We kept him drugged up until we could see his quality of life wasn't worth keeping him around for our own selfish need to hang on. Samson was the best dog, agreeable, friendly. Happy.

We rode in the cab of my husband's tired pick-up to the vet that day. Jeff couldn't even look at Samson. I couldn't let go. I hugged him and tried force-feeding him pieces of a raw hot dog I'd snagged from the fridge on my way out the door. That dog looked at me, one eye puffy and swollen shut, as if to say, "Not a chance, lady." *He couldn't do it anymore. I didn't want to believe it. His tail was wagging, telling me he was content to go along for the ride. I remember wanting to scream at him and Jeff. I wanted to tell my husband I wasn't strong enough, demand he pull a U-turn and take Samson right on home. I wanted to say,* "He's really not suffering that much. Let him stay with us a little longer. Die at home. Happy." *I said nothing.*

I wanted to tell Samson this would be his last ride. "Stupid dog, this isn't an ordinary ride! Eat the damn hot dog! It will make me feel better."

I know, selfish.

Jeff said nothing either. Even when he carried Samson's body, wrapped in his favorite quilt from our bed, to the backyard, leaving his loyal friend only to find a shovel. Samson's been buried in our backyard under our favorite apple tree for eight years now, two months before the routine physical that changed everything. I still wince when soggy November apples drop, thinking they are hurting Samson. I picture them plopping onto the ground, hitting our family dog in the head, interrupting his peace. But nothing would hurt him like this. In fact, I'm glad he's not around. I can't imagine how he'd handle losing Jeff. They were best friends. Where Jeff went, Samson was sure to follow, always with a wagging tail and good intentions.

My husband? Not so much. He isn't like either of us, Samson or I. He isn't agreeable, and he is even less selfish. No, my husband is a breed of his own. It would take me all day to find a word to properly describe him, but I'm not wasting our last hours together doing that. I'll follow his lead, like I did the day we put Samson down, and pretend that everything will work out okay. Like when he taught me how to dance, I'll be his silent partner. There will be plenty of time, the rest of my life, for tears and regret and telling the story, the other side of it, later.

I grip his shaking hand, look him in the eyes, and ask him what he'd like for breakfast—twice. I wonder if anyone else would understand his garbled response, not that it matters now. I don't miss the grin that used to worm itself across his lips to thank me. It's been months since that's been around. You can't miss what you no longer expect. I rub his head, tossing a handful of coffee-colored hair, and get up from the tiny table in our dreary motel room. I need to focus on the mission at hand–making my husband his last real meal. Trying not to dwell, I am extra careful, skimming the pulp out of the orange juice and grabbing the biggest spoon to feed him. I hope he won't fight me. He does that, especially lately.

Jeff was the cook, until he lost his balance and nearly burnt half his body with boiling water for chicken alfredo. It was a fluke accident, I'm sure, but he tells it that someone pushed him. Jeff has a crazy imagination. Regardless, Martha Stewart, I am not. It's not easy making eggs sunny side up in a motel room. Yet I'm not the type of woman to argue, which is a big part of my problem. Plenty of time for self-improvement books later. I make do with a hot plate and try to remember if Jeff's even supposed to eat today at all. I'm tempted to grab the paperwork or pull the prescriptions out to read the bottles. The thought makes my stomach lurch.

Does it matter, really? I mean, someone will clean up the mess.

I always clean up the messes. It's what I've done our whole lives together. I miss New York. I miss home.

The worst that can happen is we lose our room deposit. What's ten bucks? Who would notice a few stains in this place anyway? It's littered with them.

We've been here, on the West Coast, for two years now. You have to establish residency before you can move forward with the, well, the other stuff. Currently, Oregon is the only state where this type of medically assisted suicide is legal. The Death with Dignity Act was signed in 1997. Two years and a few acquaintances later and it still doesn't feel right. Aurora, Oregon, is not our home. I can't wait to get out of here. The fact is we never really fit in here. As hard as we tried, it was clear to everyone in our tiny new town that we were here for the same reasons as so many dignity pilgrims before, to get residency and get out: me in the Subaru, Jeff in a hearse. It's the agreed upon plan, the one we decided on three years ago before he lost his…'pride.'

Pride. That's the word he used. I'd call it 'fight.' Doctors would write either term off as the 'natural progression of the disease' and call it Parkinson's Disease Dementia–like "…*no big deal, lady, exactly what we anticipated. We warned you it could come to this. Have you made plans?"*

They'd go about their day, writing on clipboards and asking what the special was in the hospital cafeteria for lunch. I would know. I've heard it more times than I can count.

I'm not sure what it will be like returning east without him. I'm thankful that our children Ella, JJ, and Nathan got their own rooms. Soon, they will be knocking on the door, and Jeff and I won't have much more for alone time. It's funny. All those years, I fantasized about leaving him or of a life without him. Now, as he faces his final hours, I have never wanted to be with him more. It's the classic codependent dance, I suppose. I've spent enough time in support groups to know. Sometimes Ella asks me how I feel about my decision to stay with him, to put up with his declining health and failing mind or even his chronic substance abuse before we'd ever heard of Parkinson's. She wonders, I know, if she'd have done the same. For her sake, I hope not. I wouldn't blame her if she did. Love is a powerful thing. So is need. I feel both for Jeff. And many other things. To mention those would be inappropriate...insensitive...now. One of the gifts in dying is that your flaws are buried with you.

My husband was diagnosed with early onset Parkinson's disease three days before his 42nd birthday. The past eight years have been a whirlwind. Watching his mind and body fail has been the hardest thing I've ever experienced. There were many times I wanted to quit. But, just like I stayed with him through his rollercoaster battles with alcohol and cocaine, I'm here now. In this moment, I'm not sorry. In fact, I wouldn't have it any other way. I'm like Samson, a loyal dog, to the bitter end.

For Jeff, living with advanced stage Parkinson's until the natural end was never an option. A guy who prided himself on his ability to handle virtually any problem that came his way, he wasn't about to accept limited physical and mental abilities. Personally I think it's stupid. He used to call me a "life lover," meaning someone who would choose to live no matter what my limitations. He's right. I would never sign a living will. I'd want hope that one day I'd wake up from a coma and learn to walk again. I'd eat the hot dogs all the way to the vet, tail wagging, even if only in spirit. I get it, though. I understand because I know my husband. I support him, as I always have. For better or worse, right? Honestly, even though he's been trapped in his body for several years now, I still can't fully imagine him as anything other than my hardy wanna-be-lumberjack, out in the yard chopping wood or building an animal shelter from trees he milled himself. Although it's been a long time since I've taken in that sight, it feels like yesterday.

It's how I see him, even now, even when helping flip pages in a paper he can't read.

Jeff

Today, I'm going to die. I've been stuck in this body of mine, the "House of Horrors," for eight years. My horror story began with a doctor's appointment. I was starting a new job that required a routine physical and drug testing. "No problem," I told them, relieved to have earned my three-year chip and sure there was nothing to worry about. My biggest fear going in was the prostate exam. No guy gets too excited about those. Sure, my hands had begun to shake. I've been shaking for years. *You* try living with a psychopath. It makes you shake. It makes you paranoid. It makes you need drugs or a good stiff drink to help you get through the day. Peace. A week later, they called and said they wanted to do more tests. I wasn't worried. I figured it was all routine. I was over forty. I didn't even have high blood pressure, amazingly enough. There was nothing physically wrong with me, I told myself.

Another phone call came. This time, they wanted me to come in. I had no idea that that day—January 4, 2008—would change my life so drastically. More tests. A second opinion. A third. Three weeks later, I learned I had early onset Parkinson's Disease. Three years later, I couldn't work, couldn't even walk without Lisa asking me if I was "using...again." I'd been left with a memory requiring I kill a tree a week in Post-It notes.

Now I'm confined to a wheelchair and helpless to do anything on my own. My mind, though, is still here. You see, I'm not as bad off as I lead people to believe. It's the one advantage I have, her and the doctors thinking I'm so out of it that I have no "quality of life."

It's true. My quality of life *has* diminished. The House of Horrors betrays me every day. A man has no dignity left when he can't be left alone on the toilet. If I were a normal guy like any other man and didn't have this stupid disease, I'd have been able to leave her when the kids moved out. I had my chance and kick myself for not taking it when I should have. I could have divorced her, given her the house and all the other things she cares about. I could have walked away. I had too much guilt. For what? I have no idea. So this thing, Death with Dignity, is my only out. Today, I can finally be free. It's hard not to smile and instead pretend it's merely another Tuesday. I'm good at pretending.

Finally, I'll rest in peace.

For twenty years, I've faked reading the newspaper. Why should it be any different now? I'll do anything to avoid talking to her. My wife, that is. Especially today. Whether I like it or not, the power's in her hands. Sure, I have to be the one to swallow the death serum myself, but I need her help. The doctor is meeting us here at three. The day can't move fast enough. My greatest fear is that something will go wrong and change everything. Change can happen in an instant.

For Lisa, 'the change' happened after our youngest, Ella, was born. Lisa went from being a doting mother and wife to someone out of a horror movie that I didn't recognize. I'm telling you on my grandmother's grave, that's how it happened. Just that fast. The first red flag went up the day she called me shouting that if I didn't get home from work "this minute, Jeff" that my "screaming witch of a daughter" was going to die. Her ear-piercing shrieks and the uncensored names she called me made me believe her.

"How dare *you leave me alone with these three monsters all day!" she'd screamed, holding a red-faced Ella out to me when I arrived home exactly twenty-eight minutes—I made great time at eighty miles per hour—later. That day I came home to a complete stranger who's never really left.*

You see these sorts of things on the news. There was that mother who drowned her kids in the tub. The other who drove her kids into a lake. That's what I worried about with Lisa every day after that one phone call. The calls didn't stop, and if I had the chance to do it over again, I would have taken the kids and left her. But fathers don't get custody. Men don't have rights. That's what I told myself. I white knuckled between jobs, trying to be sure I was always close to home for one of her dreaded hate calls.

She wouldn't get help. She didn't think she had a problem. The problem, she said, was me. The scariest part of it all is that she claims she doesn't remember it. She says I have a vivid imagination and pets my head like I'm her dog and tells me not to worry about it. It wasn't until years later, when Nathan and JJ were old enough to protect their sister, that I stopped worrying. That's when I started getting into troubles of my own. Things I'm not proud of. I needed to unwind, when I finally could. Unfortunately, those ways of relaxing weren't the brightest. I never claimed to be all that smart. I'm simply your average guy.

I watch her wend her way through our tiny motel room, digging through the miniature refrigerator with burn marks in the shape of an X on the side. We've been here nearly five weeks. She insisted on this room, this place, something about her writing. I told her we'd need something bigger. I was right. Being in such a tight space this long has only made biding my time harder.

I remind myself to drool, unsure if that'd even be a symptom. Luckily, Lisa's not medically inclined. I can't see her looking it up. Not now, anyway. We're too close to the end, and she's more worried about figuring out the bills, I'm sure. This won't be cheap. Maybe that's why she chose this place, on the edge of town, bookended between one-night junkies and prostitutes. Maybe she wanted to save money. Or she figured that the cheaper it was, the longer I'd stay around. *Oh, joy!* I'll be glad when the kids can get out of here. I can't imagine they're enjoying the view either, especially Ella.

What's the doctor going to think? The Coach Motel isn't exactly the type of place most people would want to die.

I try to tell myself that she's a good person, deep down. It's hard not to be nostalgic when you know it's your last day. My wife's not all bad. When I first met her, she loved life more than anyone I had ever met. She brought with her an energy and spin on things I'd never felt before. I see it still, every now and then. I'll miss that. She's great with trivia and can retell a story so it's fresh, even if you've heard it, even if you were there. She's captivating. She's not bad to look at, either. Even good in the sack, or was, until I couldn't do that anymore either.

Fucking House of Horrors.

Sure, time's taken its toll on her. But she still walks with a straight back, tits to the sky and a smile that could charm the pants off nearly anyone. Her hair is dyed a charcoal black and down to her shoulders. I used to play with it as she slept. Used to, as in twenty years ago. Or, more recently, on a good day when her demons were tucked away. So not often.

Some say the dead watch over their loved ones, sometimes coming too close for comfort. I don't know about that. I hope it's true, minus the smothering part. Maybe Lisa won't look so bad—so crazy—from afar. I hope to watch over Ella. She'll be the most hurt by this. She's the only reason I've held on as long as I have. She wanted to be here sooner but had to defend her dissertation. She's finishing up her doctorate in philosophy. I can't imagine her thoughts on assisted suicide. I haven't asked. I learn fast. For a demented dude, I'm well aware that Ella could say the one thing that could change everything and derail my plan. If she mentions me not walking her down the aisle, I'm a goner.

I like my eggs scrambled and a little runny. I miss pulpy orange juice and never minded when it got stuck between my teeth. Lisa's always hated that. Pulpy orange juice reminds me of my grandmother. She died in 1979. I spent every summer with her as a kid. She left me her prized possession, her sterling silverware, even though I was a kid. She knew I'd take better care of it than anyone. I put it, full place settings for twelve, at the bottom of my sock drawer. Then, as a married man,

I did the same. Lisa gave it to the Goodwill when I was at work six years ago. She said it was taking up too much space. It's something I'll never be able to forgive her for, even when I'm dead.

I'm coming, Grandma!

I watch her burn my eggs, the ones she'll feed me with a baby spoon, and remind myself this is my last meal. Never again will I choke down her sloppy attempts to give me what she calls 'love.' I call it 'revenge.' Maybe it's a combination of the two. They say love and hate walk a tangled line. I tell myself to focus on the good things, something she's told me to do a thousand times over. Like her, I don't listen. I hate sunny-side up!

Lisa

We could have done this anywhere. I picked this place, the Coach Motel, because of its history. Our home lease in downtown Aurora ran out a month ago. We checked in here, a tiny motel at the edge of town reeking of skunk and menthol, without a date in mind. We only knew it was close. I thought today would come much sooner. It's okay. I'm flexible, or I've learned to be. Juggling three kids, nearly alone, does that to a person. There's something about a place with antiquity that gets my curiosity going. I figured while I waited I could at least get some writing done. I'm writing a thriller about hauntings.

They say the Coach Motel has the scariest history in all of Oregon. The entire West Coast, really. If you don't count the haunted hotel one town over, that is, which I don't, because people say the hauntings there are staged.

As the story goes, it was 1930 when one of the travelling laborers who built the Coach Motel was killed. His body was never found. He was staying in room 18—our room. I made sure, booked it a month in advance, and paid extra for it. The only trace of him was bloody sheets and a half-eaten ham sandwich on the night table. Since then, guests report seeing the ghost of a woman, believed to be his widow. They call her the "Ghost Widow of Coach Motel." They say after you see the widow, it's likely you'll go missing. She's looking for her husband and won't give up until she's found him.

The last sighting of her was six months ago, according to the wide-nosed, uninterested clerk at the check-in desk.

"That old ghost?" he said. "She's harmless. She's just stuck here. Can't find her old man. Lonely, I suppose."

I haven't seen anything so far. I've felt some shakes, just the planes coming out of the old state airport down the road, but I often think about why she'd still be here. I mean, come on, lady, move on. You're dead by now, too.

The Ghost Widow of Coach Motel is only one of the stories people here love to tell. Over. And over. And over again. When you're stuck in a town with a population of 1,018, torn from friends and family who love and need you, you have a lot of time to do your research. The big news in town this week was that there will now be a street sweeper on the fourth

Wednesday of every month. Residents must move their cars.

Gee, sounds exciting, sorry I'll miss it.

I've always been one to look under the rug. The quieter a place, the more you might dig up, if you look hard enough. In fact, since 1930, the five murders that have occurred in Aurora have all been at the Coach Motel. Even better, none of those five bodies have been found. All have been men between forty and sixty years old. All have had brown hair, brown eyes, and been over six feet tall. All of the cases are cold. No one's even looking for the victims. Well, except maybe the Ghost Widow of Coach Motel.

It's 9 a.m. It's hard to believe that in less than a working day's time, my husband will be gone. Of course, he's fighting me on breakfast.

I'd like to see Mr. Perfect pull off bacon, eggs, and oatmeal in a place like this. No appreciation.

I shove the spoon in his mouth, forcing him to take it. He narrows his eyes at me but relents and swallows. I'm tempted to make airplane noises and make him chase it, like I did for the kids when they were little. However, I'm not a cruel woman; I wouldn't want to steal his pride.

Breathe. Count to three.

"Come on, honey, open wide."

He relaxes his jaw and makes a garbled sound. I take the opportunity to fill his mouth with oatmeal.

"The kids will be here before lunch. We have a little time together. I thought we might take a nap. How does that sound?"

His head to the side, he nods, only a little, but

enough for me to know he agrees.

"Perfect. I know you *love* your naps."

It's passive aggressive. I'm aware of that. It's not like he'll catch on anyway. I have a right to be upset. He's about to abandon me. Since the dementia began, he naps every day for several hours, even in the middle of a conversation. Sure, the conversations are mostly one-sided. Not much I can do about that.

It takes a good forty minutes to finish feeding him and help him into bed. I close the thick, dingy curtains. The room is nearly dark. It's a warm burgundy. Painted, I guess, to keep the stains on the walls to a minimum by a well-intentioned owner to give it a richer feel. It hasn't worked. I cannot wait to get out of this stuffy place. I'm tired of listening to the neighbors scream at each other and am beginning to believe the widow is a tale made up by bored townspeople wanting something, anything, to put Aurora on the map.

He stares at me for only a second, averting his mocha eyes when mine connect. I wonder if he has something to say, but he's silent and closes them. I lay beside his curled body, remembering how long it once was. We used to sleep with tangled legs. Now he stays on his side of the bed, me on mine, to the right, by the nightstand. I wonder if it's the same night table the sandwich was on. No, it can't be. This one is made of laminate. Back then, they would have used real wood.

He's snoring within ten minutes. I resist the temptation to talk to him. There's really nothing more to say that hasn't already been said. I glance at the metal door, checking that the latch is turned to the left. It is. I move slowly, so as not to wake him, to take the room phone off the hook. I've never been able to sleep like Jeff. In his younger days, he could go from running a marathon to sound asleep in the same half hour window. I need a book, noise from the TV, or something to get me out of my own head to lull me to sleep. I watch him, envious.

Jeff

I focus on my breathing. Deep, long, steady breaths. I open my throat, faking snores. If I do this long enough, I'll be asleep in no time. Here's hoping she has the mercy to *let* me sleep. It will make the day move faster. I can't risk letting my mind drift. Lately, that's been dangerous. I have to concentrate—*in, out, in, out*—on my breaths. She notices these things. Crazy? Yes. Stupid? No. My wife is anything but stupid.

I dream the oddest of dreams.

I'm a carpenter or builder. The month is June. The year is 1930. My body works. I'm younger, late twenties. I'm putting up trim on this very motel. It's fresh and optimistic, despite pessimistic times, set to open in only a few weeks for people coming through by train. I want to reach out and touch my legs, which also have hope. I'm torn between two worlds somehow. I want to wake myself up so I can stretch and run. I'm moving quickly, a hammer in one steady hand, nails in the other. My teeth hold the spares.

Bang! Bang! Bang!

I bury each nail with two swings. They land perfectly down the trim line. Soon, my dame and I will be moving on. It will be another project, hopefully closer to home. A whole new chance to start again. First, I'll take some time off to rest. A day or two. Although I need the work, I also need some time for peace and hooch.

It's noon. The bell at nearby Colony Church tells me so. I begin my descent down the ladder, headed straight for my room, where there's a ham sandwich, my doll Rory, and a fresh newspaper waiting for me. I hear Hoover's signed some tariff act. I'm not sure what to think of it. I want to decide for myself.

When I reach ground, I fill my tool pouch and lay it on loom that will soon become grass. I can't keep Rory waiting; she has no one but me. A by-marriage decedent of the man who founded this town, William Keil, Rory shares his impatient nature. This land and this project are important to her because William's home was once on this very lot. It was lost to demolition after the communist colony he built became an incorporated city. My wife, who never even met this man, still carries with her some sort of ownership of both the town and place. I'm hoping when we finish the job, she'll let it go. I miss home. I miss the Apple.

"What took you so long?" She shakes a finger in my face, her black hair falling from a bun. I want to push it back in place. I know better. You don't mess *with Rory when she's mad.*

"I had to get off the ladder."

"I made you your lunch! There!" She points to the night table, brought in last week by the guys from the Portland mill. What a bitch that had been, unloading between scaffolds.

"Thank you." My hands shake. I trip over the edge of the bed, reaching for my lunch, a ham sandwich and cup of city juice. I hesitate to take my first bite, hoping for mustard. It's dry. I glance at the paper next to it, which mocks me. I tell myself I'll read it later. Maybe, if I'm nice enough, she'll settle down. She's a heck of a sweet patootie. Maybe it'll work. Maybe, if I'm nice enough, we could roll around together a little before I head back to work.

"Are you okay?" I ask, knowing this is risky. I ignore the bread caught in my teeth but cover them with my upper lip. She hates things stuck in my teeth.

"No! I'm not okay, Henry. Waiting around all day—alone—for you to come back from working."

"I brought you with me, doll. None of the other men do that. I brought you here so you wouldn't have to be alone. Do you have any idea how much grief I get for that? They call me a soda jerk."

She crosses her arms over her chest and is silent. She turns her back, digging into a drawer, also new from the mill, and ignores me. I sit on the bed and take another bite, resigned to the fact that there's no chance of a lunchtime quickie. I have no idea what she's looking for. I don't dare speak or move. It could set her off, and it's not worth it. I don't know what I did wrong. She said she wanted to come along. She said this was important. She called this—Aurora—her "real" home.

I wonder if she's still angry we'll have to go back soon. I can't understand why anyone would want to stay here in this two-horse town. There's nothing for miles but a market, the church and a museum. The last time we discussed it, she said she would never leave. She said I would never leave either. I've learned to ignore those things. Rory can be a cranky broad.

There's nothing for us here. She needs to be glad that at least I have work. Many don't. It's not like I'm a joe college. And it's only getting worse. It's been eight months since Black Thursday. I keep telling her it's going to get worse. She doesn't believe me.

My thoughts are interrupted when she finally turns around, the hem on her pink dress spinning out enough to catch a peek of those fine legs that help me put up with her. She has my spare hammer in her hand. I'd been looking for that. Why would it be in a drawer?

Bang! Bam! Bang!

The guys keep hammering. No one notices I'm missing.

Bang! Bang! Bang!

The church bell rings, marking the end of lunch hour.

I want to wake up. But I can't. Half in and out of sleep, I groan. I don't know if I groan out loud or in my dream. They seem to be the same thing.

Lisa

Bam! Bam! Bang!

I jump.

Jesus. Is it noon, already? I rub sleep from my eyes.

The room's too dark to find my cell phone. The motel's too cheap to provide a dollar store clock.

Bang! Bang! Boom.

Nathan thumps on the door.

I check on Jeff, still snoring. Of course.

I creep out of bed, stubbing my toe on the sitting table to unlatch the door.

"Ssssh, your father's sleeping!" I whisper through the crack in the door. "Hang on!"

Bang! Bang!

I turn the latch to the right, creaking the door open so as not to let in too much light. A woman in her thirties stares directly into my eyes. I gasp, averting my own and taking in the full sight of her. This is not some random woman. I'm looking at my own reflection, only different. I gasp again, this time covering my mouth. Fear bites my stomach. I feel like I'm going to puke. I look closer. The woman at the door is my identical, younger self, minus make-up. She's sporting a pink dress with butterfly sleeves, belted at the waist, ending below her calves. Her dress, her legs, classic brown pumps, and even her hands are covered in blood. I slam the door in her face.

She starts right back up: *Bang! Bang!*

I slide down the metal door, tempted to open it so I can see I've been mistaken. If this is only in my mind. Jeff struggles to roll over, groans, and goes back to sleep.

Useless. As usual. I have *to be dreaming. There's no...the Ghost Widow of Coach Motel. No. This woman is my mirror image. I* have *to be imagining this. It's the stress of Jeff. Of today. Of what today means.* Why *is she covered in blood?*

Bang! Bang!

There's no way I'm dreaming. I'm much too light a sleeper. I would never be able to sleep through all this banging. I lean my full weight against the door, praying she isn't strong enough to push it open, begging she won't try. Slowly, I rise, never taking my weight off the door. I turn the latch to the left and sink back to the floor. I need to get to my cellphone. I can't remember if I left it on the counter in the tiny bathroom or on the night table.

Bang! Bang!

My heartbeat, echoing between my eardrums, is almost as loud as her persistent thuds. I close my eyes, trying to think of what to do. I can't concentrate.

Go. Away.

I squeeze my eyes tighter, as if pinching them shut hard enough will make this one wish happen.

Go. Away!

It doesn't.

"Talk to me and I'll go away. We can both go away," she whispers through the track in the door, like she's read my mind. "I'm not here to hurt you." Her hushed, gentle voice is so opposite the banging, it makes me want to trust her. This confuses me.

Nothing says she's a ghost. I mean, I saw her plain as day. She wasn't transparent. She was there, all of her, and I slammed the door in her face. If it wasn't for the blood, I would have welcomed her. I'm being paranoid. Stop. Breathe. She sounds nice enough. Maybe she needs help. Maybe she's a neighbor from next door. Her old man beat her up or something. Talk to her. The banging will stop.

"What do you want?"

"I want to come in."

"What do you *need*?"

"I need to talk to you."

"Why are you covered in blood?"

"I need to talk to you."

"I can talk to you from here. Do you need help? I can go find my phone." Words are rolling off my tongue as if they were predetermined. I feel like an actress in a script. Like I'm watching this, not part of it. My sprinting pulse tells me different.

Get up, Jeff. Get up! Speak! Say something!

"I need to talk to you. Inside."

"Why?"

"If you don't open the door, I'm coming in. Ghosts can do that, you know."

I spring to my feet, hurdling the leg of the sitting chair and leaping onto the bed next to Jeff. I bury myself in stiff covers and shake him. He won't wake up.

"Did you hear that? Did you hear her?" I scream.

He may as well be dead already. It's like he's already swallowed the death serum. But that can't be. The doctor has the other half of the equation.

The stuff we have here, the prescription alone, won't do it.

"Jeff! Wake up!"

"He won't help you. Men never do. You and I are alone."

I curl my toes, wishing I had socks on. I bury my face in my husband's chest, sorry for burning his eggs and battling him at breakfast. "Jeff! Please! Please! You have to wake up!" I have no idea what he'll do for us. He can't even move. I need him, anyone, to be here, to see what I'm seeing and hear what I'm hearing. I want him to look out the window and tell me if she's real. I want him to tell me if she is the widow I've read so much about. And if so, why does she look so much like me?

He snores. I jump again.

"I'm coming in in three. It's *rude* to keep me waiting. I don't like waiting."

Let yourself in, then. I'm not letting my feet hit the ground. I'm not waiting to find out what's under the bed. Why did I pick this stupid motel? We could have done this anywhere. There are plenty of five stars in Portland. Stupid, stupid me.

"…three."

And there she is, sitting at the tiny table, next to Jeff's dirty breakfast plate, like the door never existed. She merely sits there, staring at us, an uninvited house guest waiting to be served. I clutch Jeff's chest and bury my face in the crook of his neck.

"What do you *want* from me?"

Aurora

"You really need to work on your manners, Lisa. Times sure have changed. In my day, no *proper* lady would let someone stand outside like that. It's *rude*."

She leaves *his dirty breakfast plates? Doesn't wash them? No wonder he hates her.*

I flatten my dress over my knees, crossing my legs at the ankles. I've learned to look past the bloodstains. Yesterday's unread news. Today I need to focus on the present and, more importantly, the future. So much has changed. These folks are planning on sending him out of here in a Chicago overcoat. Seems a little unfair, don't you think? I've been stuck haunting this place for eighty years for doing the same to my husband and, soon after, myself. Of course, you didn't take drugs for these matters back then. A hammer did the trick. I don't see how it's different.

Look at her. So much older than I was when I took Henry's life, watched him take his last breath. Look at her, shaking on the bed. Hiding behind her husband. I was wise, you see. I didn't want to waste my life waiting around for a man, popping out children. I had my own dreams. I wanted to take over this land, bring it back to my family. It was stolen from us, a wonderful colony where people shared and did things for each other. Nothing like the world today.

My dreams, my very life, crashed with the market. Seeing him dead, the man who promised he'd build a life for us but failed, wasn't as satisfying as I expected. It was only a few years later that the motel had no guests, when paint started peeling and no one cared to do anything about it. The trains stopped. Beggars slept in the very doorways Henry slung himself, where grass should have grown but never did. Shameful, all of it.

I never planned to take my own life. It just happened. I lost my pride. I lost my fight. I had no way of knowing the price you pay for taking a life is giving back the same. I've tried five other times and failed. I can't find my Henry. I miss him so. I've spent years trying to get people to understand that you have to do the right thing, even when you don't want to. This time, I have my chance, a two-for-the-price-of-one opportunity no broad who lived through the start of the Great Depression could ever pass up. If I can get them to reconcile, to admit their flaws and faults and walk out of here alive, I'll finally be free to rest. In peace. Maybe I'll even see Henry. If, of course, he's forgiven me.

"Do you expect me to sit here all day with you peeking out from under the covers? I will, you know. I've got nothing better to do. But then, how will you explain it to the doctor? You can't think he'll go through with it, not with me here, covered in blood. We're on a timeframe, dear. Speak." I lower my voice, softly adding, "Please."

"I ...I don't know what you *want* from us," Lisa finally says.

There's no point going slowly with this. We only have a few hours. I jump right in. She's invited me. If you don't want the answer to a question, don't ask it. That's what I always say.

"I want you to rethink things. Do you *really* want him dead? Is he *really* ready to go? To leave you? It seems to me that you have some making up to do. And what about your daughter's wedding?"

The great thing about being a ghost is there's plenty of time for research. I'm not limited to the Google world library. I can also access thoughts. I use this to my advantage whenever I can. I'm not about to spend another eighty years at the Roach Motel.

The man's eyes spring open. Because he's on his side, turned toward me, I don't think she notices, although I can't be sure. I can only access thought when I'm focused, concentrated.

Was he ever asleep at all?

"Welcome!" I say. I want her to know he's awake. He stares at me, remaining silent. His face is frozen, like Henry's when I dragged him out of here that night, after dark. I shiver. Something about him is familiar, but I'm sure I've never seen him before. I'd remember his frail limbs.

Lisa comes out from the covers, sitting up enough to glance at her husband, whose deep brown eyes, so like Henry's, are fixated on the hem of my bloody dress. She nudges him and whispers, "She's a ghost. She's the one they talk about."

"Aurora. My name's Aurora. Like the town. Named after the town. Pretty neat, don't you think? However, that's neither here nor there. And, yes, I am a ghost."

I think I hear Jeff thinking that he's seen me before, but I can't be sure and don't know how that would be possible. I must make my presence known for the living to see me. It's harder than you think. I'm not like an ordinary ghost; I'm a ghost in purgatory. There's a huge difference, but I won't bore you with the details. I wish he would speak. I know he can. I'll let him hold that secret a little longer.

"Well?" I prompt.

"Well, what?"

"Well, are you going to answer me? Are you really ready to let him go? I should warn you, answer carefully. I can hear your thoughts. I know the truth, about both of you. Go on, take your time."

"No, I'm not ready to let my husband go," Lisa says without hesitation. Despite everything I know, I believe her.

"Then why are you here?"

"He is suffering. He hates living this way, stuck in a body he has no control over. You don't know him like I do. You don't know how he used to be, so capable and grounded."

"True. I do not. Go on."

"I don't understand what your point is. We've made up our minds. Our children will be here any minute. You need to go. This is hard enough."

I shake my head, sighing. "That's not possible, dear."

"Then what do you *want*?"

"I want you to make peace with each other. If you decide, after forgiveness, that it's still the right thing to do, then far be it from me to stop you. That was not the story with Henry and me. Henry was my husband."

Lisa nods. "You *are* the Ghost Widow of Coach Motel."

"Dear, titles mean nothing to me. I should warn you, should you proceed, should you determine this is your only way out, letting him die without making peace of the situation, you too will be stuck. You too will be talked about for years to come. Do I look like the sort of broad who'd lie to you?"

Lisa's face goes white. She shakes her head from side to side. I stop myself from laughing, thinking she's paler than me, a ghost.

"That's not possible. What about the others? There have been four, five other men. Wait, you *killed* him? Your husband? *Killed them*?"

"Semantics, dear."

"That's not possible. The other men died long after you did. One was only six months ago. I don't understand."

I pick at my fingernails. I'll never get used to the blood underneath them. I wish I'd thought to polish them before I killed Henry, but one could never predict being stuck in my current state. Had I known, I would never have picked this dress. These stuffy shoes either. I would have gone for open-toed sling backs. I would have showered, not only used it as a place to catch the mess. I was trying to be courteous.

"So what you're saying is that we need to forgive each other before Jeff takes the serum or I will die and kill random men too? Impossible."

"They say coming through metal doors is impossible too, dear."

"But—"

"Look. I've been here eighty years. I'm a patient woman. I've learned to be. I can leave now and you can see for yourself. I've had chances to leave before. None of the other woman have believed me either. Not surprising, really. They were all scarlets, unmarried and shacking up for a night here, a night there. Shame, shame on them. Hussies, every one. So unattached that no one's looking for them either. No value in women then, and nothing's changed with that. You can believe me or not. I cannot force you. What I'd like to know is what your husband's thinking?"

"He can't talk. And I thought you could read minds?"

"He can't?" I stare at her, my eyes as wide as they can stretch. I repeat my question. Twice. And then, "Are you sure about that?"

Lisa's head snaps to look at Jeff, who lets out a garbled groan.

"Oh, be serious! Tell her!" I want to hit him, to make him speak.

He says nothing.

"Tell him to speak! Do you really want to be stuck in a place like Coach—Roach—Motel forever? It's not like it once was, like it should have been. Back when the land was beautiful, not this cement stuff. When William owned it. Look at this place! *Make* him speak! You want to end up like me? I died here too, you know. Yes, it's true. This very room. In the shower, if you must know. Others too. You think I don't know a thing or two about all this dying business? Trust me, there's no dignity in it. None at all."

A wave of anger comes over me, something they say ghosts shouldn't feel. But like I've told you, I'm not an ordinary ghost. I stand, ripping the dresser away from the wall, reaching for my hammer. Lisa hides under the covers, clutching her husband.

"You think he's going to help you?" I shout. "He won't even *speak*!"

"He *can't* talk! He has a disease. It's why we're here!"

"Oh really? Ask your daughter about that. Go on! Get on the horn and call her!" I leap to the night table, pulling the loose receiver from the horn, thrusting it at her, receiver in one hand, hammer in the other. I'm not afraid to use either of them. I have nothing to lose. "Do you need me to dial for you? It's room 12, isn't it? Or shall I pay her a visit? I'm not afraid to use this, you know. I've done it. Couple of times." I hold the hammer up, grinning. I rub my hand along its bloodied handle.

Lisa dives toward me, pulling the receiver from my hand. She sits on the edge of the bed holding the phone. "One second, please. I'm getting her." The man does and says nothing.

Typical.

Lisa

This bitch has lost her fucking mind. She says Jeff can talk, shaking that bloody hammer all over the place. Jeff hasn't been able to speak in nearly three years. I grab the phone from her hand and remind myself to breathe. I still my shaking hands enough to call Ella. I tell her I will call; I need a minute. I remind her she said she was patient. I tell her I believe her. I hold the phone in my hands, telling myself to calm down.

I can't call Ella. Ella will come here. Ella will come here, and this psycho will use her hammer to kill her too.

I hang up the phone, ducking to avoid the hammer I'm sure is about to come down on my head.

"Jeff! Can you speak?"

I shake him. I see a flicker of life in his eyes, which is not unusual. What makes this different is that his eyes are wet, like he's about to cry.

"Jeff! If you can speak, fucking speak! Do you want Ella to *die*?"

The ghost-freak laughs. I ignore her.

It comes out raspy at first, like a growl, the sound of a wounded animal, guttural. He says, as clear as the hammer freak-bitch holds, "Yes."

I don't know what scares me more. The long ago lost sound of his voice or the hammer. Ghost-freak won't stop laughing, like she wouldn't stop banging. I want to rip the hammer from her hand and cave both their skulls in with it.

"There! See? The power of a father's love. Miracles happen every day. You're cured." She looks at my husband, putting the hammer to her side. Her face softens and she lowers her voice. "You can speak. That's more like it. I'll leave you two to talk. Don't make me come back! Make peace, so we can all have it. Don't worry,

Abyssina." With those words, she is gone.

Who the hell is Abyssina? Freak.

"You can *talk*? *All these years*, mumble, mumble, grunt, and you can *speak*?" I'm seething. I can't even look at my husband, this man who has made me take care of his every need all this time. Hundreds of one-sided conversations flash through my head, like an old movie minus the subtitles. Silent on one end. I feel so stupid. I wish she'd left her hammer. I'd kill him myself. Why wait for the doctor? That's too merciful.

He's shaking more than usual. His wet eyes overflow as he sobs.

"Ella knew?"

He nods.

"But why, Jeff, *why*?"

Who cares why? Freak could be back any second. I need to call the police. I've got to know what time it is. It has to be close to noon by now. What if the kids show up? What was it that ghost-freak said?

"Who the hell is she talking about, Abyssina? Does she think that's my name? Maybe she has the wrong people. The wrong room. Maybe this is all a misunderstanding."

I have no time for his atrophied answer. I rush to the bathroom, searching the tiny space for any sign of my cell phone. Nothing. The bathroom's cramped, more so, it feels, than usual. I can barely fit myself in without turning sideways. I can't believe I've dragged Jeff in and out of here all these months. I'm afraid to look behind the yellowed shower curtain. It's not like my phone will be there.

342

Some morbid part of me wants to look anyway, wondering if one of the bodies was cut up there, or if she's hiding there, reminiscing about her own suicide.

Stop. There's no time for that. You have to find your phone. Focus.

I don't know why it doesn't occur to me to use the land line. I scan the back of the toilet, catching my reflection in the mirror. I grimace, thinking of how similar I look to her. Time stands still. The mirror's cracked, and I wonder how many people have used the rusty sink to dye their hair or make sure there's no coke left on their nose. That's what a place like this is for—hiding out, hook ups, and disappearing. The stories this room could tell. The people who've stared in this very mirror.

Have they met her too? What's become of them?

"I can't find my fucking phone!"

I run out of the bathroom, looking to Jeff for answers. Old habits die hard, I guess. He's sitting up, all on his own. Normally, I have to prop him with pillows. I don't bother to ask about it. I don't think I want to know the answer. Hell, he probably goes running at night and has full conversations with the moon. I grab the land phone receiver and dial Ella's room. I breathe in through my nose, out through my mouth, before I speak.

"Hi, hon. Listen, your father and I need a little more time alone. What time is it?"

"Only eleven. I thought you wanted us there at noon? Are you okay? You're, like, panting."

"Let's say two."

"Two? But the doctor's coming at three." My

daughter's never been one to accept an answer without questioning it.

Breathe. In. Out. Keep your voice steady.

"I know, hon, but remember, we don't have to do it right away. Your father will have as long as we needs. No rush today, okay? Why don't you and the others go out for a while, maybe drive up to Portland and check things out? Even if you're not here until three, that's okay. We'll make sure everyone has plenty of time."

I want to ask her why she didn't tell me that Jeff could speak. I want to yell at her for it. More important, though, is getting her off the phone.

"We're not driving all the way to Portland! That's, like, an hour or something! By the time we got back it would be five, if we wanted to see anything at all. We'll go out to lunch and be there no later than two," Ella says. "Dad wants us there too."

"I know. Okay. Sounds good. See you then."

"Mom? Are you okay?"

"Yes. I'm fine."

"Are you sure? And why are you calling me on this phone? You know my cell. You scared the shit out of me. This place is so creepy."

"Yes, Ella, I'm sure we're fine. We just got a slow start this morning. I need to get your father dressed and make his breakfast. Running a little behind, that's all. Don't worry."

"You didn't answer my question about the phone. It's weird."

"I can't find my cell phone. I've had other things on my mind."

"Okay. I'll help you find it later. See ya."

"Ella? Love you."

"Love you too."

I exhale my relief. I have three hours to figure out what to do. I sit on the edge of the bed, as far away from Jeff as possible.

"Do you know where my phone is?"

He extends his arm, fingers balled up, motioning in the direction of the nightstand. All I can see are a box of tissues, cough drops, my reading glasses, and that stupid rotary phone, circa 1980. I wonder what year they put the phones in and if Ghost-freak was around to see it. I stand and move the table. Sure enough, my cell phone is behind it. I have no idea why I forget to call the cops. Stress, I guess.

Jeff

Abyssina.

If I wasn't in this situation, I'd chuckle. "I'll be seeing ya," is what she meant to say. There's no point in explaining this to Lisa. I'm sure she's forgotten her question by now. I have more important things to focus on. Like this ghost, for starters. And my plan falling to shit. I have five hours to die, abyssina. Or *had.* This is exactly what I worried about. And Ella. Fucking Ella. Since her very conception, exactly three years and two months *after* Lisa got her tubes tied, that kid's thrown us for a loop. I wouldn't be surprised if she hired this ghost, an actress or something, to screw things up. I knew she wouldn't let me die.

No wonder she's been so accommodating about all of this. But the dream. Where did that dream come from?

In that dream, I was Henry, the ghost's husband. In that dream, she killed me. How could I have known, dreamt, that?

Is she screwing with my mind? Is that possible?

"Found it! Thanks." Lisa produces her cell phone, shoving it in my face like I'm supposed to do something with it. Okay, so I exaggerate symptoms a little, but I really *do* have Parkinson's Disease. It's been five years since I've used one of those things and certainly not the smart kind. What does she think I want with a cell phone?

"We might need it. If she comes back," Lisa whispers. She leans down, only inches from me, and pushes her finger—hard—into my chest. "You start talking. What is this 'yes' shit? You haven't been able to say yes or no for years. Now suddenly you can speak? What the hell, Jeff? What else have you been keeping from me and why?"

She takes her finger back. I wish I could break it. Not that I'd have any idea how to go about doing such a thing. Not stuck in the House of Horrors. She stares at me, waiting. There's nothing more dangerous than keeping an angry woman waiting, at least not in my experience. I tilt my twitching head to the side, trying to use the pillows and its weight to shift my body away from her. It's useless.

I have to find my voice. Sure, I've managed to communicate with Ella from time to time. It's our little secret. It's got to be the real reason why she never argued with me about the plan. She knew, more than anyone, that I was still serious and still fully competent to decide. I've been alone with Lisa for months now. My vocal cords are wrapped around themselves, twisted and useless like the House of Horrors. I have to find a way. I'm not getting marriage counselling from a black widow, hell, a ghost.

Just what I need, not one, but two psychotic women determining my fate. Fabulous.

Bang! Bang! Bang!

Lisa throws her body against me. The anger in her face only seconds ago has turned to panic. Aurora enters the room, through the door, without opening it. I can rule out the idea of her being a hired actress. I guess the knocks were courtesy taps. Someone must have told her that it's rude to enter a room without knocking first. I suppose they left out the part about it being impolite to carry a bloody hammer like a handbag. I haven't the time to figure out why she's back so soon before she's seated, again, at the tiny table by the window, pushing my breakfast spoon aside. I wish Lisa hadn't drawn the curtains for our nap.

"Well? What have we decided? Is all forgiven? Is everything well? Can we finally be free? Or will we be hanging out together for, oh, infinity?"

"You just left," my wife barks, sounding much less afraid than her clammy skin tells me she is. "We haven't had a minute to speak."

"You've had nine minutes, to be exact. That should be enough. What is there to discuss? This isn't a tough one. Do we want to die, or do we want to forgive each other and go on with our lives?"

"It's complicated."

"Sure, sure. So was learning the Carolina Shag, but my Henry managed to pull that off. You should have seen us, whirling around. One night, even in this very room. It wasn't always bad, you know."

What the hell is going on?

I closed my eyes for one second, a habit of mine when I'm thinking hard. I close them again and I can see it, like it was yesterday.

I dance with Aurora. She forces me to move the bed into the corner of this very room. The room is different, lighter, brighter. It smells of paint and potential.

"Dance with me, Henry," she says.

"My husband has a disease! Okay, so he can say little words. That doesn't mean it's okay for him to suffer."

A slow smile spreads across Aurora's lips. "Do I look like the type of woman to make a man suffer?"

"Eat the sandwich, Henry. I made it for you. You work hard. I don't want you out there on an empty stomach, suffering. Do I look like the type of woman to make a man suffer?"

"R…rory?" Fear spits out the word for me. I nudge Lisa off of my chest. "Rory?"

Aurora's mouth hangs open. "Henry? Is that you? *My* Henry? But how…?"

Lisa looks between us, back and forth, back and

forth, trying to make sense of our words.

I shake my head. How? I do not know.

Aurora lunges toward me, hammer above her head. "Henry, you kept me waiting!"

Bang! Bang! Bang!

Epilogue

Henry

They say the third time's the charm. The funny thing about being almost dead is that you get closer to the other side. In all my plans to die, I never considered that I was nearly there, all on my own. Now, after another killing by my first wife—Aurora, the Ghost Widow of Coach Motel—I understand. I was never Jeff. I was Henry, round two, trying to live a life as close as the one that'd been stolen from me as I could. All that time, waiting, to be with Rory again. My body and circumstances may have left; however, my spirit did not. For better or worse, they say. Rory was right; Aurora is my home. I'll never return to New York. When people come, it'll be the two of us, haunting the Coach Motel. I plan to fix it up. And we shall

350

dance, oh, how we will dance! Never again will she make me a sandwich without mustard. Never again will I keep her waiting.

About the Author

Erin Lee is a freelance writer and therapist living with her family in southern New Hampshire. She is the author of *Crazy Like Me*, a novel published in 2015 by Savant Books and Publications, *Wave to Papa*, 2015, *Nine Lives,* and *Alters*, 2016 with Limitless Publishing LLC. She holds a master's degree in psychology and works with at-risk families and as a court appointed special children's advocate. When she's not busy writing about the human mind, she's obsessively taking pictures of her rescue dog and muse, Milo. Her work can be found at www.authorerinlee.com.

Facebook:
https://www.facebook.com/gonecrazytalksoon

Website:
http://www.authorerinlee.com/

The Virus: Prequel to the AM13 Outbreak Series

By Samie Sands

Dylan
February 1st

7.32am.

I blink. Are my eyes deceiving me? Is this some kind of dream? Or *nightmare*?

What the actual hell? I *never* wake up at 7.32.

I always, always without fail, open my eyes at 7.29am. I don't even have an alarm clock; it just happens. I wake at 7.29 and get out of bed at 7.30.

Every. Single. Day.

Except today.

Why? What's so different about today? The panic starts as a tight knot in my stomach, slowly expanding until my whole body is consumed in terror. I'm literally shaking. I try to figure out where exactly I went wrong and what impact it'll have on the rest of the day.

While this might seem like an adverse reaction to waking up a few minutes late, for me, every single second of my life is planned out meticulously. It *has* to be. I won't bore you with all the exact details of my routine (7.44am drink coffee, 7.58am brush teeth…). However, if anything—and I mean *anything*—doesn't go exactly to my plan, bad things happen.

Wow, I sound insane, even to myself.

My mum always said I was an odd little boy, organising everything obsessively, making sure everything was clean and 'in its place'. For that reason, I never had many friends. You can imagine that, can't you? People don't like to be controlled, and I can't bear to just 'go with the flow', to do what others want. In fact, the thought of letting things 'run their course' fills me with an unnatural, sweaty, paralysing fear.

Yes, before you ask, I have been through numerous therapy sessions and seen many, *many* doctors to help me with this. However, what they don't understand, what no one seems to get, is that this isn't something plaguing my mind. This is real.

When things don't go to plan, bad stuff really does happen.

I started to take things a bit more seriously when I reached the age of eight. Before then, I merely liked things to be *just so*. At first, I started to notice that I absolutely *had* to do things equally with both sides of my body. For instance, if I touched a stone with one hand, I *had* to touch it with the other. If I didn't, my chest would get tight and I'd struggle to breathe.

Then the pain would start.

Whatever side of my body had not been 'included' would ache like mad. A constant reminder that everything was unequal, unbalanced.

Mum first cracked and got me examined by a medical professional when I turned eleven. The doctor convinced me everything was in my head, that I simply needed to change my thought patterns and it would all be okay. I took his advice to heart, sure that if I tried my best, I could start being 'normal' like all the other kids in my class. They didn't seem to be plagued with any of the issues I had, and I longed to be carefree and fun like them.

The next morning, I woke up at 7.29am. Instead of getting out of bed like normal, I squeezed my eyes shut, willing them to go back to sleep, just to test the doctor's theory. My breaths got shallow and ragged, my heart pounding so hard I was certain it was going to burst out of my chest, my legs twitching, itching to get up. I resisted, determined to win. I lay there for the longest two minutes of my life. Then, eventually, I opened one eye, fearful of what would greet me. To my surprise, everything appeared normal.

Calming down, I went downstairs, proud of my

huge achievement, expecting praise from my mother. It turns out she hadn't noticed the time difference to my normal arrival at the breakfast table. I guess two minutes isn't a long time for other people. After that, the day continued as normal; I started to relax, *really* relax. I was over the moon with myself and happy that I could *finally* be like everyone else.

Until I got home from school that evening.

I walked in to my mother crying, a grim atmosphere encasing the room. My stomach fell to the floor. Although I had no idea what was wrong, I *knew* it was my fault. I cursed myself for not trusting my instincts, for forcing myself to listen to someone who knew absolutely nothing about me. As I wrapped my arms around my mum, I discovered the grim truth. My father had been killed in a car accident, hit by a drunk truck driver.

My whole world fell apart at that moment.

The number 29 came to haunt my whole life after that. Mum has never recovered; she's still a shell of her former self. And me? Ten years later, here I am, being tormented by the same thing, waking up late. This is the first time I've made the mistake since that fateful day. Don't get me wrong; I've caused all sorts of other illnesses, accidents, and problems with my slipups, though nothing like the first time. They've all been the result of me forgetting to lock the door three times or being unable to kick the football equally with my left and right foot in gym class. I've never, ever allowed anything so tragic happen since.

Until now.

This is bad. This is really, *really* bad.

I'm wringing my hands in terror. I don't know what this means for me, my family, everyone I know…

What do I do first? I can't exactly try and rectify the problem; it's far too late for that. In fact, it's already 7.42am. Oh God, it's all gone to hell now. Should I ring my family? Run outside and warn everyone to be careful?

My eyes set on the television remote. I don't know why, but for some reason I know it holds the key. It has the answer to whatever I've done. I stretch my stiff hand to pick it up, knowing that I need to discover the truth. I deserve this punishment; I need to know who I've hurt this time. With one last tremble, I hit the 'on' button, and the news flashes up before my eyes…

Laura
February 3ʳᵈ

"Dolly, will you sit down and eat your dinner? Mummy can't do that right now. She's on the phone."

I turn my back to face the wall, tugging at my hair, which is matted with sweat and baby food. I think back to a time when my hair was always styled to perfection, and I'd never dream of going outside without my full face of makeup on.

"Honestly, why does anyone have kids?" I laugh

mirthlessly. "They're *such* hard work."

"Yeah, and it unfortunately doesn't get any easier," my best friend Pippa replies knowingly. She has two teenagers, which give her no end of grief, whereas my four are all under the age of ten. The future does *not* look good for me.

We continue our conversation about the letters all the parents have been given by the schools about a new bug going around. It's not unusual for this to happen. Teachers always have to be overcautious, to stop illnesses spreading as rapidly as head lice does among children. This one, however, seems…I don't know how to describe it, more severe?

"It's basically telling us that if our kids show *any* sign of illness, anything at *all*, we have to keep them off school. Do they not understand? What are we supposed to do with them? I have a job, you know."

I nod along, agreeing with Pippa's whining, though also trying to read between the lines of the letter. I'm a little more concerned than Pippa because I watched the local news yesterday. I always try to do that, so my life isn't completely and utterly consumed by my children. It's the closest thing I get to adult conversation most days. I heard about this bug thing then. Honestly, it sounds dire. The report freaked me out; even the news reporter sounded worried. I always notice these things, because before I was a mother, I was a psychology lecturer, so I decided to do some more research into it.

I searched the Internet for hours and couldn't find a single thing out about it, which I find strange.

You can find out about *everything* online but not a peep about this. It's on the news but not online. Something is off, although I don't know what.

"All the other mums are kicking off about it too. We *need* school to give us a break. We have the children all the time, and school hours are our time. Now we're supposed to sacrifice that over every sniff and tummy pain?" Pippa's words skim my ears, though I don't take them in. My mind is too consumed with trying to figure out the link...the thing that's all wrong about this. It's probably something simple, something obvious. I just can't place it.

A tugging on my t-shirt pulls me out of my trance.

"Mummy, I feel..." I shake my head at Dolly and mime at her to sit down.

That child will do anything to get out of eating her dinner sensibly. My one year old is easier to manage than her.

"I guess, maybe..." I try and organise my words carefully so as not to anger my already riled-up friend. "Maybe we should do as they say. Maybe it would be better to avoid—"

"Oh nonsense!" Pippa interrupts. "The teachers are just worried about getting ill themselves. Our kids go to school poorly all the time. Moping around at home won't do them any good. It only teaches them to be lazy."

I let her continue with her rant, knowing I'm not going to change her mind. Once she's set on a campaign, nothing will shift Pippa's opinion.

I scan the room, looking at the faces of all my

children in concern. I have to look out for any signs of being ill; I need to be extremely vigilant now, more so than before. Glancing at all four of them in turn, I don't spot anything unusual, no snotty noses or pale faces.

Hopefully, they'll be fine. I'll be careful and hope all the parents with children in their class will do the same. According to this letter, if even one of them gets it, they *all* will.

I sigh deeply and try and find a gap to end this conversation. If I don't eat something soon, I'll faint with hunger. I can't remember the last time I got to eat my food when it was first cooked. Cold fish fingers have become my staple diet.

"Okay, mhmm, yeah, well I have to—"

A loud bang interrupts me, and I whirl around, wondering what on Earth the kids have done to each other *this* time. I find Dolly collapsed in a heap on the floor. I'm about to shout at the others, to ask her who pushed her off her chair, when I notice she's convulsing…and foaming at the mouth.

Evan
February 6th

"Testing, testing, one, two…" I grin. I don't need to test my microphone, I'm only a television news anchor, but the sound girl is super cute and I've been trying to get her attention for a while now.

When she smiles back shyly, I wish I was better at flirting, then I might've worked up the courage to ask her out by now. In front of the cameras, I'm cool and confident since I *have* to be to get the job done. Real life is a different story. I've always been shy without a teleprompter to give me the words to say.

For the last couple of days, news of this 'super bug' has been one of our smaller pieces. Tonight it's about to be our headline news. According to our researchers, it's becoming a much bigger threat, and there's even the fear that it's killed someone.

I push my hair behind my ears, the way I always do when I'm concentrating. I need to get tonight *right*. I need to be detached, yet sensitive at the same time. It's so difficult to not let emotion get in the way sometimes, especially with some of the more awful stories, and that's something I need to master if I want to reach the big leagues.

My mind instantly flicks back to a gruesome homicide from a few months ago. The details were horrific, and I couldn't get it out of my mind for ages afterwards. It even gave me sleepless nights, not that I'd admit that to anyone here. The only way to make it in the media is to be thick skinned and unemotional.

I often wonder if I'm truly cut out for this cutthroat industry. Although you'd never think it of me, being important is all I've ever wanted. Being known, helping others, and this seemed like the best way to achieve that goal.

Time is counting down, and I begin to feel slightly nervous right before being on air. Live shows can be unpredictable, and that terrifies me.

10, 9, 8...

My brain shifts into gear.

...7, 6, 5...

Deep breath.

...4, 3, 2...

And we're on!

I repeat the words as they flick up on the screen in front of me.

"Good evening. It's time for the 10 o'clock news. My name is Evan Parsons."

Cue music.

"Tonight's top stories: local celebrity contests super injunction, house prices sink to their lowest rate yet, and the newest viral bug is poised to affect 75% of the population."

Is that true? I think to myself as I mechanically read what's written in front of me. That's frightening! As I read the other stories, my mind is elsewhere, firmly fixed on finally finding out more details about this virus. I want to learn more about what's going to happen, what we need to do to protect ourselves. I hope this isn't merely another media scare, because even *I'm* worried about this one.

I find myself trying to rush, to hurry the rest of the news along. Is everyone else the same? Sat on the edge of their sofas, screaming at the screen for me to shut up about the depressing recession? I know I would be. We all know everything sucks with money at the moment; no one needs to be told that the housing market is still crashing.

And finally I'm there. I'm concentrating on the words so hard that they almost don't come out right. I hope I manage to relay the details in a suitable manner, because when a crisis like this comes along, giving people information is the best way to stop anything spiraling out of control.

Sitting at home later that evening, my mind is still reeling. I'm trying to organise my thoughts, work through the fog of tiredness to figure out what the hell is actually going on.

The news never reveals the whole truth; we all know that. It only reports enough so people feel informed. I hate that. I wish I could tell everyone everything, especially with something as important as this. But I can't. I say whatever's put in front of me.

Like a puppet, I guess.

From what I can work out, some strange illness has come from God knows where, affecting everyone differently, all in a *very* bad way, and we need to do all we can to avoid contracting it.

How vague is that? Don't get ill. That's all they could give me to convey?

I need to find out more. What if I have it now? Am I *really* tired, or do I have this bug? Maybe I should get myself checked out, just in case. You never know; it could save my life.

I look down, realizing the phone is already in my hand, the doctor's number dialed, as if my body already knows what I need to do.

Jasmine
February 7th

I've been planning this day my entire damn life. Well, for the last eight months anyway, and now this?

I finally found the right dress, the perfect dress. It took months of tears and tantrums to get there. Yes, I may have gone a little Bridezilla along the way; who doesn't? Planning a wedding is *so* stressful.

This dress, it's unbelievable. It makes me look like a princess; soft silk spinning out at the waist, covered in tiny crystals which sparkle when I move, it makes me smile merely thinking of it.

When I saw it in that tiny boutique, I couldn't wait for the moment I'd get to wear it, walking down the aisle of the church my parents married in, surrounded by white carnations, my absolute favourite, with all eyes on me.

I kept imagining myself elegantly gliding toward my super handsome—and super rich—fiancé. I pictured my bridesmaids, dressed in conservative teal-colored dresses, behind me looking gorgeous enough to keep the aesthetic good without drawing any attention from me.

Yes, I am the sort of girl who picked her wedding party based on looks rather than friendships. Don't judge me; I barely have any female friends.

My eyes snap open, the fantasy day blowing up in a puff of smoke. This day is nothing like that. Everything is going wrong. *Everything.* I swear if anything else happens I'm going to lie on the floor and pound my hands and feet on it, screaming like a toddler. Why do bad things only happen to good people?

First my hairdresser phoned to say she couldn't make it because she's ill. I screamed at her, but she didn't change her mind. Luckily my makeup artist stepped up and did a semi-decent job.

Then, just as I averted that disaster, the photographer called to say he'd heard something worrying on the news, something about a virus, and he wouldn't come out and mix with people who could have it; after all, he *'has a family to think of'*. Honestly, how selfish can you be?

Luckily, my maid of honour, Sephy—I know, what a ridiculous name! I only got her involved because she's my fiancé's stepsister and she's quite pretty—is a journalist and has great connections and set me up with a photographer.

Then to top things off, I'm in the middle of my spa treatments, a facial, a mani-pedi, a hot stone massage, all the standard things before you get married. I was starting to calm down, and the florist rings me saying a huge roadblock has been set up and they can't get through.

It's a complete and utter disaster. This blockage has also stopped a lot of our guests from arriving, and I don't know what to do.

I wish I'd stuck with the wedding planner we originally hired, but after I called her a bitch and threw a shoe at her, she left and refused to work for me again. She also told others in the business that I'm 'impossible and high maintenance', which meant no one else wanted the job either, leaving everything to me.

I thought I could do it. Now I'm really beginning to panic. This is *my* day, and it's supposed to be perfect. All the people I know are supposed to be witnessing me making my life's biggest achievement, marrying a millionaire.

Well, he might not quite be a millionaire, but he is very rich. I just like the sound of the word 'millionaire'.

I switch on the news, trying to work out what's wrong, trying to figure out a solution. I need this day to go as I wanted it to, and the only way I can do that is by finding out the details.

Urgh, the news is so morbid. Why does anyone ever watch it? It's gone so overboard about this stupid virus, no wonder everyone's freaking out. Although I may have solved every other problem that's cropped up today, this one feels a little out of reach.

Maybe I should cancel the wedding, try it again when all these problems go away. But it was *so* expensive, and I might not be able to get it the same again. This is exactly the wedding I wanted, and I'm not sure I'll be able to settle for less. Plus we fly to Bora Bora tomorrow on our honeymoon, and I have wanted to go there forever.

Can the wedding go ahead anyway? My mother-in-law won't even be there. Wait a minute. This is great! My mother-in-law hates me. She called me a gold-digging tramp and said she wanted to stop the wedding from happening. Now she's stuck somewhere behind a roadblock, unable to do anything.

Ha! In your face, Beatrice. I *will* get married today just to spite you, even if the wedding sucks.

A smile crosses my lips at the realization this might be the best thing that could have happened. Thank you, virus; you've just made my life amazing.

Augustus
February 9th

Haven't I been telling 'em for years and years that this was goin' to happen? They always laugh at me, call me names when I stand out with my sign preaching from the Bible. They're the ones who're gonna get punished first now, aren't they? I was only trying to help 'em all. I didn't know how else to do it.

I've been a bad lad. I ain't perfect by a long shot. In fact, I was in the clink for aggravated burglary when I found Him. I was bored, to be honest; stuck inside those cramped cells twenty-four hours a day ain't fun by anybody's standards. Especially knowing I still had five and half years to go. I took up reading, found a Bible, and it all started to make sense to me. I realised everything bad that's happened to me was my own doing. If I do good, He will make sure good stuff happens to me.

That's been my life ever since.

When I got outta prison a year early, thanks to my newfound good behavior, it was still tough. I couldn't get a job or a decent place to live due to my past. So I spent my time people watching, seeing what others were doing. Even though times were rough, I refused to turn to alcohol or drugs this time to get through my problems. I started to see how rotten this world is, how awful the people in it are. All everyone cares about is material crap, things that don't matter. No one is nice to each other anymore, not without something to gain. It ain't right.

I decided to start my one-man campaign to make the world a better place, and boy did I try. I went out every day, reminding people of His teachings, telling them they could bring a better life upon themselves simply by being a better person. I know, I might seem annoying to others, but all I wanted was to give people the enlightenment I'd had, to help 'em.

No one listened. I'm not surprised. In this day and age, belief has taken a back seat to technology and fast-paced living. You won't believe how few people attend church every Sunday nowadays, which is an absolute travesty.

And now this!

They've caused this with their sin. This virus will wipe out all the bad people, just you wait and see. He has unleashed this upon us, to punish our sinful lives.

Why are you surprised? He's done it before, and people are a lot worse now. You wouldn't believe some of the scum I met in prison.

It's not only the *real* disgusting people that will meet their death with this. Oh no, the Ten

Commandments are very basic and have been broken by everyone at some point or another. Everyone has something to hide these days.

Reading between the lines of the news reports, it's started here, in this very town. Of course it has. There isn't a single good person left in this hellhole. Sure, the reporters are trying to pretend it's everywhere, that the roadblocks are being set up to keep the bug out, but I know the truth. It's to keep it *in*. He has picked this very place to unleash His wrath. We are being made an example to the rest of the world. Even if I die, I hope His message is heard, that the rest of the world learns a hard lesson.

While it's too late for these people to atone for their sins, if I let them know they need to show some remorse, He might forgive them, may let them into Heaven. I don't know why I'm still helping these ungrateful people who have mocked and ignored me, except that I feel it's my purpose. It's what He wants me to do. I still have some making up to do, and this is my last chance. I'm putting my life in danger in the hope of saving others.

1 John 2:2 - And he is the propitiation for our sins: and not for ours only, but also for the sins of the whole world.

Tia-May
February 10th

Seriously, how is it possible for people to be so

lame?

My parents suck. They know full well that if I don't go to Quinn's party tonight, I'll be a social outcast forever. They're trying to ruin my life, and I have no idea why. Argh! Just because they're old now and have nothing worth living for, they have to make me miserable too?

All because some stupid, idiotic news report said that we should only go outside when necessary because of this bug thingy going around.

God, no one else's parents are taking it this seriously! Everyone else is still going. It's the social event of *forever*, and I can't miss it. The social suicide argument got a laugh out of Dad, though. He instantly started on the whole 'your school days mean nothing in the long run of your life' lecture.

Whatever. I want to go to this party; I might have to sneak out…

I've received the best text message, like, ever. If I don't go to this party now, my life will not be worth living.

From: *Tyler*
Time: *8.35pm*
Message: *Hey Tia-May,*

Can't wait to see your sexy self at Quinn's. I fully intend to start an epic game of Spin The Bottle, and if you aren't there, it'll be a total let down ;) x

I've wanted to hook up with Tyler *forever*! He's so hot, and he's hardly been with any of the girls in our year, so he's this major challenge too. The respect I would get if I could land a snog from the elusive Tyler would be amazing. Totally worth being grounded for the rest of my life. I *have* to go now; it's become a matter of life and death.

Luckily my bedroom window is next to a tree, which has come in handy many times in my life. I've needed to sneak out on a variety of occasions. If only my parents were cool, there would be no need for this. It must be because I'm an only child. They're so obsessed with what I do all the time. Quinn's parents have the decency to go on holiday, like, all the time, leaving her to do as she pleases. That's how she has managed to wrangle herself the 'most popular girl' in school title.

Plus, it's also how she's managed to hook up with so many boys. Even though she's kind of a slut, that only adds to her popularity. Everything she does adds to her allure.

As I walk down the road, wearing an oversized jumper to hide my short dress, I'm delighted with myself for pulling this off again. I played the whole 'pillow body' under my duvet trick, after making a big point of 'going to bed', which I pray will work. Butterflies are going crazy in my stomach, and I am buzzing with anticipation of tonight. So much could happen. You never know with these house parties how they're going to turn out. Even the bad ones usually have some funny stories to discuss the next week at school.

I can already hear the loud music playing, which is a sign that I'm close. There's so much noise and screaming, I'm surprised no one's complained yet.

Mind you, overly excited teenagers always seem to end up making a racket, and none of Quinn's parties have ever been broken up before.

When I turn the corner, I can tell this time something is different.

Police cars are scattered in her back garden, an ambulance is in her driveway, and people are being dragged out of the house covered in blood and dirt.

What the hell…?

My heart jumps up to my throat when I see my best friend Harper screaming and crying, being bundled into the ambulance. Her hair is matted against her face, her makeup streaming, her outfit torn to shreds. Her leg looks broken, at a weird angle. As I examine it closer, it makes me gag. Bone is sticking out, and her flesh is hanging off. The screams I mistook for fun are actually of terror.

Something terrible has gone on here…

Quinn is collapsed, sobbing on the lawn watching everyone being taken away. I want to go to her, to comfort her, but my legs won't move. I'm frozen to the spot. When I open my mouth to call out to her, nothing save a whisper passes my lips. My heart is pounding in my mouth, and the butterflies that were swimming in my stomach have taken over my entire body.

I don't understand. Any of it.

Then my eyes find *him*, as if they're drawn to his presence. Tyler. He's in handcuffs, being held firmly by four police officers. He's making weird noises, sort of growling. His expression is weird, like nothing I've ever seen on a person's face before.

It's then the fear takes on another level, and my legs start sprinting faster than I ever could've imagined they were capable of. I need to get home. My parents were right!

I push past people on the street, my face cold and wet with tears. I don't look at anyone, even the people who try to communicate with me. How can they be calm when something so weird is happening? I can't be around anyone. I need to be safe, indoors. I need my family.

I fall onto my bed, panting hard, trying to get my head around what I've just witnessed. Could it be the virus? I thought it only made you really ill if you got it. I know Mum said it was contagious, but seriously?

That was like something from a horror film or another world.

Nurse Leigh
February 12th

"I know, sir, and I'm sorry to hear that…mmhmm…yes I get that, and under normal circumstances we would admit your wife. Unfortunately…uh huh…well, we *are* overrun at the moment, as I've already explained to you, so you need to wait until she…"

I turn away from Donna, smiling to myself. Do people not realise the chaos we come under every single time a medical news story pops up? We get swamped and can barely work, all because hypochondriacs are unable to cope with a little media scare.

And this morning, they told everyone to go to a hospital if they're feeling unwell! That's like offering a red rag to a bull.

The waiting room is predictably filled with people chattering, panicking, and riling each other up. I hear the phrase, *"Well, I heard that…"* more times than I care to remember.

Sure, this virus is suspicious, I admit that, especially since I keep hearing about mysterious roadblocks being set up. However, that doesn't help us here at the hospital.

I glance around the room, trying to figure out the most important cases—the people who *actually* look like they could be ill. This time, they're difficult to pick out. Normally, it's obvious, though right now it looks like no one is healthy.

I take a deep sigh, trying not to let the situation overwhelm me. Panic in this job can get people killed. I can see the surveys we have especially for these situations have already been handed out and filled in, so by collecting them in I can stall, give myself a bit more time to get my head together.

We quickly realised that our usual methods were not going to work today. This was something different, something serious. For once, the media got it right. The beds filled up quickly with people unable to move, in desperate need of medical attention, and now we have nowhere left for people, yet many patients needing us.

To say it's chaos would be an understatement.

I want to stand on a chair, scream at everyone to shut up, to give us time to do our job, that their constant demands are only slowing us down. If this were a film, I'm sure that's what I'd do. However, this is real life, and there are no simple solutions.

I'm exhausted. I have no idea how long I've been working—longer than my shift, I'm sure. When a crisis like this comes about, the medical staff doesn't matter. We have to plough on regardless, not making any mistakes.

Mistakes cost lives.

However much I want to stop, to cry and try and figure out what this bug is, I can't. We don't even have a name for it yet. It must be the same thing, for everyone to be affected like this, all on the same day, although everyone is reacting differently to it. My manager spoke to a few other hospitals earlier today outside of the town, and none of them seem to be going through what we are; they hadn't even heard of this bug. I think that's weird, but I don't know if I'm too tired to see the obvious answer.

Now the phone lines are down.

Everyone's in extreme panic mode; it must be because of too much activity. How are we going to get help or solutions now? Argh, this is insane! There must be something I can do.

A wave of nausea hits me. I feel woozy, and my vision goes blurry. I can't stand up straight, and my voice doesn't work. I'm falling. I'm acutely aware that I'm falling, but I can't do anything to stop it. No one else notices; there's too much going on around me. Am I fainting? Is this what passing out feels like? It's all in slow motion; everything dissolves around me. It must be the exhaustion, and I can't even remember the last time I ate…

I'm not ill. It can't be that. I'm a nurse, for crying out loud! We don't get ill. Even when a bug is as contagious as they say this one is.

Anxiety shoots up my spine as I realise that I'm bound to have this…*thing*. In our haste, we've done nothing to protect ourselves from it. None of the medical staff has. And if it truly can spread as quickly as they said, we've made everything a thousand times worse.

This sheer terror is the last thought that goes through my mind before my body slams against the floor, taking all my memories with it.

Bill Richard
February 13th

"No, no, no, *no*…" I know something isn't right, so why won't they listen to me?

I'm perfectly aware that everyone thinks I'm a bit odd. I've overheard the whispers: "You must be a bit strange to manage a funeral home…" I don't know why they can't see that *someone* has to do it, and if I can get through each day without going insane, surely that makes me one of the good guys? I have the right amount of empathy and professionalism that everybody can get on with during these difficult times.

The police brought in a load of bodies from the hospital yesterday, and I mean a *real* load, too many for me to deal with alone. I'll be very surprised if there's anyone left in the damn town! This illness has spiraled way out of control; I have never had so much business.

Still, something isn't right, and however long I spend at the station, the officers aren't going to listen to me. I'm trying to tell them that all these people are not dead, but will they have it? Of course not. I deal with death every single day, and they're trying to tell me *I'm* wrong.

No, they want the problem passed onto me so they no longer have to deal with it. They have no idea what to do about all of this; they've never experienced anything like it before. None of us have. Plus there's been a massive increase in crime, people taking advantage of a bad situation, so they simply don't have the time. That isn't *my* problem; I can't do a lot about a bunch of sick people. That's the hospitals' forte.

Except I guess there *is* no hospital anymore. It all went to hell yesterday, got overrun with the virus. Everyone there was affected. Damn doctors, can't even get themselves organized.

So now what? Do they want me to wait for everyone to die so I can get on with my job? What a grim thought. Not like I have much choice though; no one is prepared to help me.

I wander slowly back up to the funeral home, noticing that the streets are pretty desolate. I haven't seen a single person outside today. They can't all be in my building, can they? I was only joking about that part!

I pull the keys out of my pocket, deep in thought. I've never seen anything quite like this bug before, and it's difficult to wrap my head around. The door creaks open, the familiar sound soothing my ears. After the stress and arguing this morning, it's nice to be back in this place I've made a sanctuary. I shrug off my coat, already mentally putting the kettle on for a cup of coffee. I think I'll have three sugars in this one. Sugar is my one vice, and the amount I have in each drink depends on how badly my day is going.

Before I make it to the kitchen, a noise makes me jump. I'm so used to the silence that it echoes in my brain for a while after. I'm perfectly still, breathing heavily, trying to figure out if it was a real noise or simply my imagination.

Again.

It's a door opening. Obviously I was right!

Someone has finally got enough energy to get up and move around. I'm pleased to be proven correct and also glad that someone is alive, despite what people think. *"Look at him, just waiting for the next person to die…"*

I rush up the stairs, eager to help out in any way I can. A shadow looms above me. "Hey, are you okay?" My voice sounds extremely loud in this building that's always filled with quiet. No answer. "Can I…?"

I am unsure of what I'm seeing. This person, a woman, I don't even recognise her. Whoever it is, isn't…*alive* exactly, although she *is* moving around, so she can't be dead either.

My feet are frozen to the spot. She's getting closer, followed by someone else, an elderly gentleman. They're reaching out for me, clawing at me, snarling. Her eyes look lustful, but not for me, for my blood, my flesh. I want to scream, and nothing comes out. My pulse is pounding, drawing them in quicker; my head feels like it's going to explode, and still I can't move.

More of them pile out, heading toward me. Terror doesn't even begin to describe how I'm feeling. Nothing will take away this sensation.

Until hot teeth clamp down on my arm and the physical pain takes over everything else.

Burning.

Burning...

Ella Louise
February 15th

"Mum? Mummy?"

It's too loud out here; my mum will never hear me over all this noise.

We were running, I don't know where, and my mum looked really, *really* scared. So when she pulled my arm to move, my legs raced as fast as they could, down the stairs and out of the house.

I'm still in my pajamas; my bunny Flopsy is still tucked under my arm. Mum was screaming at me, *"Move, move!"* and I wanted to ask her where Dad was, and my big brother, then before I knew it we were out here among all these people and it was too noisy for me to talk.

Now I don't know where she is. I'm desperately trying to find her, but I'm too small. I only come up to everyone's chests, so I can't see over anyone. I don't even know what Mummy was wearing! I'm being shoved about left and right, pushed everywhere. I shout louder and louder, and I cannot be heard. There's too much noise.

My heart is beating like crazy, but I don't know why. Everyone's screaming and shouting around me; something bad must be happening. I don't know what. I wish I knew where Mum was. I don't know why she let go of my hand. Did she mean to? Or was it by accident? Did she get pulled away from me?

Everyone around me starts running again, and a pair of strong arms grip around my waist. I try and shout 'no', call out for my mum louder. I can't get a word in; I'm being shaken about far too much. I look over the shoulder of the man carrying me and am faced with some truly disgusting, sick-looking people.

They look like the people in that horror film we watched at Lisa's sleepover after her parents had gone to bed, all bloody and bits falling off them. Some of them really need a bath. They're making some strange noises, growling and snarling, and a few of them are baring their teeth, like animals do when they're hungry. I feel a bit sick. I think because of the smell more than anything. It smells like the sewer works are broken again.

I close my eyes tight, trying to pretend I'm still in bed, that this is all a bad dream. I imagine that my bed covers are pulled up to my chin, and my nightlight is flashing stars up on the ceiling above my head. I hold Flopsy up to my nose so I can smell her. I always do that when I have a nightmare, to remind me that it isn't real.

When I peek, I can see it *is* real.

I've lost my mum and we're being chased by monsters. It's worse than any nightmare I've ever had in my *life*! It's scarier now; some of the ill people have caught up to the slower ones and they are eating bits off them. It's so gross! I screw my nose up, trying to think if this is something I've ever heard about in school. I can't remember the teacher ever telling us about people eating one another.

We've stopped. I look around again, trying to find Mum. I'm dizzy, so it's hard to focus. I can hear shouting and thumping. Everyone seems to be banging on something. I try to spin around to see what's happening, but the strong arms grip me tighter, making it impossible.

"Let us out now!" one voice booms over the others. "You can't make us stay here. It's inhumane!"

A lot of people agree with this man. I still can't see Mum. Isn't she looking for me at all? A lot more shouting happens, but I don't care about that; I want to get down and have another search. Although I struggle and push, whoever has me refuses to let me go.

Suddenly there's a crash followed by what sounds like fighting. It's only then that my feet hit the floor. Everyone's gone mad, and I've been dropped in all the chaos.

Finally!

I push and shove as hard as everyone does to me, all the time screaming out for Mum. I need to get out of this crowd so I can breathe properly and get a look about.

Push, shove, knock.

I'm out! I heave a sigh of relief. I glance up, and I think I can see her. I'm not definitely sure, but there is a lady shuffling toward me in what looks like Mum's nightdress.

Thank goodness!

I run up to her, tears splashing down my face. I've never been so happy to see her, and I promise to myself never to argue with her about chores again.

I crash into her, flinging my arms around her. "Mum! Oh, Mummy, I'm so glad to see you…"

Then I realise this isn't my mum. Not really. She's one of the monsters, and there are hundreds more behind her. I spin around in a panic to see everyone on the other side of me is too busy arguing and fighting to realise what is about to happen to them…

Officer Margent
February 17th

When the orders came from the higher ups a couple of weeks ago to stop anyone coming in and out of this small town, I thought it was strange. The army doesn't do things like this, not in our own country anyway.

Now the tales I've heard from the other guys, men that have *seen* things, have made me realise this is no drill or test; this is necessary for our survival. This virus is dangerous, more dangerous than anything I've ever seen in my life, and I've been in the depths of war zones.

Apparently, the tiny nothing-town on the border of Mexico is absolutely full to the brim with sick people. *Really* sick people. People so ill, they look like the living dead, wandering around in a mist of rage and desolation, attacking each other with no provocation. It sounds truly crazy, and I know how stories get exaggerated, even by the best of people, so a sick part of my curiosity wants to see it for myself, just to clarify if what I've been told is true. Standing here guarding a town is boring. We've been doing it for a while now, without knowing why. Maybe I should find out the truth, so I know what I'm fighting for…or against. I like to know my purpose.

Maybe these thoughts are me trying to justify to myself what I've already decided to do. Our orders were strict: *Only be where you're told, and only do what we say.* So basic, so easy. They *want* to be broken. If I could get a peep, simply look over the roadblocks we've set up, just once, I can carry on with my job, interrupted, no longer plagued by these concerns.

I scan the area, finding no one around. If I'm going to look, it has to be now. I'll take a quick glance, only for one second. There's no way a single second can make any difference or cause any harm. I jump up, my eyes in line with the wall. One more push and I'll be able to see, to confirm the truth. My heart is pounding at the thought of being caught; it could cost me my job. Disobeying orders is so strictly forbidden. For a second I think of my ex-girlfriend and our child back home and quickly force that thought out of my mind. I can't let myself become distracted. I need to focus. If I'm quick, nothing bad will happen.

Heave.

I blink. I must be dreaming.

There must be something wrong with my eyes. There's no way I can see what's before me. My brain must be making it up. It's worse than I could have ever imagined.

I fall to the ground with a thump, crying out in shock rather than pain.

That town…it's worse than any of the horrible places I've fought in the past, and there have been many. It looks like a lawless wasteland with broken buildings, stolen goods, burnt-out cars, and blood.

Lots of blood. Everywhere.

That's not what got to me, though. The people, I shudder. They aren't merely ill; they look inhuman, alien. Certainly no longer sane.

I've never in all my years seen anything like that. I've witnessed terror attacks, brutal murders, people blown up by bombs. But nothing, *nothing,* has ever made my soul feel so cold. No one could have described that to me; no one could have prepared me for what I was about to see.

This is worse than I thought.

I realise that I need to act. I need to do something, anything. I need to make sure the other guys are aware of what we could be getting ourselves into. This is more than any of us expected. Could this illness get to us? We're pretty close; I don't see why not. Then what? Will we die? Become like those people I saw? Is there a cure for something so unusual?

I quickly write a note, detailing what I saw, with sketches to accompany it. The more information I can get out now while it's still fresh in my mind, the better. I've never pushed boundaries before, never been one to take major risks; I've always taken orders and done what needs to be done.

Not this time. This time I feel like I need to do this. If I don't, no one else will. I'm not sure where the courage, or maybe stupidity, is coming from. I could simply be in shock. I cover my face with my scarf and shove my helmet over my head. I place the note on top of my backpack and climb up the wall again, this time with the intention of flipping over the other side.

I'm going in.

Owain
February 18th

If only I had the Internet, this situation would be perfect.

I've seen every single zombie film and TV show ever made. I've read every novel, comic book, manga…you name it, I own it. I even run my own zombie blog. The photographs and video footage I've managed to get while all this is going on are *amazing*. Literally, all my followers would go wild for it. I'll have to save it until this blows over and then upload it. Can you imagine, real life footage?

My blog is going to become famous!

I know, I know. No one has said the beasts shuffling along outside are zombies, that word hasn't been used once, but just *look* at them. It's so obvious that what this illness has been all along.

Luckily my house is very secure; no zombies are getting in here! I've been preparing for this for years. I always knew it would happen eventually. When you spend as long as I have researching zombie viruses, you realise it's a ticking time bomb that could explode at any second. And how right I was. I've got enough got food to last me forever; I have medical supplies and weapons that I've gathered over time. My defences are high.

And now it's here; it's *really* happening.

When I first heard about this virus, nothing about it sparked excitement within me. It didn't sound too different than the bird flu, which turned out to be nothing. But as the news reports started becoming more panicked, and the streets more out of control, I started to become intrigued. I got all my filming equipment out, ready and…jackpot! I have my very own live action horror film to watch whenever I want in my home town.

It's all I've ever dreamt of!

It's definitely harder to watch in real life than it is in the cinema. I usually spend the whole time admiring the special effects and wondering how they've achieved them, but sitting here, watching the zombies tear chunks off people in front of me, it's a lot harder to digest. I certainly don't have popcorn in my lap, put it that way.

The thing with this is, I'm constantly wondering if it is actually the zombie apocalypse, or if it's only happening here, in only this town. I know people have tried to get out and were refused, which makes me very suspicious.

If that is the case, do they expect us all to succumb to this illness? Do they expect every single one of us to die, wiping out the problem with us? I won't, not unless they eventually drop a bomb on the place to make absolutely sure we're all gone. That's always a possibility, especially if we're some sort of testing center for the whole thing. It could be a nuclear weapon for all we know, something to hold over the rest of the world.

I wonder what made them pick here to test it. Maybe that crazy religious guy that's been roaming the streets recently is right; maybe it's because we're all evil and deserve to die. It's not like I think God has sent this to us or anything, yet the basis of his theory could be right. This town is filled with dickheads. Although I don't know what *I've* done exactly. I guess I did start that computer virus a while back, but I didn't mean to.

I've always loved my home, and watching the events unfolding on the streets, I realise this house is the absolute best place anyone could be during this time. I don't worry about someone trying to take it over, although that could be a risk. I more think about trying to contact other survivors, to offer sanctuary. I have more than enough to share, and I could be here for a very long time. Some company might be nice.

I dig out my old radio transmitter, as there are no other methods of communication available for the time being. While I'm aware that others might not love old technology like this, I have to try.

"Hello, if anyone is still out there, my name is Owain. Please let me know if you're safe. I live at 119 Wesley Road on the East side. Come to my house if you need food, water, shelter…hell, even just company. I'm currently alone but have enough supplies for others if you need it. Let me know if you need help getting here. I'll leave this radio on so you can contact me anytime. Over."

Static. No reply.

I feel more disappointed than I thought I would be. Though I didn't necessarily expect a response, it's a shame I didn't get one.

I try and keep my upbeat attitude for the next few days, carrying on as before—filming, eating, and relaying my message. Every lonely day makes me increasingly disheartened, until finally, I get what I'm after.

"Hello? Hello…?"

Kurt McFaddon
February 21ˢᵗ

I'm sitting with my head in my hands and an empty bottle of whiskey by my side. How did my great life become *this*?

I used to be the bassist in the band Burning Innuendo. You've probably heard of us. Everybody around here has. We were right on the cusp of becoming absolutely huge, I mean *massive*, when our lead singer overdosed on drugs. Heroin, of all the damn things. Even though it's still a shock, deep down I'm not totally surprised. We were all into a bit of it, loving the lifestyle of being a rock star—the drinking, the girls, the general bad behaviour, and the drugs.

I thought we all handled taking drugs well, kept it within reason, enough to have fun but not enough to be known for it in the business. Until a month ago when Jack died. It turns out he was doing a lot more in secret than any of us knew. I can't believe it. He never seemed like a typical addict. He was always in top form at rehearsals and gigs. How could this happen to such a nice guy?

The band immediately went our separate ways without even discussing it, the grief of the situation too much to bear. I started drinking and haven't stopped since. I've only started to sober up now because I ran out of booze in the house, and when I tried to step outside I was cornered by some weird zombie-like things. Now I don't know if I was hallucinating or if I'm insane. Obviously that wasn't real.

So I sit here, unable to move, unable to make a decision like a normal, functioning human being.

Maybe I should just end it all. I don't have

anything to live for anymore. Music is…*was* my life. Now I have nothing. I'm sure I must be about to lose the house; I don't even know the last time I paid a bill. My long-term girlfriend Marie must have finally left me, because all her stuff is gone. I didn't even notice her going in my drunken haze. I don't blame her really; I spent way too much time cheating on her. It was too easy with all the girls throwing themselves at me. On stage I was sexy, I was alive! That charisma drew them in like flies.

Now I'm just a sad old drunk, too miserable to even move because the juice has stopped flowing. How pathetic. I could have been someone. Now I'm…*this*.

A static sound makes me jump. Where is that coming from? The noise makes my headache worse, so I decide to search for it to shut the sound off. I throw everything around in frustration, messing up my already very untidy house.

Shut the hell up already! Don't you know I have a killer hangover?

Huh, a radio. I remember this. It's an old police device I stole on a wild drunken night out a while ago. I can't believe this thing is still working.

"Hello? Hello…?" A female voice interrupts my thoughts. *"Hello? Are you there?"*

I hit the button quickly before I change my mind. "Erm, hi?"

"Owain?"

Oh no, this call isn't meant for me. "Er, no, it's Kurt, sorry I didn't mean to—"

"Oh, are you trying to get hold of Owain too? We've been hearing his broadcasts over the last

couple of days but haven't been able to get an answer from him. He says he has supplies, a sanctuary...something we could use about now." She follows this with a laugh, and I tentatively join in, unsure of the joke.

"I don't know what's going on...?" I hate how idiotic I sound, but I don't know what else to say.

"Oh my goodness, what have you been doing? It's the end of the world, I think. They won't let us out of this damn town, and that virus is going to kill us all if we don't do something about it!" I'm silent, still totally dumb. *"You do know about the virus, don't you? The thing that's turned the whole city into cannibals? It's like a freaking movie out there."*

So what I saw before was real? That's more frightening than any of the possibilities I'd come up with. I can't get my head around everything; even without my foggy mind, this would be difficult. So there really are zombies or whatever?

"So this Owain guy? We need to find him, right?" I ask with a newfound determination in my voice.

"Yeah, he lives over on the East side. That way is teeming with infected, and we haven't been able to get through. We have no weapons or anything to protect us, so we don't know what to do."

I wrack my brain, trying to think of a solution. I need to help these people, and possibly myself too. If I can figure out a way to get us all to that guy's house, maybe we can stake out there until it all blows over.

Got it! I speak into the radio, discussing my plan

with the unknown girl.

The funny thing is I start to feel a sense of purpose again.

Dr. Hishman PH
February 22nd

I feel so guilty. I never meant for this to happen. I truly didn't think the virus I created would lead to this. It was only an experiment, one that went too far.

A lot of people, people with power and money, will pay more than you could ever imagine for something like this, a disease that could wipe out a huge portion of the population virtually undetected. I would hope these people would only use it as a threat, a bonus in the ever-changing power struggle of the world. I wouldn't expect anyone to go ahead and unleash it. How messed up would you have to be for that?

I was only attempting to create it because the recession has hit our field hard. I usually spend my time trying to find *cures* for diseases, not *create* them. People have no money now, and with no money they can't donate to the charities that fund us. Combining that with minimal government funding, our job is virtually impossible. With no results to speak of, people are even less inclined to help us out.

It's a vicious cycle, one I was determined to

break.

I couldn't find a viable solution, and believe me I tried. I couldn't find a way to earn us enough cash to actually make a difference to the world.

Until this insane idea hit me.

Everyone knows about black-market scientists, the ones who do the jobs you really shouldn't. The rich ones. I started thinking, if I was doing something for the greater good, would it really be that bad? I would make sure the person I sold my creation to wasn't truly evil, and I'd do my best to sell it to the highest and nicest bidder. I justified my decision to myself, even though I knew it was morally wrong. Somewhere along the line, I decided that it was the only way.

I knew the most money I could get would be for creating a deadly illness, so I figured if I was going to do this, I might as well go whole hog.

I worked in the evenings, when I finished my real job, barely leaving the lab at all. I even slept here most nights to get the most out of my time. I made mistake after mistake, but finally—shockingly—I managed to create something real. Something dangerous. Something worth a lot of cash, but also a lot of lives.

That night I went home. I needed a decent night's sleep before making my final decision to go through with it. My conscience was finally stepping in and shouting loud and clear into my ear. I tossed and turned all night, talking myself out of it and then back into it. The morning came and I was still unsure. The power I'd created, it could be too much for the world to handle. Every time I thought about it getting into someone's hands, my heart started racing and my palms sweating.

I knew I had to be totally sure before I could go through with anything, that even a teeny tiny doubt would plague me forever, even if I never heard of it again. I had to wait; I couldn't pass this deadly illness on with an impulse. I needed to lock it away safely until the time was right.

I entered the lab first, before anyone else could get to it. I needed to lock it somewhere and soon. My breathing would not return to normal until I did.

It was gone.

I have no idea how it happened, who took it, or why they decided to do this, but someone has bought hell upon this town.

I sit here, watching through my laboratory window, and I'm horrified. At myself for creating such a monstrosity, at the evil bastard who took it, and at the disgusting beasts roaming the streets. I've heard people shouting and screaming as they're being chased, calling these things 'zombies'. I guess they're right; what else could they be described as?

The worst part is, however disgusted I am at myself, a small, scientific, clinical part of my brain is impressed. Amazed at myself for creating something that works so damn well. I'm fascinated with this disease and everything it's done. I wish I could grab someone and do tests…see how this thing *really* works.

Can I? Can I do that? Go out there and grab one, cage it up, and experiment further?

Or would that only make me sicker than I already am?

Tom
February 25th

I wake up, head pounding, cotton mouth, rumpled clothing…and in a hedge.

Huh, must have been a good night. I've had quite a few of these since I started university a few months back. You've got to, haven't you? First taste of freedom, new mates…it's the done thing. I've never had one quite this bad, though. I've never completely blacked out and fallen asleep outside. On the stairs, in the bathtub maybe, yes, but always inside somewhere.

I can't even remember what happened, however hard I wrack my brain. I need water, painkillers, and more sleep. I'll worry about figuring everything out after that. I must've been alone when I slept here. I know my friends like to play pranks, but they'd never have left me here by myself. We all start the night together and end it together. Unless a hot girl comes along…all rules fly out the window then.

I stagger upwards, the motion making my stomach heave. Urgh! This hangover is so bad. I might have to slow down the drinking for a while. I run my fingers through my hair, trying to get a grasp on reality, when a sharp pain makes me jump. I pull my hand away and realise it's completely covered in blood. I touch my face; I'm bleeding there too.

I guess I must have been in a fight or something? Or I fell and hit my head. That would explain a lot, I suppose.

I want to be back in my dorm, tucked in my bed. The walk there feels like the end of the world. I don't even know where I am. I wish my vision would stop blurring; then I could figure it out.

I start walking, trying to work it out as I go. Flashes of memories cross my brain, but they can't be real. They must be what I dreamt last night in my knocked-out haze filtering into my brain. Zombies, lots of them, chasing me…killing my friends that were too drunk to run. Shuffling, bloody, and stinking of rot. I shiver at the thought, convinced I can actually smell the revolting scent now.

I really need sleep!

When I finally make it out onto the streets, I feel a sense of relief. I can get back to a bit of reality now. I look up, flicking my eyes around, and I am flooded with dread. Everything is weird: burnt, littered, broken. What the hell happened? The images I saw in my subconscious are becoming my reality.

I open my eyes, my whole body aching. I try to sit up. The shock of everything must have caused me to faint. How embarrassing is that? I will never, ever tell anybody that happened.

I look around, trying to get a grip on myself. It looks like I'm in a different place than before. I can't be sure though; I only got a tiny glimpse before I passed out.

It's completely deserted here, and for some reason that fills me with more terror than if there were a thousand zombies here. I stand up, everything pulsing and throbbing in agony. That smell…I swear it's up my nose; I can smell it everywhere.

I walk slowly, cautious not to make too much noise, scared of what I might attract. Every step hurts; every movement causes me to cringe. Eventually I reach a corner, frightened of what I might see, what I could come across. I can hear noises—low groans, crunches—so I know I won't be alone. Should I turn around and go back?

No, I need to figure out what is going on. Zombies can't be the answer…they aren't real!

I tentatively take a step, fearful, but needing to know all the same.

Curiosity killed the cat.

Maybe that saying is more accurate than anyone could have ever guessed.

I'm not in total shock about what I see, although it is surreal. I feel as if I already knew about them. The zombies, I mean. I even have a brief moment of déjà vu where I remember fighting them, but the memory is gone so quickly I don't know if I'm just making it up.

The blood and gore is far too much. The zombies are eating the remains of humans, a sight which equally disgusts and fascinates me. I move forward. I don't know why I don't run in the opposite direction; my body makes the decision for me. I need to see more. The noise of me moving causes a wave of disturbance among them. They all turn to look at me, and my heart jumps up into my chest. I stop breathing.

In that moment, I know I'm about to die.

The moment passes as quickly as it happens.

They all return to what they were doing. This confuses me. If they're eating people, then why not me? I look down at myself and realise the state I'm truly in. I am covered in blood and dirt, my flesh torn to bits, and my arm is broken; I can even see the bone hanging out. How am I still moving? How the hell did I not notice?

I glance between myself and the infected, realisation taking over, clouding my mind. I remember it all now. The fall, the broken bones, hot teeth clamping down on my skin, my friend distracting them and then being torn to shreds himself, thinking he'd saved me.

He hadn't.

In fact, he got to die, whereas I'm left like this. Like the monsters I've been looking upon in horror. I'm one of them. We're the same.

That's the last coherent thought that passes through my brain before the virus takes me in completely.

Councillor Bailey
February 27ᵗʰ

I've pulled it off. The ultimate test.

I'm going to be so rich!

I smile to myself whilst watching the CCTV footage from cameras set up around the town. Although I've created some serious chaos, that's the price everyone had to pay. I'm safe here in my bunker. It's been set up so securely, nothing is getting in here. Every single knock at the door has gone unanswered; every scream has been ignored. The public is insignificant to me. They're merely pawns in this game.

A game I've just won.

As soon as I found out that the geeky scientist guy was creating an illegal, deadly illness, I sprung my plan into action. It felt good to finally have a fight. I'd been out of the battle for so long. Competition between politicians is so fierce, and none of the others play by the rules, so why shouldn't I play dirtier than any of them? I spoke to some 'contacts' and managed to find a guy willing to pay dearly for something like this, someone our country has been at war with for God knows how long. And there you have it.

My 'contact' insisted that I needed to test the virus in the real world, with proof so he can see its true capabilities. Well, that's definitely been achieved. I have all this footage recorded and ready to send as soon as everyone dies, leaving no witnesses but me. I made sure roadblocks were set up, keeping everyone in and out. I also have contacts in the military, people willing to do anything for the right price. I even secured a media blackout on this whole thing. The only news it has even been mentioned on is local, and it's flagged and removed if spotted anywhere online. This isn't getting out, so no one will know what's coming until it does.

It's all gone better than I could ever have dreamed. When I finally spotted the guy muttering to himself in a state of panic on my secret camera in his lab, I leapt into action. When he finally went home, I knew he must have been finished. With the vial in my hand, I've never felt the world at my feet so clearly. Everything was finally falling into place.

I decided to unleash it in the school. I know, that sounds evil, but to be fair everyone was going to get it anyway. It had to be contagious, otherwise what would be the point? I thought it would go undetected for a longer time among children. Everyone knows illnesses spread like wildfire among kids.

It affected everyone a lot quicker than I thought it would.

First the hospital collapsed under the strain, then they assumed everyone was dead. *Great*! I thought. Time to pass on all the information. Then the ones who died were…coming back from the dead. Can you believe my luck! Just like zombies, I suppose.

I think I can ask for a lot more than the original offer. After all, this virus comes around in two waves. This is an amazing killing machine, and any government worth its weight would do anything, *pay* anything, to stop it from being released. It could stop all the wars.

Or it could create more, but that isn't my concern.

I'm getting impatient now, waiting for everyone to hurry up and die already. Then I can make up some fake disaster that finished everyone off, and the rest of the world will be none the wiser. It's taking longer than I can bear. I want my money, my power, my *real* life to start.

I've considered bombing the town, finishing

400

them all off quickly; however, I don't think I could do that without people taking notice. I need to be more subtle. I guess I could always get the military in to shoot everyone. Hopefully they won't get too worked up about how contagious the virus is.

I need this done, and I need it now. I pull my radio out and demand the job be done...

Katy
February 29th

When Kurt picked up me, my sister, and my auntie in his car, the first thought to cross my mind was *'Whoa, a Porsche'*. I know, how inappropriate, but it was a lifesaver. If it wasn't for him randomly turning on his radio that day, we'd all be dead now for sure, one way or another. We'd been surviving on the streets after the town was swarmed by the infected. We were starving, tired, and ready to give up. It was only by chance we stumbled across an abandoned police car, unfortunately for us out of fuel, and managed to get in touch with everybody.

Kurt drove us to Owain's, where we all stayed for a while, living on a knife edge, just waiting for something to happen. While it was terrifying for all of us, being safely inside and together made it easier. We didn't argue over petty things like you'd expect five strangers thrown together would. We got on well, helped each other through this difficult time, working together to survive. Thank goodness for Owain's forward thinking, who knew the crazy, geeky, zombie enthusiast would be right?

Then yesterday, the gunshots came.

Part of me was relieved, because it was so obvious the government wasn't going to let things go on the way they were forever. We knew this virus was only infecting people in this town, so we knew some action had to be taken. At least it wasn't a bomb!

Obviously they need this thing to be kept hidden, whatever *it* is.

We all dropped to the floor, trying to hide from stray bullets, whilst trying to decide what our next move should be. One thing we all realised was that we couldn't stay put. It was pretty obvious that they weren't going to leave any survivors.

So we left.

It took a lot of planning, a lot of organising to get there, but we made it. We managed to get past the roadblocks now that they're no longer being manned, and we're out. We haven't made it much further, but it's better than being inside *there*. We went on foot, knowing the Porsche was a bad idea, and it was extremely treacherous.

We have a tent, a roaring fire, and weapons. Owain is going to teach us to use them properly because we may need to defend ourselves from a number of threats at some point. Our little group which has come such a long way. At least I'm not alone; at least I'm with friends.

Now, we just need to wait.

Wait for the military to leave.

Wait for the infection to burn itself out.

Wait for an escape.

Epilogue

"An unidentified virus, believed to have originated in Mexico, has caused a widespread national pandemic. Military, trying to stop the infection from spreading further, inadvertently carried it out to the rest of the world with them. No one knows how dangerous or contagious this virus is. All we know at this time is the current death toll has already reached the hundreds of thousands in a matter of days. For now, if you're **sure** *you're not infected, you are advised to head to your nearest refugee camp until further notice. The refugee camps are clearly marked all over, so you should have no trouble finding them. Until then, please stay safe."*

About the Author

Samie Sands is the author of the *AM13 Outbreak* series—*Lockdown, Forgotten* and *Extinct*. She's also had a number of short stories published in very successful anthologies. To find out more about her and her work, check out her website at http://samiesands.com.

Facebook:
http://www.facebook.com/SamieSandsLockdown

Twitter:
http://www.twitter.com/SamieSands

Website:
http://samiesands.com/

Goodreads:
https://www.goodreads.com/SamieSands

The Six-Foot Ladder

By Luke Swanson

I'm Ramona Price. Twenty-one years old, born October 1934. I'm always on the run, my nerves are always on edge, and I've learned to sleep less than five hours a night.

Why?

Because I've always seen the specters.

For as long as I can remember, they've walked along with me, staring straight ahead, paying me no mind. They talk to one another, laugh, nod, and cry. Sometimes they disappear, soar through the air like wraiths, and contort into horrifying shapes. But they never look at me. That's almost worse than it would be if they targeted me or something like that. I know that's ridiculous; why would I want to be haunted by ghosts?

When their crystal eyes pass right over me, though, it's as if they don't even want to waste their endless time on me.

That's worse. A great deal worse.

I sit in the driver's seat of my Ford Coupe, barreling through Podunk-Nowhere, Oklahoma. Nothing but horizon, the occasional spindly tree, and the asphalt ribbon stretching on and on and on in front of me. "Rock Around the Clock" by Bill Haley is stuck in my head, which I'm grateful for, because there is absolutely no scenery to keep me occupied. I've already run through all of "Singin' in the Rain" twice.

The ripe orange sun in the center of the pale sky makes everything shimmer and flicker like images on a projected screen. The heat is unbearable, and the open windows only succeed in mussing my hair and letting in uninvited mosquitos. I've heard that a lot of the brand-new Chryslers and Cadillacs now come with systems that regulate the temperature inside your car so you could shiver in July or wear a sundress on Christmas. My dirt-brown '35 Ford, on the other hand, needs a kick and a prayer to get started, and it looks like it's winking when I drive at night.

It's a cruddy car, to be sure, but in this new place, I'll need any sort of familiarity in order to not spiral into insanity.

I glance into the backseat. Six dresses on wire hangers; my old high-pop automatic toaster, charred crumbs still stuck in its belly; a few pairs of brown house shoes and my blood-red stilettos in case I need to gussy up; and a mid-sized suitcase, its hinges and locks straining from its contents.

Yep. Everything I own in the world, in my backseat. While not exactly a pharaoh's treasure trove, it's gotten me this far.

Why?

I shake my head to dislodge that nagging question, but it remains all the same.

Why did I leave the city?

The worst part is, I know the answer. I know without a doubt that I needed to leave Oklahoma City, and the specters make it easy to not look back. The streets are haunted for me; the tall buildings are more like Valkyries than sentinels. The city used to be so full of promise, bustling and energetic, thrumming with the rhythm of a million souls, a million heartbeats. I could stroll down West Main Street and see joy embodied in the people. Businessmen, young mothers, nomadic artists, dogs on leashes…OKC was a fascinating amalgamation of Manhattan and Mayberry, a sprawling city with the tenderness of a small town.

Was.

It had been like a light switch. On one second, off the next. As warm as OKC had been, it abruptly became twice as arctic. I had never felt so alone, despite being surrounded by people. The population began to reject me like a failed kidney transplant. I would walk along West Main in a desperate attempt to recapture my previous sense of contentment. Nothing changed. The businessmen jostled past me; the young mothers scoffed and turned their heads away. The dogs even bared their crusty teeth as if threatened.

The specters sure didn't help. Usually they avoid crowded areas, preferring to show up when I'm alone. However, the coldness of the city drew them out. Ghostly figures staggered among the population, huge, toothy grins stretched across their faces, cackling like madmen. Or aggressive, poisonous eyes, itching to attack. Or blank stares, as if lost in a supermarket. Still, they never looked directly at me.

I couldn't take it anymore. In addition to the hostility of the living, the terror of the dead sealed the deal.

So when the winds changed from pleasant to dusty and wet laundry dried almost instantly on the line, I decided it was time to leave. I stripped my apartment bare, loaded all my worldly possessions in the back of my Ford, and left.

I had no destination, no plan. I simply needed to leave.

So here I am, bulleting through the empty plains of dusty Oklahoma. Nothingness stretches in every direction, flat as a pancake. I'm almost impressed. It's like some sort of purgatory from a Kafka novel.

I smirk to myself. At least the college degree stuffed in my suitcase is good for something—if only making obscure literary references in my head.

Then I see one. A strange man in a strange suit, standing in the middle of the road. A specter. The very thing I'm running from.

My Ford screams onward, directly toward the specter, like a locomotive careening along its fixed tracks.

Time seems to slow. I get a good look at this man, this Earth-bound shadow shackled to my world like a prisoner of war.

I'm a hundred feet from him and closing fast.

He is tall and lanky like Jack's beanstalk, with wide shoulders that could knock in a locked door—that is, if he needed to use a door. Dark hair stands up straight from his scalp like it is trying to escape, and his eyes are wide and round, vibrating in his skull. He staggers across my path, jerkily stomping one foot in front of the other as if crushing a procession of cockroaches, like a demented version of a chicken-crossing-the-road joke. His clothing is strange, as though from another country that isn't to be founded for another century, familiar enough, though also completely alien. I can even see his clenched jaw, balled fists, and gray, bumpy skin.

I'm fifty feet away.

He is a wraith, a reaper, a phantom, to be sure. But he looks like a man, and that is what thrashes my nerves.

Twenty feet.

Of course, he doesn't look at me, the automobile speeding directly in his direction. I am nothing to him. And *that* is what turns my blood to ice.

Ten feet.

I clench my eyes shut and brace for impact.

Of course, I don't feel anything. My Ford keeps cruising along. I pry my eyes open and see the ribbon of road, the horizon, the dusty Okie landscape and the ripe orange sun.

Yep, I passed right through him. I always do. But

I can never help it; I always think I'll hit them, hurt them, kill them. They don't even mind me running over them.

My hands would be trembling if I weren't grasping my steering wheel so tightly. This is a strategic move, but my white knuckles and bulging tendons start to unsettle me, so I force my muscles to relax.

This isn't easy to do. I'm a bit like a jack-in-the-box—tightly wound within my own box, always waiting to pop, wearing garish clothes and probably ruining someone's day.

That's not all true. I think I dress pretty well.

I shake my head to clear my wandering thoughts. The road in front of me demands my attention.

Even so, I glance in the grimy rearview mirror. The specter is gone.

Their existence is still a mystery to me. I've lived amongst these misty, grotesque apparitions for as long as my memory can stretch, yet I don't know their purpose. Who are they? Why are they so disfigured? Where do they come from? Where do they go? Why am I the only person plagued by their presence?

I have no answers. The specters, the phantasms that define my life and temperament and reality, are one gigantic question mark.

It drives me insane. Hence the less-than-five-hours-of-sleep-a-night thing.

Then I see a road sign up ahead, a squat, blue notice emblazoned with the three words, ***"Welcome to Crawford."***

A town this far out in the middle of limbo? I

squint and, sure enough, I spot the silhouettes of buildings, structures, and even a few trees in the distance.

Should I pull over here, call Crawford my new oasis? I've never even heard of this town. My foot leans a little further on my Ford's accelerator. Maybe the next city…

The residual memory of the specter practically slaps me. His wild eyes, the ramrod-straight hair…

I switch my foot to the brake and decide to give Crawford a try.

Why not, right?

The air glistens as I pull my car onto the side road leading to this unknown township, like a flowing current suddenly disrupted. Deep creaking sounds rumble from under the Ford's hood, causing the entire car to tremble around me. I groan. After years of being faithful, it picks *now* to croak? I caress the dashboard like it's a nervous pet and whisper, "C'mon, old lady. Just a little bit more." As if that'll help. Hey, it's only a superstition if it doesn't work.

It only gets worse. I grit my teeth and will my car to keep going, but it's shaking like a newborn foal using its spindly legs for the first time, and it seems it'll buckle any second.

"Go, old lady, I believe in you!"

Sputter.

"Don't do this to me…"

It does it to me. The engine goes quiet, the car's momentum continues for about forty yards, and I roll to a stop in the middle of the road.

The sun beats mercilessly on me, forming a layer

of sweat on my skin. I rub my temples with my palms, forcing myself to focus, to block out the ridiculous heat, the fact that my car is dead on the outskirts of an unfamiliar town, and the specters that are sure to be lurking nearby.

My situation is smothering me like a pillow. Or a noose. I punch the dashboard and growl, furious, wary, scared, lonely, and tense. I am drowning within my own mind.

I sit in the front seat for a moment. Only a moment, but it stretches into an eternity. I pull my breath in and push it out slowly, decelerating my heart rate bit by bit. Gradually, I regain control.

You will not win.

I banish the specters from my mind. I refuse to let them burden me.

Before the dismal thoughts can sink their hooks back into my brain, I kick open the car door and clamor out into the sandpaper air. Not only is it sizzling, but the Oklahoma wind slams into me like a pro linebacker, hopelessly mussing my long curly hair, and even worse, whipping my dress up over my face. Now I'm blindfolded by a floral pattern and my bloomers are exposed before God. I quickly shove my dress down into its proper position and hold it there against the deviant gusts. While there may not be anyone around to see, I still consider myself a proper lady.

Plus, I don't want to put on a peep show for any specters who might be passing by. We haven't quite reached that level yet.

The town of Crawford looms about a mile away, flickering and waving at me through the heated air.

Although Oklahoma City may not be New York or Los Angeles, it's practically the golden age of Rome compared to the itty-bitty collection of buildings that calls itself a municipality. There couldn't be more than five hundred people in the whole area, and that's a generous estimate.

Still, I was on the run from the big city in the first place, my Ford Coupe isn't going anywhere without some motivation, and the specters tend to avoid groups of people.

Looks like Crawford, Oklahoma, is the place to be.

I throw a glance in my back seat at the bulging trunk. The dresses, the stilettos…it can all sit tight until I get a mechanic out to fix my old dirt-brown tank. I get the feeling it's safer out in the middle of this Midwestern desert than in a Swiss bank vault.

I fix my gaze on the distant shadow known as Crawford, crack my stiff neck joints, and start walking, ignoring the misshapen, grunting specter to my left just as it is ignoring me.

This town is a snow globe. Small, contained, daintily designed, and ornately painted, as picturesque as a postcard from Heaven. But small can be stifling. Contained can be restrictive. Dainty and ornate can be fragile and weak, and picturesque is often a mere façade disguising a husk, a withering cocoon that once held a butterfly. One abrupt movement could send everything into chaos.

This is Crawford, Oklahoma. I tiptoe on the

sidewalk, afraid to place my full weight on my soles in case the footfalls might awaken a slumbering beast. I pass a street sign signaling that I am walking along Main Street, which appears to spear the entire town, running from end to end. There is a boutique advertising both manicures and shaves, a squat gray bank that seems to frown, a handful of wrought iron streetlamps that look pulled from the pages of a Dickens tale, and even a huge brick monstrosity branded the "Hughes County Mortuary" with a cardboard sign in the window reading *"You bag 'em, we tag 'em"* in polished calligraphy.

However, not a sound. No birds or footsteps or revving car engines or rattles of bicycles.

No one is in sight. Not a soul. No mothers with children, no businessmen hustling to and fro, no families with faithful canines.

The entire town stands perfectly still, like a sprawling monument to some past tragedy. Like a dollhouse waiting for its god to manipulate it.

Like a snow globe, idyllic and ersatz all at once.

A darkness blankets the street, and the hairs on my flesh prickle. I glance up to see a thick cloud swallow the orange sun, completely blocking its heat and engulfing all of Crawford in an ethereal embrace. I clench my fists against the chill.

Something's wrong. My eyes dart across the buildings lining Main Street. Even beyond the absence of people, there's an atmosphere about this place that makes my bones tingle. Something…off, like department store mannequins that look only halfway lifelike. I can't quite put my finger on it.

Then it hits me.

There aren't any specters here.

None. Usually I see at least a handful at any given time, even in the heart of lively Oklahoma City. Here there are none.

Even they seem to know this town is wrong.

Click clap click clap.

My heart leaps. Footsteps.

A person!

I'd never dreamed that someone's loafers thumping against asphalt would sound so glorious.

A man rounds the corner out of an alleyway onto Main. His watch is an inch from his furrowed face, and his frenzied gait is that of a king late to his own coronation. His black suit is neat and pressed, including a snazzy waistcoat, although his haircut is as polar opposite as it gets—jagged, uneven, more akin to ole Albert Einstein than a CEO.

Still, in the middle of this void, I couldn't be happier to see him. His cheeks are rosy and his eyes flash like azure lighthouses. He looks nice enough.

I call out, "Mister! Hello?"

He slows for a moment, ear cocked curiously, then goes on his speedy way.

I huff, more than a little frustrated after my automotive woes, the trek on foot into town, and my encounter with the wide-eyed specter on the road. Digging for my most authoritative voice, I yell, "Hey!"

That stops him in his tracks. His shoulders clench and he looks around, searching for the source of the greeting. I take a few steps toward him, raising my hand for easily identification, although it can't be too hard to spot me in the middle of this empty, life-size toy set of a town. Then his eyes land on me.

The rouge drains from his face immediately. He opens his mouth to speak, but only guttural gasps escape.

"Sir?" I walk toward him.

He raises his arms toward me and shrieks, "No!" He staggers backward as if I have the plague, tripping over his own feet in haste. "Stay away!" he hisses.

Then he twists 180 degrees and sprints out of sight.

Click clap click clap click clap click clap.

Deafening silence smothers Main Street, and I stand frozen beside the mortuary. My feet are bolted to the sidewalk, which is a good thing, because I think I might topple over otherwise.

I don't understand. Why did that man act so...*afraid* of me? My knees tremble under the weight of my confusion. Or is it fear? Both? I can't even pinpoint my frame of mind. All I know for certain is the cold sweat on my brow and the bile in my throat.

"Good afternoon."

I yelp and spin toward the new voice. Leaning against the doorframe of the mortuary entrance is a long-limbed fellow in a white coat that tickles his ankles, which are pasty and exposed by his too-short trousers. Round bifocals with inch-thick lenses shield and magnify his green eyes like spotlights pointed directly at me. His frizzy hair reaches for the sky like he stabbed one too many sockets this morning. He is certainly a gawky fellow, to say the least, perhaps the kind of guy to keep his seatbelt fastened at a drive-in movie.

But that voice…it sends shivers down my spine, then all the way back up. Deep as a bassoon, soothing, silky, it practically wraps itself around me like a snake. The voice of God Himself.

I realize I've been standing in silence for an uncomfortable ten seconds. "I-I…Hello, sir," I manage.

The man nods once, and his hair bobs forward like a wet sponge. "How do you do? Are you new in town?"

I clear my cobwebbed throat. "Yes, sir. My car…" I gesture down Main and out of the city limits, vaguely toward my shell of a Ford. The man cocks an eyebrow as he listens—and a coldness taps me on the shoulder.

Was this lanky man in the white coat standing behind me the whole time? Could *he* be what frightened the businessman so?

"Well, I have a telephone just inside. Would you care to use it?"

My feet are quickly fused to the ground again. The man must see my reaction, because he shakes his head, embarrassed, and chuckles, which makes my heart flutter a little, to tell the truth.

"I'm sorry, Miss, I must appear pretty kooky right now, popping outta nowhere, right?" He adjusts his wiry glasses and stands up straight, casting a rail-thin shadow on me. He must be at least six-foot-six. "Dr. Milt O'Connor. I run this little shop."

I glance back at the signage of his 'shop,' grandly pronouncing itself the morgue of the entire county. Then there's the piece of cardboard, making a mockery of the whole thing in immaculate penmanship.

The doc follows my gaze. "As Oscar Wilde said, *'Life is too important to take seriously.'* Well, I feel the same way about what comes after."

I look back at him. "You know Wilde?"

A smirk. "I have more time on my hands than I know what to do with. So yes, I read anything I can. And you are, Miss…?" He extends a hand.

I realize I haven't offered my name yet. "Ramona." I smile and shake his hand. It's cold, as if he'd been holding a beverage for a long time, but kindly and sincere.

"It's nice to meet you, Miss…?" He fishes for a last name.

"The pleasure's mine." I give his hand one last pump and retract my own, definitively keeping my surname to myself for the time being.

The doc catches my signal and raises his hands in mock surrender. His smile is good-natured, and I see that his bottom teeth overlap crookedly like old wooden fence posts. I return his smile, but the chill from the shrouded sun and my encounter with the suited man keep me alert.

"So would you like to use my telephone?"

Should I trust this strange man? His wry grin appears genuine, but the suited man feared the very sight of him.

"There are no auto mechanics in Crawford," he continues. "I do have the number for the best man for the job. He's here in Hughes County."

The cloud passes and a sliver of sunlight catches the doctor's eyeglasses, transforming the lenses into yellow discs. In that moment, he looks like a grinning jack-o-lantern, fire illuminating his hollow eyes from within.

After the trying morning I've had—the car, the specters, the cold rejection of OKC and the eerie snow globe that is Crawford—this strange coroner's kindness is a welcome change in tone. So I find myself relaxing and saying, "Yes, doctor, I'd appreciate that."

He smiles as if I had made his day, opens the door wide, and gestures for me to walk through. The frizzy hair atop his head reminds me of the tiny hats bellboys wear in fancy-schmancy hotels, and I can't help giggling as I enter.

"Welcome to my humble abode."

Plush carpets soften my footsteps and rich scarlet curtains adorn the windows, making this place look more like that aforementioned fancy-schmancy hotel than a small-town morgue. A staircase on the far side of the room leads to a second floor. It's bit jarring, even—I'd had visions of dead bodies and bloody bags, not soft lighting and...is that a hint of jasmine?

The doc steps in and closes the door, shutting out Crawford. "Can I offer you a drink? Juice, coffee, Coca-Cola?"

"Umm, water?"

"Of course." He smiles.

I crane my neck to look up at him. "You live here?"

O'Connor nods slightly, his glasses sliding down his blocky nose. "Yep. I have a small living quarters area upstairs. Washroom, stove, bed, reading light…It's all I really need. This way."

He strides to a cabinet and withdraws a glass bottle of Malvern drinking water. "From the granite hills of England. Only the best for my guests." His glossy voice actually raises my heart rate, but his awkward exterior and ill-fitting clothing remind me of the begrudging bachelors at my senior prom. I find him endearing and friendly, nonetheless.

"Thank you very much." And I mean it. I take the bottle and drink its crisp, clear contents, nourishing my scratchy throat. I hadn't realized how parched I am.

"You're welcome, Miss." He pauses for a moment, then abruptly switches back to the previous conversation, like a record that had to be flipped over for the B-track. "The quarters upstairs are a bit too stuffy for my liking. I actually spend most of my time in the king's suite here on the ground floor." He gestures to another door, this one tucked in a corner and hidden by shadows. "I rarely go out because I'm so…buried in my work, you might say."

"The king's suite?" I gulp.

"Mhmm. Back there is where all our A-list clients spend the night until it's time for them to climb down that six-foot ladder."

"Wait. Behind that door is—"

"Are," the doc quickly corrected. "There *are* multiple dead bodies lying in large metal drawers."

His bluntness catches me off guard. "I thought

you saw the funny side of death."

"What can I say? I'm a complex fellow." O'Connor laughs, which shakes the entire structure, and saunters further into the plush antechamber. "Yes, this is the lobby of the mortuary, where the architect and interior designer felt the need to lull visitors into a sense of safety and pleasantry before opening that door and entering reality."

With a flourish, O'Connor pushes a palm against the door and floats in, and I follow, completely entranced.

He wasn't exaggerating. Stepping from the plush, womb-like anteroom into the morgue proper is like entering another realm entirely. This floor is tiled in a checkerboard pattern, and the walls are a tired, smudged plaster. I definitely don't want to know what the smudges are. Reflective metal tables sit in the corners, carrying flasks, rulers, blank tags, and all sorts of menacing instruments that make my skin crawl. A few adjustable lamps with craning, spindly necks eye me as I enter—watch dogs sensing a trespasser with equal parts aggression and curiosity. Harsh white light bulbs in iron cages dangle from the ceiling, bathing the room in a dull brightness, as well as long, thin shadows like prison bars. The whole thing feels airy and ethereal, like a dream. Or a nightmare.

The drawers are what immediately capture my attention. Dozens of little square doors fixed to the walls, stacked three high, hinges well-worn but sturdy, with handles like a refrigerator's. And locks. Why do these drawers have locks?

They are numbered from *001* to *085*, wrapping

around the room, a perfect circle of death. Surrounding me. A boa constrictor—

"Breathe, Miss." The doc places a hand lightly on my shoulder.

I hadn't realized I was holding my breath. I exhale, releasing the air, yet my chest is still tight.

"These are my house guests." He nods to the drawers. "Unique in every way. Who they were, their occupations, their passions, their vices, how they went belly-up…" We stroll further into the morgue, and his rumbling words are fascinating. "But they all converge here, and they all are now nothing more sacks of flesh stacked in a wall, waiting to take a dirt nap."

I shudder and not only from the chilly draft. "These were people. Why are you so nonchalant about their deaths?"

"Because it's the way of life, Miss. Humans cloak the monstrous in euphemisms. People call it 'unspeakable' or 'unthinkable', designations that are true simply because in using them we make them so. But death isn't unthinkable. It happens millions of times every single day. And the sun still rises."

"Isn't it sad to see people who were once so vital, so…human, reduced to inanimate objects lying on a slab?"

The doc's shoulders deflate slightly. "Everything ends, Miss." He swivels his head to look at all the drawers, and an impish smile tugs at his lips. "Number 16," he nods to the metal drawer, "was a clown."

"Well, that's not very nice."

"No, I mean he was a *clown.* He wore white makeup, baggy pants, and danced around with elephants. And he was a buffoon, too. Stupid, I mean. Stood on a rocking chair to try and adjust a crooked painting. Leaned too far one way, flailed like a seagull for a second, went airborne, and the rest is history.

"Number 33. Klansman from Georgia, passing through on his way west. He roughed up a few innocent gentlemen on his trek, as well as kicked a puppy, I believe. He was asleep in a motel when an artery burst behind his eye. Didn't feel a thing, simply slipped away. No one has claimed his body. No one wants him, but his passing was quite peaceful.

"Number 64. He was in his early forties, the prime of his life. Exercised, ate a good balanced diet of fruits and meats, never touched a drop of alcohol, nor a puff of nicotine. He tithed at this church every Sunday, refused to say an ill word to any person he met, especially his lovely wife and two adoring sons. Was on the board of the Oklahoma Children's Hospital. Oh, I forgot to say he was a surgeon who volunteered at clinics on the weekends.

"Did he simply stumble and crack his neck or slip away in his sleep like those two other dodo birds? Nope. He got cancer in his small intestine. Wasted away from the inside out for years. *Years.* His family watched. His friends mourned. He was in absolute agony, wondering why God was letting this happen. Eventually, he passed on, only after three surgeries and losing nearly fifty pounds.

"Yet, here they all are, under the same roof, reaching the same fate, booked for the same ticket on the Gravesend bus."

I'm numb, disbelieving. But he has a point.

"The euphemisms and synonyms are all well and good, but death is a natural part of this life, whether we choose to accept or flee from the very thought of it. We're raised to see it as a tragedy, but it comes for each and every human. Many don't accept it, and that simply leads to an existence of fear and bitterness."

I ponder his last statement. "Why do you say that?"

"Well...imagine denying that gravity exists. Or the wind. Something that others see as plainly obvious. Every time an apple falls from a tree or clouds move across the sky, your paradigm would be proven wrong. You'd be angry, resentful, and fearful of what else you're wrong about."

"Wow. That's...an incredible view of life, Dr. O'Connor. Or death, rather."

"Milt," he corrects genially.

I look up at him. "Dr. O'Connor, I hate to sound rude, but where is the telephone? It's been a very long, trying day."

He nods once. "Certainly. It's on this far table." He signals across the room to a boxy telephone, the numbers worn off its dial from years of use. "The number of the automobile mechanic I mentioned earlier is written on the tag pinned to the wall. I shall give you some privacy." He tips his head and bows out of the morgue, leaving me alone.

Well, alone, plus a few dozen chilled corpses

tucked in their beds.

I clear my throat and take a breath, doing my darnedest to focus on the black telephone rather than the unseen—yet incredibly present—bodies. Like a rook across a chessboard, I move directly to the metal table, refusing to even acknowledge the drawers.

I pick up the telephone's receiver and lean in to read the slip of paper tacked to the plaster wall.

"*Scott, mechanic…*" followed by a letter and five digits.

I pause.

That's the only thing written on the note. Why did the doc have this mechanic's number pinned right here?

As though waiting for me?

Suddenly, I want nothing more than to leave Crawford. Leave the mortuary. Leave this godforsaken room of death. With a trembling finger, I turn the dial six times, press the receiver against my face, and wait.

A brief musical note scratches my ear. In this moment, my lungs feel smaller than seashells, unable to catch a full breath. Beads of sweat slide down my back, and they feel like slimy fingers caressing my flesh. I shiver and tighten my grip on the telephone.

I tap my fingernail against the metallic tabletop. It sounds like a ticking clock. Or a time bomb.

At last, a pleasant female voice responds: "I'm sorry, this telephone number is currently unavailable…" It is a cold and mechanical voice, like an actress reading a script. "If you would like to hang up and try a different number—"

I pound my palm on the table, which booms against the tile floor, and hiss, "You've gotta be kidding me!"

"Now, now, Ramona," the robotic female voice continues, "there's no need to get emotional."

My blood freezes.

"You need to go, Ramona. Accept it."

The cordial voice's threats hit me like a slap.

"Don't turn around, either." Then, static. The automaton had hung up.

I'm stiff as a board. The dull lights intensify, making me squint, doubling my vision, churning my stomach.

Don't turn around...

I slow my breathing and listen. The morgue is silent. The air vibrates with an electric charge, holding its breath. Waiting.

Tick.

A footstep. Someone is behind me. Something...

I need to leave, to run out of this sanitarium nightmare. But I'm rooted, clutching the plastic receiver, staring at the smudged wall, the handwritten phone number staring back.

Another *tick*. It's still there. I hear a slow, almost imperceptible inhale. For a moment, I think I may have imagined it, my frenetic brain trying to push me over the edge. Then, an exhale.

I grit my teeth, throw down the receiver, which boomerangs back up thanks to the tangled cord, and spin to face the exit.

Nothing is there.

I groan. Wow. All these years running from the

specters really has messed with my head.

Regardless, this place still gives me the heebie-jeebies, so I head for the door, stepping across the checkerboard tiles with no regard for the game rules.

Tick. Behind me again.

A skeletal hand grabs my shoulder. Frigid. Coarse. Strong. Before a scream can escape my throat, it yanks me around.

I'm face to face with an old woman who appears to only be half-there, like when I put the dial midway between two radio stations. The deep wrinkles in her face are filled with dust and flecks of copper. She pulls me close with surprising power in her frail fingers, so that I am centimeters from her ragged face.

Her breath. I almost gag. The stench of an ancient crypt.

She clacks her marble teeth together and then croaks, "Leave this place." Her eyes flare with the intensity of an exploding sun, then blacken like charcoal.

I want to yell, to kick, to flee, but my limbs are paralyzed. A specter has never so much as looked at me, much less attack and shriek like this.

She bellows, "NOW!"

I sink to my knees as the old woman's shrill voice becomes a siren, wailing and wailing until my ears become numb. The medical instruments tremble on their tables, and the walls appear to ebb.

The door flies open. The lanky doctor in the white coat bounds in, a grimace etched into his face. He glares directly at the old woman and balls his

428

fists.

No one else has ever seen a specter…

"You," he growls, the voice of God unleashing His wrath, "release her!"

The old woman's smoldering eyes snap from me to O'Connor, wide and defiant. Her gaunt fingers let go of my shoulder, and I crumple to the tiled floor. She stands tall and moves toward him, her wrinkly expression contorting so that her scowl stretches her cheeks.

O'Connor doesn't flinch. "I'm not afraid of you. Go."

At that word, the woman stops immediately, twitches once, and sinks into the checkerboard floor, disappearing in an instant.

The morgue is still again. Deathly still.

O'Connor runs over to where I'm collapsed on the floor, kneels, and gently helps me into a sitting position. "Miss, are you alright? Miss?"

I stare at him, slack-jawed, barely able to string a sentence together. "You saw her…D-Do you see them…?"

"I see them, yes. All of them." He adjusts his eyeglasses.

"How did you command her to leave?"

"Years of practice. C'mon, Miss, let's get you on your feet." He shifts to a squat, places his hands under my elbows, and we stand together. He rises to his full height, and I throw my arms around his torso.

"Thank you, Milt." Tears poke the backs of my eyes, but I rein them in and set my jaw. Still, I smile. The first genuine smile I've had in a long time. "I just…I've never met anyone else who can see these…well, I call them the specters."

We move out of the sterile morgue, back into the lobby with the plush carpets and scarlet curtains. The bile clings to my throat, a foul reminder of the attack I just escaped, or really, I was rescued from.

O'Connor nods, his mop of hair bobbling. "Yes. These beings, these…people—"

I shudder and eye the door to the morgue. "That was no person."

"You'd be surprised. I've been dealing with these things for a long, long while. They're trying to get by, like you and me."

I cock an eyebrow. "You sympathize with them?"

He mulls over his response, swirling it like brandy in a snifter. "I can see where they're coming from. They're lost and confused. Imagine if you were forced into a realm you didn't understand, a dimension you may not have even believed in. How would you react? Doomed to walk the night and confined to fast in fires?"

That breaks my stony face and makes me smirk. "Thanks, Hamlet."

The doc grins too. "I knew you would catch that little snippet." His silky voice sobers again. "Honestly, though, Miss, there's a spare loft upstairs. I think you should stay there until your car is fixed and you can get on the road again."

I'm taken aback. "Really? You want to give me a room?"

O'Connor stutters and looks self-conscious. He paces around to face me directly, his back to the mortuary's exit. "J-Just as a friend, truthfully, I didn't mean it like that." His words tumble out like he's trying to dam a river with over-explanation. "I-I think we should look after one another. Plus, there's already another tenant in there. He's an old chap called Gunner, completely harmless. There are two bedrooms. He's in one, you'll have the other. And my quarters are down the hallway. You wouldn't be alone."

His embarrassment makes me giggle. I smile up at him. "Sure, Milt. I appreciate it." I put on a mockingly stern face and raise a finger. "Just no funny business," I tease.

He doesn't realize I'm kidding and nods. "Of course, Miss Price."

Miss Price...

I never told him my last name.

The doctor continues to smile at me, eyes big and wide like a doll's, his teeth gleaming. My mind is in a cold sweat. Who is this man? How did he know my name? Why is he helping me? Suddenly, although he doesn't change, everything about the man is different—his white coat is sinister; the emerald eyes behind the bifocals probe instead of beam; his deep voice isn't God's anymore, it's a demon's.

There's only one thing now: *Run.*

I scan the lobby for an escape. But O'Connor has positioned himself between me and the only exit. Sneaky fellow...

I muster up a smile to keep him from getting suspicious. "So where's this room, Doc?"

What's his end game, his goal? Why is he—

I shut off my mental inquisition. I need to get out of here first.

Where will I—

Shut up and focus, Ramona.

He's facing me, and it doesn't look like he's caught wind of my shift in attitude. Good. Although the mortuary's exit is about twenty feet away from us, I'd have to bob and weave around him to get there, and his bungee arms will snare me for sure. Can't get out that way. Yet.

The door to the morgue is only a few steps behind me. Nowhere to go or hide in there, and the telephone doesn't want to cooperate. Dead end. In more ways than one.

That leaves upstairs. The staircase is diagonal from my position. I'll get him to lead me there, keep my charade up for the moment. Maybe I can take cover somewhere and wait for the doc to give up and leave, or maybe shimmy out a window, or maybe get the old man Gunner to help. I need something though—this is my only option.

O'Connor tilts his head toward the stairs. "Right this way. I'll show you, then we can go get your bags from your car."

I hadn't told him about leaving my luggage behind either.

I giggle to cover up my frayed nerves. "After you!"

Too cheery. He'll notice for sure. He'll snap and go crazy and throw me in one of his big metal drawers.

He nods and holds out his arm toward the stairs. "After you, Miss." He arches an eyebrow. "I insist."

Alright then. It takes all of my concentration to lift my leg and move toward the stairway at a natural pace. I want to run like a maniac, sweeping my foot under O'Connor's stilts as I go, but I need to keep my head on straight.

The white coat floats directly behind me, a specter wearing a fleshy disguise. Step by creaky step, I work my way up the stairs. The electric lights from the lobby fade into the distance as we move further upward. Shadows lengthen, the air bites my exposed skin, and a static buzz rings in my ears.

We're almost to the top. The second floor consists of a short hallway containing three doors, two on the left side, and one on the right. O'Connor said his residence was small, so I deduce his room is on the left. I'm not sure which room is Gunner's—I'll have to follow my gut.

"Why did you stop, Miss?"

I hadn't realized it, but I've halted at the top of the staircase, legs locked like an Olympic sprinter before the starter pistol fires. The doc is a few steps behind and below me. I gulp and make my move.

I lift one leg and twist, smacking O'Connor in the jaw with my heel. It's a solid hit, trembling all the way up my body and undoubtedly leaving quite the bruise on the doc's face. He doesn't cry out, instead falling backward down the stairs. I don't wait to see him tumble like a runaway boulder, I race up the remaining stairs and land on the second floor.

Which door to try?

The seconds tick by. Precious seconds. O'Connor will be back any moment, and he'll know

433

my mindset is less than compliant.

The lone door on the right. That one. I dart to it.

I barely realize I didn't hear O'Connor land at the bottom of the staircase. I didn't even hear him hit the ground. No thumping, no tumbling. Like he didn't touch the floor.

Go. Run.

I lunge for the door handle and scarcely manage to turn it before barreling into the bedroom.

It's arctic in here, instantly numbing my hands. And pitch black. I rub my hands together to generate some warmth, but I can't even see them through the inky shadows. The static buzzing intensifies.

A purple light emanates from across the room, and the sudden illumination stings my retinas. I squint and turn to leave, figuring this place to be a waste of my few remaining seconds.

The door slams shut, booming in the small, dark space. Like a tomb.

I grasp the doorknob and instantly recoil. It's searing hot, despite the frigid air.

I've had just about enough of Crawford.

Gritting my teeth, I look back at the violet glow, which is radiating from an easy chair sitting in the middle of the room. I crane my neck for a better look, but the high back of the chair is blocking my view.

Inch by inch, I orbit around the chair. The purple glow bathes the room in an alien shade, morphing a common bedroom into a scene from a dime store science fiction novel. The blacks are blacker, and all other colors—my dress, my skin, the floor—are a strange hue, from another world entirely. Now the buzzing noise is starting to make my eye twitch.

I finally circle around to the front of the chair. In its fold sits an old man, head bowed to his chest, dressed in corduroy trousers, a dusty old shirt, worn-out suspenders, and a moth-eaten tweed flat cap that hides his face. He is withered, bent like a tree that has withstood decades of torrential winds, and his clothing hangs on his thin frame. His hands lie on the armrests like the Lincoln Memorial, and he is just as statuesque, not moving, shifting, or even breathing. This must be Gunner, O'Connor's elderly flat-mate.

The purple light emits from his skin like an ethereal lantern. I can hardly believe my eyes, but as I stare and stare, it doesn't change. I clear my throat and do my best to sound confident as I say his name: "Gunner?" I don't succeed at the confident part.

His hands jolt as if I had awakened him from a deep slumber. Then, his head begins to rise. Slowly. Very slowly, a coffin's lid gradually creaking open.

I see his face. I stagger back and stifle my scream.

His skin is waxy and creased into an eternal scowl, revealing teeth as black as obsidian and stocky enough to crush the same. Wisps of lavender hair cling to his powerful jaw, waving in an invisible breeze.

His eyes rest upon me. Eyes filled with fog, a broiling storm staring right into my soul.

For years, I had wished that these specters would simply look at me.

I was wrong.

"What do you want?" His voice is rough and reedy, the voice of a tobacco addict. It thunders with absolute malice, shaking the entire Earth.

Although my heart hammers as if I'm already running, my feet don't budge. I am trapped in his purple glow, his misty gaze.

"How dare you…" he rasps, his boney hands pushing against the armrests. He begins to stand, stormy eyes never wavering from me. "You come in here, trying to drag me down *there*." Spite drips from the last word. "Did he send you in here? I'll betcha he did, that soulless hellhound."

He raises his arms, his odious glare strangling me. The violet light shifts with his movement like a cyclone, swirling around the room and shepherding us closer together without either of us taking a step.

"I'll never leave, ya hear? You'll have to lug my cold body outta this room. Despite what the slimy sonuvawhore downstairs says, I'm staying put."

He keeps drawing nearer, and despite his monstrous appearance, I'm spellbound. The light zips around us with a mind of its own.

I have no idea what he's talking about though, and I open my mouth to say as much. "I—"

"*No!*" The purple light explodes as he bellows, and the noise reverberates like we're in a cavern. His jaw elongates, the teeth gleaming like bullets. "*You know nothing*! Run back to that nocturnal demon in his white cloak and tell him," his feet leave the floor, and the violet glow turns into a supernova, "*I'LL NEVER LEAVE.*"

A bolt of lightning streaks across the room.

Finally, I scream. I run. I barge right through the door, charging down the stairs two at a time.

I'm back in the lobby, dim and gloomy now, the thick curtains drawn across the windows. My hair sticks to my skin with frantic sweat, my heart pounds in my chest like a piston, almost shattering my rib cage. O'Connor isn't in sight. I don't know where he is, but I don't care. I just need to run.

I trample the lush carpeting as I rush to the exit and grasp the handle. It won't turn. I whimper and lean all of my weight against the door. It's like beating my fists against a stone wall.

The windows! I grab the blood-red curtain with both hands and rip it down. I almost retch.

Where once there was an opening to the town of Crawford, there is now gray cinderblocks. The mortar is old and cracked, as though it had been there for decades.

I'm trapped.

My brain knows it is futile, but I punch the cinderblocks with all my might. Though I hear my bones crack against the solid brick, I feel no pain. I scream but hear nothing. I call—

The telephone!

It's worth a try. I'm desperate at this point, not thinking logically. I spin and run back into the cold, austere morgue.

The drawers and lamps glower at me, surprised to see me back so soon. The checkerboard tiles distort my vision, twisting and turning; I'm tumbling down Alice's rabbit hole.

The phone, Ramona. Get the phone.

But it's not there anymore. The metal table

where it once sat now holds a yellowed newspaper, its corners curling like a beckoning finger.

My heart slows, along with my breathing, curiosity mixing with my fear.

From across the room, I see a monochrome photo of a girl on the front page. A woman, really. I know who it is, but I deny it. Even as I shuffle closer, I refuse to see what is directly before me.

The hair, the build, the face shape and expression.

It's me. Beside the headline,

"Woman killed in collision."

"Ramona." The deep, silky, rumbling voice of God. Behind me. Soft and tender. Like a father breaking bad news to his daughter.

I look at him. The eyeglasses. The frizzy hair. The white coat and ill-fitting slacks. I can describe him down to the minutest detail, yet I know nothing about who this man is.

In his hands, he holds a file, gently, like it might crumble in the air like a dandelion. He opens it and reads:

"Ramona Price. Twenty-one years old, born October 12, 1934."

He practically whispers, forcing me to lean forward, to listen. It's as if he's opening my hand, giving me the words, and closing it up again.

I know what he's going to say next, but it still slaps me.

"Died July 2, 1955. Head-on automobile collision in Oklahoma City. Driving a dirt-brown 1935 Ford Coupe."

He lowers his eyes, almost ashamed, truly disheartened to be the one telling me this, and closes the file.

I take a ragged breath. "I'm dead." I realize it's not a question.

"I'm sorry, Ramona. It's…" O'Connor struggles to word the next sentence in his head. "Miss, it's not 1955. Today is August 28, 2017."

"I…" When my knees begin to shake, I quickly still them. I refuse to show my fear. "*I'm* the specter."

O'Connor nods sadly. "The beings you see walking around you, the ghosts wearing clothing and jewelry you find strange, these specters that straddle their world and yours…these are real. *They* live in the physical world. They are people going about their lives, oblivious to your presence. For the most part."

The man in the street earlier today. The one who had blanched and yelled, "Stay away!" He'd seen me. He'd thought I was a ghost. A specter.

Which I am.

I look at O'Connor, straight into his emerald eyes. "You. Are you…?" I can't even say it. It's too ridiculous, childish, insane. I gesture to the drawers.

The doc chuckles lightly. "I may not have a black robe or a scythe, but yeah. That's me." His dark humor disappears. "I'm sorry, Miss. I really am."

"What am I doing here?" I murmur, suddenly exhausted. So, so exhausted.

"When a human dies and doesn't accept it, they're left behind. Trapped halfway between realms. Doomed to walk the night, confined to fast in fires. When they realize the truth, they can move on. Upgrade to the king's suite, if you will. I do what I can to help the lost find their way."

The electric lights sputter in their iron cages. Otherwise, it's silent.

He resumes. "The old woman here in the morgue, Gunner upstairs…they've been here for decades. As I said earlier, not accepting death leads to an existence of fear and bitterness. In their ghostly forms, these negative emotions distorted them, transformed them into the beasts you encountered. I thought, maybe, seeing them might persuade you."

"Persuade me?" I freeze. I see where this is going.

"Don't be like them, Ramona. Angry, resentful, fearful. Please…"

I wipe a hand across my eyes.

2017…My family is dead. My friends are gone. I couldn't even find them if I wanted to—no one can see me. If they do, they see a spirit, something to be feared.

My head feels as if it's rapidly emptying. I clench my temples between my palms.

I hear a scraping sound. Metal on metal. O'Connor has pulled out an empty drawer from the wall. He stands next to it, hands clamped before him. Dutiful, but with kind eyes. He glances at the

steel slab, then back to me.
"Ready, Miss Price?"

About the Author

Luke Swanson was born and raised in Yukon, Oklahoma. He loves nothing more than a good story. He currently attends Oklahoma Christian University, studying English writing, history, and international studies. *The Ten*, his debut novel, combines elements of mystery, thriller, and comedy.

The First of Thirteen

By Sara Schoen

Prologue

I started to come to, but it wasn't fast enough. I could feel panic building in my chest as my breathing starting picking up to the point of hyperventilation. The darkness slowly lifted from my vision, crawling away from the center and eventually to the outer edges until I could see again. As the darkness cleared, I tried to remember what happened. I remembered talking to Steve, a peer from Psychology class, about the final exam we had just finished. We had studied together on occasion, though I had never suspected him of anything other than friendly flirting. However, when I left and started toward home, I knew he was following me. I tried to brush it off, thinking that he was going to get food or heading to his car. He wasn't following me. I was just being paranoid, at least I thought I was, until he grabbed me.

I tried to fight. I struggled, attempting to summon the self-defense training I had learned only a few months earlier. I couldn't recollect any of the training. I guess fear really can make your mind go blank. I remember the sheer panic, my body tightening and freezing as I tried to scream, but no sound came out. I could still feel his hands coming past my neck from behind and the pressure as he held a cloth tightly over my mouth. The strong acetone scent burned my nostrils before my vision faded to black. I recall looking up as I fell back, staring into his eyes, cold, calculating, and unfeeling as he whispered something unintelligible to me.

I had been kidnapped right off my college campus. Had anyone seen it happen? Did anyone know I was gone? Would they even look for me when I didn't show up to graduation in a few days?

I tried not to think about it as I went to move, discovering my arms and legs were immobile. I glanced down to see that I was tied down, my wrists and ankles bound tightly to the wooden chair beneath me. Each attempt to escape only made the binds tighter. I looked over the empty house, devoid of photos or furniture, and I knew I had to get out. A kidnapping days before I was set to move out of state, no one to look for me, and the windows I could see from my seat were boarded shut. Nothing good could come from this. I had to escape.

"Good," a voice called from another room. "Glad to see you're awake."

A chill raced through me; my body froze as I searched for who spoke to me. I couldn't tell where the voice had originated from because it seemed to bounce off the walls and reverberate through the whole house. It sounded as if it was trapped in the building as I was, unable to escape the confines of the walls and forced to remain here against its natural desires to echo into the world.

A shadow emerged from the hallway. The tall figure remained cloaked by the darkness until he stepped into the room, allowing Steve to slowly reveal himself in a grand gesture seemingly what he wanted judging from the smile on his lips. First his dark washed jeans, which had holes in them, then up to his medium build chest and muscular arms, until his square jaw and jet black hair came into the light. The smile gracing his features made my stomach churn. Something was very wrong. What did he want from me?

"Steve, what am I doing here?"

"I've been following you for a while now, Kelly. To put it simply, I saw you at the start of this semester and decided in that moment I had to have you for myself. You're here because I want you to be, and you'll stay for the same reason."

I wanted to ask more, and I couldn't bring myself to force the words out. I feared his answers and the repercussions they would bring if I dared to ask what I was thinking. I wanted to know the extent he had been following me and how far he'd taken it, what he meant by wanting me here, and how long I'd be staying. I shuddered at the thought. I already knew those answers, and each of them made me wish I was dead instead.

"I visited you almost every night," he explained as he approached me. His soft smile convinced me that he didn't think what he had done was wrong. Then the smirk returned as I struggled against the binds, and I knew he didn't regret it. "I know you felt me there. You knew I was there and welcomed me."

I thought over all the strange occurrences over the last few weeks. Suddenly they all made sense. I thought I had been going insane, that I was the one leaving windows open, feeding the cat and then forgetting, leaving the door unlocked, even leaving the water running in the kitchen sink. I thought it had been me, when really he was making himself at home in my apartment. I shuddered as I recalled the dark voice which had haunted my dreams. He would talk to me at night. I'd hoped I had dreamed it, but the more he spoke, the more I knew he had been with me at night. Every night.

"You're so pretty," he whispered, lightly stroking my cheek. Exactly as he had done almost every night for the past month. I had been stupid enough to believe it was all nightmares. I should have listened to my instincts while I had the chance. Perhaps then I wouldn't be here now. What could I have done? He had been visiting me at night and never made himself known. The police wouldn't have believed me, no one would have, and I would've ended up here anyway. However, if I had said something, at least someone would know I was missing.

A tear slipped down my cheek. Now no one would know what happened to me. They'd think I simply left town. Maybe they wouldn't even look for me. I should have said something to someone, anyone, simply so someone knew. I couldn't shake the feeling of being watched when I was heading to classes, coming home, or running errands. It hadn't escalated further than that. I was constantly looking over my shoulder, looking for someone who wasn't even there. No matter what I did, I couldn't shake the feeling. Maybe that was because he was never far from me.

"I'd come to your apartment while you were gone, live in your home, be with your cat, and smell your clothes to feel close to you. I always made sure to leave everything as it was when I came. Sometimes, though, you would show up unexpectedly. More than once you almost walked in on me. I would hide in closets, under your bed, and at times behind the shower curtain. You never knew I was there, no matter how often you searched for me. And I know you tried. You could feel me there, couldn't you?"

I shuddered at his words. How many times had he been with me? Had he stayed while I thought I was alone?

"I'd wait for you to fall asleep. I'd steal a glance, maybe a quick touch, and leave the moment I had a chance." As if to prove a point, he produced a crumpled photo, worn from folding and refolding before being roughly shoved into a pocket, from his back pocket. He turned the picture to me, revealing me curled up under the covers, unaware he was there. "You look so beautiful when you sleep. I wasn't ready for you to know I was there, and I had more to do before I could make you accept your fate."

"What's my fate?" The words left my mouth against my best judgment. I couldn't hold back my curiosity. Why me? Why now? He had lived behind the scenes, lurking in the shadows and waiting for the right moment for me. Why? What made him want me? I wasn't anything special. Why couldn't he let me graduate and live the life I had planned?

"You know, the photos do you no justice." He fingers lightly grazed my cheek again before he caressed my face in his hands. He slowly lifted my head to force me to look at him. I could see his emotions in his eyes, pleasure and lust. "You have a natural beauty that can't be captured correctly on film. No, in person is so much better. I never enjoyed the photos I took of you, yet I kept them, saved them for when I needed them." His gaze drifted over my body at an agonizingly slow pace that made it obvious what he wanted from me. I held back the bile that threatened to come up. "Soon I won't need them anymore. Now that I have the real thing, that is."

He leaned down and roughly took my hair in his hand, forcing me to kiss him. His kiss was sloppy, wet, and messy, similar to how I imagine kissing a dog would be. I wanted to pull away, to escape and never be in his hold again. The way he held me as I fought against his grasp told me I'd never get away from him. I had my chance before he took me, I could have stopped this, and now I never would be able to escape him. He pulled away slowly, lingering too closely for my comfort.

"What's my fate?" I asked again. The question lingered over me like a dark cloud. Steve refused to explain anything other than his stalking. I wanted to know why he picked me and what he planned to do with me. I'd have to wait. I couldn't take all the answers at once. I'd crumble and suffer from whatever he said.

"To stay here with me, forever. All those thoughts about your future that you've been worrying about are gone now."

"What about school? Classes? My family? Steve, this is ridiculous. Let me go and we can pretend this didn't happen. I won't tell anyone; no one has to know. Let me go now and we can forget all about this."

Despite knowing those words never helped anyone escape, whether in movies or real life cases, it was the only thing that came to mind. I knew that there was a slim chance he'd let me go. I'd have to find another way to escape once he turned his back or left me alone. I'd figure something out.

"Kelly, your parents died when you were seventeen. You talked about it in class, and from what I remember you are an only child. There's no family to worry about you. We just finished classes, and it will look as if you chose not to walk at graduation. By the time anyone knows you're missing, it will be too late. Any trail to you will be long gone. I'll go back to your apartment and collect a few of your things. Other than that it's done. Trust me, I've been thinking long and hard about this. It's perfect."

My jaw fell open. He had planned it all. He knew no one would miss me, no one would look for me, and he knew when no one would notice I was gone until it was too late. My lease wouldn't end for another three months, and if no one noticed I was gone before then, what hope did I have? I didn't have a family or roommates, only my cat who had been with me since the start of college. She was all I had, and now I felt like I had nothing. I had let too much of my past show through to him, and he took advantage. That's why he chose me; I was the perfect target. The only one that made sense.

"I'm glad I don't have to sneak around anymore to be with you. You have no idea how long I've waited for this. Welcome home, Kelly."

He leaned in and planted a kiss on my cheek, as if sealing my fate with a kiss.

Chapter One

Three Years After the Kidnapping

My story isn't unlike so many others who had been taken. I've heard about girls being taken on the news, seen it in movies and on television for years prior to my kidnapping. It had been shown so often it had started to become normal. It's true. Everyone had gradually become desensitized to the horror of kidnapping and what typically came with it. Even though girls and guys were taken, sometimes for the same sick reasons, no one will talk about it unless it's on a popular show, and even then it's merely entertainment. We never want it to happen to ourselves or anyone we know, but we never talk about it. What happens if we are taken? What do we do? It's not something the movies really prepare you for.

I'm coming to realize that the short answer is, do whatever you have to in order to survive. At first you're in shock, complete disbelief. Eventually you'll have to come to terms with it and start living through it.

It will be hard, damn near impossible at times. Trust me, I know. Steve had moved some of my stuff into the house, including my cat, who refused to leave her carrier for days because she was so terrified. I couldn't blame her. I wished she would have come to comfort me as she did after a long day of classes.

A single tear trailed down my cheek as I thought of my old life, what had been and could have been. There were so many things I could have done differently. If I wasn't so nice to everyone, a little more guarded and aware of my surroundings, maybe I would have seen the signs. It had started innocently enough. Steve and I were study partners for our class. Although I knew he had an interest in me, I didn't reciprocate.

I hadn't been careful. Even if I thought we were friends, I should have guarded myself more. He had come to my apartment, learned I lived alone, knew my class schedule, and followed me everywhere. I had walked right into it. Another tear slipped out, and I quickly wiped it away, along with my thoughts of self-pity. It wasn't my fault. I shouldn't have needed to think about what could happen; he shouldn't have taken me. Though I *should* have been more aware. Maybe then I could have saved myself. Was there ever a way to know for sure? No, I could have simply been more careful, been around other people instead of alone with him.

Now look at me.

I glanced up at the mirror in my room. *Our* room, I mentally corrected myself with disgust. My once blonde hair was dirty, my face was grimy and bruised, and I had lost a lot of weight from lack of food—his punishment for me attempting to escape. I used to have my own room, a concrete box with nothing except a bed and a closet. I was moved in here a few months after my capture. This room had a nice bed, carpet, photos on the wall, and an en suite bathroom. I never had to leave if I didn't want to. If I could lock him out of it then it would be perfect.

It must have been the escape attempt that finally broke him from trusting me. Though which one was the question. I had tried to escape multiple times; each time he'd seal off the exit I had chosen to prevent another attempt and meted out the punishment he thought I deserved, one of which included killing my cat for disobeying him. I had to get out and wanted to go back to my life, even if no one was waiting for me.

I've been in this house for years, maybe a decade. It's impossible to really know since I rarely go outside or see anything with a date on it. He didn't bring newspapers back to the house anymore after work. The last paper I had seen with a date had been a few months after my initial capture. He had only brought it home to taunt me. There was a brief article asking for any information on my whereabouts, but there wasn't a missing flyer or anything. It really looked as if I had vanished into thin air.

That's when I tried to escape again, and when he caught me he shackled me in my old room until he broke me so I wouldn't try to run again. He had taunted me with his stories of how he would watch me and what he wanted to do to me after the first escape attempt. It made me sick. Then after trying a few more times, he let the fantasies come to life.

I had hoped it had all been talk to scare me, and I learned quickly it wasn't. He wanted a good wife, one who followed his rules, his every order, and never tried to run away. He got that eventually. I did what I had to in order to stay alive.

To keep us alive, I thought as my hand instinctively fell to my once swollen stomach, which had now gone back to normal after the miscarriage. He had told me he wanted a family, and he had finally gotten it after a few attempts. I couldn't fight him anymore. It kept me alive, and at this point I'd do whatever it took to survive. Not only for myself, but I would have done it for my son, Noah.

He hadn't asked for this. Neither did I, and look how that turned out.

I shut my eyes, shielding myself from my image. I could barely look at myself without feeling disgusted. While I did what I needed to in order to survive, I still felt disgusted with myself for being used. I swallowed to suppress the urge to throw up as I thought about all the things I had done for him just to live a little longer. They all made me want to crawl in a hole to die.

The rules were easy enough to follow. In fact,

there weren't that many, only one. The unspoken rule of "do what I say, or else."

I sighed, forcing myself to look back in the mirror. The bruises couldn't be ignored, and maybe that's why he didn't let me out of the house. I hoped once I could do what he wanted without screwing up and the beatings would stop. He was always careful not to harm the baby. Until I tried to escape again.

He had gone to work. I was about six months pregnant, and I knew I couldn't let the baby be born into this life. Poor Noah. What would his life have been like growing up here? I had to do something, and the only thing I could do was run. I didn't make it far enough.

I barely made it two miles down the road before a police car stopped me. I thought he would help me. Officer Rivers, how could I have trusted you?

My gaze fell back on the mirror. The reflection of my glare was heated with anger. I had always been told to believe police could help me, but the cops around here were no good. They seemed to know what was going on and would fake it for those around them, and they let it happen. I'm not sure whether Steve paid them off or not, but all Officer Rivers did was take me right back to Steve, and he had been furious.

I had done everything he said to keep Noah safe, and I still failed him in the end.

Steve had taken me back to my old room and let me suffer. He beat me until I bled and then he left me alone. When the pain started, I knew something had gone wrong with Noah. My stomach had been in so much agony, the pressure and constant shooting pains made it impossible to remain silent, and when I caught sight of the blood between my legs I called for the only person who could help. Steve.

At first, he seemed reluctant. He thought I was upset because of the beating. Once I told him something happened to Noah, he raced up the stairs. There was nothing we could have done, despite my pleas for him to somehow save Noah. Steve refused to take me to the hospital and eventually I lost the baby, along with a lot of blood. I had hoped it would kill me, free me and my son once and for all, but it didn't. Steve had brought in a friend of his to check on me, and together they kept me alive. Here I was, trapped, with no way out, waiting for Steve to give me another child who he'd eventually kill when I tried to escape to save my child and myself. I wouldn't stop trying to escape, especially when it wasn't only for me, but also for something so innocent. I didn't want a child to be raised in this environment. I couldn't let it happen.

He had tried to get me pregnant again and thus far had failed. He even had the same doctor friend who had been there after the miscarriage come check me over. He believed I could no longer bear children, and I hoped he was right. No child deserved this life.

"Kelly, I'm home!" Steve called. "Come here, I have a surprise for you!"

I got up without a word, displeased to have him back and unenthusiastic to see what he had with him. With my luck, it would be his cop friend again.

This time payment would be me instead of money. I walked away from the mirror, away from my thoughts and shame as best as I could. When I approached my captor, the guilt returned in full force as I laid eyes on a blond boy no older than two years old in Steve's arms.

"Who is this?" I questioned, unable to take my eyes off the child he was carrying. "What did you do?"

"This is Garrett. He's ours now. That's all you need to know."

Chapter Two

Seven Years After The Kidnapping

Garrett ended up being everything I wanted in a child. I had spent years with him, watching him grow into a playful six-year-old boy, and he almost made living with Steve tolerable. I got to see him grow up as I never got the chance with Noah. His loss still pained me even years later. I tried not to think about it or the depression would set back in. Garrett needed me; I couldn't let it consume me again as I had before he arrived all those years ago. I didn't want him to worry any more than he did. It was my job to protect him, and I needed a clear head for that.

As Garrett grew up, I started lying about my life. Our life. I did it to protect him…or so I told myself. In the end, I was only protecting myself, but when he asked me at the tender age of six how I met his "father," I couldn't bring myself to tell him the truth. I shook the flashbacks of the day Steve kidnapped me and the years of horror I had lived through since.

"Mommy, Mommy!"

"Yes, Garrett?" I loved Garrett, and Steve knew it. He used Garrett as leverage, and I obeyed without hesitation. I couldn't be responsible for his death as I had been for Noah's. I did everything I could for Garrett, and I would continue to until my dying breath, no matter what it took to protect him.

These days Steve let me outside under his supervision with Garrett close to his side to make sure I didn't try to escape again. I knew it was the small freedoms that would save Garrett and me one day. If I could keep Garrett under control, then we had a real chance to escape and move forward with our *real* lives.

"You never answered how you and Daddy met."

I prayed he never found out the truth; it would tear him apart. At least if I lied, he could grow up with some resemblance of a childhood.

"Well, sweetheart," I said, noticing Steve watching me, "your father and I…" I paused; this would be the last chance to turn back. Tell the truth or lie. "…we were high school sweethearts. We met our first year and knew right away we'd be together forever."

Literally until death took one of us away, most likely me.

"Then a few years later, we got you." Not a lie, though not the whole truth either.

"Where did I come from?" Garrett's eyes sparkled with intense curiosity.

"New Jersey," Steve replied coolly from the kitchen table.

I shot him a glare and turned back to Garrett, whose curiosity had been replaced with confusion thanks to Steve's comment. I couldn't think of anything to say except, "Your father found out about you while he was in New Jersey." *After he stole you from your real parents and brought you here to live with us in permanent hell,* I added silently to myself. "You were a surprise to me especially."

"A good surprise?"

I hesitated. I knew the real reason Steve had brought Garrett back with him was because of me. He did it because I had been devastated over losing Noah because of *him.* He killed our child and feared I'd do something drastic if he didn't do something quickly. Garrett was simply a pawn in Steve's game to keep me in line. Otherwise I'd either run again or try to kill myself in order to escape. Anything was better than living here with him. Garrett wouldn't understand that, not yet anyway, and I couldn't explain even if I tried.

"Yes, you were a very good surprise. I'm happy to have you here with me."

Garrett smiled and hugged me around my legs. The familiar feeling of love and appreciation for him swelled in my chest. He loved us as if we were his parents, not that he knew any better. Steve had taken him away at such a young age that he had no hope of remembering his real parents. Soon it would be too hard for him to return to his real family unless I found a way to get us out. He'd be too attached to me; it would hurt him to have me leave alone. I also couldn't bring myself to leave him; he couldn't grow up here. He'd live like an animal in captivity, beaten and tormented for the enjoyment of his captor.

I couldn't risk running yet, though. I wanted to take him with me when we escaped, and for that I needed him to understand if we were caught he had to go on without me. I needed to know that he would follow my orders and run without me, but he wouldn't understand until he was older, when I could really sit him down and explain what happened, where he actually came from, why I lied to him while he grew up, and what had to be done for us to escape. I knew his family, at least their name and where they were from. The Thomas' would look for him. If I was his actual mother I would never *stop* looking for him. I hoped they could wait a few more years. For now, playing into Steve's desires kept us safe; I couldn't break from them without punishment. I had waited this long to try escaping again. I could wait until Garrett could come with me.

At least I hoped I could. There was no telling what Steve was truly capable of, especially when he was angry.

Garrett raced upstairs to play with his toys. I had been so distracted by my own thoughts that I hadn't even heard Steve tell him to leave us. My stomach clenched and turned to knots when Steve rose from his seat. My heartbeat raced as his footsteps came closer to me. These were the moments I dreaded most, the fleeting minutes which felt like days when I was alone with him.

"That was a nice story you told, Kelly. I honestly almost bought it myself." His hot breath attacked the back of my neck before his hands grabbed onto my waist. "You have such a way with words. They slip through your lips so easily and smoothly, even a lie to our beloved son."

"I had to tell him something." My voice cracked dryly as my throat contracted in protest. I shouldn't have to explain myself to him, but coming in a better light would only help me in the long run, despite my desire to tell him to fuck off.

"Yes, and the truth is dangerous. You were right to say what you did. I don't want him telling others the real story, would you?" His grip tightened around my waist. I knew the threat well and gave him the answer I knew he'd want.

"No, we wouldn't want anyone to find out and break us apart," I said emotionlessly. The words were tasteless on my tongue except for the hint of venom lacing the edge.

"Good," he cooed, brushing my hair to one side of my neck. "I'm glad we agree on something. If you keep behaving this well, we can try another trip outside with some of my friends."

I forced down the bile rising in my throat. His *friends* were just as disgusting as him. They knew he had taken Garrett and me, and none of them did anything. The cops turned a blind eye; the others laughed in my face and told me if I ever escaped from Steve they'd find me and do worse.

"I don't want to take Garrett on those trips until he's older. He can't do much, and going to the lake is dangerous because he can't swim. Let's at least wait until he's older to take us out with your friends again. We can just go outside in the forest and play together. Like last week."

Steve had taken us to a park, unfortunately with one of his friends to keep me in line, but Garrett was safer out with me. When Steve's other friends came, they would try to pull me away from Garrett, and I feared the worst if they got a hold of him. Steve took him sometimes, and I would be left alone with his friend of choice. Although what they did to me was never pleasant, it wasn't worse than what Steve had done to me. Even when we were forced to take a photo as a "family," I couldn't even manage to fake a smile anymore.

"We will see. He has to behave, and only when I think he's ready will we do anything. I have to make sure he knows the rules and follows them as you do." His hand trailed lightly up my torso. Another threat if I didn't behave.

I was about to respond when something dropped from upstairs and Garrett cried out in pain. Steve pulled away from me, and we both ran upstairs, Steve wondering what broke while I feared for Garrett's safety.

We found that he had broken one of Steve's glass awards from his job a few years ago, back when I knew what he did for a living. These days he kept everything that occurred outside of the house separate from me. It seemed that he was living two separate lives after he brought Garrett home. He must not have wanted anyone to ask questions.

"That little shit." Steve leaned down to collect the pieces of glass, cursing Garrett to Hell and back.

I picked up Garrett, who had started crying, which only turned Steve's anger toward me.

"Put him down. He has to be taught a lesson!"

"You can't hit him, Steve! He's only a little boy. He did it by accident; he's a *child*. I told you when we moved his toys in here that you should move all of those out of the way. He could have gotten seriously hurt!" I knew Steve wouldn't take him to a hospital, and if I lost Garrett I wouldn't be far behind. I wouldn't live here without him.

"He broke it. He has to be punished. Now put him down!" His eyes grew wider with the command. His posture turned rigid, and his hands balled into tight fists. I knew what was coming next, and I refused to let him harm Garrett.

"Punish me. I should have raised him better; it's my fault. Don't hurt him because of something I did. That's not the kind of punishment you deal out. Do it to me so I raise him better."

Suddenly I understood motherly instinct, willing to put Garrett's well-being before my own. Dangerous and stupid, but my need to protect him overruled every other emotion.

"If that's how you want it, Kelly." His voice turned dark and ravenous. "Put him in his room and come receive your punishment."

I raced to put Garrett in his room. I told him he would be safe, that I would protect him, and as he cried I felt my heart torn in two. He asked what his supposed father was going to do to him and me, and all I could tell him was, "He won't do anything to you while I'm alive. I'll keep you safe."

Without another word, I sealed Garrett in his room and went to receive the full punishment. Anything to protect him.

Chapter Three

I could barely move, and even when I had to I didn't want to. Everything hurt, my legs especially. Each subtle movement sparked a sweeping pain throughout my body, first emanating from the beating I had taken. Steve had landed a few well-placed blows to destroy any resolve I had to take his beating proudly for protecting Garrett. I had crumpled to the floor by the second blow, directly in the gut, when the air left my lungs and I struggled to take in a full breath. Tears stained my face through his repeated blows, alternating between kicking and forcing me to stand so he could knock me down again.

The scene played out for what felt like hours, though maybe only lasted at most an hour. He had dragged me to our bedroom when I begged him to stop. I told him I didn't want Garrett to hear, I didn't want him to worry about his parents fighting,

466

and thankfully Steve had agreed, although when Steve agreed with me there was always a darker reason for it. I shuddered at the memories flashing behind my closed eyelids. I wanted to forget and somehow move on, but that wasn't possible. In the end, Steve got what he wanted again. He always did. No matter how hard I fought, he always won.

I could see every disturbing detail of the attack and the ones before it. This wasn't how my life was supposed to be. This wasn't what I planned, and now I was barely surviving. Even that small flicker of desire to live was slowly diminishing. It only continued because of Garrett.

I sighed. Poor Garrett. What would his life become here? Did he understand what was happening? Was he old enough to understand, to run, and somehow survive? After Steve threatening him, I couldn't hide the truth from him anymore. He had to know what happened and why, even if I had to explain how we both got here. Could I ruin the innocence of a young boy only to open his eyes to the horrors around him? Soon he'd be punished because Steve wouldn't get his fill merely from beating me. He hadn't gotten that since the first few years of Garrett being here, and soon him taking advantage of me wouldn't satiate his anger.

This couldn't backlash onto Garrett. I had to do something, even if it meant telling him the truth and tearing myself apart once more to explain Noah and why Garrett had been taken from his parents. I prayed I could be strong enough to tell him the whole truth.

I willed myself out of bed. I hadn't moved since

Steve finished with me last night. When he got up this morning he brought me breakfast, which I hadn't eaten, and told me to take it easy. That's how it always was with him, furious one day and acting like a caring husband the next. It made me sick and let my hatred fester. One day I'd make him pay. I'd see him rot and then burn in Hell if I had my say. When my feet touched the hardwood floor, a chill raced through me, quickly followed by a searing pain when I started to walk. I fought through the pain in my legs as best as I could, though my breathing quickly became erratic. I wasn't in any shape to move around, and while in pain, I didn't feel as though anything had broken. I simply didn't have the strength to move through the empty house.

Garrett had remained locked in his room after Steve took him breakfast this morning. He told me if I felt up to it I could go see our son, but he told Garrett not to come downstairs. With each step, my body threatened to give out. I fell to the steps to rest for a moment when I heard Garrett call down to me. He sounded as if he was in the main room playing with his toys. At least he stayed upstairs. Thank the Lord. I don't think I could have made it all the way up like this.

"Garrett, sweetheart, you can come down. I need to talk to you."

I heard the patter of his bare feet race toward me and down the stairs.

"Are you okay, Mommy?" His eyes held so much sorrow for his age. He had seen so much but thankfully dealt with none of it personally, and if I got my way I'd keep it like that.

"I'm fine. I'm just tired." I stroked his hair gently. "I have to talk to you about your father."

"What about him?"

"Well, you saw that he gets angry, right?" He nodded. "You have to be very careful not to upset him. I don't want you getting in trouble with him."

"Is that why you yelled?"

"Yes. I told him you didn't do anything wrong, so we had a small argument." I could see guilt overwhelm him, and I felt terrible. I didn't want to tell him, but I had to. "Well, you know how I told you that your father and I met in high school?"

"Yes."

I took a deep breath, trying to gain control over waves of emotion crashing over me. Tears pricked in my eyes, threatening to spill over. "Well, Garrett, I have to tell you the truth so—"

I heard a car door slam and cursing emanate from outside and panicked; Steve was home early and that was never a good sign. I couldn't make out what he was cursing about, but I knew he'd be furious when he came in.

"We have a secret hiding spot I found a few years ago, and we are going to play hide and seek from your dad, okay?" I said urgently. "He came home early to play with us. Come with me." I took his hand and then kissed him lightly on the cheek as I led the way.

"What's the hiding spot?" he asked skeptically as the stairs creaked beneath our combined weight.

"It's one I found and made for you," I explained, fighting through my pain and leading him to the wall.

He watched me pry at the edge of the wooden slat to reveal the hiding spot.

"It's right here. I have a blanket in there for you and some snacks in case I can't come get you right away. Remember, we are hiding from Daddy. Don't let him find you no matter what, okay? I'll come get you. I promise." I lifted him in the hole, barely big enough to fit him. I had found a large hollow part of the wall in my escape attempts. It had a beam for him to rest on, and I had prepared it while Steve was out. We hadn't used it before because Steve had been around and I didn't want him to know where it was so it could keep Garrett safe.

Garrett grinned. "Okay, Mommy!"

"I'll come get you really soon. Until then you stay quiet and be brave." I kissed him one last time before sealing the paneling back into place and covering his hiding spot. "I love you, Garrett," I whispered softly right before Steve walked in. He had pushed the door with such force it slammed against the wall behind it, echoing through the house.

It didn't take long for him to notice me standing, nor did I miss the intense anger in his eyes when he saw me.

"What are you doing out of bed? I told you to take it easy!"

"What happened, honey? Did something happen at work?" I asked, ignoring his comments.

"Well, since you asked, I got fired, so I'll be around the house for a few days. Apparently to teach you to listen to me." His voice turned dark and menacing. He glared at me, a mix of anger and lust entering his eyes before he flicked his gaze toward the stairs where Garrett should be.

"Where's Garrett? I don't hear him."

"I don't know. We were playing hide-and-seek before you came in. He's been told not to make a noise so I can look for him."

Fury took over his features completely. "Find him before I come back inside and have him upstairs in his room. We need to talk about you disobeying me, and I need a distraction from my day."

He walked out to get something from the car. *We have to run*, I thought as I watched him from the window. He was punishing me more often, and it was only a matter of time before it turned to Garrett. I had to try and save him.

Chapter Four

I grew to hate having Steve around all the time. I thought it was bad when he came home from work, but when he was around all day I lived in a place worse than Hell. I didn't know that was even possible. Each day was worse than the last. Garrett hadn't been allowed downstairs in almost two weeks because Steve wanted us to be alone so I could be his distraction; however, the whole time I was waiting for him to leave, just for a few minutes. I had a plan, and while it wasn't perfect, it was better than this.

I knew to escape I had to leave Garrett behind. Steve used him to force me to obey his rules; Steve only wanted me. He didn't want Garrett. For Garrett to live, I had to sacrifice myself or risk killing us both. The best thing I could do to save him was to sacrifice myself and give him the chance to escape. I'd escape through the loose window in the basement and slip out without being seen. Steve would look around for me, but hopefully by that time I would be long gone. He'd leave Garrett here, and then Garrett could escape and make it somewhere safe, with a note I had written out explaining the situation to whoever found him. I knew if I was found I'd be dragged right back here, dead or alive, and I needed Garrett to escape. Thankfully, one of Steve's friends had managed to get him an interview for a new job. He left early that morning, and I prayed I would never see him again.

"Garrett, can you come downstairs?" I called up. I had been thinking about it long and hard and still wasn't sure how to tell him what I was about to do. Although I wanted to take him with me, I couldn't. I had a better chance of delaying Steve than actually escaping, and that would give Garrett plenty of time to escape. It killed me on the inside to leave him here alone, but at the same time he'd have a better chance of living if he didn't come with me. While I may never be able to see him again, at least one of us would be out of this hell and live to tell the tale.

"Yes, Mommy?"

"We have to go, Garrett. We can't stay here anymore. I'm leaving, and I need you to be a big boy." I knelt down, getting as close to his level as possible. We didn't have time to waste, and if I tried to ease him into this I would lose my nerve to tell him everything.

"Where are we going?"

"Away from here. Hopefully far away where we will be safe. You have to listen to me very carefully.

We can't go together." His eyes grew wide in horror. He was too young to understand. No six year old should have to go through any of this, but this was how it had to be. If I took him with me, we'd both be caught because he'd refuse to leave me. He had to be strong enough to leave and I'd sacrifice myself to let him live. I'd rather just me die than also kill him. "I'm going to leave and your father will follow after me. When he's gone, you run and find someone to give this note to." I placed the note in his delicate hand and forced his fingers closed around the note. "Find anyone except the police officers you see here. Tell them what happened and you'll be safe." Tears welled in my eyes. Sacrificing myself was for the best if it meant I could save him from a life with Steve.

"What about you, Mommy?"

"I'm going to slip out and distract him. I'll make sure you have time to escape and make it somewhere safe."

"But why not come with me?"

"Garrett, you have to understand that this isn't your real life. You have to escape. You have to survive. In order to do that, you have to run and leave me behind. I'm going to save you one way or another. So please listen to me and be ready to run far away from here."

"Why are we leaving?"

"We have to, honey. I don't have time to explain everything to you. I have to go before Steve shows up, and you have to be ready to run! Be brave and strong. You'll survive this. I love you." I gave him one last kiss on his cheek and a tight hug, letting a few tears slip over my eyelids before pulling away. "I have to go. I'm sorry I can't explain more. Once Steve leaves, run and don't look back. Just keep running."

He nodded as if he understood. Did he really understand, or did he think I was abandoning him? I couldn't think about that. I had to go. The more distance I put between me and this house, the further Steve would have to go to find me and the more time Garrett had to run.

I raced down to the basement and leapt onto the chair I had placed down there. The window opened easily, and I slid through the tight spot after a little squirming. My hands rested on the grass as I forced myself out of the hole and into the sunlight. My body slowly slid onto the dirt, and I was free. Wasting no time, I jumped up and started running. I knew the general area of town, and if I ran I could make it there in a little under a day if I got lost, which was bound to happen at least once. I didn't have an internal compass and wound up lost all the time growing up.

Racing into the trees, I heard tires crunching on the gravel driveway signaling Steve was home. He'd see I was gone in no time. I thought I had more time. I thought I could get further and buy Garrett more time.

Please run, Garrett.

I sprinted through the trees, hoping my high school track speed would come back and get me far enough away from the house before Steve could come after me. Every tree looked exactly the same. There were no landmarks for me to remember, branches and leaf clutter cut at my legs, and the sun soon began to set. I didn't make it far before Steve's voice called out to me, bouncing off the trees. I couldn't clearly make out what he said, but the anger rang through loud and clear.

I silently prayed Garrett was strong enough to make a run for it. Steve should only be interested in getting me back; I had always been his target, and Garrett could escape and live a real life.

I love you, Garrett. Please remember that.

I made it to a clearing. I spun around in an attempt to get my bearings. Nothing looked familiar. I couldn't figure out which way to go, and Steve's voice was inching closer and closer to me the more time I wasted. I spun once more before taking a leap of faith and jumped back into the woods. I knew I was heading away from the house, but I'd either go away from town or toward town. At this point it was up to luck which I had chosen.

"Kelly, I know you're out here."

Fear rushed through my veins at the sound of his voice. How did he catch up to me so quickly? I should have had more of a head start. I pushed harder, moving as far away from Steve as I could. He knew these woods well; he had hunted, played with Garrett, and explored them. I knew he'd find me; however, I didn't think it would be this fast. On the bright side, it gave me hope he had left Garrett alone. He wouldn't have had time to interrogate Garrett, tie him up in the house, and catch up to me. For now, Garrett was safe. If I could just make it to town then maybe I could see Garrett again. If I couldn't, I prayed Garrett could be strong enough to save himself.

"There you are, Kelly. I was worried about you." Steve stepped out of the trees a few yards ahead of me, huffing in exhaustion. "You should come back home now." His eyes narrowed, daring me to challenge him. "You can come back and take your punishment and Garrett will be spared."

I smiled lightly knowing Garrett was safe. He had a chance to escape, unless Steve had done something to him. Grief crashed over me, before I pushed it away, forcing myself to hold on tightly to the last bit of hope I had. He wouldn't kill Garrett; Garrett was his bargaining chip. If he killed Garrett, he knew I'd take my own life before living with him a moment longer. Garrett had to be alive or gone, which meant I had to stall to give him time to escape.

"No, Steve, I'm done. I'm not going back to that hell hole, and you can't make me!" I cried. "You may be able to drag me back to that house of horrors, but I won't stop trying to escape. I'm going to get out, and I'm going to save Garrett from growing up with you as his father. You took him from his real family to give him a life of living in Hell. You've ruined him, and I won't stop trying to save him!"

"Then why not take him with you?" he asked, taking a few steps forward. I took a few steps back to keep distance between us. "You left him alone at the house to fend for himself. He's still there. I can go back anytime and punish him for your escape, or you can come back and I won't touch him."

"That's where you're wrong, Steve. Garrett is

escaping right now while you're messing around with me. *That's* why I left him. I knew you'd come after me. I knew you'd find me, and I'd be forced to come back with you if I had him. By leaving him, I'm giving him a chance to escape. I'm the bait; I'm sacrificing myself because I have nothing to lose except him. My life means shit after living with you for so long. I lost any life I could have, everyone already thinks I'm dead, you killed my cat, you killed my son, and you've killed me! I left him so he could run away from you and actually get away. I left him so I could die and finally get away from you! You can't have both of us, and now you'll have neither of us. He'll escape, and I'll kill myself before I live through another day with you."

His eyes reflected pure hatred and anger. He didn't like that I had managed to beat him, that I had found a way to finally take control. There was nothing Steve hated more than losing control, and now he was about to lose everything.

I spun and raced through the trees. He released a guttural cry, almost animalistic, then heard him chasing after me. I zigzagged through the trees, hitting a dense part of the woods. I aimed to lose him as I slid down beside a large tree and waited. If I could throw him off, not only would I distract him longer for Garrett's sake, I had a better chance of living to see tomorrow. His footsteps drew near. My breath halted and my body froze as I prayed against all odds I wouldn't be found. After a few tense moments, he passed, and once I felt he had gone a fair distance I raced in the opposite direction. The trees started to thin after a few minutes. I hoped it meant I was close to a road, but instead I entered the same clearing I had been in before.

I turned around and tried again. I didn't see or hear Steve, which worried me. He was a hunter, and as his prey, I wanted to know where he was so I could avoid him. Trees sped by as I raced through the thickening woods. The deeper I got, the easier I had hoped it would be to avoid him, although it also meant he had more places to hide.

He lunged out of the trees at me, and before I could move out of reach, he grabbed me. I knew the moment his hands latched onto me this was it. Between the anger in his eyes and the cruel grin on his lips, I knew I had pushed too far. He forced my chin up so I would meet his gaze. Despite the desire filling them as he looked me over, the anger remained. I'd be punished and forced to live with whatever he did to me, or I could push harder and end this now.

I hope you made it somewhere safely, Garrett. My time is about to run out.

He leaned down. "Kelly, you have one last chance to come home without repercussions. This is it. Make the right choice." His words held a warning when read between the lines: live in hell or die right now. I didn't need to think it over, especially with his other hand traveling up my body. I didn't struggle; I knew he enjoyed that, and I was through giving him what he wanted so I could survive. I was done, and nothing would make me go back to that house.

"Don't touch me!" I shoved him off of me, turning to face him.

He smiled, enjoying the last challenge I would ever give him. "Fine, have it your way, Kelly. I don't care. I can drag you back there. I don't need Garrett to control you. Your fear will help me." He pulled a knife from his pocket and clicked the release, allowing the blade to spring to life. "Even if you do end your suffering, I'll go find someone else. This has been fun, but I can move on. You, on the other hand, can finally get what you want." He laughed, as if he truly believed I would go back to him.

"Might as well kill me now, Steve. You'll get caught. You won't take anyone else. Garrett will find someone who believes him, and you'll go to jail. I'm your first and last girl." I stepped toward defiantly. "You might as well kill me now."

His eyes narrowing, he grabbed me and forced me against a tree. His hand hesitated slightly as he pressed the blade to my neck. "Have it your way. But you're wrong. This isn't over. Garrett won't make it far; you should have known that. I'll find him and take him back home. You've left him now to fend for himself, and I'll find another girl to take your place. All you did was start the torture and death for young girls. Take the guilt to your grave." His voice dripped with venom as he forced the blade into my skin. Pain rippled through me as he sliced my neck. His eyes never left mine as I gasped for breath and my hands rose to my neck to stop the bleeding. Sheer panic took over as I screamed in pain, but only a gurgling sound emerged from my lips.

He stabbed me in the gut and moved the blade

up. I crumpled to the ground, and my vision caved in. It slowly went black, and the last face I saw was Steve's. This was the end.

I'm sorry, Garrett. I wasn't strong enough to escape. I hope you did. I'm sorry to the girls who come after me. I was the first, but I know I won't be the last.

About the Author

Sara Schoen is a college student studying Biology, who writes in her free time. She has published numerous titles and hopes to continue writing throughout her life.

Facebook:
https://www.facebook.com/profile.php?id=10000 5224038610

Twitter:
https://twitter.com/SaraNSchoen

Goodreads:
https://www.goodreads.com/user/show/36172080 -sara-schoen

The Challenge

By Sophia Valentine

Chapter One

Welcome to the biggest show on Earth you've never seen before.....

Carla shoved the rest of her sandwich in her mouth and eyed the glossy flyer. The Royal Circus and fairground was back in town to celebrate its grand opening. The page was adorned with slightly odd-looking, wide-eyed, caked-on make-up trapeze artists, wacky clowns, peculiar magicians, and a creepy ringmaster, all under a white and red striped tent, surrounded by scary rides.

Carla had grown up to love the circus, until around the age of eight, when it strangely stopped visiting her town. In fact, it had stopped visiting *any* town.

"You need to eat more than just a sandwich for dinner."

Her mom's stern tone made her straighten her posture.

"Mom, I'm late for class. I'll grab something at McDonalds later."

Her mom shook her head in disproval, pulling on some rubber gloves. She confronted the pile of dirty dishes before her. "Cody's excited about the circus, if you fancy taking him tomorrow?"

Carla rose to her feet and pinned the flyer back under a magnet on the fridge, where she had found it. "I suppose I could. Where is he?"

"He's supposed to be sleeping, but I doubt he is with that racket going on upstairs."

Carla smiled as she approached the stairs. Her five-year-old brother Cody meant everything to her. She was often filled with guilt, knowing she didn't pay him enough attention due to evening school and her job at the restaurant taking up most of her time.

"Cody!" she called out, pushing the door open to his bedroom. All she saw was a clutter of toys and no cute brown-haired boy in cartoon pajamas. She grinned, heading toward the wardrobe. "Where's Cody?" Her brow furrowed in confusion, her hand on her hip, she scanned the room. Hide and Seek was a game Cody loved to play. "I wonder if he's in the wardrobe." She yanked open the door and stuck her head in. No sign of him. Shutting the door, she spun round.

She noticed the curtain billowing from the gentle breeze seeping in through the open window. "Hmmm. I wonder if Cody is here." She pulled the curtain across, surprised not to find him crouched on the floor, staring up at her with red cheeks, holding in his laughter.

"I bet he's under the bed," she said, dropping to her knees. He wasn't there. "Wow, you're getting good at this game." She stood back up, her eyes trailing over every possible area that he could be hiding. The toy box. She strolled toward it.

"Boo!"

She jumped when she felt something cling to her ankles. It took her a moment to catch her breath. She looked down and giggled. Cody was wrapped around her legs, laughing uncontrollably.

"I scared you!" His soft-sounding voice made her melt.

"Where were you?" She bent down and picked him up, balancing him on her hip.

"There." He pointed a chubby finger to the gigantic wooden rocking horse.

"Oh, so you were behind the horse." Carla nodded, impressed. "Good hiding place."

She carried him to the bed, where she lay him down. Cody asked her repeatedly for his stuffed monkey. Ensuring he was wrapped warmly in the covers, she grabbed his toy and placed it beside him.

"Guess where we're going tomorrow?" She sat

down.

His eyes shot open in excitement. "The circus?"

Carla nodded. "You like the circus, don't you?"

"I love it!" he squealed.

"What do you like most about the circus?"

"Um…" He paused, deep in thought. "I dunno." He shrugged.

"You like it all, don't you?" Cody nodded. "You do know there's a real live monkey there?"

"Can I stroke him?"

"If you be a good boy and go to sleep now, I'll ask the ringmaster if you can."

"Thanks, Carla." He buried his head under the quilt. "I'm sleeping now."

She laughed as she tucked him in one last time and switched off the light. "'Night, Cody. Love you."

Silence. She descended the stairs. Her mom had finished cleaning and was now before the television, engrossed in some drama show, which was probably depressing and completely unrealistic. Slinging her bag over her shoulder, Carla advised her that she was leaving.

"Okay, sweetie. Drive safe."

"Mom?"

"Yeah?" She looked up.

"You know how the circus stopped coming to town all those years ago?"

"Yeah."

"It was because a few children went missing, wasn't it?"

Her mom stifled an incredulous laugh. "Don't be ridiculous. They were having money problems, I heard. Apparently they'd expected a bigger turnout than they got, and it just got quieter and quieter."

Carla crossed her arms across her chest. "Well, as much as I do love that circus, it's a bit odd, don't you think?"

"In what way? All circuses are quite peculiar if you think about it."

Carla shrugged. "No, it's something else." She screwed up her nose. "I can't put my finger on it." The sound of the bells on the wall clock dragged her back to reality. "Anyway, I better go. Bye, Mom."

"Bye, love."

Chapter Two

Carla stretched her aching limbs and let out a loud yawn. Rolling onto her side, she massaged her temples, wishing she hadn't gone to a bar after class. She'd downed one too many sambucas and had nothing but a throbbing head, dry mouth, and churning stomach to show for it. The sound of Cody's excited cries filled the air, and she remembered the circus.

Fuck.

She yanked the covers over her head, blocking out the bright rays that stung her eyes. She desperately wanted to tell Cody that she was sick, that she couldn't take him, but she couldn't bear to see the disappointment in his eyes as a result of her always breaking promises.

After a few more moments of lying there, she jumped out of bed and fled to the en suite bathroom. Her chest heaved; her shoulders bounced uncontrollably as she vomited down the toilet. The acidic feeling in her throat burned. Sliding to the floor, she screwed her eyes shut.

"Carla." Cody's voice pierced through her brain painfully like a sharp sphere. "We're going to the circus! We're going to the circus! We're—"

"Okay, okay!" she shouted out. "Yes, we're going to the circus." She grabbed hold of the edge of the bathtub to support her jelly legs as she rose. "Go have breakfast. I'll be down in a minute."

"I've had breakfast. Cheerios."

"Okay, well go and watch TV for ten minutes."

"Mom said I can't watch TV until I've cleaned my room."

Carla moaned inwardly. It was way too early for conversation. "Go and clean your room then, or I'm not taking you anywhere."

"Okay," Cody responded sulkily, then she heard him plod off.

Carla peeled off her clothes, dropping them to the floor. A nice warm shower would do her a world of good. She twisted the tap, and it didn't take long before the room was filled with steam, the warmness washing over her naked body pleasantly. Climbing under the water, she allowed it to cascade down her long blonde hair and slim frame. The smell of Pink Sands filled her nostrils from the Yankee Candle soap. Her hangover became a distant memory as her muscles began to relax and her headache subsided.

Half an hour later, Carla was dressed in blue skinny jeans and a black t-shirt, with matching leather jacket and boots. Her hair hung silkily down her back, and her make-up had been perfected to accentuate her green eyes and full lips.

Not bad for three hours' sleep, she thought, giving the mirror a final glance.

"Cody?"

"I'm here." He came rushing toward her faster than lightning.

This kid had better lose some of his energy before he tired her out. She made a mental note not to supply him with any fizzy drinks or chocolate. In fact, screw anything with sugar, period. The kid could have a cracker.

"Can I have some candy gloss when we get there?" Cody beamed, tugging at her sleeve. His wide puppy dog eyes met hers, and she lost the battle before it even began. How could she deny *that* face anything?

"Sure," Carla mumbled. "Let's go."

The chatter, screams and laughter hit her like a punch in the stomach. She should have known it'd be busy, but it was more than busy. It was chaotic. Anyone would think it was an Eminem concert. She tightened her grip on Cody's tiny fingers and wove through the crowd. Flashing lights of fairground rides blinded her, music filled her ears, the smell of hotdogs hung in the air, and childhood memories invaded her mind. The Royal Circus. She took in the sight displayed before her, and her eyes lit up like a child's at Christmas. She was simultaneously filled with anticipation, excitement, and fear. The place hadn't changed one bit.

The red and white tent stood tall and intimidating, the doorway luring you inside to experience many of the wonderful and extraordinary delights.

Carla joined the queue of ecstatic children and parents, equally as eager to see the show. At the entrance, they were handed a complimentary drink. Carla swirled the blue crushed ice around with her straw and then took a sip. It cooled her throat and she downed more, the bubble gum flavour delicious.

When she and Cody finally got seated on one of the uncomfortable wooden benches, the lights dimmed for a second and silence loomed until a high-pitched cackle followed, preceding the beam of a bright spotlight. Carla tensed when she saw three clowns dancing around, yanking at one another's braces and pulling stupid facial expressions. Carla wasn't a big fan of clowns. She shouldn't have watched *IT*. In fact, she probably shouldn't have watched most of the horror movies she had. Her mind was haunted by sick and twisted images, spirits, clowns, psychopathic murderers, and more.

Funny how the mind plays tricks on you. Why is it that whenever you have to enter somewhere dark and alone, even if you tell yourself not to be a baby and force yourself not to think of scary stuff you've seen, it all explodes out of your mind, to freak you out? Every little thing. Every little nightmare. Every single fear. It was always the way.

"Look, Carla. The monkey!" Cody screeched.

"Oh, yeah." She drew in a deep breath in a bid to rid the fluttering butterflies in her stomach. It was the ringmaster, the same man from all those years ago. He'd aged, but beneath the red hat that matched his suit, his eyes were as secretive and manipulative as ever.

"Ladies and gentlemen! Welcome to the greatest show on Earth!" His voice echoed around the room. "Be prepared to be surprised this evening. We have things that you have never seen before. Acrobats that can bend in ways that don't seem possible, animals that can dance, clowns that can sing, a man that can lift this entire tent, and a magician that can make it all disappear with a click of his fingers." The ringmaster removed his hat and bowed before the cheering crowd. "Anything your mind can imagine, you *can* see." He placed his hat back on his head and waved his arm in the air. "And now, I bring you Rory!"

The crowd gasped as a menacing tiger appeared. Its fierce eyes swept over the crowd, its lips pulled back over sharp teeth, drool dripping from the corners of its mouth. Rising on two legs, it jumped against the metal fence in which it was encased.

Chapter Three

When the show finally finished an hour later, Carla accompanied Cody on several fairground rides. The spinning teacups played havoc with her stomach, but seeing Cody doubled over with laughter made every second worth it. The big wheel was next, and the view of the sparkling lights against the night sky was spectacular. Everything was one big blur of smiley faces.

"Can we try and win a teddy?" Cody pleaded.

"Sure."

Carla smiled at the twenty-something boy that stood behind the counter of stuffed animals. He flashed her a grin, and she was certain she saw a flicker of recognition in his eyes. Eyes that seemed to hold some sort of dark secret. It was the same look she noticed on everyone that worked on the grounds, like they were all in on something. It made her feel uneasy, causing her heart to slam against her chest and goosebumps to race over her now chilly skin.

"Um, how much is it?"

"Five pounds for three balls."

She dug into her pocket and retrieved a fiver. Handing him the money, she knelt down to Cody and explained that he had to knock all three tins off the shelf in order to win a teddy.

While Cody did as instructed, Carla examined the boy again. She also found him vaguely familiar. Surely it wasn't the same little boy she'd seen on many occasions, running around the circus, wild, dirty and barefoot?

"I lost," Cody huffed, his shoulders sagging.

"Never mind. Let's get you some candyfloss."

When she turned to leave, the boy called her back. "Here, he can have a clown."

He pushed the toy into Carla's hand, and she closed her fingers reluctantly around it, not breaking her stare from his. There was something sinister about his kind act, as if by her accepting the toy she would somehow have a price to pay. She let go of it like it had scalded her hand. When it fell to the floor, Cody grabbed it desperately, hugging it to his chest tightly.

"He said I can have it."

"No, Cody. You didn't win it," Carla said firmly. "Give it back."

"I insist." The boy's eyes were now ice cold, and his tone had a chilling bite to match.

Carla tore herself away from him and told herself to stop being paranoid. The circus was there to ensure children made happy memories, that they enjoyed it, that they would return.

What about the children that hadn't returned, though? Regardless of her mother brushing it off, *something* had happened at the circus in the past. The media splashing the faces of those young missing children all over the front pages had been unusual for their town. People didn't just go missing. The town was small, friendly, and everyone knew each other and kept a lookout. It was so safe that you could leave your front door unlocked and never have to worry. It seemed far too much of a coincidence how the circus had visited, and on each occasion, another child had disappeared into thin air. Carla guessed there was no proof. The ringmaster had made an announcement that a lack of money was the root of all their problems, preventing them from being able to return.

"Which colour candyfloss do you want?" she asked Cody at the candy stand.

A thin lady with a pointy nose and a smile plastered on her face greeted them. Again, even though she seemed friendly, there was something odd about her too. Carla wanted to get out of there.

"Erm…pink," Cody responded. "No, no…white."

"White candyfloss, please," Carla said to the woman.

"No, actually, pink," Cody said.

The woman's smile remained, although Carla sensed the irritation in her eyes. It was as if they were all wearing false masks, that if you removed them, you'd see the monsters they really were.

"Okay, we've had enough for tonight. How

about we go home?" She ruffled Cody's hair.

"Not yet." His mouth turned downwards. "Please, Carla. One more ride."

She sighed heavily. "Which ride?"

"The ghost train."

"No, you're not allowed on those sorts of rides. You're too young."

A sly grin crept across his face. "You don't need to tell Mom."

"No, Cody, pick another ride, and then let's go."

At that moment she felt her stomach churn. The bubble gum flavour from the drink earlier came back up in her throat.

"Cody, do you feel okay?" she asked him, trying to figure out if it was in fact the drink that had upset her tummy.

"Uh huh." He beamed.

She put it down to the McDonalds she had eaten yesterday. As Cody dragged her toward more fair rides, she groaned inwardly. She felt a hot flush spread though her body, then a cold gust of air. She felt feverish. All she wanted was to be tucked in bed, The Royal Circus another thing to tick off her "Cody list."

Chapter Four

"Cody!" Carla screamed, wincing at the loudness of her own voice.

Where the fuck is he? Panic spread through her as she pushed through the crowds, her eyes darting frantically everywhere. She'd looked down for *one second* to put her change in her pocket. Grabbing every small brown-haired boy by the shoulders, and none of them being Cody, tears stung her eyes. If something happened to him, she'd never be able to forgive herself.

She searched the entire place for a good twenty minutes. She rushed into the circus tent, which was dark and empty. She checked every single ride. She peered through the windows of many campervans and vehicles. She checked the animal cages, and nothing. Cody was nowhere to be seen.

Her heart tightened painfully inside her chest, and bile rose in her throat. Unable to refrain from crying any longer, she burst into floods of tears. She'd lost her baby brother. Anyone could have snatched him. What they would do with him was another thing that filled her with sickening dread. Inhaling air, she regained her composure and told herself to get a grip. Standing there snivelling, at a loss of what to do, wouldn't bring Cody back. Wiping her eyes and nose, she stepped forward.

A shiver ran up her spine. In front of her was an imitation of a haunted house. It was tall and grey, with shabby-looking windows and doors. A red glow cast on the ground, as if nothing but pure evil lurked inside. Surrounded by cemetery stones, skeletons, and freaky characters in masks, Carla knew it wasn't real, but it felt every bit as though it was haunted. She silently prayed that Cody hadn't entered the House of Horrors. Feeling something touch her shoulder, she yelped, spinning round.

"Are you looking for Cody?" a smooth, silky, creepy voice asked.

"Who are you?"

Black eyes peeped out from a jester mask. The type that entertainers used to wear before kings and queens centuries ago, which Carla found more terrifying than anything else. It was all white with a large nose and a wide smile. She didn't get how something that had a happy face painted on it could look so devoid of emotion, for you didn't really see the smile. You saw the peepholes beyond it, and you wondered what and who was underneath. Bells hung from the top, which let off a spooky jangle each time the jester moved his head, the same sound a chime made when it sang in the wind that was meant to be relaxing, pleasant to the ears. This was anything but.

"Where's my brother?" she asked through gritted teeth. "If you've hurt him…" She clenched her fists, her blood boiling.

"We have your brother," the jester responded casually, as if they weren't talking about the kidnapping of some poor young and probably frightened boy.

"Take me to him now!" she screamed, lurching forward.

"It's not that simple, Carla."

Her head snapped to attention. "How do you know my name? Did Cody tell you?"

Silence.

"I'm ringing the police." She fumbled in her bag, hurriedly. "You've kidnapped my brother."

"Where's the proof? No one will believe you." His soft chuckle made her want to punch him in the gut.

Ignoring him, she dialled 999 and held the mobile to her ear. Unfazed, the jester stood there calmly. Carla shouted out to the crowd that they were holding her brother captive, but people only looked at her like she'd lost her mind.

"Hello?" she said shakily.

"Hello, ma'am, what is your name and your emergency?"

"I'm Carla Reid…" She held back tears. "I'm at the circus, and they've taken my brother…please, you need to send someone out here before they hurt him. The address is—"

"Ma'am, please calm down. How long has your

brother been missing?"

"Um…" She scratched her head. "About half an hour. I've looked everywhere, and they've got him. The jester told me they've taken him."

"Miss Reid, although you're more than welcome to come down to the station and tell us what happened, we can't file a missing person's case and undertake a search until forty-eight hours have passed."

"It will be too late then."

Catching sight of the jester's eyes that now danced with merriment, Carla ended the call.

"Give me my brother!" She slammed her fists into the jester's chest, but he gripped her tightly around the wrists, restricting her from moving. She shouted for help, casting a look over her shoulder. The crowds were oblivious to the commotion, and the workers appeared to be looking over, regarding her cautiously, as if waiting for a sign to come to the jester's aid. Carla knew there and then that she was all alone, with no one to help. This couldn't be happening. This couldn't be real.

"What do you want from me?"

"If you want to see your brother again, there is something that you can do."

"Anything." It was out of her mouth before she had time to stop herself.

The jester slowly made his way toward the House of Horrors. "Are you prepared to face a challenge?"

"What sort of challenge?"

"A challenge…" He turned to face her.

Her eyes widened in alarm. "What are you

talking about? You're not making sense."

"If you want to see your brother again, then you must take a tour in the House of Horrors. You either make it through to the end and be reunited with your brother, or…" He took a step closer so that his face was only inches away from hers, his hot breath sweeping against her cheek. "You fail to make it to the end and don't survive."

Chapter Five

Carla drew in a deep breath. She lifted her head slowly to take in the House of Horrors again. Every horror movie she had ever seen invaded her mind. Freddie Krueger, Jason, IT the clown, Michael Myers, Pinhead, Leatherface, and more terrifying faces that had caused her many sleepless nights.

What did the jester man mean by "she wouldn't survive if she didn't make it to the end?" Would whatever was lurking inside actually kill her? It didn't make sense. The circus couldn't go around killing people. Her eyes widened, and she licked her suddenly dry lips. The missing people. Maybe the circus *had* done something with them! Maybe they were so good at hiding the evidence, they were never caught.

"Did you take those other children?" she asked.

The jester mask moved from side to side as the man shook his head, jingling the bells. "The circus

502

never tells."

"Is there another way I can save my brother?" she pleaded desperately.

"Your time is running out, Carla."

"Okay…okay." She buried her hands in her hair. "How long does the tour usually take?"

"It depends. The brave get out in ten minutes."

"Ten minutes." She nodded vehemently, gathering her courage. *I can do this.*

The man led her toward the house. Carla's knees trembled with every step that she took, and she inwardly scolded herself. It couldn't be that bad, surely? The man was toying with her, trying to scare her. Once she was at the door, she noticed him hang a sign on the fence: ***This ride is temporarily out of service.***

"Will you be coming in with me?" she asked.

"Oh no." He chuckled. "This is something you have to do alone."

"If something happens to me, you do know my mom and dad will be looking for me, right? They know I'm here. You'll never get away with it."

With amusement in his eyes, the jester replied, "Tell us something we haven't heard before."

He pushed the heavy door open, which creaked loudly. Carla could see nothing but darkness inside. Her heart tightened inside her chest.

"Good luck," the jester whispered.

Carla tentatively took a few steps inside, and gasped when the door slammed shut after her. She couldn't see a thing. She smelled something damp in the air. She was almost certain that she heard the faint sound of someone breathing. Wrapping her arms around herself protectively, she scanned the room. No way could she go on a tour in complete darkness. She expected things to jump out anyway, but not being able to prepare for it or to know where to flee made it so much worse. Besides, what if there were holes in the floor or things to trip over?

"I need some light!" she yelled to no one in particular. "I can't see where I'm going."

She sighed in relief when some lights flickered on. They weren't too bright, but they helped. Surveying the room, she could see that she was surrounded by mirrors. She felt her shoulders visibly relax. A mirror maze. She could do that.

She passed the first mirror and held in a laugh. Her reflection appeared stretched, as if she were a giant. Tucking a strand of hair behind her ear, she passed the next mirror. Her image appeared extremely small. The next mirror made her look wide and the one after that she saw no reflection at all. She couldn't help but think how odd it was. She lifted a hand and waved in front of it. Still no reflection. She wondered how it was possible. She could see the wall behind her reflected in the mirror. She turned around and examined the wall. The bricks were crumbled and there was a painting of a skull. Turning back to face the mirror, she could see the crumbled bricks and skull image clear as day. Waving her arms about again, she saw nothing.

She stepped in front of the next mirror. Her heart raced at a frenetic pace, a yelp escaping her lips when she noticed a clown in the reflection. Squeezing her eyes shut, she prayed it was gone when she reopened them.

A white face with black eyes, a red nose, and painted on red mouth glared at her. She glanced over her shoulder. There was nothing there. Facing the mirror again, she cried out. The clown appeared to be behind her. Closer this time. She moved away from the mirror as fast as her shaking legs would take her.

Pushing open another door, her eyes had to adjust to the change in lighting, which was even dimmer than the previous room. She noticed a dirty, worn sofa, and a table holding a record player. Her mouth fell open when the needle moved across to the record, settling on it and making it play. There were probably wires somewhere, or it was made to work by itself. The music, however, sent chills up her spine. It was a spooky-sounding song.

She looked up at the ceiling, and at each wall, her breath held tight in anticipation. Then the door creaked open. A body wobbled toward her. It was pale, foaming at the mouth, and making a groaning noise. Its hair was tangled, its complexion grey. She bit her lip. A zombie. She screamed out when she felt hands on her shoulders. Turning around, she spotted another zombie. Before she had time to brace herself, another zombie entered the room, followed by another. When there were five of them wobbling toward her, their eyes black, their faces devoid of emotion, she backed toward the door. The smell of them caused her stomach to somersault. They smelled just like rotting corpses.

"Get away from me!" She exited the room, pulling the door shut behind her. They banged on the wood repeatedly. When her knuckles turned white and she could no longer hold on, she let go, waiting for it to burst open. Silence descended in the air. Certain that they had gone, she spun around.

A man wearing a torn leather mask caught her eye. He was easily 6'4", with big, stocky shoulders. She saw he had four sharp knives in his hands, which glinted under the lights. The heavy sound of his breathing alone made the hairs on her neck stand to attention. He stepped toward her. She edged away. He lunged for her, the knives missing her by a millimetre.

"You can't hurt me," she told him, although her voice came out shaky and not confident as she had intended. "I'll get out of here and go straight to the police! They'll find you and—"

She screamed out in pain and shock when the knife plunged into her arm. She clamped her other hand around it to stop the blood from flowing. She was unable to stop the tears from streaming down her cheeks. She couldn't believe that she had really been stabbed. What if she *didn't* get out alive? What if these people got away with it? What would happen to Cody?

With all of the force she could muster, she punched the man straight in the face, causing him to tumble backward. When he jumped back to his feet, she dove through the door. Pulling it shut behind her, she was relieved to see that it had a lock. With shaky fingers, she locked it quickly. She glanced down at her arm again. It stung like hell. Removing her scarf, she wrapped it around her arm tightly. She yanked a knot in the end, praying that it would stop the bleeding.

Something tickled her neck and she scratched it, then something tickled her arm. Then her back. Looking down at her feet, Carla's jaw dropped open. She kicked off the large black spider that was crawling up her foot. She hated spiders more than anything. Another spider ran up her leg.

She brushed it off. "Ah!"

Four more ran up her feet and legs. Spinning around, she flicked them off as fast as she could, all the while more latched onto her body. There were now thousands of spiders roaming the floor.

Oh my god!

She raced through the door and slammed it shut behind her. Brushing the spiders off her body, her heart felt like it would explode in her chest. She remained rooted on the spot for a moment, feeling dizzy at the sight of blood seeping through her scarf. Inhaling sharply, she wiped the tears from her face. Her spine stiffened when she heard a woman humming. Shooting around, she saw a transparent lady floating in the air, humming a song. When a gust of air swept her hair out, Carla looked beside her. A transparent little girl was staring up at her, clutching a teddy bear.

"Miss, can you help us?"

Carla swallowed.

"Miss, can you help us?" she repeated in her low, chilling voice.

Carla neared toward the other door. Both the lady and the girl's eyes bore into her. When they floated in her direction, she fled the room.

She whimpered at the scene before her, almost wishing she'd stayed in the last room. A man was lying in a bathtub full of blood. His gaze met hers, and he laughed loudly. Pulling something up from the depths of the water, what appeared to be a heart, he shoved it into his mouth. As he tore into it with his teeth, Carla's stomach churned. Tossing it to the floor, the man felt around in the water, pulled out a finger, chewing on it.

She was surprised when he rose to his feet, his clothes drenched in blood. He took a step out of the bathtub, the blood gushing off him, soaking the tattered carpet. Carla yanked on the door handle. It was locked. She banged on it frantically. The man was now laughing hysterically, his shoulders bouncing up and down. Holding a hand out, his evil eyes locked with hers. Carla stood against the door, her back to it, banging with her fist.

The man was now in front of her, his hands around her neck. Carla's heart banged in her chest, her stomach flipping. His stench brought bile up in her throat. She swallowed it down and tried to keep in the vomit that was threatening to spill from her lips.

The man's fingers tightened around her neck until she was struggling for air. She dug her nails into his hands and tried to kick at him. It was no use. He was much stronger than she was. He towered over her. When he smiled, she got a glimpse of his rotten teeth.

Struggling, she tried to push him off. Her eyes were bulging. Her lungs tightened. She desperately needed air.

When he released her, she sucked in a deep breath. She didn't get a chance to try to defend herself. He dragged her toward the bathtub and pushed her head into the filthy water.

Carla thrashed about. She clamped her lips and eyes shut, praying that the blood wouldn't seep in. The hands were forcing her head lower and lower into the water.

Cody. Help Cody!

With all of the force she had left, she placed her arms on the bottom of the tub, dug her heels into the floor, and pushed herself backward. She tumbled on the floor, landing with a sharp thud.

Panting and gasping for breath, she searched for the man. He was gone. The cold air was now bitter against her soaked body. She rubbed her nose with a soft cry, wondering if she could take much more. She had to, though. There was no way that she would fail Cody. She *had* to get out alive.

Chapter Six

"Carlaaaaaa…"

She bolted up.

"Carlaaaaa…" the singsong voice repeated.

She surveyed the room. She couldn't see anything or anyone. When it was silent again, she entered the next room. It was pitch black.

"Shit," she muttered, taking slow steps forward.

She shrieked when fingers wrapped around her arm. Jerking out of the way, she felt another hand on her leg. She spun around. More hands were on her, pulling her, yanking her into the darkness of the room.

"Nooooo!" she screamed, feeling herself being pulled to the floor. She clenched her fists, punching each of the hands on her body.

"Carlaaaa…"

"Get off!"

She scrambled to her feet and saw light seeping

through the bottom of a door. Climbing over the bodies beneath her, she darted out of the room.

Dead bodies were hanging from the ceiling, bloodied and swaying gently. Their mouths were wide open, and their tongues had been cut out. On closer inspection, their eyes too. She placed a hand over her mouth, sick to her stomach.

On the bed was a corpse. It was a woman's body. It appeared to have several stab wounds. All of her fingers and toes were missing.

"Take a seat," a stern voice said, causing Carla to jump.

A man dressed in a white doctor's overcoat stood behind her, a white surgical mask over his mouth. A table before him was laden with sharp knives and other equipment Carla couldn't identify. She stepped away from him as he approached her, gasping when she felt a chair against the back of her legs. Stumbling, she landed in it.

She didn't get a chance to stand up. The man quickly secured her arms to the chair with leather cuffs.

"Please..." she begged, "don't hurt me."

Her legs were then tied to the chair. She wriggled frantically, trying to free herself. It was no use. She was completely captured. When a blindfold was placed over her head, restricting her vision, she begged again for the man to let her go. Not knowing what he would do next made her fear him further. "You won't be needing these for much longer."

Something sharp pressed against her hand with a stab of pain, and she realised that he was attempting to saw her finger off.

"Please! No!" She tried to yank her hand back, but the cuffs prevented her from doing so. She grabbed onto his white coat, pulling on it as hard as she could, and with a tearing sound, some of the material came off in her hand. It didn't deter him.

"I beg you, please! Let me go!"

The sharpness of the blade sent an excruciating pain up her arm. She kicked her legs out, thrashing her head side to side, unable to take it. She heard the grinding sound of the saw against her bone and was unable to help the vomit that flooded from her mouth, drenching her top. The acid of it burnt her throat. The smell of it caused her to puke again. She clenched her teeth, screaming out. She had never felt pain like it in her life.

"Please…" she sobbed.

When he stopped, she knew that her finger had been cut off completely. She wiggled her hand and screamed. As soon as the blindfold had been removed, she looked down. She cried even harder. Her finger was gone. Blood oozed from the wound.

"You won't be needing these for much longer either."

When the man picked up a spoon, she sank further in the seat. The coldness of the metal against her cheek made her whimper. He was aiming for her eye.

No, no, no, no, no!

She squeezed her lids shut, and the man forced one eye open with his fingers. His evil face peered down at her, clearly enjoying inflicting pain.

The spoon was now on her lower lid, being

pressed down harder. She couldn't let this man scoop her eyes out. No way. She kicked her legs wildly, thrashing her arms forcefully. When one leg was freed, she booted him as hard as she could in the shin.

Instead of tumbling to the floor, he punched her hard across the face, obviously consumed with anger. Carla kicked him again and again. She didn't stop kicking him until he fell backward.

The leather cuffs automatically sprung open. She closed her eyes for a second, thanking the lord above that she was free. For the moment anyway. She pocketed the material patch from his coat to wipe up her bloodied finger later. She then grabbed a knife from the table, and without giving it a second thought, she plunged it straight into the man's heart.

Blood spluttered from his mouth. She drove it into his chest once more. Before she left the room, she grabbed another knife, the sharpest and biggest one she could find, locking the door behind her.

The wound in her arm and where her finger once was sent stabbing pains through her entire body. Her cheek was sore. Her limbs started to feel weak, and she knew she soon wouldn't have any fight left in her. She needed to get out of the House of Horrors as fast as possible.

"Carla! Help!" Cody's voice pierced through her brain.

"Cody!" she screamed out. "Where are you?"

No answer.

"Cody?"

The silence was unsettling.

Shit!

She spotted three clowns before her. Their eyes were huge, their teeth long and sharp. They were tossing a ball to one another, playing. Carla tried to quietly creep past them; however, the floorboard creaked. She froze. Their heads snapped up to attention. When they threw their heads back with laughter, Carla shuddered. She could see deep inside their mouths. Snakes squirmed out of them, past their rotting teeth.

Carla shook her head.

It can't be real. It can't.

They sauntered toward her, the snakes getting closer. Opening their mouths even wider, hundreds of snakes were released, heading in her direction.

She waved the knives in the air, managing to cut the heads of a few. Then the snakes grasped hold of the knives, wrenching them from her grip. She was again weaponless.

Carla dived into the next room, crying. She tripped over the carpet and fell to her knees, buried in a heap of skulls. Struggling to stand up, she tried to feel for the floor. She couldn't help but notice that some of the skulls were small, obviously belonging to children. There were animal heads too, cats, dogs, cows, everything she could think of.

Who are *these people?* she thought, desperately trying to push herself to her feet.

When she finally found balance, the lights flickered on and off continuously. Coffins lined the walls, and not wanting to know what was inside them, she fled for the next room, the skulls crunching under her feet.

A man was hacking into bodies with an axe. Bloody limbs were everywhere. Blood sprayed up the walls as he chopped off an arm. Carla contemplated going back into the previous room and giving up, shouting out that she couldn't continue the tour. Then she thought of Cody. She couldn't let him down.

A cry left her lips when an axe was flung at her. It sunk into the wall right by her head. The man then picked up another axe and threw it at her. Carla scurried for the door, bending down and standing up repeatedly, trying to miss the axes being flung her way.

"Ahhhhhhh!"

An axe sliced right through her shoulder, pinning her against the wall. Carla squeezed her eyes shut tightly, willing herself not to faint, although she was sure she'd die on the spot from the pain alone. When the man picked up another axe, with her free hand, she grabbed the wooden handle of the one that had her captive. She gritted her teeth, gripped it, and pulled it out with a scream. She ducked the axe that was flying through the air toward her and escaped through the door, locked it behind her, and collapsed to the floor. Her vision went blurry, her mouth dry, and her heartbeat was slow, as if it didn't have the power left for her survival. Blood gushed from her shoulder. She didn't think she had the energy to stand. She was losing a lot of blood fast.

"Please!" she cried out. "Let me out! Please!"

The sound of the door unlocking behind her chilled her to the bone. With what little power she had left, she crawled away, a trail of blood spreading on the floor behind her. Her face was bruised and swollen, her finger was gone, her clothes were soaked in blood, and her shoulder was cut wide open, and her clothes were soaked in blood. Catching sight of her face in a cracked mirror, she could see that her eyes were also swollen and puffy.

She managed to bring her attention to the door, and she sucked in a breath. The man that had thrown the axe was standing there, as was the freaky surgeon, the little girl and lady ghosts, the zombies, the clowns, the man in the torn leather torn mask, the bloody man from the bathtub. And they were all heading toward her. Thousands of spiders also raced across the floor in her direction.

Carla pulled herself to her feet. She balanced against the wall, believing that her trembling legs would buckle beneath her. She slid across the wall, using it for support as she stumbled into the next room. The freaks of the House of Horrors followed her.

"Cody!" she cried out. "Where are you?" She was sobbing so hard that her chest hurt.

She gripped her shoulder firmly, trying to stop the bleeding. The next door she opened led her to a black corridor. She inched her way along it, knowing that she was still being followed by the sounds of heavy breathing, panting, humming, sadistic laughing, and her name being whispered.

"Carlaaaaa…"

She ignored them and continued to walk on her shaky legs until she touched a door handle. She grabbed hold of it and pulled it open. She bit her lip, cursing, as tendrils of pain shot up her arm.

Once on the other side, she pulled the door shut, hastily locking it. The freaks banged on it from the other side, demanding for her to open it. She twisted around to take in her surroundings. The room was empty. Her muscles relaxed for a split second, until she realised that there wasn't a door.

No!

She raced over to each wall, stroking her palms over it, trying to see if there was a secret door of some sort. There wasn't. With tears rolling down her cheeks, she grabbed the tatty corner of the carpet and pulled it up. Examining the floor, Carla prayed that there was an exit.

Again, there was nothing.

The laughter at the other side of the door made her crumple. The laughing grew louder, more sadistic, as if her being trapped was the funniest thing in the world. She slid to her knees and buried her head in her hands. She cried harder than she ever had before. She could feel the life slowly slipping away from her as she was losing blood. Before her vision went, the last thing her mind presented her with was her baby brother, Cody.

Chapter Seven

Carla blinked her eyes open. Sunlight blaring through a gap stung her eyes and heated her face. She felt disoriented. She swallowed the lump that had lodged in her throat. She needed a drink, urgently. She examined the room, not knowing where she was. Then she noticed the bare walls, tatty rolled-up carpet, and a wooden door, which was locked. Feeling something wet and warm on her hand, she glanced down.

Blood.

The sight of it made her feel woozy. She drew in a sharp, deep breath. As she took in her bloodied shoulder, arm, and missing finger, it all came back to her. She was in the House of Horrors. She had no idea how long she'd been out cold.

A cry caused her head to shoot up. A little girl was sitting in the corner of the room, wearing a yellow jumper, blue jeans, and yellow sandals, her brown hair in pigtails.

Carla blinked rapidly, and the room was empty again. She sighed heavily, feeling completely bewildered and not knowing what the hell was going on. Turning back to the light, she noticed that the gap was too small, way too small to escape from. Slowly climbing to her feet, she took steps toward the door. Were the freaks gone? She pressed her ear against it, trying to hear some movement beyond it. She gasped in fright when the banging, shouting, humming, and laughing started again.

"Let me out," she groaned, knowing that if she didn't get to a hospital soon she'd die. "Pleeeeeeease!"

She remained rooted to the spot for a moment. Then the gap grew bigger. Light burst in through the room. With a soft laugh of relief, Carla dragged herself to the gap. She clutched her shoulder tightly, trying her best to ignore the smell of her blood.

When she stepped out into the daylight, she was met with a busy fairground and circus. Families strolled together eating candyfloss and laughing, children running around excitedly. A blur of colourful lights filled the air from rides, and the different songs were being played everywhere.

She stared at the House of Horrors. Children poured out of the doors happily. Even adults exited it, seeming completely unharmed or distressed. Gone was the **"out of service"** sign.

She had passed the challenge. She had survived the House of Horrors.

"Carla!" She spun around to see Cody racing toward her.

Her heart skipped a beat. "Where were you? I've been looking everywhere!"

He pouted.

"I was looking for you. Where were you?" she snapped.

"I was winning toys. I got you this." He thrust a yellow teddy into her hands.

Carla swallowed. No longer feeling the moistness of blood, she checked to see if the bleeding had stopped. Her mouth fell open. She checked herself over, confused. There was no blood to her shoulder, no wound. Running her hand along her arm, she found no stab wound there either. She opened her hands and counted her fingers. None were missing.

What the hell?

She rubbed her aching temples. It didn't make sense.

"Anything your mind can imagine, you *can* see," the ringmaster's words echoed in her brain.

She remembered the complimentary drink she had received at the circus and how she had felt slightly sick afterwards. Had they drugged her? Or had she imagined everything? Retrieving her mobile from her pocket, she checked the call log. Her heartbeat increased, her breathing suspending. There were no dialled calls to the police.

Grabbing Cody into a hug, she squeezed him tightly. She buried her head into his hair, holding back the tears that were threatening to show.

"Don't you *ever* run off like that again. Do you hear me?"

He nodded.

Grabbing hold of his hand, she started to lead him through the crowd. Feeling something pressing against her leg from her jeans pocket, she pulled it out. It was a ball of white material. Inspecting it, she swallowed. It was part of the coat that she had torn from the freaky surgeon. She felt the blood drain from her face.

With a glance over her shoulder, she noticed the man in the jester mask. His eyes were dancing with merriment. He gave her a knowing wink.

Tightening her grip on Cody's hand, she continued walking toward the exit. The man at the toy stall also gave her a wink, and so did the lady at the candyfloss stand. Lastly, she saw the ringmaster waving.

"See you next year!" he said, his tone menacing. Then he smiled widely and winked.

The Thompson News.
18/04/2016
FRANTIC SEARCH FOR MISSING GIRL, 8, WHO WAS LAST SEEN CYCLING IN RANGE PARK

A frantic search is underway for a missing girl who vanished after cycling in Range Park, Birmingham. Raina Summers was last seen Saturday afternoon at 3 p.m. Due to The Royal Circus taking place across the road, Raina's sister stated she had turned her back for a split second when Raina was lost amongst the crowd.

Investigators and Police searched the area for

the missing girl. At the time, Raina was wearing a yellow jumper, blue jeans, and yellow sandals. Her brown hair was secured in pigtails. If you have seen Raina, or have any idea of her whereabouts, please contact the police immediately.

About the Author

S. Valentine grew up in England. Studying English language and literature as well as law, she worked in a law firm for many years before moving to Spain. She does, however, still visit the UK which, in a way, will always be home. She writes contemporary fiction, including erotica, thrillers and romance.

For more information, please visit: www.s-valentine.wix.com/books.

Facebook:
http://www.facebook.com/SophiaValentineAuthor

Twitter:
http://www.twitter.com/SophiaVAuthor

Website:
http://www.goodreads.com/SophiaValentine

Mirror Man

By Jackie Sonnenberg

Jean Conway sat up in bed, ears perked. She strained her hearing in the night and listened again to the sounds of the voice talking a mile a minute. The bright red letters at her nightstand clock told her it was four o'clock in the morning.

Jean got out of bed and made her way down the hall to the room with the faint glow of the nightlight beaming underneath the door. She didn't have to press her ear against the door to know that her daughter was awake. She eased inside.

"Avery?"

Jean came into the room full view and saw her six-year-old daughter at her vanity. She had switched on her lamp which only lit her surrounding area, making her look like an old time movie star about to go on stage. Her play cosmetics case was opened, and she was drawing all over her mirror with the little lipsticks. Red and pink stick figures decorated all the glass, looking like colorful little children floating in a giant bubble.

"Avery, what are you doing?"

The child turned in her seat, not at all concerned that her mother was there. She looked happy to be caught awake. "Playing."

Her mother crossed her arms. "Do you know what time it is? It's four in the morning. You should be in bed."

"I'm not tired."

"You need to get in bed and go to sleep. Right now. And tomorrow you're going to clean up the mess you made on your vanity mirror."

Avery pouted. "But we couldn't find paper!"

Jean was taken aback. "We? Who's we?"

Avery swung her feet at her stool. "Me and my friend."

"Who is your friend?"

Avery pointed to the mirror. Was she pointing at one of the stick figure children? If so, Jean couldn't tell which one and it did not matter.

She crossed her brow and shook her head. "You need to go to sleep, honey. It's late. You can play tomorrow."

"Okay, Mommy."

The child hopped into her unmade bed, and Jean left, satisfied yet confused. On her way back to her own room, she heard the murmurs of the little voice again but just shook her head and went back to bed.

Jean worked her shift the next day as a corrections officer at the prison, while her husband served as the honorable Judge August Conway. When they came home that evening, they at first could not find their daughter. She was not in the family room watching TV, and she was not in her room. They questioned the neighbor, an elderly lady who sometimes watched her when she came home from her morning Kindergarten.

The lady shrugged. "She's been playing quietly by herself all day. I barely heard a peep out of her."

Jean and August eventually found Avery in an unlikely place: the family dining room, the place they were only ever in twice a year for Thanksgiving and Christmas dinner. Avery was standing before the long mirror that stretched horizontally by the table. Her face was so close to the glass it was almost touching.

"Yeah," Avery said, "I think that too sometimes."

"Avery?"

The child turned around and looked at her parents, while they looked at the mirror. Of course, the only thing in it was the reflection of their daughter. She had cropped sandy hair that reached her ears, a haircut that Jean regretted as it made Avery look more like a boy than the baby doll she'd imagined.

"What are you doing?" asked her father.

"Talking to my friend."

The parents' darted eyes at each other, but they didn't move their heads.

"And who is your friend?" her father asked.

"His name is CJ and he lives in the mirror."

"That's your friend you were playing with real late last night, weren't you?" Jean asked.

"Uh-huh."

"Oh, I see," said August.

"Can't you see him?"

Jean and August shook their heads, which only delighted the child.

"He must be your invisible friend," Jean said.

Avery suddenly spun around to the mirror, looking at it for a minute, and then nodded.

"You're right." She looked back to her parents. "CJ says that I'm special because only I can see him."

"Okay, honey, you...play, and we'll call you when dinner is ready."

Avery already had her back turned and was having an animated conversation with the mirror, and every once in a while she would turn around behind her to see if her parents were there or if they were listening.

At dinner, Avery ate a little, as any finicky child would. Her parents talked about their lives in criminal justice work. They noticed that Avery turned completely around in her seat to stare at the mirror in the foyer.

"Avery, finish your dinner."

"Mom, can I go play? CJ is waving to me, and he wants to talk."

"No, not until you've finished eating."

The child ate a little more until they finally thought it was enough and excused her from the table. She scampered off from her chair while they continued their dinner and conversation. At one point they stopped because they heard her talking in the foyer. "No," they heard her say. "But sometimes they do. Sometimes they let me do whatever I want."

Jean and August were asleep by midnight. Their daughter was not. Their door creaked open and the little girl stepped in. Her nightshirt was an old t-shirt of her father's, and it dragged on the floor as she walked, nearly tripping her. Avery made her way to her parents' bed and quickly to her mother's side.

"Mommy?"

Jean made a small noise.

Avery shook her on the bed and spoke louder, more alarmed. "Mommy?"

Jean sat up, and August did as well, turning on the lamp.

"What's wrong, baby?" asked Jean, brushing her hair out of her eyes.

Although the sudden light from the lamp hurt their eyes, it did not hurt Avery's as she had been awake for some time. She climbed into bed with her parents and snuggled up to them in the covers.

"What's wrong?" Jean asked again.

"Mommy, I don't want you to go to work

tomorrow."

"Why?"

"Because somebody stabbed a police officer at the jail."

Jean and August looked at each other in shock.

"What are you talking about? Where did you hear that from?"

"CJ told me."

Her parents just stared at her.

"He told me that you're gonna get stabbed too because you're mean."

Jean hugged the child close. She and August looked at each other again, each hoping the other would say something so that they wouldn't have to. They both noticed that Avery was legitimately afraid the way she had her hands curled close to her chest in a protective instinct. It did not matter if she made it up in her head, she believed it would happen.

"Honey, you have nothing to worry about. I do have a dangerous job, but I am safe. It is my job to keep other people safe. Okay?"

Avery nodded hesitantly, not entirely convinced. She twisted her face into her mother's chest and refused to let her go, even after Jean rubbed her back and promised her that she would be okay.

"They can kill you," Jean heard her muffled voice. "They do it all the time."

"Sweetie, the bad guys are locked up and they are watched by police."

"No." Avery shot her head up and looked at both of her parents. "They can kill anyone," she said, with such seriousness, and such truth, that Jean wanted to curl her own hands to her chest.

"It's okay, Avery, it's okay." August hugged both his wife and daughter close, instantly thinking that he needed to monitor everything Avery ever watched on TV.

She went back to her room after some more consoling, after she felt convinced enough that everyone would be all right. On her way out, she looked at her parents one more time before opening the bedroom door, lifting up her large t-shirt like a ball gown.

Jean and August looked at each other once she was gone.

"Why would she say something like that?" Jean blurted out.

"Because she's a kid, and kids invent stories all the time," reassured August, although it had jolted him as well.

"Where would she get that idea from?"

"The news? Kids see stuff on TV all the time; it probably scared her."

"But why is she using this imaginary friend as an excuse to tell us that?"

The next day both Jean and August came home in a rush to see each other.

"Officer Vick was wounded last night. A prison shank," Jean told him. "Just like Avery said. How would she know that?"

August shook his head. "Don't think of it that way. Of course it wasn't Avery. It's a coincidence.

Just a coincidence. It has to be. There is no way she would know. It happens all the time and she probably gets scared and thinks about the possibilities."

Jean nodded, not wanting to think about it anymore. The first place she wanted to go to was her daughter's room.

Avery was sitting at her little plastic table with a jumbo box of crayons and a pad of paper. She had already drawn a few pictures, and they were all the same subject. Jean circled around the table to get a good look at the scratchy stick figures in imagined landscapes made of fluffy clouds, at the park, at the beach, and in front of the house eating cotton candy and ice cream. The smaller figure was no doubt the self portrait of Avery, the messy yellow scribble and red jacket she wore. The other figure was only a tad taller than Avery, and it appeared to be male. He had thicker legs and wore all black clothes. He had short red hair and a longer nose, similar to Pinocchio.

"Is this what he looks like?" Jean asked casually.

Avery nodded. "Yeah and he's got a freckle face and a pointy nose."

At that point she turned around to her vanity. "You do too."

She considered the mirror for a minute, looked at her mom, and then laughed. "No she doesn't."

"What did he say?" asked Jean, only a little bit amused.

"Nothing!" the child proclaimed.

Jean stared at the face created out of Avery's mind and Avery's crayons. The smeared black and red and peach made a crude face even though it was not intentional. The more Jean stared at it, the more she realized she did not like this face. She did not like this face at all. She looked toward the mirror and instantly imagined that face peering out from it, and it made her stand up and leave the room. She could not help but shudder a little as she left her daughter's room, both at the child's authenticity of believing someone was there and her predicting that incident that happened at the prison.

Jean was home before Avery scampered off the school bus. She came through the door and instantly dropped her backpack, heading straight for her room. Jean thought nothing of it and resumed reading on the couch. Soon August joined them at home as well, and everyone seemed quite settled that afternoon. After finishing a glass of water in the kitchen, August went upstairs to change his clothes and Jean joined him to find a sweater. He retreated into the bathroom while Jean headed for her dresser. At almost the same time they both jumped back and screamed, both staring at the face in the mirror.

August saw the one in their bathroom and Jean saw the one above the dresser, and they were both eerily similar if not exactly the same. The face was the one Jean saw in Avery's drawings: the disheveled face with the messy hair and pointed nose and crudely drawn eyes nothing short of evil. The face was smeared with red, and Jean and August both figured out that it was done with lipstick: Jean's brand of bright cranberry that perfectly matched a pair of shoes she owned. August and Jean met halfway and only stopped because they both heard the muffled sounds of giggles outside their door. They caught Avery before she ran back to her room and fully intended to brush that mischievous smile from her face.

"Avery!"

The child tried to hide her smile.

"Why did you draw on the mirrors with Mommy's lipstick? You know better than that! You ruined both the mirrors and the lipstick!"

"CJ can see you," Avery said, which stopped both parents short. Goosebumps ran up their arms whether they wanted them to or not. "CJ wanted to play peek-a-boo. He said it would be funny to scare you."

"Give me my lipstick," Jean snapped.

Avery reached in her pocket and pulled out her graffiti tool. By now the perfect, pointed lip shape Jean mastered with each use was down to an ugly, flattened stub. Some lipstick still remained which would take some work to put back into usable form.

"You are going to clean up your mess and go to your room," she said sternly.

"But, Mommy, it was just for fun! And it's not a mess 'cause CJ wants you to know what he looks like!"

"Listen to your mother!" August said.

They monitored Avery's cleaning while she pouted and frowned. They stood behind her, subconsciously maintaining a distance from the mirror. The lipstick marks smeared down the glass with every spray and wipe Avery did, but no matter what, as she worked, the parents saw that spending any time in front of the mirror was not a punishment for Avery. When she thought they were not looking, Avery was smiling widely at those smears. She even hid a giggle or two.

During dinner, the family ate mostly in silence, eating up and finishing what they could without mentioning the mirrors, or anything else for that matter. When most of the meal was completed, August looked over to Jean, and Jean looked over to August, as though they could conjure up a proper signal. They both looked at Avery.

"Sweetie, we want to talk to you about this CJ problem," August started.

The child played with her spoon.

"It's all right to play pretend and make believe, but you need to understand the difference between make believe and reality."

"CJ is real," Avery stated.

"He may seem real to you, because he is your imaginary friend, but he is only in your imagination."

"No, he *is* real!" Avery insisted.

"Avery, anytime you want to do something that is bad, you can't think that saying your imaginary friend told you to do it will mean you won't get in trouble. That's baby stuff, and you're not a baby anymore. You can't pretend to blame something on someone else that is pretend."

Avery just folded her arms. "He *is* real!"

"Go to your room," August said.

Avery flew out of the chair and thundered up the

stairs. She slammed her bedroom door as hard as she could and immediately went to sit down at her vanity. She let the tears fall and her eyes turned to angry slits. She was not looking at her own reflection. She was listening.

"I know they're wrong," she said to the mirror. She folded her arms and then nodded. "Yeah. Yeah I do."

In the dead hours of the night, both Jean and August were jolted out of sleep. They shuddered along with the rest of the house as the gunshot echoed through the walls. Both Jean and August grabbed their Glocks from the nightstand and rushed out their bedroom door. Jean barged into her daughter's room first while August crept down the stairs.

"She's not here!" Jean hissed.

August's eyes bulged as he lent an ear toward the office downstairs and motioned for Jean to follow. They descended with their weapons in hand, and both wanted to drop them in heartbreak to the sounds of their daughter's frantic crying.

She was in the office that both the parents used from time to time, the double glass doors both open, as was the safe in the bottom left hand drawer. Avery was a crumpled ball on the floor, no doubt from both the impact and consciousness of the activity. The revolver lay on its side where she dropped it, facing Jean and August in a cry for help.

"Avery!" both parents screamed as they rushed

to her, at once putting their own guns away in both relief and horror. Their daughter sat up, still shaking.

"Avery, what are you doing in here?"

"Are you okay?"

"How did you get the gun out of the safe?"

"*What* are you doing with the gun out of the safe?"

"Didn't we tell you to stay out of the office?"

Their questions came at rapid fire and the child still cried, keeping her fingers near her ears like she wanted to be rid of the loud sound that penetrated them.

"I…was…trying to…practice getting bad guys with CJ…"

Jean held the child as close to her as she could while August picked up the revolver to return it to the safe.

"Avery, how did you know the combination to the safe?"

Avery sniffed and looked up, specifically to the wall behind her father's head. "CJ told me," she whispered. "He said he needed my help killing…"

Their hearts froze. It was one thing for Avery to play with those plastic guns from the Dollar Tree that made cracking noises; this was completely different.

"Killing *what*?" August dared to ask.

All Avery did was sniffle and did not provide an answer.

"You know the difference between real and pretend," Jean managed to say through tense lips.

"But CJ said—"

Both August and Jean sighed in frustration, knowing that would be her excuse for everything and she would never own up to anything.

"You need to stop with this!"

Avery sniffled some more, still going from looking to the floor to the wall.

"This is dangerous, Avery. This is a real weapon. A real weapon that hurts people and it is *not* for children!" exclaimed August. He put the weapon back, all the way back to the end of the safe, and shut the door.

"Come on," Jean said, picking her up. "You are going back to bed right away, and you *will* be punished for this."

Jean carried Avery out of the office and peered behind her to see that August checked the room out. The gun had fired at the wall where the bullet left a lovely little hole that any tacked-up postcard could hide. Jean noticed something else too. The minute August moved his head, she saw the tiny mirror that faced the desk. It stood in direct view of the desk as a whole, and there was a subtle smudge of a child's handprint on the bottom, like a high-five.

Avery stood at the spot in the foyer, tears running down her red cheeks. She sniffed each tear away, still worn out from screaming, unsure of what to do next. She stared at the shadow on the wall from where the mirror used to be, the outline of the frame a perfect rectangle. She'd learned about shapes in school today. Her favorite shape was the rectangles.

She ran from the foyer and into the downstairs bathroom, once again met with the former shadow on the wall. This shape was an oval, like an Easter egg. She learned that in school too. CJ was going to tell her where the Easter bunny hid eggs in April. She knew he would. She knew they would have a lot of plans together. He'd told her so. How could they now?

Avery ran all throughout the house and discovered that they were all gone. All of the mirrors. All of the shapes on the walls were the ghosts of the mirrors that used to be there, the paint on the walls a shade lighter having been protected from dust. The foyer, the bathroom, the dining room. She ran upstairs with her little heart thundering in her chest. She let out little whimpers as she checked the bathroom, the hallway, and finally, her own room. Her little vanity mirror was gone, torn out so that there was a giant blank space where she sat to put on play makeup and brush her hair.

Avery's whimpers escalated into full out screams. She collapsed to her bedroom floor and punched and kicked. The last time she had a temper tantrum was when she was two and wanted the dollhouse from the toy store. Throwing a temper tantrum was only for babies, but Avery didn't care at the moment because she felt as helpless as one. She cried and cried, believing she was all alone.

Jean and August hauled the last mirror into their bedroom closet, all covered in bedsheets and positioned safely behind the shoe racks.

"That's the last of them?" August asked, putting a shoe rack back into place.

"I think so," Jean said, ticking them off on her fingers. "I really hope this doesn't last long."

Avery sat on her bed with her legs to her chest, her head resting on her knees. Her emotional well was dried out, and now all she could do was think by herself. All she could do was sit and listen to hear if her mean parents were going to come in her room and tell her she could have CJ back if she promised to be good. She would promise to be good. She would have to be sure to tell CJ he had to be good too. Of course CJ would be good, because he wasn't bad. He was just naughty and wanted to play.

Avery raised her head because she did hear something, and it wasn't her parents. She heard a quiet voice from a corner in her closet. She leapt off her bed and started to rummage through her playthings, tossing aside Barbies, Legos, dress-up clothes, books, and games, until she came across a little bag. She opened it to find nail polish, nail stickers, and a little pink plastic compartment with a jewel on it. Avery petted the compartment lightly, because she heard her name again. She didn't hesitate to pull out the compartment and open it up. What she saw inside made her light up.

"I knew it!" she said to it. "I knew you weren't gone!"

Downstairs, Jean and August hung their heads

over their glasses of wine. They took sips each time they wanted to talk, like it was providing the conversation for them.

"Are you sure about this?" August said.

"Well, what other options do we have? It's become a serious problem, and most people I've talked to about it agree with me," answered Jean.

"What if we don't like what this doctor has to say?"

Jean smiled weakly. "Then we look elsewhere."

August took a gulp. "Fine."

"If we don't do something now, she could get herself or someone hurt and keep blaming this imaginary friend, possibly developing some major mental health issues. I've seen it. I don't know how we can make this go away."

"It's got to go away," August said. "It's got to be just a phase; it probably is something that is common with an only child. Once Avery gets used to being in school, she'll make real friends and then forget about all this nonsense."

They made an appointment, waited for Avery to get home from her A.M. Kindergarten class, and broke the news gently.

"Avery, honey, we're going to visit someone today."

"Who?" she asked innocently, dropping her Frozen backpack to the floor.

"Someone who is an expert on imaginary friends," August said carefully. "He wants to talk to you about CJ."

"Really? Why?"

"Because he wants to learn more about him,"

Jean answered.

"Oh. Okay. Be right back." Avery disappeared and a moment later came back downstairs with her plastic cosmetics mirror snug in her pocket. Her parents didn't notice.

The man behind the desk had no hair on his head but plenty on his face, covering so much of his nose and mouth Avery wondered if he even had one. She couldn't understand why. She snuck a peek at the little compact in her pocket while he was talking and giggled one too many times.

"Avery?"

Avery looked up. "Sorry. CJ was telling me a joke."

"How about you tell CJ you'll talk to him later and talk to me some more?"

"Okay."

The girl whispered in her pocket and snapped the little mirror shut. She looked at the man who was looking at her curiously.

"So what kinds of things do you and CJ do together?"

She let her legs swing lightly at her chair. "We color, we play tag, we tell jokes, and we play pretend."

"Is CJ a good friend?"

"Yeah, we have lots of fun."

"Do you think that anything you do seems like fun and is actually dangerous and gets you in trouble?"

She licked her lips. "Sometimes."

"And is that usually CJ's fault?"

She looked down at her pocket. "Sometimes."

The man leaned forward. "When did you first meet CJ?"

"In the mirror in my room. He was in it one day when I was bored and lonely. He said he lived in the mirror and that he was bored and lonely too. He said he needed someone."

"So then you started to play together?"

"Yep, and Mommy and Daddy don't like it so much. CJ thinks they're mean."

"What kinds of things does he tell you?"

Avery thought for a minute. "He tells me stuff that he sees from other mirrors. He can spy on different people from different places, but he can't leave the mirror."

"Why not?"

Avery shrugged. "He's stuck in there. He's stuck in there until he can find a way out."

"Do you think you can help him?"

Avery looked down at her pocket. "I think so. We just have to believe in him."

"Do you believe in him?"

"Yes."

"But nobody else does, right?"

"No. But CJ is real. He really is."

"Well," the doctor said, shuffling papers at his desk. "Avery doesn't just think of this CJ as an imaginary plaything; she considers him to be a real human being. He just happens to be her source of knowledge for everything. She has told me that he lives in the mirror and he can spy on other people via mirrors."

"Is that what she says about knowing things?" Jean asked. "We can't figure out just *how* Avery would know certain things. Like the prison stabbing and the combination to the safe."

"It is possible that she saw one of you do the combination herself, and the prison incident could just be a coincidence? Look, Mr. and Mrs. Conway, it is obvious that Avery is using CJ as an excuse to get away with things, but he might be coming from somewhere else other than her mind. She acts like he is real and might be based off a real person, someone close to the family perhaps. What we need to do is try to get to the core of the matter and figure out where CJ came from and why. What exactly does he represent?"

Avery was quiet the rest of the evening, not saying a whole lot during dinner. When her parents tried to get her to open up about her session, she mostly shrugged.

"I told him me and CJ play together and do fun things," was all she said.

August and Jean were not sure what to make of the situation themselves, and Avery left to go play in her room.

Tiptoeing past her room on their way to their own, August and Jean could see her through the small opening of her door. She sat on the floor next to her bed, clutching her compact mirror.

"Yes," she whispered. "I can."

The rest of her whispers were inaudible, but her head was bent down in a very involved conversation. Her parents left her doorway without saying a word.

Avery had sheets of paper spread across her table, but instead of using multiple colors for her drawings, this time, she only used one: black. Avery had to draw the same thing over and over again until she got it right. She'd stop and position her mirror toward it and then had to listen to direction.

She held up a finished drawing of a skeleton figure with drawn-on bones, a mask with big, hollow eyes, and only a few teeth. The mask looked dreary and haunting, like it was a reflection of the face behind it.

"It is very scary," Avery agreed, letting the black crayon roll off the table. She cradled the mirror and gave it the rest of her attention. "I love Halloween! Really? It's my favorite holiday too!"

She was quiet for a minute, then, "I don't know yet. Last year, I was a cowgirl, and I had a hat and boots that matched."

Avery paused for a minute, staring at the mirror with full attention. Her eyes widened.

"Do you think that's when I can do it? It is?"

She perked up. "Yeah! We can go! You can come with me and nobody will know."

Avery squeezed the mirror a little, out of nervousness or excitement, or both.

"I can't wait, either."

Jean came home from work before August and went straight to the fridge for a glass of water. She stopped in her tracks at the face taped up to the fridge, mesmerized by its large hollowed-out eyes and gaping grin. She sighed and rolled her eyes, mostly at herself. All of Avery's other drawings were gone, and this one in particular took front and center. It was definitely not like her other drawings. Those were colorful and carefree and happy, much like any child's Crayola scribbles would produce. This one was anything but. It lacked color, for one, which did not make it happy at all. Jean couldn't help but stare at this figure, which she concluded was disturbing. It was a skeleton figure with hard black strokes outlining the bones that made up the arms and legs. These arms and legs were spread eagle across the page, making this skeleton looking like it wanted to leap out from the page at any moment. That face with the empty eyes held her stare. Jean did not want to give it more attention and tried not to let it unnerve her. It was, after all, Halloween time. Of course some spooky things would be showing up. She got her water while avoiding eye contact with the skeleton drawing. It was foolish, really, but she felt like that drawing was looking right at her.

"Mommy?"

Avery pranced into the living room where her mother was reading a paperback. Jean glanced up after sliding her finger under the page.

"What, sweetie?"

"Can we go to the park today?"

Avery seemed more bouncy these past couple of days and wanted to go to the park more and more, which didn't bother Jean one bit. In fact, it made her euphoric ever since the disappearance of the mirrors. She smiled at her daughter when she saw her shoelaces were barely tied the right way. She put the book down, spread open on the chair.

"Come here."

She tied the girl's laces and then stood up, taking the book with her. "Sure, let's go."

Avery skipped to the door, and Jean had to rush to keep up the pace. The park was a short walk from their house and a quick run for the child. The sidewalk curved left and right like an active concrete snake, a tree shedding its leaves on every side and littering the path, eventually curving at an end to the park. It was grounded in a rock pit that made it look like it fell on that path snake's head and finished it off for good. Avery ran to the swing set and slides while Jean sat down. Avery took herself across the monkey bars with ease. Jean immersed herself with her book.

Once in a while, Jean would look up from her book to make sure Avery was safe. The next time she looked up, she saw that Avery was in chase and laughing. She kept looking behind her and giggling, but when Jean looked to that direction expecting to see a child playmate, she saw nothing. Avery looked back again and darted up the steps to go down a slide. When she reached the bottom, she pointed and laughed and declared, "Beat you!"

Although there were other children running around, it was hard to see who Avery was playing with, and Jean could not connect her with any of them for some reason.

While Jean read, Avery went past the swing set to where a multitude of multicolored leaves sat in big heaps. Avery jumped in a heap and rolled around, allowing the excess leaves to sneak into her jacket and hair. She giggled and kept saying things such as, "This is fun!" and, "I love jumping in leaves too." At one point she sat up in her leaf pile, and then she turned directly to the pile next to her. "I know," she said softly. "I think so too." Avery played in the leaves and once in a while would nod. Avery at once shot out of the leaves and ran around the playground again. She soared across the monkey bars, and when she landed she stopped and proceeded to have a conversation. Jean looked up and watched Avery play with the drawstrings on her hoodie.

"Yeah," Avery said. She nodded and said some more things that Jean couldn't hear. The more Jean watched her, the more the knot in her stomach began to grow in anxiety. She got off the bench to view the scene at the monkey bars.

"Avery?"

"Yes, Mommy?"

Jean tried not to let her voice quaver. "Who are you talking to?"

Avery smiled, the devilish and boastful smile.

"CJ."

"I thought he lived only in mirrors?"

It was when Avery's boastful little smile grew bigger that Jean's stomach tightened to the core.

"He doesn't anymore. I let him out."

Jean acted natural for the day and all the way back, just in time for August to come home to see his wife sitting on the couch with a perplexed look on her face.

"What?" he asked her.

Jean sighed. "Well, your daughter and I went to the park today, and guess who she spent all day playing with?"

"Who?"

"CJ."

August rolled his eyes. "Are you serious?"

"She told me she let him out of the mirror."

Her husband stayed at the doorway to the living room.

"What is that supposed to mean?"

"That she has a one-up on us now and decided this imaginary friend doesn't live in the mirrors anymore? Now he is just out and about, and Avery is going to cause more trouble because of it? We've got to have another talk with her, as soon as possible."

"I wonder what Dr. Whatshisface would have to say."

"We need to see what we can find out for ourselves first."

"The so-called experts don't really have much to say about kid imaginary friends, do they?" August muttered.

"Not really," Jean answered. "They all just say that kids sometimes invent imaginary friends because they have social issues and a hard time fitting in, and we both know that's not Avery. Sometimes kids are just kids and like to pretend."

"This is beyond pretending."

"Well, when should we take her again? Obviously, we should make an appointment after this weekend."

"Yeah," Jean agreed. "Let her have a fun Halloween first."

Avery came into the living room, clad in her purple and orange skeleton costume and mask.

"Isn't it cool?" she asked her dad.

"It is cool," August agreed, flashing Jean an amused smile. Jean still had the tags in her hand from when she cut them off. "It was the one she insisted she wanted," Jean said.

Avery spun around so that everyone could see the cool purple and orange bones. She couldn't wait to be out until it got dark because everything glowed in the dark. She thought it was the coolest costume ever.

"CJ has one too!" Avery boasted proudly.

"Is that why you wanted to be a skeleton this year?" her father asked.

The child nodded, and her mother smiled. "She's

going trick-or-treating with Molly Henderson and her family."

"*And* CJ," Avery stated. "It's his favorite holiday."

"And CJ," both August and Jean said.

Avery announced she was going to her room to find her favorite trick-or-treat bag, the pumpkin-shaped one she had last year. She searched through her closet and the baskets by her bed.

"Don't worry. As soon as I find it, we can go," she said.

Avery looked under her bed.

"Oh, we'll be ready really soon. I promise!"

Avery stood up and looked to her right.

"Of course," she said, nodding.

Avery looked in her closet again and found her trick-or-treat bag on one of the shelves. She pulled it down and proudly held it out in front of her.

"Look, CJ! I got it!"

She smiled at no general direction.

"Yeah, I am ready!"

Once she found her bag, she put her skeleton mask on to finish the deal. Avery adjusted her costume a little bit, suddenly feeling a little lightheaded. She moved her legs like she did not know they were her own, like she was walking for the first time. She felt strange but was comforted at hearing her friend CJ's voice again. He was very close. She could hear him more clearly than she ever could, more than when he was trapped in mirrors.

On her way downstairs, something changed in Avery's manner. She lost her childlike spunk and instead marched down the steps with a great sense of purpose. She ended up not going back to the living room. Instead, she went straight to the kitchen and pulled out a butcher knife. She carefully ran her fingers across the blade and took note of its sharpness. She nodded to herself, like she was satisfied.

Her parents announced that the neighbor friends were there, the adults in jackets and a few kids scampering around as robots and superheroes. Avery slid the knife in her trick-or-treat bag and scampered off a little more enthusiastically. She was smiling behind the mask, but no one could tell.

With not much else to do, Jean and August made their way downstairs to the office. Paperwork in different colored folders lay scattered all over the desk. These accumulated so much during the past few weeks they had forgotten the color of the desk. They all contained the same information: brochures and various printed articles on child psychology the doctor had given them. They were also files of criminal justice. Several were old newspaper articles about the people who had come and gone through the system.

While shifting through paperwork and files, August came across a newspaper article that was nearly a year old. His brow crossed when he looked at the man's picture and felt compelled to reread the article:

Trick or Treat Serial Killer Got His End in Prison

Renowned serial killer Clancy Jerome Thurman

was stabbed to death by fellow inmates last Thursday. Thurman was often the target of abuse and ridicule by other inmates because of his smaller size. Thurman is the man responsible for 28 deaths of both adults and children on Halloween night when he dressed as a trick-or-treater and went door to door for all tricks and no treats, brutally stabbing whoever answered the door. Thurman masqueraded in a black costume and skull mask and blended right in with other children. He was caught and sentenced to prison by the honorable Judge August Conway.

"Jean," August said.

"What?"

August showed her the article and waited to see her reaction. She looked at the picture of the inmate staring back at her: the long pointed nose, messy hair, and hollow eyes…and since the image in the paper was rather blurry, it was almost the identical picture to the drawing their child had sketched.

"I remember this guy," Jean said. "He was in my wing. He's the one who did all those Halloween murders."

"And he…" August didn't finish his sentence. Instead, both his and his wife's thoughts turned to Avery out trick-or-treating in her skeleton costume.

About the Author

Jackie Sonnenberg is the author of the *YRESRUN SEMYHR* book series, telling the dark side of Nursery Rhymes. The first novel, *My Soul to Keep,* is the story of a boarding school cult with paranormal activity…and deathly secrets. Jackie lives in Orlando as a writer and actor for Zombie Outbreak, a year-round haunted attraction.

Facebook:
https://www.facebook.com/authorjackiesonnenb
erg

Website:
http://www.jackiesonnenberg.com/

Goodreads:
https://www.goodreads.com/author/show/326811
7.Jackie_Sonnenberg

Acknowledgements

Limitless Publishing would like to thank all the authors who shared their stories with us to make this Horror Anthology.

We are very proud of the wonderful team we are able to work with every day.

#TeamLimitless